In consequence, I mentally summarized, I was now

1) surrounded by a gang of ruthless heavily armed killers, and
2) confident that all of these gangsters would have been briefed on how to true-kill me.

To true-kill me, of course, they needed to use explosive hardtip bullets not plasma blasts on my hardmetal frame, and they also needed to shoot the bullets into the centre of my torso, where my cybernetic brain was housed, not into my skull.

And, most important of all, when I was dead, they needed to rip out my inner core and gouge out the contents and smash them, and then destroy my databird—the backup memory device that would otherwise allow me to save my personality into a new body.

Grogan's people would, I posited, know all this. And they were of course skilful warriors, fighting on home turf, with the odds overwhelmingly in their favor—one cyborg Cop against more than two-score heavily armed gangsters.

Swiftly—in less than a trillionth of a second—I ran a scenario analysis based upon all the above data, and reached my final conclusion:

These poor sorry bastards didn't stand a chance.

VERSION 43

PHILIP PALMER

orbit

www.orbitbooks.net

Orbit
Hachette Book Group
237 Park Avenue, New York, NY 10017
www.HachetteBookGroup.com

First U.S. Edition: October 2010

Orbit is an imprint of Hachette Book Group, Inc. The Orbit name and logo are
trademarks of Little, Brown Book Group Limited.

Library of Congress Control Number: 2010910439

ISBN: 978-0-316-01894-4

10   9   8   7   6   5   4   3   2   1

Printed in the United States of America

For Zanna

THE COP

Version 43

I was in a cheerful mood. The sky was a rich blue. The twelve moons of Belladonna shone, it seemed to me, like globes on a Christmas tree in the daytime sky. I could smell heliotropes, growing in banks beside the moving walkways, and orchids and lilies and peonies growing in baskets that hovered above the pedestrian boulevard.

I was one day old. I would, my database warned me, grow more jaded with the passage of time. But for the moment, life felt good.

It was a short walk from the spaceport to the crime scene. I was in constant subvocal contact with the Sheriff, Gordon Heath, and the crime-scene photos scrolled in front of my eyes as I walked. But the air was fresh, and the heliotropes and the orchids and the lilies and the peonies were fragrant, as were the roses and the summer lilacs and cut grass in the parkland that led off the boulevard. A woman was sunbathing naked on the grass, and I registered her distant beauty, and felt a faint stirring of remembered regret.

Then I walked on, another five blocks. Most of the citizens were using the moving walkways, twin rivers on either side of the pedestrian thoroughfare. Flybikes and flying cars zoomed above me, rather lower than was prudent or indeed (I checked this on my database) legal. The Belladonnans, I noted, dressed soberly but elegantly. Many of the men had grey or black waist-coats and ornate buckled belts and armoured jackets. The women tended to wear long silver or gold or scarlet dresses and high-heeled boots, apart from the courtesans who wore jew-elled gowns.

"I'm Sheriff Heath."

"I'm aware of your identity," I said. I was now at the crime scene, and I filtered out my olfactory sensations to focus on the case.

"Pleased to meet you too," the Sheriff chided, and I registered the hint of irony but decided it would be politic to ignore it.

The Sheriff and I were standing outside a twelve-storey hotel made of black brick. Police officers had cordoned off the area with holos proclaiming POLICE and MURDER SCENE – KEEP AWAY. The citizens on the moving walkways gawped at the sight, secretly thrilled (or so I posited) at the glimpse of a terror that had passed them by.

"Sheriff, feel free to call me Luke," I added, in a belated attempt to build a rapport.

In fact, "Luke" was not and never had been my name.

"Sure, I'll do that. 'Luke'."

This time, there was open scorn in the lawman's tone, but I chose to ignore that subtextual nuance also.

Sheriff Heath, I noted, looked shockingly old – too old perhaps for cosmetic rejuve? – though his body was fit and strong. He was bald, heavily wrinkled, with a grey walrus moustache and peering blue eyes. I had been impressed at the diverse range of his bio: soldier, pirate, artist, scientist and bartender. Now, he was Sheriff of the Fourth Canton of Lawless City.

"Through here."

The holograms of the crime scene didn't do justice to its horror. Blood and human flesh spattered the walls and ceilings. A screaming severed head swam in a pool of blood on the bed. And inside the mouth, which gaped unnaturally large, was a human heart, squeezed and squirted. It was evident that multiple murders had occurred, and that the killings had all been frenzied.

I switched on my decontam forcefield and hovered back and forth a centimetre above the ground. I used my finger-tweezers to take samples of blood and flesh, and carefully counted and collated the scattered limbs and organs in order to make a tally of the corpses. (Final count: five, of which two were male, three female.) The chaotic dispersal of body parts at this crime scene was far from typical: I found two legs and all five livers in the wardrobe and a pair of hands and six eyes underneath the floor panels in the kitchen, and the entrails of all the corpses were enmeshed and interconnected to form effectively a vast colon. In addition, one set of lungs had fallen under the bed.

At one point I glanced behind, and was startled to see that the Sheriff was pale and looked nauseous.

"Murder weapon?" I asked.

"We found nothing. We don't know what could have done this."

"Plasma beam? Samurai sword?"

"Look closer."

I looked closer. I'd assumed that the heart in the mouth of the severed head on the bed had been inserted by a psychopathic ritual killer. But an eyeball-tomograph told me that the heart was actually occupying the space normally reserved for a tongue, and was organically connected to the throat. I took pin-prick microsamples and analysed the DNA, and found that the DNA in the head's staring eyeballs didn't match the DNA of the head itself, and neither was a match for the heart. I then performed a dissection of the heart, and found, inside it –

– an erect penis.

For the first time in many years, I wished I could desire to vomit.

"What *is* this?" I marvelled.

"Our best guess," said the Sheriff. "These bodies were quantum teleported, and got jumbled up along the way. That's why we called you in. A quantum teleport weapon, we ain't never hearda such a thing. So we reckoned, must be banned technology, your kinda can of worms."

"Amongst other things. Do we have any idea who these victims are?"

"I recognise this one," the Sheriff said, gesturing at the severed staring head.

"Who is it?"

"It's my son," the Sheriff said, barely a quaver in his voice.

I processed that fact for a few moments, and decided not to comment on the horrific coincidence.

"His name?"

"Alexander. Alexander Heath. We didn't get on so well. He was a stubborn bastard, just like me."

"Enemies?"

"Just me."

"What gang did he work for?"

"He was clean. He was a doctor at the City Hospital. Two convictions for violence as a boy, but they were gang-related *mano a manos*, and since then, he's lived the pure life."

"What about you? Do you have enemies?"

"None. I'm corrupt as hell. No one could fall out with me."

I processed this too; it tallied with all my data. I nodded.

"I've identified two men, including your son, and three women. Could they be colleagues?" I asked.

"Worth checking out."

I checked it out, cross-referencing the DNA of the corpses against the City Hospital personnel records.

"They're all medics," I said, a few seconds later. "In addition to your son, the corpses are: Andrei Pavlovsky, Jada Brown, Sara Limer, Fliss Hooper. Know them?"

"Fliss was my son's girl. Pretty as hell. He thought I was hitting on her; that was one of our fallings out."

"Were you?"

"In my dreams. She was a looker."

"Did you love your son?"

"Oh yes."

I felt an emotion inside myself, and identified it, and marvelled at its richness and its power:

It was Rage.

43

Lawless City had a real name: Bompasso. After John Bompasso, one of the three creators of *cute-o*, the Quantum Theory of Everything.

No one ever called it that.

It was a city built on hills, and riddled with rivers — five of them, intertwining like rats' tails — and dominated by black-stoned towering buildings decorated with jewelled carvings by master artisans. Many of the buildings teetered precariously on thin pillars, or even floated above the ground. It was forcefield architecture at its most inspired: the marble and the stone were clad over a diagrid of unyielding nothingness.

I had, my database told me, visited this city three times before. Once I had been ambushed by desperadoes and killed. The second time I had arrested and then executed those desperadoes. And on my last visit, I had successfully smashed the entire crime cartel. Four gang bosses had been killed, eleven more had been brain-fried. A democratic government had been appointed, and incorruptible cyborg judges had been placed in charge of the criminal justice system. And an army of street cops were hired to enforce the rule of law.

That was a hundred years ago. Now, the gangs were back in charge. The dons were all new immigrants, with souls seared by frequent brain-frying on one of the Home Planets. They were ruthless, hungry, and full of dangerous exhilaration at having survived the fifty-fifty.

It was a wretched state of affairs, but I didn't feel even a twinge of despair at the prospect of working on such a planet.

For I had expunged Despair from my circuits long ago, considering it to be a purposeless and dispiriting emotion. Instead, I felt Excitement at the challenge ahead. I would solve this crime; and when I had solved the crime, I would solve all the other crimes that I might happen to stumble across. I would restore peace and justice to Bompasso.

Then I would leave, and peace would reign for a while.

And then, after a slightly longer while, the violence would return. And Bompasso would once again be known as Lawless City.

"This is your hotel," said the Sheriff, and I craned my neck.

"Which room?"

"Any room. It's yours. It's fully staffed."

I continued to stare up at the hotel. It was a double bay-fronted mansion decorated with gold-inlaid sgraffito and ruby bosses, set in the ubiquitous black stone. It shimmered like a rainbow that has snared a pot of gold.

"I don't need a whole hotel."

"It's yours. You're our guest."

"I don't even sleep. I just need a socket to plug myself in to at night."

"You *recharge*?"

"I'm kidding. I don't recharge. My batteries never run out. I kid, sometimes."

"Remember to warn me."

"I will, Sheriff."

"We've given you hologram facilities. You can speak to anyone you like anywhere on the planet."

"I don't like holograms. I prefer to interview suspects in the flesh."

"Flesh?"

"I'm still kidding."

"Ho, forgive my hilarity, ho. Did they ever tell you—?"

"I'm not at liberty to answer personal questions."

"So they didn't, huh." The Sheriff grinned, knowingly, with a hint of condescension.

I was used to this kind of treatment from living humans. I had once analysed the reasons for it, and had recorded my conclusion on my database: *humans like to think they are better than cyborgs, despite being, in every relevant specification, less efficient, less effective, and inferior.*

"My personality," I explained gently, "is a template for my consciousness. It really doesn't matter *who* used to own it."

"I can't imagine—"

"What?"

"Living on in a robot body. Forever."

"My personality does not live on. The human I used to be is dead. It's me now. Just me."

"Yeah. The hotel door is set to your codes. Just give it a hard stare, it'll let you in."

"I need to start interviewing."

"Who? We have no suspects."

"We have a city full of suspects, Sheriff. I want to get to know them all."

43

This was a city of high and low tenements, narrow alleys, cluttered side-streets, and tall, magnificent, needle-like soaring spires. There were no churches in Lawless City, and no religion. But the spires were the homes of the city's *ancien régime*, the original Founders. A hundred spires loomed high over the city's affairs, brushing the soft pink clouds of this small and once-arid planet.

I hired a flybike to carry me across the city. In the distance, like sentries guarding the horizons, were red mountains and vast savannahs of yellow dust dotted with meadows of vividly green grass.

I wove a path through the sky-scraping spires and looming tenement blocks of the black-stoned city. And then I landed in the vehicle park of the City Hospital.

The hospital was the key to it, I had decided.

All five victims had worked at this hospital: therefore, I theorised, all five victims must have been involved in a medical fraud. The fraud went wrong, the expected profit targets were not met, and the poor dumb fraudsters were eliminated by the evil gang boss who had conceived the whole enterprise. That was my working hypothesis.

This still left the mystery of *how* the medics had been killed: I assigned a subroutine to worry away at that.

My primary consciousness, however, focused on finding the motive, method and opportunity for the underlying fraud, which would then allow me to draw up a list of the most likely suspects for the murders.

Medical fraud of course meant organ theft or rejuve theft. What else could it be? I was aware that Belladonna had an appallingly inefficient medical system: some citizens waited decades for rejuve therapy or organ and limb replacement. The rich lived for ever on this planet, but the poor had to steal to get money to jump the clinical queue, even in cases of dire medical emergency.

As a consequence there was, my database informed me, a shockingly high true-death rate on Belladonna. On Earth it was rare for more than ten or eleven people to true-die a year, out of a population of two point three billion. On Belladonna, by contrast, there were more than five hundred thousand true-deaths a year, out of a population of eight hundred and fifty million.

This created, I concluded, the ideal conditions for a black market in stolen body parts.

My database reminded me of a case on Calabria where hospital patients suffering minor digestive ailments were sedated, and had their eyes and genitalia removed. The traumatised victims had to wait nearly twenty years before they could receive the intensive rejuve therapy that allowed their missing organs to grow back.

I strode swiftly out of the vehicle park, entered via the hardglass door into the hospital reception, then moved swiftly past the robot porters. And I marvelled at how patiently the crowds of citizens were waiting to be seen.

I went through four levels of security until I was admitted to the large and oddly deserted administration office. There I spoke to the deputy hospital manager in charge of admissions, who was named Macawley – just Macawley – in her holo-walled office that offered a dazzling animated array of angry rock stars.

Macawley looked younger than her actual age which, my

database informed me, was twenty-five. She was a genetically engineered wild-looking girl with claws instead of fingernails. She wore a silver bodysuit, tightly fitting, with green flashes on the arms and breasts to match her green eyes. I considered her to be rather eerie. She smiled at me tentatively. After .05 of a second had elapsed, I realised she was afraid of me.

"Your name is Macawley. You are the DHMICA," I said.

"Yes, that's me," she said, and the tentative smile was now just an anxious twitch of the lip.

"Hello Macawley. I believe that you were born on this planet. Your mother was transported after being convicted on capital charges, she died when you were five, you are estranged from your stepfather, Ron Barclay, who is a drug dealer," I told her, chattily, attempting to put her at her ease.

"Yes – how did you – fuck, I know how you knew that! You have a database?"

"I'm just guessing," I said, with an attempt at humour. The fear flickered in those green eyes again.

"It's a nice planet," I volunteered.

"Is it?"

"I've been to many. This is nice. Too much desert, though. There's one place I've been to—"

I stopped talking. Macawley was virtually spasming with anxiety. "I'm here to enforce the law," I pointed out. "You have no need to fear me."

"No?"

"No."

"They say you're a cold killer," Macawley said, and I stifled an emotion: Scorn.

"Maybe I am," I told her softly, and touched her hand with my robot fingers. She didn't flinch, nor did she shove my hand away.

"Look at these photographs," I told her, and with my eyes I projected images of the five dead medics into the air in front of her.

"I'm looking."

"Do you know them?"

"Why do you want to know?"

"Answer the question."

"Yes I do know them."

"Who are they?"

"I'm not telling you that, unless you tell me why you want to—"

I interrupted: "This is a murder investigation."

She blinked.

"They're dead?"

"Yes."

"All of them?"

"Yes."

"Murdered?"

"Yes."

A strange look came over her face: I identified it as Shock.

"They—" she said, and cleared her throat. "They all worked here. Three of them were doctors – Dr Alexander Heath, Dr Fliss Hooper, Dr Sara Limer. Jada Brown and Andrei Pavlovsky were nurses."

"What were they like?"

"They were—" She cleared her throat again, vigorously, and continued: "They were like doctors, except the ones who were, duh! like nurses." Her tone was snide, but I overlooked it.

"Did they live extravagantly?"

"How would I know?"

"Did you see them socially?"

"I knew, um, Dr Hooper – Fliss Hooper. She, um . . . I knew her pretty well."

I checked my database of Belladonnan hotel and restaurant receipts. "She was your girlfriend," I asserted.

Macawley wiped away a tear.

"What makes you think that?" she said, in a terrified whisper.

"You ate in nice restaurants with her, fairly often, on average two-point-five times a month. You went on holiday together, on quite a number of occasions, seven in all in the last six years. And you purchased good-quality champagne once a year on or around the same date, which I presume was the anniversary of you two becoming a sexually active couple."

Macawley stared at me. Then she spoke angrily, in what sounded to me very like a snarl: "You are such a fucking creepier-than-creepy fucking creep! She was my friend! Not my fucking—"

"The data," I pointed out, "is consistent with—"

"Friend, get it? Not lover. Not even fuckbuddy. We were *pals.*" Macawley was becoming hysterical. I reminded myself that the brutal death and dismemberment of a close friend was liable, in many emotionally inclined humans, to lead to trauma and distress.

"Very well," I said mildly. "I concede that I may have interpreted the data wrongly. So let us postulate that you were indeed friends, not lovers. But would it be fair to say, 'close friends'?"

Macawley stared. "Yeah."

"So what else can you tell me about her?"

"Nothing! Everything." Macawley wiped away another tear. Then another. Then suddenly the tears had gone and her voice was cold. "How long have you got? She loved TV, we both did. We had our favourite shows, all the wild ones, *Death Girls*, *Xandra*, *Witch World*. We went to TV cons together. She liked red wine, so did I, especially Chateau Nova, the syrah *and* the pinot noir. We shared good times and bad. And we drank, not too much but we knew how to fucking— Look, I married an evil charming-bastard-that-dumb-girls-fall-for kind of guy, okay am I perfect? No! So – fuck – skip it, you wouldn't – he was violent, the prick, I left him. And so – I'm sorry, I'm rambling – what I'm trying to say is – that's why Fliss and I drank champagne. Every year, on the anniversary of the day I ditched the fucking jerk."

"Ah."

"Any other bits of my life you'd like to filthily dabble in?"

"Who could have killed her?" I asked.

"How the fuck should I know?"

"Will you help me find her killers?"

"No."

"Why not?"

She looked at me with contempt. "Because this is *Belladonna*," she explained, with more scorn than I had ever encountered before in a human's voice.

"That's a defeatist attitude," I advised her, and she glared more contempt at me.

I wondered if I could have handled this interview differently.

I came to no conclusion.

"This is what you will do," I told her curtly.

"I'm busy."

"This is not optional. Do you have a camera?"

"What does 'not optional' mean, tin man?"

"It means it's a criminal offence to hinder a Galactic Police Officer in the performance of his duties. Also, your friend was just murdered *and you ought to help me find the killer*."

Macawley winced.

"You just had to ask nicely," she muttered sulkily.

"No, I do not have to ask nicely," I explained. "I do not even have to ask, I am authorised to order citizens to do what I need them to do, promptly and efficiently. Remember, there are sanctions for non-compliance, and the fines can *really* add up. Now: get your camera. Patrol the wards. Every single one. Send me the images. Look in my eyes."

"No."

"Look."

"No!"

"Look."

She looked. Her green eyes flickered then fixed as she stared into my empty black pupils, and I downloaded my access codes into her mind.

"Subvocalise GPC453, and the images will reach me. It's a secure line."

"Did you just enter my brain?"

"Your brainchip. Not your brain. I can't read thoughts. Just brainchips."

Macawley shuddered, and the look she gave me would have curdled water.

I leaned over the desk, and she flinched; our cheeks were so close I could smell her skin.

Then I put out my arm and accessed the hospital's computer system with a handtouch on her desk databox. I downloaded all its data, and transmitted an authorisation for a full audit of all the hospital's medical and financial records. I then reviewed the hospital database of all Patient Admissions in the last five years. It took me almost ten minutes to process this information. During this time, I stared blankly into space, while Macawley fidgeted and twitched, clearly longing to leave her desk but afraid to do so.

In those ten minutes, after accessing the personal emails and MI conversations of every member of hospital staff, I learned that Alexander Heath had been in love with Fliss Hooper. I also learned that she had become pregnant with his baby, and had opted to have the fertilised egg removed and placed in storage.

The Sheriff would have a grandchild one day. I wondered if I should subvoc this information across to him, but decided that lay outside my remit.

Fliss Hooper, I learned, had been a pretty, clever and entertaining young woman. I watched, in my mind's eye, office-party footage of her dancing. Her eyes leaped out across at me, and impaled me with their energy. I, too, had once known—

I refocused my thoughts, and assimilated social networking and other personal data about the life of Alexander Heath. I registered that this had been a young man of exceptional promise. He had loved Fliss very much indeed: this was recorded in detail in a large number of inter-office emails and subvocs, and several elegant and touching poems that I retrieved from his encrypted file vault. One of these poems dealt with—

I had all the data I needed. I logged off.

"You may go," I told Macawley, and she twitched, and then fled.

I made my way out of the administration block, and down into the basement of the hospital. At every level, I was stopped by security guards, and obliged to holo-project my warrant of authority. It was, I would have thought, fairly *obvious* I was a Galactic Cop since I am six foot five with plastic skin and dead eyes, and there were no other cyborgs on the entire planet.

However, I had to admire these citizens' devotion to mindless bureaucracy. It was one of the few encouraging signs of civilisation I had encountered here.

Finally, I reached the lower depths of the hospital, where the organ banks for the entire city were housed. Microcameras tracked me, and I was aware of each and every one of them. A pair of sullen guards glared as I passed them, shrouded in my holo-warrant.

I passed through the final security door, and closed it loudly behind me. I surveyed the scene:

Kilometre upon kilometre of corridors ran beneath the hospital, in every direction. And each corridor was stacked high with hardglass vats containing limbs, hearts, livers, kidneys, eyes, intestines, oesophaguses, ovaries, penises, skeletons, and whole-body skins.

I walked down one corridor and surveyed and counted and classified the body parts; then I counted the corridors, and was moderately impressed by the scale of this storage facility. There were enough organs and limbs and skins here to replace the bodies of at least thirty thousand people; all of them grown from foetal tissue and ready for transplant. For this was a dangerous planet, and rejuve was a slow healer.

And yet, I mused, even *this* wasn't enough. Dozens of citizens true-died every day because they'd had to wait too long for a heart or a liver or new lungs. And the death toll from duels and random murders was staggering.

I checked the inventories I had downloaded into my database, and cross-collated them against the organs I was walking past. It took me two days in all to walk/hover the whole length and width of this underground labyrinth. I checked the contents of every vat in every corridor and every alcove; I even smashed through sheer rock walls with my fist to check for hidden organ vats, but found none. Then I transmitted a message to the works department to make the necessary repairs, citing the grid references to aid them.

At the end of this long search, I had found no discrepancies or unexplained losses. There was therefore no prima facie evidence of organ or skin theft.

I decided to explore the possibility that the hospital's computer records had been falsified.

However, after a detailed analysis of the records of Admissions and Surgical Procedures, I found no anomalies, or evidence of data-tampering. Furthermore, I determined that none of the dead medics had any recorded connections with organised crime figures. None of them had been receiving large money transfers from covert untraceable accounts; nor did any of them have expenditure patterns that were inconsistent with their income flows.

My organ-fraud hypothesis was accordingly downgraded.

Was there some other reason for the killings?

I could think of none.

Which meant, I concluded, that I had no notion whatsoever about the motive behind the murders.

I took to the streets again. I programmed my flybike to return to my hotel without me, and walked across town to the Black Saloon. It was a vast bar, with tables on the sidewalks and oval keyhole windows that made it resemble a castle abandoned by its defending bowmen.

A chef was cooking burgers on the outdoor griddle, and some of the regulars looked as if they had been there for days on end. It was, after all, a pleasant spot. It rarely rained, and there were no cold winds on Belladonna, just warm summer zephyrs bearing the scent of flowers.

I walked inside and sat at a bar stool. I glanced around and admired the mosaic floors and the garishly nude statue-pillars, and smelled the booze and the bodies of the drinkers, and remembered the taste of beer.

"What can I get you?" asked the woman at the bar. She was a black-haired, dark-skinned, stunningly beautiful woman with a single brow and lips that hinted at a smile.

"Information."

"You're a Galactic Cop?"

"Do I look like a Cop?"

"Six foot five? No manners? Plastic skin?"

"I'm a Cop," I sighed.

"How's that feel?"

"I'm old. And very smart. And I will never ever die. It feels – I have no view on how it feels."

"Yeah? You know, tin man, you are one sorry son of a fucking bitch," said the barmaid, and grinned. It was, I noted, a superior kind of a grin. I was being patronised once again.

"So," the barmaid added, in more friendly tones, "what's your poison?"

Suddenly, I found myself overwhelmed by waves of melancholia.

It alarmed me severely. In the usual course of things, my emotions were carefully calibrated to assist the functioning of my cybernetic intellect. My slowly shifting moods enhanced ratiocination, allowed me to access "gut instinct," and enabled me to make lateral leaps of deductive brilliance. And hence, I valued my emotions, for I knew they served a useful function and made me more than just a machine.

But this – this! This – black, dark, void, empty – no word for it! – this ghastly self-loathing feeling – what function could it possibly serve? What did it mean? What did it—

Swiftly, I erased Melancholy from my emotional repertoire.

"I don't drink," I said, aware that I had skipped a beat in my conversation with the barmaid, but hoping it would pass unnoticed.

It passed unnoticed.

"Don't, or can't?" said the barmaid.

I thought about it. "Don't."

The barmaid drew me a beer, and passed it across. White foam stood proud on golden bubbled lager. "Drink this," she said. "You look like you need it."

I drank three pints, then cleansed my fluid-system of all traces of alcohol, and transpired the toxins through my pores. "I'm looking for Filipa Santiago," I said.

"That's me."

"I know."

"There are kids who were born on this planet; they don't know what it was like, in the old days, you know?"

"Yeah, I know," I murmured.

"We came in on the fifty-fifty. We risked—"

"I know. I know what you risked."

"—everything. Fifty-fifty. A flip of a coin."

"Tell me about it."

"You wouldn't understand."

"No? No?" I stared at her, coldly. "I should inform you that you don't know anything about me, or what I can comprehend, or the depth and detail of my experience. So do not presume to say what—"

"You're a fucking cyborg."

"Even so. I understand. Plenty. Tell me about this city, please. Tell me—"

"My boyfriend died in hyperspace."

"Ah."

"Scrambled. It turned him into – I don't know what."

"I comprehend."

"I loved him."

"It's the luck of the draw."

"He was facing a murder charge. I was his accomplice."

"Were you guilty?"

"Hell yes. We were wildcats in those days. Then they gave us the choice. Death, indoctrination, or the fifty-fifty."

"Brainwiping is not so bad."

"How would you know?"

"I'm a cyborg. It's what they do to us."

"Ah."

Filipa was silent, waiting, and I felt impelled to talk.

"I was born from a human brain," I explained to her, and Filipa sipped her drink, and looked at me. Her dark eyes were intrigued, and her brow furrowed as she listened. "And, because it is beneficial to the working of my intellect, I retain trace elements of that human personality," I continued, aware I was interrupting my own interrogation, but doing so anyway. "My human was dead, of course, true-dead, of natural causes I am assured. But after death, my human mind was preserved and then merged with the self-aware consciousness of a cybernetic intellect and attendant hard drive." I paused, and wondered why I was explaining myself to a witness who had no reason to know this data. "But to create me, as a chimaerical man-machine entity, they had to wipe my human memories. They turned me into a new-born. That's when Version 1 was created."

"Who were you? The human you, I mean?"

"They never told me that," I admitted, for the second time that day.

"You could find out."

"Why? What would that achieve? I am who I am. I do what I do."

"Yeah, but without memories," said Filipa, "I wouldn't know how to . . . hell, I have so *many* memories . . . I have . . . oh, fuck it."

"Tell me about the Mayor, please, Filipa," I said. "Your expertise, my database assures me, is second to none."

I was aware that, as well as working at the bar, Filipa was the planet's Archivist, the official chronicler of politics and crimes. It made her a first-rate information resource; hence my visit.

"So many fucking memories," she said, forlornly.

"Is he involved in gangland activities?" I insisted.

Filipa grinned: "Hell, of course not," she said, in a tone which implied she was jesting.

I waited.

Filipa shrugged.

"Yeah," she said eventually, "the Mayor takes bribes. I should know, I pay him – to protect this bar. I also know that he over-turned a major police investigation into extortion rackets. He gave a Dark Side gangster immunity from prosecution, after he slaughtered his own family. He pretty much turns a blind eye to all that the gangs do. The old Mayor, he never mixed with the gangs, never took money, never received favours. He was incor-ruptible. He lasted two days."

"According to your Archives," I said, "he's never lost an elec-tion. Why is that? Voter intimidation?"

"Voter apathy. Only the criminals vote."

"Is he popular?"

"Hell yeah. He's a larger than life figure. He tells us we're a great city, and the citizens of Earth aren't fit to wipe our arses. What more do you want from an elected representative?"

"Who are his closest associates, amongst the gang bosses?"

"He's thick with Dooley Grogan. He knows Kim Ji too, he used to work for her as an enforcer. Beyond that, I don't know."

"Does he drink here?"

"Sometimes."

"Will he be here tonight?"

"Yeah, he'll be here tonight. Can we stop this now?" Filipa was looking weary. "You see, tin man, I really don't give a shit any more. I've done so much, I'm drowning in fucking memories. Sometimes I feel my head will explode."

"I'm sorry."

"Not your problem."

"You can tell me, if you like, about the memories," I said, in a tone laden with kindness.

"What do you care?"

"I care. Tell me."

And so Filipa Santiago told her story.

Born in the shantytown slums of a brutal planet. Enslaved. Brutalised. Raped. Pimped out. Abused by friends and family. Sold to a drug gang. Forced to work as a mule. Till the day that she and José stole the drugs and killed a gang leader and ended up in a shootout with the crooked police.

They were lucky not be assassinated in the local jail. Luckier still to be tried in front of a Star Court, with cyborg judges teleported from Earth. Luckier still to be offered the fifty-fifty — with a chance of escape, freedom, a new world, a new start.

It turned out, though, that José wasn't so lucky after all. For Filipa knew, as all transportees knew, that quantum teleportation is an inexact science. It makes it possible to travel trillions of miles in less time than *this*. But it has one drawback: quantum travellers only survive fifty per cent of the time.

Thus, Filipa arrived on Belladonna in the blink of an eye. And José was standing next to her, smiling. But when he spoke, his words made no sense. He stared, but he did not see. And he tried to move, but he could not move.

Later, she learned that the cells in his body had been replicated intact, but without cell membranes. So as he tried to move, his body turned to mush. And he sagged and slurped to the ground in a wet heap of organic matter.

He didn't die in front of her, he was already dead. José was no longer human within the first trillionth of a second of the teleport process. He was just misaligned cell-meat.

But Filipa told me she would always remember the moment he looked at her and smiled, and started to speak, as if his body were stubbornly trying to live.

"Tell me about your happier memories," I said, using my "gentle" intonation now.

But Filipa didn't answer me. She just stared blankly: and I deduced she was lost in memories of that moment, when José smiled and tried to speak, and then turned to pathetic slobbering mush in front of her.

43

The Saloon was getting crowded. A tall man with a metal skull entered, followed by an entourage of bodyguards. Filipa was serving a beer to two women at the far end of the bar, but she whistled, and I caught it and followed her gaze across. And I checked my database for background information on Abraham Naurion, Mayor of Lawless City, formerly a farmer on Mars, convicted of mass genetic manslaughter and banished to Belladonna.

The man indicated by Filipa didn't in fact resemble the photograph in my database, and he was six inches taller than his official height. But that was body morphing for you. These days, no one ever looked like what they used to look like.

I eased my way across. It was busy now, and I had to squeeze my way past drugged and drunk partygoers who mostly wore tight leather body harnesses with bare midriffs and arses and breasts. Thus, my progress through the crowd was slow, and replete with inadvertent intimate contacts.

I remembered, but I did not feel: Lust.

"I'm a detective officer of the Galactic Police," I told the Mayor, once I had reached him.

"You don't say! Join us," said the Mayor, smiling.

He beckoned to his two lady friends; I photographed them with my eyes, and ran a swift records check. One was a prostitute, the other was the Chief Financial Officer of the City Council. Neither was armed, and I discounted them. I was more wary of two heavy-set men who stood behind the Mayor, arms folded. They were both ex-mercenary soldiers, and their job was to protect the Mayor at any cost.

"I'm taking you in, you big ugly motherfucker," I told the Mayor, with carefully calibrated rudeness.

"What?"

"You heard," I snapped. "You're under arrest."

"What charge?" The Mayor was almost flustered.

"Corruption."

"Can you prove it?"

"No."

"You can't prove anything against me! You – what?"

"I said no," I clarified. "I'm arresting you, without evidence. I'm banking on a confession. You look like a guy who's gonna crumble easily. So come with me, now."

"What if I refuse?"

There was a terrifying pause. I looked at the Mayor with my black empty eyes.

"Then I can kill you for resisting arrest," I pointed out, slowly, and longingly. And, finally, the Mayor saw my logic.

"Why don't you interrogate me here? The beer's better." The Mayor beamed.

"Don't get smart with me, metal-head!" I sneered. And I towered intimidatingly over the Mayor.

The Mayor stood up from his bar stool. He was nearly seven feet tall, half a foot taller than me, and his shoulders were as broad as wings. I wondered if he was bio-engineered to fly.

"Sure, I'll come with you," he said mildly.

"Hey," said one of the girls, the accountant, a blonde with the face of a reptilian alien skilfully tattooed over her own.

"I won't be long," the Mayor reassured her.

"Don't bank on it," I advised him.

"You can't do this, you fucking robot tyrant!" said one of the Mayor's bodyguards, and I flicked a glance at him. The bodyguard glanced away. My glance, I have been told, is full of nothing: few men, even very dangerous men, can withstand it.

The second bodyguard looked away too, a sideways glance that was his letter of resignation.

I led the Mayor out of the Saloon. All eyes were on us.

Outside the Saloon, the twelve moons of Belladonna Christmas-treed the sky once more.

"Is this about the Sheriff's son?" the Mayor asked, casually.

"It concerns the murders of Alexander Heath, Andrei Pavlovsky, Jada Brown, Sara Limer, and Fliss Hooper, at 43 Lafayette, Canton 4, Bompasso," I explained.

"I had nothing to do with that."

"You know they were murdered?"

"Hell, we've all seen the police footage." The Mayor grinned. "Someone fucking butchered 'em, right?"

"That's correct," I said. "Now tell me: who?"

"I don't know."

"Why were they killed?"

"I don't know."

A robot police cruiser glided to a halt in front of us. I beckoned the Mayor to get in.

"I can have you terminated," the Mayor pointed out. "I still have connections on Earth. I can bribe some bureaucrat to have your licence to exist revoked. They'll wipe your database and feed you into a crusher. No more rebirth. I could kill you! Don't you fucking know that?"

"I do know that," I said, in bleak tones, and the Mayor got it.

Death held no terrors for me.

"Ah," said the Mayor, and he got into the cab.

43

Five hours later the Mayor was released without charge.

Mayor Abraham Naurion had proved to be a pliable and garrulous witness. He had told me everything I needed to know about the gangs and their leaders and their foibles and friendships. The Mayor had also calmly admitted to taking bribes from all the gang leaders, and he shamelessly condoned the culture of crime and corruption that existed on Belladonna.

The Mayor was in a chatty mood when he finally left my custody. "I'm a realist," he said.

"And what does that mean?"

"It means there is no justice in this fucking universe," he told me. "So don't waste your time looking for it."

43

A hundred years ago, I cleaned up Lawless City.

It was a dangerous, but a glorious time. I was programmed to bring law and order to the Exodus Universe planets, and back in those days no one queried my methods. I arrived to find Belladonna was in the grip of frontier frenzy. Bitter wars were being fought between rival ranchers. The city of Bompasso was considered fair prey by rival raiding parties. All the houses were fortified, and the citizens carried guns and wore forcefields as a matter of course.

At one point, I fought a pitched battle with the local gangsters, running through the houses in a Fourth Canton street to get cover from their explosive bullets – punching and kicking my way through interior walls to get from one end of the terrace to the other.

Fifty-five gangsters died that day, judicially executed by my guns. Afterwards, I convened a meeting between the rival ranchers and city gang bosses. I imposed a set of land registry decisions upon them to determine who should own what. I passed judgement on all those who I felt deserved to die for their crimes against humanity. And I either executed the guilty ones or (if they were still on the loose) hunted them to death. Then I imposed democracy and freedom and a new civil service structure.

And then I left.

But, as I had learned from the City Archives, and from my long conversation with the Mayor, in the years after my departure more and more "immigrants" from the planets of the Solar Neighbourhood had continued to flood into Bompasso. And the governments of Earth and Kornbluth and Pohl and Cambria and all the other planets of human space continued to use the rest of the infinite Universe as their trash can.

For nowadays in the Solar Neighbourhood – this idyllic, civilised, peace-loving sector of space – murderers are no longer executed or imprisoned or brain-fried. Serial killers and psychopaths are no longer subject to personality reversals. And genocidal maniacs are no longer interned in centuries-long hibernation. In this new and liberal regime, all offenders get a second chance, *somewhere*, in what bureaucrats called the Remote-Zones of the Human-Habitable-Universe; and which the transportees called: The Exodus Universe.

Somewhere like Belladonna. A planet colonised by convicts and felons, where the dregs of humanity clustered and festered.

The Mayor had told me about Dooley Grogan, who had arrived in Lawless City nearly forty years ago: the celebrated Butcher of Lyra. Dooley bought a tech-store, then a liquor store; then he went into the drug and shebeen business. And now, he was the undisputed king of brutality in Lawless City, as well as controlling all the robbery gangs in Belladonna's other major cities.

Kim Ji – so the Mayor had explained – was a bio-engineered Cat Person/Dolph mongrel with psychopathic tendencies, who was also a whore of consummate ability. She saw a gap in the market and set up a host of brothels in Lawless City and twelve other cities, as well as founding her own city, Jiville, in the deserts of Duende.

Fernando Gracias, I learned, was a former Soldier in the

Cheo's space navy. He had created a protection racket that terrorised every legitimate business in every city on the planet, and
which extended to the ranches and the wilderness areas too.

And Hari Gilles – whom the Mayor openly despised – had
created his own unique niche of vileness, in which he pandered
to the freaks and the sadists and the fetishists and the necrophil-
iacs and the "animal-lovers."

These four saw a power vacuum, and they swept in, and took
charge. In the century that had passed since I last came to town,
they had turned a civilisation into something truly barbarous.

And they had every right to do so. It was, after all, a free society. My programmers had given me authority to investigate mass
serial murder, alien genocide, AI cyber-fraud and the use of banned
technology. But beyond that, I was just a tourist in someone else's
culture. I was not allowed to do what I wanted to do: eradicate evil.
Instead, I was obliged to merely uphold the law, according to the
rules and regulations defined by my programming.

However, there *was* a course of action which would allow me
to achieve my goal of liberating Belladonna.

For I knew that if I could pin the Mass Murders (Utilising
Banned Technology) of Heath, Hooper, Limer, Pavlovsky and
Brown on one or all of these gang bosses – then, and only then,
my programming would allow me to intervene and trash their
empires. In those circumstances – and those circumstances
alone – I was authorised to use full discretionary force, including pre-emptive assassination of the guilty.

So now I needed my just cause. Without it, I was powerless
to intervene, to save the people of Belladonna.

For the unpalatable truth was this: the Four Bosses were not
outside the law. They *were* the law, in Lawless City.

43

The woman was tall, slim, naked, and bound with shackles.
The man beside her was muscular, and also naked, and had been

adeptly hog-tied. They both groaned with pleasure as they were kissed and fondled and whipped by the giggling girls in the hen party.

Elsewhere, similar acts of violence and lust were being performed between paid and paying consenting adults in a wide variety of acrobatic variations. The whores, male and female, were beautiful, agile, and tireless, and capable of enduring extraordinary amounts of pain. And the paying customers were good-looking and toned, but lacked the easy grace and poise that a lifetime devoted to sensuality will bring.

"Nice place," I said, and smiled. That always unsettled people. My plastic face has, pretty much, the texture and sheen of human skin, but it is still plastic. And I rarely smiled, because I knew that when I did, it made my eyes look blanker.

"It's a service," Hari Gilles said, defensively.

Gilles was an eerie-looking man: thin to the point of being skeletal, extensively tattooed, with eyes that did not focus, and lips that were always moist.

"Some people find this a turn on," I mused, as I watched the orgies and the beatings and the whippings and the flesh-mutilations which took place to a soundtrack of ceaseless groaning and expletive barks. A curtain was pulled back and three female courtesans appeared, in richly coloured Arab robes that swirled around their naked bodies, and began to dance inside a haze of hallucinogenic mist.

"They do, indeed," leered Hari, and I felt – or rather, quite dis-passionately, noted the presence within my psyche of: Contempt.

"How about you? Does it turn *you* on?" I enquired.

"I'm a businessman."

A scream rang out. The dungeon was dank and dark and steeped in evil, and bodies sweated, and semen oozed, and rain dripped from the ceilings, and rats scurried about underfoot licking blood off the black flagstones.

And, for me, the cumulative effect of the whole ghastly *mise-en-scène* was curiously . . . *amusing.* How strange these humans were! How abjectly driven by their bizarre passions and obsessions!

I had counted fourteen sexual perversions new to me since I first entered through the slimy stone corridors that led down from the House of Pain's reception area. The stone arches of this underground cavern were pitted with metal hooks from which chains dangled. The air was thick and fuggy and rank with incense and aphrodisiac spices. And TV screens unobtrusively placed in alcoves gave the punters a tantalising fast-cutting overview of the wickednesses of the day.

"There was a time," I said – for I pride myself on my historical knowledge – "when sadistic acts that led to death were considered to be criminal."

"No one dies here," Hari protested, "not really. The brain doesn't die. Our performers are all insured, and everyone who pays our prices can afford to replace their limbs and organs. Where's the harm?"

I sighed. I actually had no answer to that. A hell-hole of depravity like this one always rocked my moral values, but logically, where *was* the harm?

"Why?" I marvelled. "What's the appeal of pain?"

Hari Gilles smiled coldly; no, it was not a laugh, it was an evil snicker.

I decided to make my play.

And so I stared, with blank eyes, into Hari's eyes.

It didn't work. Hari met my glance with a sneer of contempt.

"You'd love to be able to experience this, wouldn't you?" he taunted. "Because to feel pain is to be *human*. Whereas you, you're just a fucking—"

"You're under arrest," I interrupted, tersely.

Hari blinked. "You're kidding me?"

"No, I am not, you slimy son-of-a-whore," I snarled.

He blinked again, and licked his lips in a swift, nervous tic – hence, the always-moistness of his lips.

"What's the charge?" Hari demanded.

"There is no charge."

"You're just going to arrest me, for the hell of it?"

"You can resist if you like."

"What happens then?"

I paused, and smiled again, for maximum effect.

"I gun you down, like the vile hound you are."

Hari laughed, and relaxed. I felt: Rage-at-Myself. I'd over-played my hand.

"In my circles," smiled Hari, "that counts as erotic flirtation."

I smiled a third time, eerily. I took out my right-hand gun – a dual-use plasma and explosive bullet pistol that I wear sheathed to my body-belt – and I prodded the muzzle into Hari's mouth.

"No one would care," I said, "if I killed you now."

Hari goggled his eyes, unrattled by my taunting.

I withdrew the gun muzzle. A few punters cried "Hurrah" and "Do it again!" at what they took to be my sexual game-playing.

Hari licked his lips, and swallowed, and smiled naughtily.

I sighed. "Forget it. You're not under arrest. Just tell me this – did you kill the Sheriff's son?"

"No. But I know who did."

"Who?"

Hari's tone was calm. His face was tattooed with magic sigils; his skin was unnaturally pale, with cord-like veins clearly visible; his body emaciated. I felt uncomfortable in his presence. He looked like a man who treated his body as an evil farmer treats his dogs.

"The Sheriff himself," said Hari. "He's corrupt. So was his son. They were in a racket together, it went sour. Sheriff Gordon Heath killed his own son, and then he butchered his son's friends to cover it up."

"You just made that up on the spur of the moment, didn't you?"

"Yeah," said Hari, proudly.

43

Dooley Grogan's place was an Earth-Irish theme bar carved out of the side of a mountain. Goats ran up and down the grass slopes and shat at the customers' feet. Piped music played, and a real fountain bubbled in the centre of the bar, filled with a potent blend of gin and water. When the water splashed, it created a haze that could be sniffed and gulped, so that breathing the air in this place was enough to make you drunk.

Dooley was a broadly built Golgothan who bragged of his Earth-Irish descent, and who ran a riotous bar. Prostitutes, male and female, disported themselves, semiclad and less than so. The heavy drinkers sat at the bar consuming beer after beer, washed down with shots of whiskey and tequila and liquid morphine. Loud insistent and addictive brainmash music blasted out at sternum-shaking levels of volume. Potent drugs in brainspray form were openly on sale, and a few of the bleary boozers had catheters in their temples or scalps.

I felt an emotion, no, not an emotion, a pang: *déjà vu?*

"I don't know anything about any fucking murders," Dooley snarled.

At that moment, I felt consumed with Despair – even though this was an emotion I had previously purged from my programs.

"Any more fucking questions, I want my fucking lawyer present," added Dooley, with a sneer.

And Rage.

"You fucking tin monster; were you a man once?" Dooley mocked.

Rage, Despair, Scorn: a trinity of base emotion.

According to my database, Dooley was a legendary bareknuckle boxer. A workplace bully. The father of five children. He had three brothers, all of whom had been murdered, and there were widespread rumours that Dooley himself had ordered the hits on them.

"You useless fucking plastic-skinned machine, you got a fucking nerve on you, coming in here!" Dooley taunted, as the bass line from the brainmash metal song shook the glasses on the table.

"Did you know Alexander Heath?" I said flatly.

"Of course I fucking knew him. He was the Sheriff's jerk-off son."

"And Fliss Hooper?"

"She came to my bar a couple of times, with Alex. A looker. No more fucking questions."

"And Andrei Pavlovsky?"

"I said no more fucking questions."

"Why not? Do you have something to hide?"

I stared into Dooley's eyes, and Dooley flinched.

"I didn't fucking murder them."

"I know," I said, though I knew nothing of the sort. "But I want your help."

"Go fuck yourself."

I threw a money belt on the table. Dooley opened it out. Gold nuggets tumbled loose.

"Money. For information. How does that appeal?"

"I'm not a fucking stool-pigeon."

"Yes you are," I said, having previously accessed the Belladonnan police informant files, in which Dooley featured largely.

"Yes I am," said Dooley amiably. "Now you're talking my language. Who do you want in the frame?"

"I just want the truth."

"The truth? Someone's trying to get at the Sheriff."

"Why?"

"He's getting old. And soft. Interfering with business that ain't his fucking business."

I considered this possibility.

"Who?"

"I'll find someone."

A powerful emotion crept up on me at this cavalier offer to frame an innocent. I recognised it, a compelling compound-emotion with a distinguished historical lineage: Righteous Wrath.

"You're under arrest," I told Dooley, in neutral tones that concealed an avalanche of anger. And I grabbed Dooley by his shirt front and shook him like a rat.

Dooley reacted instinctively. He broke my grip with a powerful wrist-twist, rolled off his chair and backflipped expertly, and came up with a pistol in his hand. His bodyguards also had guns which they aimed steadily at me.

Then more of Dooley's men and women appeared, carrying pistols and rifles; they emerged from doorways like termites fleeing a mound, forming a semicircle in the bar, and glaring at me past their guns. Grogan had subvoced for help, and his entire army had come running.

In consequence, I mentally summarised, I was now

1) surrounded by a gang of ruthless heavily armed killers, and
2) confident that all of these gangsters would have been briefed on how to true-kill me.

To true-kill me, of course, they needed to use explosive hardtip bullets not plasma blasts on my hardmetal frame, and they also needed to shoot the bullets into the centre of my torso, where my cybernetic brain was housed, not into my skull.

And, most important of all, when I was dead, they needed to rip out my inner core and gouge out the contents and smash them, and then destroy my databird – the backup memory device that would otherwise allow me to save my personality into a new body.

Grogan's people would, I posited, know all this. And they were of course skilful warriors, fighting on home turf, with the odds overwhelmingly in their favour – one cyborg Cop against more than two-score heavily armed gangsters.

Swiftly – in less than a trillionth of a second – I ran a scenario

analysis based upon all the above data, and reached my final
conclusion:

These poor sorry bastards didn't stand a chance.

I stifled a grin.

"Put your weapons down, or else you will face a penal sanc-
tion," I said, in a deliberately mocking tone, and was rewarded
by a hail of sneers.

But then, to the astonishment of all present, Dooley shrugged,
and lowered his gun. "Hell, I'm sorry," he said. "I didn't . . ."

I plunged my hands diagonally and – in a fraction of a fraction
of a second – was holding my two pistols. I rolled off my stool,
kicked it in the air where it flew wildly as chaff, knelt, and fired
both guns simultaneously at different targets. I blew off Dooley's
head with the first six explosive-bullet shots, and simultaneously, with the other gun, nailed the five nearest bodyguards
with torso shots, and then fired a fusillade of plasma bolts into
the bar, shattering every bottle and glass on the shelves.

Explosive bullets and plasma blasts rocked my armour, from
the shooters on the balcony and elsewhere. But though the bullets punched holes in my arms and legs and head, none of them
connected with my cybernetic brain. And so I swiftly rolled and
shot, rolled and shot, then was out of the saloon.

"Threatening a Galactic Police Officer with a deadly
weapon," I called back at them, "is a felony under Section
Fourteen a) (iv) of the Solar Neighbourhood Penal Code!"

The lawyers came for me at the hotel, but I projected film
footage of what had happened out of my eyes, into the air in
front of them. Dooley had pulled a gun on a Galactic Cop; his
death was therefore justified. The bodyguards were all dead,
but not braindead. In a year's time, if all went well with the
rejuve and organ transplants, they'd be able to reinhabit their
bullet-torn bodies.

But I had blown out Dooley's brains with all six exploding bullets. There was no coming back for him. An enemy to society had been eradicated.

It was assassination, pure and simple, and I knew it. But I had no qualms. Once, many centuries ago, when I was Version 1 and Version 2, I had practised brilliant detection, and solved cases of intricate complexity with astonishing leaps of logic.

But now, all these years and Versions later, I cared less and less about finding solutions to arcane mysteries, or exposing devious killers. Instead, I yearned to be, simply and remorselessly, a destroyer of evildoers.

Who had killed the three doctors and the two nurses, in such a bizarre and terrifying way?

I didn't know, and I didn't truly care. For all I wanted to do was to clean up this godforsaken planet, once again.

But then of course—

I deleted that thought, before I had finished thinking it.

And I then also deleted several of my previous thoughts, up to the point where I resolved that I cared less and less about finding solutions to arcane mysteries, or exposing devious killers; for this now struck me as an opinion that lacked both detachment and logical purpose.

Finally, I reviewed my contemporaneous mission log. It read:

> **I had blown out Dooley's brains with all six exploding bullets.**
> **There was no coming back for him.**
> **An enemy to society had been eradicated.**

I felt satisfied at both the thought, and the deed.

I stripped off my clothes and inspected myself in front of a mirror. There were ugly bullet holes in my abdomen, thighs, shoulders, and skull. I could and did poke a finger into my forehead and waggle it. But the inner cybernetic core inside my torso had not been penetrated.

I patched the holes with sealant, and watched it dry. The skin colour wasn't a perfect match, but my skin wasn't a completely convincing flesh-colour in any case. I now looked, so my style program advised me, like a patched-up action doll.

I got dressed again, and checked my appearance in the mirror. There was a circle of pale skin on my forehead, which was now the only trace of the hole where the exploding bullet had entered. And I could feel the bald patch at the back of my head, where it had exited. I also had traces of plasma-blast burns on my throat and hands. But otherwise, I looked fine.

It occurred to me that I had made no progress in the case to which I had been assigned. That, I realised, was an oversight.

So I reviewed all my data again.

And I realised I had reached no conclusions. No further hypotheses had occurred to me. I wondered if I was getting old. There was a time—

Abruptly, and shockingly, a mood of Melancholic Despair descended upon me, even though both emotions – Despair and Melancholy – had been erased from my circuitry.

I erased them once again.

I had work to do.

43

This was the Dark Side, where sex and human life were for sale.

There were no tenements here, no vast spires, just huddled rows of neon-lit brothels and cinemas and strip clubs and close-encounter joints.

I saw men and women having sex in the street. I saw men with men, women with women. Threesomes in the backs of cars. None of it perturbed me. It was a free planet. Anyone who wanted to pay for sex or be paid for sex was welcome to do so.

But the Dark Side was also home to the slave trade, and the clone trade.

I sat in a bar, and listened to the stories.

"—never thought the day would come when—"

"—the Lopers were in a killing rage by then. We could hear the police sirens. There was blood spraying everywhere. And my Loper was bleeding badly, but he rallied and—"

"—my grandfather fought the Cheo. He died before I was born, but my parents kept a hologram of him on the mantelpiece. A great fucking huge pirate with a hook for a hand. He didn't actually have a hook for a hand. That's just how those old-time pirates liked to be portrayed. He—"

"—I'll pay you twenty for the twelve-year-old, double for the baby—"

"—not a fucking virgin. Not! I've killed—"

"—so I asked her, and she said yes. And we took our flybikes into the hills. And we raced—"

"—they say it was voodoo. No *way* you could scramble body parts with any conventional weapon, not even hyperspace can do it, not even—"

"—are you fucking *joking*? You don't seriously expect me to—"

"—so what do you say? We could die together, in Glory, and—"

"—no – please – no—"

"—not to my taste. However—"

"—you owe, you pay. If you don't have money then—"

"—don't make me fucking laugh, you fucking—"

"—perfect clone of the Mayor, ideal for hunting and—"

"—I'll buy four, plus the mutant; I have an ancien who wishes to—"

"—never before been—"

"—you should take more fucking care, no one could survive that kind of—"

"—I don't care what you want, you bleating fucking girl, the contract says—"

After a few hours I left and walked the streets. A police car cruised close to me. It landed, and the door opened.

"Get in," said the uniformed police sergeant. I glanced at her.

"Sergeant Jones," I acknowledged.

"You remember me?"

"You're in my database, as a serving officer with the Bompasso PD."

Sergeant Jones stared at me. She was a raven-haired black woman, who was also, I noted, rather beautiful. And appealingly *ample* – generously curved, with laughter lines around her eyes. Something told me – though I couldn't locate the datum in my database – that this was a woman who really *loved* life, and was, in turn, loved by life.

She stared viciously at me.

"Let's go for a ride," she said.

"Sure."

I got in.

"Your first name's Aretha," I informed her, as I sat beside her in the front seat of the flying patrol car.

"That's right."

The flying car took off, and Aretha piloted it with a casual lack of regard to any other vehicles in her airspace.

"Shall I call you Aretha?"

"If you like."

"We've never met."

"Is that what your database says?"

"It is."

"Then we've never met."

The cruiser soared upwards, then flew high above the neon-lights-flashing hardcore-music-throbbing streets of the Dark Side.

"I hear you killed Dooley," Aretha said.

"He pulled a gun on me."

"We don't need your kind of law around here," she snapped.

The cruiser zoomed low over the park. Dozens of men and women were sleeping rough.

I ignored her previous comment. "What is the designated topic of this meeting?" I demanded of her, coldly.

"I'd like a progress report on the serial killing case."

"I do not give progress reports to the local authorities."

"What progress have you made?"

"I do not give progress reports to the local authorities."

"What progress?"

"I do not—"

"NONE," Aretha synopsised, savagely. "Fucking, none."

"I do not give progress reports to the local authorities."

"You went to the hospital."

"I do not—"

"Shut the fuck up Mickey, or so help me God I'll—"

"What did you call me?" I asked her and felt, for a brief moment, worryingly unfocused.

"Mickey."

"Why?"

"It's the name you told me to use. When we met last time."

"We've met before?"

"I don't mind that you don't remember," Aretha said, with a sweetness of tone that I suspected hid dark irony. "I know how it is for you *robots.*"

"You do not know how it is for me, not at all," I said flintily.

"Oh, I think I do," she crooned, with that same implausible sweetness. "They filter your database and your mission log, don't they? Hmm? Leach out all the personal stuff. Leave you with the *raw facts*. It's for your own protection I guess."

"When did you know me?"

"A while back. A century ago."

"*'Mickey'?*"

"It's not your human name. It was just – a kind of private joke between us."

"I don't have private jokes."

"You did then."

"I've never met you before."

Aretha said patiently: "Skip it. Move on. What progress have you made?"

I was silent.

"None," I conceded.

"I figured as much."

"I went to the hospital and—"

"It's not about the hospital."

"I found no evidence of organ theft. However, later evidence has persuaded me that—"

"It's Fliss. Fliss Hooper."

"—it may be a revenge attack directed at the Sheriff, whose son was among the victims."

"Listen to me, dumbfuck! It's Fliss. The rest are collateral damage."

I surveyed my database. It took about two minutes.

"Ah."

"You agree?"

"I agree. I didn't find that information on my previous—"

"You didn't fucking look."

"It is indeed true that I didn't, as you say, 'fucking look'."

"There was a time, you *would* have looked," Aretha told me, and I realised there was fury in her tone, and in her eyes. "Fliss's sister was raped by the Mayor," she continued. "Fliss was furious, fought her sister's case. She decided the police were too corrupt to help, so she put out a call for the crime to be investigated by a Galactic Cop. The call was never made. Instead, a hit on Fliss was ordered. The Sheriff's son, the other kids, they were just in the wrong place at the wrong time."

"The data may in fact be compatible with that hypothesis."

"You bet it is. Go on, metal man, access the record of the rape."

I read it from my database: **Jaynie Hooper. 23 years old. Found raped and beaten. All four limbs amputated, probably with a laser scalpel. Now in rejuve therapy and receiving psychosexual counselling.** "There's no evidence it was the Mayor," I argued. "I have nothing to confirm that allegation."

"I've got a confidential informant tells me it's the Mayor. The Mayor, you see, has control issues."

"Confidential informants can be unreliable. Their testimony is compromised by their criminality, and is frequently tainted by malice," I explained.

"It's inside information, you fucking fool! And that gives you your motive. And once you have motive, you can find your evidence, and build your goddamn fucking case."

"You've given me no evidence."

"That's your job. Find it."

"I have other priorities."

"What other priorities?"

I hesitated.

It shocked me; I *never* hesitate.

"I want to clean up this town," I said curtly.

"Why?"

"I want to clean up this town," I repeated.

"Mickey — what the fuck — we have a *case.* Crooked Mayor. Rape and multiple murders. Let's take him down."

"If we lose the Mayor, there'll be no stopping the gangs."

"Who cares?"

Another hesitation.

"*I* care. I want to clean up this town."

"What happened to you Mickey?"

"I want to clean up this town," I said, mechanically.

Aretha flipped the eject switch and my seat and I fell out of the aircraft.

The seat and I hurtled to the ground. I unbuckled, and clambered out of my seat and engaged my boot jets — but at this velocity, they were worse than useless.

A moment before I crashed to earth, my circuits went into hibernate mode. I started to lose consciousness; a sensation I experienced as a slow blackout.

I would estimate I was still five per cent conscious when I hit the ground hard and smashed a deep hole into the pavement, and then—

I recovered consciousness.

I was being lifted out of the ground by a crane.

I pulled myself free, shook the debris from my metal body. My right arm was shattered at the shoulder. My electronic mind reaccessed my database, and I could now vividly recall my conversation with Sergeant Jones, immediately prior to my crash-landing. And I reaccessed the data towards which she had directed me.

I cursed myself when I, once again, saw the clues laid out in my mind:

Criminal record check of the deceased.

Criminal record check of all relatives of the deceased.

Criminal record check of all officers assigned to the case.

Criminal record check of the Mayor and all members of his administration.

Cross-reference all criminal allegations made against the Mayor with all police reports issued on behalf of the murder victims and their relatives over the last ten years.

Call up original file on Fliss Hooper rape. It contained no mention of Mayor Abraham Naurion. But I decided to play a hunch, and initiated a command to my database to **ignore all amendments to original file.**

The file was now rewritten in my mind; the new report concluded that **the main suspect for the rape is Mayor Abraham Naurion.** But the case was dismissed due to errors in the data-filing processes, hence the re-drafting.

It took ten minutes to read and process all the data, but then I could see the story unfurl:

Jaynie Hooper, two arrests for binge-drinking excess, one reported incident of drug use prior to a school examination, expelled for having sex with a teacher in school hours, thrown out of her home, began sleeping rough, then in hostels, then acquired a luxury apartment in the Third Canton despite having no declared income. Hypothesis: she was working as a prostitute.

Her sister Fliss, I sermonised to himself, was working 12-hour days at the hospital, saving lives. But Jaynie simply coasted through her life, making easy choices and easier money.

I continued laying out the data in summary form:

Abraham Naurion, Mayor of Lawless City, accused of lewd behaviour as a student at Bompasso University, with a datatrail proving he had been downloading amputee porn via a University site. But no charges brought. And, indeed, all the allegations were expunged from the official record, and were only found when I began a deep search.

Add that together with:

Jaynie and Abraham Naurion sighted in a Dark Side restaurant, on Tuesday 14th May.

The following day Jaynie is admitted to hospital suffering from multiple limb severings. Rape allegations are recorded by Officers Williby and Glass. Her statement includes a reference to the assailant as "Abe." Forensic examination reveals micro-traces of DNA in her vagina from the condom which had been used by her rapist; the DNA was a hundred-per-cent match for the DNA of Abraham Naurion.

Hypothesis: Naurion was a sexual fetishist who paid Jaynie for sex then severed her limbs for his own sexual gratification, and then raped her, for his further sexual gratification.

I accessed film footage of Jaynie Hooper, and was shocked at how sweet and young she looked. I could see the resemblance, too, to her dead sister Fliss.

Who could do such a thing, to a girl like this? What kind of warped moral universe were these humans living in?

Despite all this, I did not, I feel, have enough evidence to convict Naurion in court: just the various datatrails, the reported rumours passed on by Sergeant Jones, the DNA evidence (easily dismissed, since the rapist could have sprayed Naurion's DNA on the condom) and a hypothesis built on all these circumstantial connections.

However, I was confident that once I arrested the Mayor, more incriminating evidence would emerge as a consequence of my diligent investigations into the accused, his friends, associates and other victims (for criminal-profile statistics persuaded me that this rape was unlikely to be an isolated offence).

I therefore resolved to arrest the Mayor.

At this point, however, it occurred to me that I was faced with four interconnected mysteries.

1) What kind of weapon could have perpetrated the massacre of the three doctors and the two paramedics? My subroutine had drawn a blank on this: some form of banned technology had been used, but it wasn't clear what.
2) What made Naurion think he was immune from the law?
3) Who else was complicit in Naurion's tampering with the police computer record?
4) And *how could I have missed all this?*

And it was Mystery 4) that worried me the most. For the clues had been there. The data had been in my head all along. All I'd needed to do was to ask the right questions.

But I *hadn't* asked the right questions. I'd been sidetracked into pursuing a private vendetta against the gang bosses.

What the hell, I queried of myself, was wrong with me?

43

"I should arrest you," I told Sergeant Aretha Jones, "for committing grievous bodily harm on a Galactic Police Officer."

"Oh my goodness? Did you fall and hurt yourself? I thought we were done, you see," said Aretha sweetly, "and that you were planning to fly home."

"I could have been damaged!"

"You self-heal don't you?"

"Well, yes," I said, grudgingly.

"I was right, wasn't I? About Fliss and the Mayor?"

"It seems so."

"Get the bastard."

"Oh I will."

"What he did – to that girl. Just fucking nail him."

"You've been," I conceded, "of some significant use to the investigation."

"Fuck off, tin man. Just do your job. That's all I ask."

"Why?"

"Why what?"

"Why—" I struggled with an unfamiliar emotion: Embarrassment. "Why drop me out of the cruiser like that?"

"I did it," said Aretha, deadpan, "to see if you'd bounce."

I wanted to experience Rage, but somehow, could not.

For reasons that eluded me, I seemed to actually like this woman.

43

"Hello Jaynie."

She was smiling at me. She was young and she was pretty, and she reminded me of Fliss.

"Are you here about my sister?" Jaynie asked.

"Yes."

The hospital room was decorated in pastel colours which, I knew, were designed to have a calming psychological effect. I consulted my database: apparently this never worked. I wondered if—

"You know who did it, don't you?"

Jaynie's words interrupted my idle wondering. I wondered *why* I had been idly wondering. That was unusual behaviour for me.

I looked at Jaynie again and thought, once more, that she looked so very young.

"I believe I do," I told her brusquely.

"All my fault." She didn't cry; her face was taut. She was beyond crying.

"I think there is no basis for that opinion. It was not your fault."

"I pushed it. I always had to push it."

Jaynie had received her arm and leg transplants after a wait of only nine months, thanks to heavy pressure from the Courtesans' Guild. Even so, it was going to take her the best part of ten years to pay for her new limbs. And until then, she would in effect be enslaved to the Guild, and would have to whore for them until her debts were cleared.

Jaynie sat in the chair, very still. She was, I observed, still in the process of getting used to her new body. She didn't gesticulate with her new hands at all, though when she had to reach for a water glass it was clear she had full motor coordination. But she looked – I searched for the metaphor – *hemmed in* by her own limbs. They weren't part of her; they were like alien creatures clinging on to her torso.

"How old are you Jaynie?"

"I'm seventeen, sir."

"It's human nature," I said, in sombre but reassuring tones. "When you're that age. To experiment. Drugs. Sex. Other –" I searched for the correct idiom, and failed to find it in my rather academically biased dictionary database – "'stuff'."

"I was a whore."

"Receiving money for sex is not a crime, and nor is it a sin. But a modern and liberal consensus would be: there are easier and less demeaning ways to make money. And you owe it to yourself to explore such options."

Jaynie winced at my words; and I wondered if she was experiencing a twinge of phantom pain in her limbs.

"It wasn't about the money," Jaynie whispered.

"I know."

"My parents have lots of money. Legitimate money. They're solid citizens. They built the City Bank, you know. They took on the loan sharks and won."

"Did they?" I asked. Though I knew that they did. I knew everything about Jaynie; it was all in my database. But I needed to hear it from her, in her own words. My eye cameras filmed every moment: everything she said would be admissible as evidence in court.

"I wanted to rebel."

"I was the same, when I was your age," I said, and wondered why I'd said that, and whether it might even be true.

"You were human once?"

"A long time ago."

"What kind of rebel were *you*, huh?"

"I guess I may have worn my hair longer than the other guys," I said, busking it now.

"I took drugs, yeah, right? Heavy ones. Reality-altering drugs. Mood drugs. Accelerants. I had group sex when I was sixteen. Well, why not? It's not like, you know, you can get pregnant, or get a disease. Not now, not like in the old days."

"I know that you like to read extensively. Therefore, that explains how you know what it was like, in 'the old days'."

"Yeah, I do. I read a lot. I love novels. I read – what? – three novels a week. More sometimes. More now. I read a novel a day now, every day."

"I'm sure that's extremely sound occupational therapy. Which novels?"

"You read novels too?"

"No," I admitted. "But I have them all on my database. Every novel ever written. Every poem ever written too. In addition, I have every—"

"I get the gist. You're a walking encyclopaedia. But do you actually *read* these things?"

"I know all the knowledge that is in them. If you name a novel, I will know the story, and the characters, and can recite every word."

"Do you take bookings?"

"No I do not take bookings," I explained.

Jaynie made a barking sound, somewhere between a laugh and a vomit. She grinned, and shook her head.

I theorised this was a sign Jaynie was becoming more cheerful. Perhaps my educative discourse was helping to lift her mood?

"Jane Austen," said Jaynie. "I love Jane Austen. I'm what they call a Janeite. Mark Forester too, I love his historical sagas. But I mainly read the classics, pre-twenty-first century. Tolstoy. Dickens. Collins. And Edith Wharton. Do you know Edith Wharton?"

I accessed my data on all the books by all the authors she mentioned, and "read" them all.

"All fine books," I observed, "though the English syntax in several of them strikes me as a little strange."

"It's an ancient *form* of English. They used semicolons then. But this is what I wanted to say. There's one book, by Edith Wharton, about a young girl who is 'ruined'. Do you know what that means?"

"I have read the book," I explained, "Just a moment ago. And yes of course, I know what 'ruined' means."

"In this context?"

I accessed my dictionary database, and was baffled. "An interesting concept, though I don't entirely see why her ruination incurred such social opprobrium," I conceded.

"It was the way they thought then. Social mores. She was ruined, and hence, disgraced. Not fit to be part of society. We don't have that concept any more, not really. Drugs aren't illegal. You can stab someone in the eye, and no one even minds. Kids my age, we all have sex, all the time. I know girls who—"

"I don't need to know that datum."

"No. You're right. You don't. No taboos in our society. Except, parents don't get that. They overprotect. You have to shake them up a bit. I shook 'em up. I was a 'bad girl'. A whore." Jaynie brushed her cheek with her finger, as if sweeping away tears. But there were no tears, and the arm wasn't hers. "I was just kidding around. I really was. I'd applied to medical school. I wanted to be like my big sister. I did. I loved Fliss. She always looked after me. Then that bastard tied me down and cut off my arms, and sawed off my legs, and he did, well you know the rest. It's in the police report."

"I know the rest."

"I'm young, I've never had rejuve. Transplants are easy for me. New legs, new arms. I was raped, but after all the other taboos I've broken, does that really matter? I mean, really, does it matter?"

I understood her logic, and her agonised irony.

"It matters," I told her calmly.

"He used me like meat," she said. "I was nothing. He didn't kill me, but he destroyed me. I'll never be good for anything ever again. No matter how long I live. I'll never fall in love, I'll never have kids. I'm not being melodramatic, it's how I feel. I'm seventeen, and I'm rotting meat, and the rest of my life won't be worth living. And Fliss knew all that," Jaynie concluded, bitterly. "That's why she threatened Mayor Abraham Naurion. That's why he killed her."

"You don't know for certain that he killed her."

"*Of course he fucking killed her.*"

"I think so too," I said. "I have to warn you that everything you say is being filmed and recorded in my database and will be used as evidence in court. If you fail to confirm anything you say in this filmed interview you can be charged with perjury and sentenced to incarceration and loss of human privileges. Everything you say must be the truth, the whole truth insofar as you know it, and must be stated without prejudice and malice exactly as the events occurred. Do you understand?"

"I understand."

"Do you solemnly swear to give a true and honest statement of the facts?"

"I so swear."

"Then let me hear your testimony."

Jaynie told her story. The rape had taken place in the Mayor's apartment. There were two witnesses, who also participated; she identified both of them, a man and a woman, from holograms which I projected in the air. They were Martha McCall, Mayor's Secretary, and Thomas Crystal, the head of the City Transport Department.

At the end of the witness statement I stood up.

I switched to my beaconband channel.

And, with all the authority invested in me by the Government of the Solar Neighbourhood, I called for the protection of a robot posse to protect me and my witness.

"*Urgent,*" I screamed at the heavens, "*assistance requested* now."

The heavens darkened as a swarm of robot battleships loomed in the sky above the City Square. A whirring sound filled the air, as the forcefield generators of the battleships whined in resonance.

The crowds in the square stared up at the sky, as the Day of Judgement dawned upon their lawless planet.

Each robot battleship had its own powerful forcefield, based on technology superior to anything available on the planet of Belladonna. Anti-matter rays and disruptor pulses could destroy the armour of any missile or weapon possessed by the Belladonnan army and navy. As a matter of strict, rigidly enforceable policy, all the Exodus Universe planets were forced to survive on outdated technology, and any attempts to invent more modern forms of warfare were punishable by the severest sanctions.

In such fashion, I mused, the Government of the Solar Neighbourhood exerted the mildest of dictatorial grips on the settler planets. Freedom and autonomy were granted to each planet; each was allowed its own legal system; each was allowed to be as corrupt, and immoral, as its citizens desired. The law specifically gave these settlers the freedom to go to hell.

But certain offences still came under the jurisdiction of Solar Neighbourhood law, and could lead to the dispatch of a Galactic Cop such as myself, with the authority to investigate and prosecute.

And to enforce the law – provided we had just cause – we were able to summon an armada of robot battleships, remotely controlled from Earth.

These were the Doppelganger Deputies, and their power was awesome.

I strode towards the hovering battleships, until I was standing in their shadow. Their hulls sparkled in the bright noonday sun. Jaynie flew by my side in her motorised wheelchair, and my forcefield subsumed both of us. A landing craft descended from one of the robot ships.

Close by, Sergeant Aretha Jones pulled up on her flybike. She shucked back her helmet, and gave a thumbs-up sign to me. Justice was going to be done.

I gave her a hand-salute, acknowledging her role of assisting me in bringing the case to a successful conclusion.

Jaynie looked up at me, fear etched on her face.

"You'll be safe with these guys," I said to Jaynie kindly. "They'll keep you in space; no one can harm you. No missile can reach you."

"What will you do?"

"I'm going to find and arrest Mayor Abraham Naurion, and charge him with your rape and the murder of your sister and her friends."

"Be careful," whispered Jaynie, and never had she looked so young.

I actually grinned. "Nothing can—" I began to say.

And then night fell, and the shadows struck.

The transition was shocking. I felt as if my mind had

suddenly malfunctioned. Blazing sunshine was replaced by blackest night. Stars now blazed bright in the sky, and the twelve moons of Belladonna loomed low, like rocks perched on an invisible wall. The robot spaceships vanished from sight for almost three seconds, then their searchlights kicked in and the ships reappeared. I looked at Jaynie who looked back at me, her expression a blend of curiosity and wonder.

"Get—" I said, and then a shadow coalesced into a human form. A black-clad warrior with hands raised. I drew my two plasma pistols in less time than a blink and I fired, but the warrior had vanished and hot clammy hands touched my head, and I rolled to the ground and turned my forcefield on to random pulse and started hurling flash grenades. Jaynie screamed and grabbed her ears, then her head was ripped off her body and a fountain of blood shot into the sky.

"*Fire!*" I roared subvocally, even though my cybernetic mind was already sending a beaconsignal to the robot battleships and all six of them laced the ground with disruptor pulses. A quantum computer controlled the trajectory of each burst and the men and women standing on the ground saw death rays rain down all around them but miraculously never hitting any innocent person. There were a dozen shadows now, and they were fast, but they weren't airborne, and these robot gunners were skilful enough to shoot the wing off a butterfly travelling at lightspeed.

But then the sky erupted as one by one the robot battleships exploded and rained down as liquid metal. Fireballs hung in the night sky, then turned into toppling sparks that plunged to the ground. I saw a shadow and lunged with a punch powerful enough to burst through hardmetal but my fist struck thin air. I briefly marvelled, and then was filled with fear.

The shadows drifted through the crowd and miraculously and appallingly the bodies of innocent bystanders exploded, and the bloody fragments became interwoven and conjoined, like snakes twisting in a deadly embrace.

Shrill screams and foul swear-words and pathetic hopeless

sobs filled the air as scores of human bodies agonisingly merged their flesh and bones. I felt my eyes being plucked out, and with my radar sense I could see my eyeballs being stretched into columns. By now I was also screaming. I closed down my brain circuits, and tried to self-destruct before the agony came upon me, but then . . . the agony came upon me.

I was crippled and contorted but could not die.

My clothes and my pseudo-flesh fell away from me until I was just a naked screaming metal shell.

And then, as I staggered blindly, my radar sense showed me that my metal carcass was becoming fused with the dead body of Jaynie, poor sweet Jaynie, and her lungs were brutally sucked into my mouth and they grew like trees inside me and my metal heart was in *her* body and was pumping coolant fluid into her dead veins. And still I could not die. Until finally—

THE HIVE-RATS

The First

I AM CONSIDERING.

The First

I AM CONSIDERING STILL.

...

...

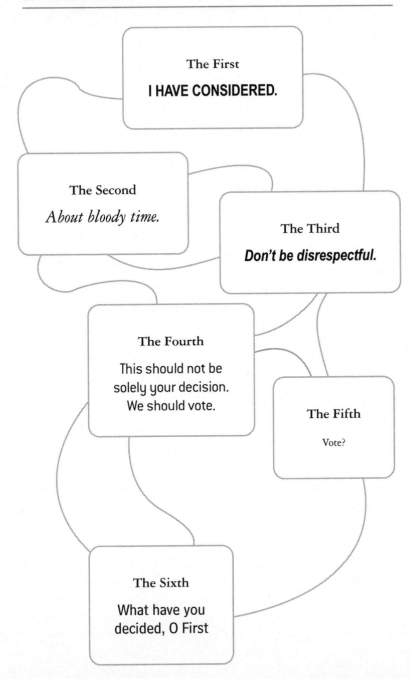

The First

I HAVE CONSIDERED.

The Second

About bloody time.

The Third

Don't be disrespectful.

The Fourth

This should not be
solely your decision.
We should vote.

The Fifth

Vote?

The Sixth

What have you
decided, O First

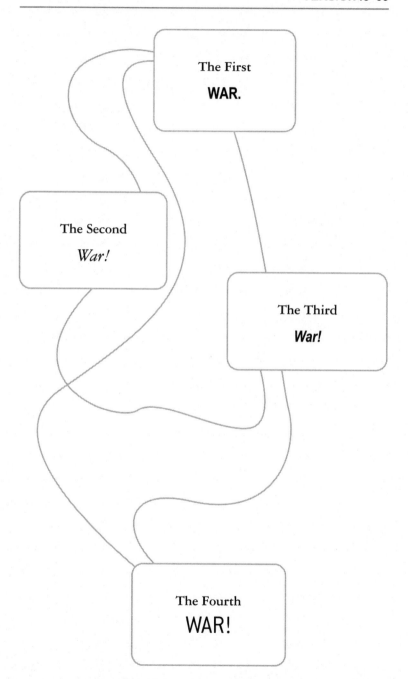

The First
WAR.

The Second
War!

The Third
War!

The Fourth
WAR!

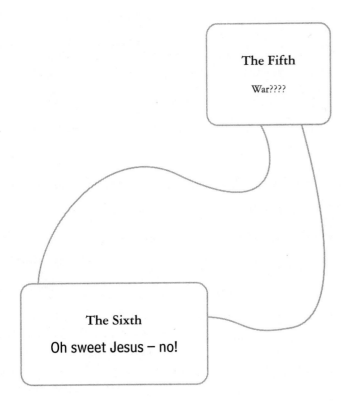

A swarm of spaceships coalesced in the sky above the planet of Morpheus; they flew and flocked in the blackness of space, until finally they formed into a single perfect V.

Each spaceship was a fighting machine of extraordinary power. There were plasma cannons. Torpedo tubes. Forcefields. Anti-matter generators. And hulls strong enough to withstand huge amounts of military punishment.

This was the Sand-Rats' armada. With these battleships they would wage war on the horror, the terror, the marauder that was Humanity.

The Sand-Rats were a swift — astonishingly swift — swifter than conceivably swift — species. From the moment that the First decided upon war, barely a Morphean year had elapsed. And in this time the Rats had invented tools, and smelted iron for the first time; they had built computers, forged unbreakable metals, and invented a system of travelling through hyperspace from first principles. Their evolution from foraging semi-rodent to faster-than-light space-travelling warriors in one of the largest armadas ever known had occurred in the period between the height of Morphean winter, and the first snows of the following winter.

Admiral Martin Monroe saw all this happen, and marvelled.

He was, in truth, growing to admire these plucky little creatures. They didn't look like much — they were smaller than a cat, smellier than a skunk, and uglier than all fuck.

And these scrawny beasts hadn't, initially, appeared to pose any kind of a threat to the Admiral and the scientific expedition he commanded when they had first arrived on Morpheus.

In fact, many of Monroe's men had used the Sand-Rats for target practice. These ugly-fuck creatures were so dumb they would stand up on their hind legs, whiskers twitching, and wouldn't run even when the plasma bolts started firing. The

Admiral once shot a hundred Sand-Rats in a single session, and had won first prize in the Most Alien Fucker Killing!! contest. The prize consisted of a yard of potent ale, which he consumed with ease in a single continuous swallow, and yet still remained sober enough to fly the space cruiser twice around the planet's moon.

Morpheus was a beautiful planet, ripe for terraforming. Instead of soil, the planet was covered by a vast variety of multi-coloured fertile sands. There were millions of species of insects, trillions of varieties of Sand-Worm and Sand-Beetles, but strangely, very few larger mammalian forms. No more than two hundred species walked the 'earth' of this sandy planet; and the most plentiful species of all was the Sand-Rat. There were so many of them! And they were so damned dumb!

And then, after two years of analysis and study, the Scientists resolved that they now had a full and complete picture of this biosphere. Some carefully selected samples were to be kept for the Zoo, in time-honoured fashion: two Sand-Rats, two samples of each of the other land mammals, a sprinkling of flying insects, and far too many (in Monroe's view) Sand-Snails and Sand-Worms and Sand-Beetles. Then Monroe gave the orders for the Four Horsemen to move into position and start terra-forming.

At this moment, the Sand-Rats staged their counterattack. They had cunningly, and in Monroe's view rather sneakily, bur-rowed *under* the hardglass dome of Monroe City. And thus one morning, a trillion Sand-Rats were inside the city, eating all the humans. It was a rout. The Sand-Rats had no weapons, they had no forcefields. But they could gnaw through body armour and they each had the capacity to eat a hundred humans or more and yet not become bloated.

Monroe had launched his Soldiers against them, wearing full body armour and firing One Suns and plasma guns and explosive-shell cannons. But in the end, the Sand-Rats ate them all.

Monroe was not afraid of dying. He had spent his entire life longing for a Glorious death. But, he had to concede, the moment when the Sand-Rats burrowed up his arsehole and began to eat him alive was a bleak one.

After hours of agonising pain, Monroe had died. But several hours later, he realised he was somehow still alive. His mind had been subsumed into a larger mind. And it was then that Monroe made three discoveries about the Sand-Rats.

1) *They were intelligent.*
2) *Their intelligence took the form of a Hive-Mind. They were Hive-Rats, not Sand-Rats at all.*
3) *There were five Minds in each Hive; and only one Hive on the entire planet.*

That's why the Sand-Rats didn't fear death. They weren't individual creatures, they were cells of a larger, *much larger*, planet-wide entity. Killing a Sand-Rat was like clipping off a fingernail.

But now there were *six* Minds: for Monroe had been absorbed into the Hive-Mind, and found himself compelled to act as advisor to the ensemble of alien intellects.

Monroe quickly deduced that one of the Minds was the original Sand-Rat. And this, he learned, was called by the other minds "The First."

And the other Minds, he gleaned, all belonged to species eaten and destroyed by the Sand-Rats. One mind from each exterminated species had been kept, and served as slave and advisor in the Hive-Rat gestalt intelligence.

All this was shocking enough. But Monroe then discovered, after a year inside the alien Hive-Mind, an even more terrifying fact:

4) *The Sand-Rats existed in six dimensions.* They inhabited, of course, three spatial dimensions. But they were also able to span three dimensions of time.

And these three temporal dimensions were:

"Normal" time. In other words, real time – time as humans perceived it.

Slow time. The Hive-Rats, Monroe learned from his fellow Minds, once defeated a rival predator species by slowing down time so much that a billion "real" years elapsed in what, for the Hive-Rats, was less than half an hour. By this point, the savage, remorseless, totally-unbeatable-in-combat predator species had become extinct. All of which constituted another victory for the Hive-Rats!

And, then, most chillingly of all from Monroe's point of view, there was:

Fast time.

This was the secret weapon that had allowed the Sand-Rats to destroy the humans on Morpheus. For every time a Sand-Rat was killed, the Hive-Rat entity entered a state of fast time. And a thousand more Rats were conceived, and, after months of gestation, were born, and over the course of ten to fifteen years grew through adolescence into maturity, and then for several decades more were trained in fighting skills, and were taught about the tactics and weapons of the humans and – a blink of an eye later, in "real" time – resumed the battle against their human enemy.

Thus, the death of each Sand-Rat generated, from the perspective of human time, the magical materialisation of a thousand more, an instant later.

It was the most terrifying war Monroe had ever fought. The enemy died – and then were reborn, a thousandfold. Savage creatures materialised constantly out of nowhere. And when the Sand-Rats moved, they blurred the air itself.

Monroe's Soldiers had fought the most deadly aliens in the universe, and had triumphed, again and again. But against the Sand-Rats, they stood no chance. For these aliens, Monroe now knew, had time on their side.

Naturally, after making these four shocking discoveries,

Monroe had tried to learn more about the creature's strange temporal gift, in order to find a way to thwart it.

But the alien mind known as the Second did not understand the origin or nature of the First's ability to manipulate time. And the Third was equally baffled. And the Fifth didn't even seem to understand the question.

The Fourth, however, being a superintelligent being, *did* understand how the Sand-Rats were able to manipulate time. However, annoyingly, he/she explained it all in terms so complicated that Monroe could not begin to fathom his/her gist.

The First, of course, did not readily answer personal questions, or yield confidential information about itself. That was why it was the First.

So Monroe was forced to accept that the First had a power beyond all comprehension. It awed him, and terrified him.

For, soon after the Hive-Rats' victory against the humans, Monroe had looked up at the stars in the sky, and found *they had moved*.

By a tiny amount, admittedly; but for a space admiral, the difference was shocking. And the landscape of Morpheus had altered – not vastly, but significantly, and Monroe was trained in spotting such details. New forests had grown. Cliffs had become eroded. Rivers had changed course. And the wrecked human dome had merged into the sands, and become almost invisible.

It was clear that hundreds of years had elapsed – maybe as much as half a millennium – in the "real" world, during the course of that (subjectively speaking) longish pause of four or five minutes.

And then, a few moments later, Monroe began to fear that his vision was playing tricks on him.

For he saw the animals that were running so wildly on the yellow and purple and pink sands start to slow down, and slow down, and s l o w   d   o   w   n until they were entirely motionless. Clouds remained frozen in the sky; birds were caught in mid-sweep. It was as if time had stood still.

And that was because the Sand-Rats had in fact made time stand still.

This had been when Monroe discovered about "fast time."

And it was during this period of fast time that the Hive Mind had applied its collective intellect to the problem of how to defeat and destroy the rest of the human race.

The Sand-Rats already knew that humans had extraordinary powers. They could fly. They could make fire emerge from tubes. They apparently had flown from the stars to reach this planet. They had extraordinary devices that could kill, shine light beams, and dig holes, and they could alter space with some kind of invisible barrier effect.

All of this was initially quite baffling to the First which was, when all was said and done, just a rat.

It evoked awe and wonder from the Second, who belonged to a feline warrior/predator species with limited technology, and who marvelled at the ingenuity of these now-dead humans.

It intrigued the Third, who like the humans belonged to a biped species, though one possessed of four arms, and not a paltry two. The Third felt envious, for these alien creatures had a civilisation so far beyond her own!

And it mystified and pleased the Fifth, though she was, in truth, often and very easily mystified and pleased.

The Fourth, however, was a scientific genius, and he/she relished the challenge ahead of him/her: to replicate the accomplishments and discoveries of human science in order to vanquish the entire human empire. And he/she was aided in this goal by his/her unfettered access to all the knowledge acquired by Monroe in the course of his long life as a spaceship captain and latterly, admiral.

And thus, as time stood very nearly still, the Hive-Rat (or rather, one of the Hive-Rat Minds, namely the Fourth) was able to devote tens of thousands of years (in subjective Hive-Rat time) to mastering classical physics and quantum physics and relativity and cute-o.

The Fourth then applied these concepts to the practical task of building space battleships, taking advantage of the formidable engineering skills of the Third, whose humanoid species had been on the verge of flying into space before being consumed by the Hive-Rats.

Once the planning stage was complete, the trillions of Hive-Rat bodies on Morpheus applied themselves to the task of mining and smelting ore, weaving hardmetal, and building weapons and space ships. The mineral resources of the planet were pillaged; in six months ("normal" time) entire mountain ranges across all the continents of the planet vanished, leaving behind barren craters and vast hordes of baffled goat-like and cow-like creatures that could not comprehend how they had so abruptly lost their pastures.

And thus, one Morphean year after the First had emerged from its long mull and declared War, the armada set sail into space.

Its mission: to eradicate humanity from the universe.

The First

STARS. SO VERY MANY OF THEM.

The Second

The beauty of infinite space is a joy like no other!

The Third

Define "infinite."

The Fourth

Let it be noted: I have considerable moral qualms about our mission.

Since you ask: The meaning of infinity depends upon one's frame of reference. I postulate that our universe evolved from a singularity generating a rapidly expanding universe unified by a multiverse founded on quantum chaos. But space is not infinite until quantal reality becomes actual, and so I propose a new concept of "limitless potentiality," herewith known as Đ.

The Fifth

I didn't follow a
word of that.

Oh I do miss
being alive and
flying in the light
of the dawn!

The Sixth

You're just a bunch of fucking rats.
How can you be so fucking *clever*?

The First

WE WERE NOT, O SIXTH. NOT AT FIRST. WE WERE LITTLE MORE THAN A SEMI-SMART HIVE MIND UNTIL WE ATE THE SECOND, AND ABSORBED HIS DEFT AND BRILLIANT MIND INTO OURS. AS I RECALL, IT FELT RATHER ODD.

The Second

Once I had claws and teeth and all feared me. I could run faster than the wind, so fast I could snatch a gliding lizardbird from the air, my roar was like thunder, my three eyes saw in all directions. Each day I fed and the vast monsters of the earth were my prey, they dwarfed me but they were powerless against my claws and teeth and my venomous darts, and no creature could defy me, and certainly not the Sand-Rats, who I regarded as my pre-dinner snacks. I ate them by the million, until — the bastards! — they sneakily evolved into lice and inhabited my bowels and ate me and all my kind from the inside out. A billion of us lay dead on the sands of our planet, and only I was left, my mind, my soul, trapped in this putrid brain.

I am shamed. And I have shamed my people. These creatures do not deserve to live, or to thrive, or to dominate our world.

And yet they now own me.

The Third

Know you this; Nature is not cruel, it is merely what it is.

Such accelerated evolution of the Sand-Rats' bodies was a remarkable feat. The rats became lice and then became rats again! No wonder, all those years later, my own people were exterminated by these monsters. We fought them with swords; and they became flying acid-spitting, poison-farted clawed monsters and slew us.

The Fourth

I am to blame for all of the horror that will ensue. I have taught these monsters all about mathematics and science and how to win a war against the humans.

But their gift of slowing down and speeding up time awes even me. How could such a talent ever evolve, in such a base and stupid creature?

The Fifth

I am just a little flying thing, a butterfly-bug, no threat to anyone. What am I doing here? Help me!

The Sixth

There is only one master race. And I was an Admiral in its fleet!

The First

**ALL DISSENT AND DISCUSSION
WILL CEASE.**

**ELSE UNUTTERABLE AGONY
WILL CONSUME YOU ALL!**

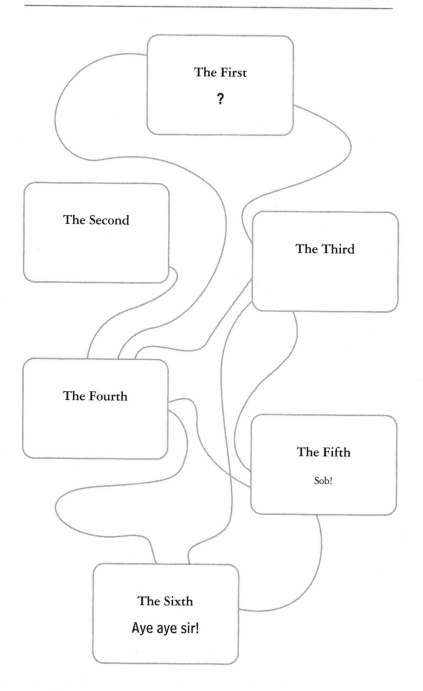

THE COP

Version 44

I was lost in deductive process as my spaceship glided into orbit around Belladonna.

It was a small dry planet, with red-tinged soil and large areas of yellow savannah. The freshwater lakes zigzagged a blue warmth into the dry land mass. There were no seas, as such.

I reviewed my database: I'd been to this planet four times before. The third time, about a hundred years ago, I had successfully eliminated the gang bosses and departed alive. The fourth time, however, my previous Version had been thwarted and assassinated before the completion of his mission.

Fortunately, my previous Version – Version 43 – had downloaded his mind into a databird two hours before his rendezvous with the robot battleships, following standard field protocol in such circumstances. So I knew everything that he knew about the case, and the witnesses he had interviewed, and his various hypotheses.

Strangely, however, I had no visual record of what had happened in the minutes just before the death of Version 43. Normally, all data from a Cop's eye cameras were automatically backed up on the home planet computer. But the wireless transmissions on the planet had ceased for a period of twenty-five minutes before, during and after the assassination. And all the local news reports of the death of Version 43 and sundry innocent bystanders seemed guarded, and confusingly expressed.

I decided that this aspect of the mystery would soon unravel. More worryingly, however, upon reviewing my predecessor's investigation into the original serial killing case, I came to a dark conclusion:

Version 43 had been defective.

He had been slow-witted and incompetent, he had perpetrated a unjustifiable and unnecessary death-whilst-resisting-arrest on a local gangster, he had failed to follow basic clues, and he had been duped by an obviously duplicitous female witness.

This woman – Jaynie Hooper – who had also been killed with Version 43 by the unknown assassins – was in my opinion almost certainly a liar. She was a prostitute, with a history of mental instability, who had been working for one of the major pimps on the planet – Sandro Barumi, an employee of brothel-queen Kim Ji. Barumi, according to copious data available on this matter, had been in dispute with the Mayor, who was refusing to accept bribes to allow Barumi to expand his business into snuff and alien-rape movies.

So, I hypothesised, Barumi had framed the Mayor, by paying Jaynie to make a false allegation of rape. Then, following through the logic of this postulation, Barumi paid some assassins to murder Jaynie's sister, in a mass slaughter that was guaranteed to draw the attention of the Galactic Police. And, furthermore, so the hypothesis extrapolated, he had paid a bribe to Police Sergeant Aretha Jones to drop a broad hint to Version 43 about how to run his investigation.

Version 43, with unpardonable gullibility, had believed every word of this elaborate hoax.

And at that point, once all the evidence against the Mayor had been transmitted via the beaconband to Earth, the dishonest witness Jaynie Hooper was assassinated, and Version 43 killed along with her.

A perfect frame! The evidence against the Mayor was on file, and the only person who could contradict the evidence, namely Jaynie, was now dead.

Any ordinary investigator would have been utterly fooled by the brilliance of this fit-up, and would therefore have ordered the Mayor to be arrested for rape and multiple murders, including the killing of a Galactic Cop. And this of course would have left Barumi free to pursue his criminal agenda.

However I was no ordinary investigator. I had assimilated all the available data with exceptional thoroughness, which included studying the biographies of every citizen in Lawless City, watching every second of TV coverage of the Mayor and his political career, and analysing and pattern-processing every crime in the city, major or minor, reported or informally alleged, for the past 100 years. Out of this wealth of information I had formulated no less than 42,037 hypotheses, involving 42,337 perpetrators. I had then performed plausibility analyses on each hypothesis, and performed mock-trials of the twelve most likely suspects using avatars in a virtual courtroom to test the evidence to the uttermost degree. Until, finally, I had arrived at my pre-ferred, and almost certainly correct (93.45 per cent likelihood) solution.

I had, in short, solved the entire case, before even landing on the planet.

I experienced a brief burst of an emotion that felt familiar to me, but I couldn't quite put a name to it.

Ah, now I had it!

It was Pride.

I debarked from the space shuttle and strolled across to police headquarters.

I liked the stark black-stoned architecture of this city, and the way some of the buildings hovered above the ground. It wasn't, by the standards of settler cities, all that bad a place. There was an Opera House, there were theatres, there were symphony orchestras. But it was still a wild town, oversupplied with tav-erns, brothels, casinos, gladiatorial arenas, and wrestling rings.

I stared at the door of the police headquarters.

"Police Commissioner Oharu," I said at the door, and it opened.

"I thought you died," the desk clerk said, and smiled at me.

I had no rejoinder to that.

The clerk – a tall sandy-haired man called Oliver Dingwall

who had an alcoholic wife and a degree in palaeontology and, who, I decided, was not worth cultivating as an informant or ally – led the way into the secure corridors, and thence into the Commissioner's office.

Commissioner Oharu was a tubby and a jolly man. He was, I estimated, twenty stone plus and almost perfectly spherical and his unlined rejuved features made him look like an overgrown schoolboy. "Sit down, sit down," he fussed at me.

"I'll stand."

"You know Sergeant Aretha Jones."

Sergeant Jones sat in the black armchair. She stared up at me. I stared back. She was rather beautiful, I observed, despite being, to put it mildly, a stranger to fashionable skinniness.

"I met you two days ago," I informed her.

"I know," Aretha said.

"You were present when my previous body was assassinated."

"I know."

"Tell me what you saw."

"Hell. Horror. Like nothing." Aretha's voice was faint, slightly cracked. There was a haunted look in her eyes.

"Why were there no cameras at the scene?"

"There were. I had a camera in my body armour. It recorded nothing."

"All public and private cameras in every location on the planet failed to record. There is no visual data available for a period of twenty-five minutes in all," Commissioner Oharu informed me.

It was indeed very strange.

"How could that be?" I asked.

"We don't know."

"And what," I said, directing my blank stare at Aretha, "exactly did you see?"

"I don't know."

"There was an eclipse of the sun," I commented.

"Artificially induced," explained the Commissioner. "An

asteroid was moved into a position that achieved a perfect eclipse."

I was lost for words.

Eventually, I retorted: "An asteroid was moved into a position that achieved a perfect eclipse?"

"That's what I said. That's what happened."

"I see," I said, and ran a feasibility study into how one could so move an asteroid. "That is an impressive piece of orbital engineering," I concluded.

"This was no ordinary assassination," Aretha pointed out. "This thing is fucking *huge*."

"I'm aware of that. My point is: no one on this planet has the technology to move an asteroid," I explained to them.

"It can be done with antigrav oscillators," the Commissioner replied calmly.

"I'm aware of that. My point is: there are no antigrav oscillators on Belladonna. It's banned technology."

"Someone has them."

"I'm aware of that." I processed the data furiously, but nothing coherent emerged out of my maelstrom of thoughts and hypotheses. "I want to see the bodies," I told them, firmly.

"I'll take you," said Aretha. She got up. I noted that, despite possessing a degree of plumpness, she was muscular and extremely fit, and brimming with energy. Her jet-black hair was pinned up. Her hands were large, for a woman, even in this day and age.

She walked with me down the corridor, and tapped a wall, which slid away revealing a lift shaft. Then we stood in the lift, which took us down to a moving walkway that took us under the city streets to the morgue.

"You say, 'Hell. Horror. Like nothing,'" I observed to her, as our walkway hurtled us along the sleek purple-tile-lined tunnels. "Would you like to elaborate, or clarify?"

"No."

"It all happened so fast, you didn't really see what happened. Would that be a fair synopsis?"

"It happened slowly; I saw what happened. It was – like nothing."

"More specifically."

"I couldn't think. I couldn't see. And yet I saw."

"More specific still."

"One moment you and Jaynie Hooper were standing in the middle of the square, as the robot landing craft descended. Then the stars came out. So many stars. So . . . many, and so beautiful. The moons were silver in the night sky. I heard a singing and a roaring and for a moment I thought I was in heaven and then the – the – the – then something cut the something, the thing, the everything thing, reality was, I don't know, split, changed, altered, and there was blood, and bodies were, and you were, I can't explain it any more."

"Hallucinogens," I suggested, "in the air, to create mayhem and confusion when the assassins struck."

"See the bodies," Aretha told me, coldly.

43

As we entered the morgue, I reviewed my data on Sergeant Aretha Jones.

Divorced three times, two children, both under ten, twice decorated for bravery. No convictions for corruption, which meant nothing on this planet, because everyone paid bribes to avoid corruption convictions.

Her stepfather Maxim had been a gangster, working for the Fernando Gracias mob, until he was killed by a drug dealer.

Her mother Jara was a singer, and still did an act in one of Gracias's nightclubs. Jara's reviews were electrifying. She clearly had an exceptional talent, though her idiom was jazz and I had no taste for it.

All this meant that Jones was compromised, an associate and relative of known gangsters. She was not to be trusted.

A large hardplastic bubble filled the room. The entire crime scene had been preserved and conveyed away from the City Square, and reinstalled in the morgue. Part of a static walkway had been chipped off, and several flybikes had been caught up in the mêlée.

I was initially puzzled, and then appalled.

I recognised shards of Version 43's body. Eyes, a face, a torso, cybernetic circuits. But they were scattered in a haze of human body parts and pieces of exploded spaceships. There were intestines, hearts pumping blood, legs, hair, muscles, all mixed together in a frozen sculpture. The engine of the flybike floated in mid-air, and had lungs. A string winding around a chunk of wall proved, on closer examination, to be a spinal cord stretched thin. Mouths were separated from faces. Sinews and muscles formed a mid-air tableau. Teeth flew like bullets. And bizarrely, many of the floating body parts must have been already static when the forensic bubble had been wrapped around them. It was as if God had clapped his hands, and frozen time and space.

Except it wouldn't have been God. This atrocity had a stench of evil about it. It was a vision of Hell. A horror.

A . . . like nothing.

"How could this happen?" I asked.

"We don't know," Aretha told me.

I stood silent, staring, for about fifteen minutes.

"Is something wrong?" Aretha eventually chided.

"I'm thinking."

Aretha waited patiently. Eventually my thought processes returned to something resembling normal.

"This is just so – strange," I said.

"Anything you say will be used in evidence. The penalty for perjury can, in certain circumstances, be death," I said, in an eerie monotone that was designed to induce panic in suspects.

"That's not true," Mayor Abraham Naurion said mildly.

I smiled, scarily.

That too had no impact on Naurion.

"If I'm forced to kill you, you should feel free to sue me," I pointed out, acidly.

"That's a threat."

"Indeed."

"Is he allowed to do this?" the Mayor asked Aretha.

"No."

"Are you going to stop him?"

"No."

"Hell, I've got nothing to hide. Ask away." The Mayor settled back cheerfully, his broad shoulders overspilling his chair, his silvery-metal skull clashing bizarrely with the coffee-coloured skin of his face and hands. The Mayor clearly had many enemies, I mused, if he felt the need to protect his brain in this way.

I reviewed my database: Abraham Naurion was once a farmer on Mars. To save his harvest, he had used illegal genetic material, creating crops that grew without water, but which had the deadly potential to mutate into cancer-spreading predators. He'd been sentenced to eighty years of corrective therapy for his abuse of the rules governing genesplicing. By this time, his wife and children and 91,245 other people had died of fast-spreading twenty-four-hour cancer, and there was nothing left for Naurion on Mars or on Earth. So he had chosen the fifty-fifty instead.

He was a well-liked Mayor, a liberal, who had built schools and theatres and had tried to instil a moral code into his lawless people. He took bribes from all the gangs, but never favoured one above another. And thus he was able to run a cash-rich administration without the need for taxes.

"We have evidence," I said, "sufficient to arrest you for rape and multiple murders. Would you like an attorney present?"

"I am my own attorney."

"We have a witness statement from a prostitute called Jaynie

Hooper who alleges you raped and mutilated her, and then murdered her sister Fliss Hooper and Fliss's four friends, including Alexander Heath."

"That's an unsubstantiated allegation from a dead witness," countered Naurion; "it's not sufficient evidence on which to charge me."

"True. But we have also minute but significant forensic traces of your DNA in her vagina."

The Mayor laughed. "That's easy as hell to fake! All you need is a spittle sample from my beer glass, and you can clone the DNA and spread it on a condom. That scam's been run a thousand times; a judge would laugh you out of court."

"I'm aware of that," I conceded.

"Do you have film footage of me committing either rape or murder?" he asked.

"No."

"Do you have an independent witness corroborating Jaynie's statement?"

"No."

"Then you have no case."

"I agree."

"Come again?" said the Mayor.

Aretha, too, was astonished, and looked at me in rage.

"I agree with you," I said. "There's no case to answer. You're innocent, in my view. My predecessor was duped. Jaynie was a liar; you are an innocent man."

"How can you say that?" Aretha said angrily.

I stared into her eyes, and Aretha flinched.

I turned my attention back to the Mayor. I smiled, to indicate that he was not under suspicion and could relax now.

"You did know Jaynie Hooper though?" I asked, casually.

"Of course."

"And you paid her for sex?"

"Hell yes."

"How much?"

"Is that relevant?" the Mayor appealed to Aretha.

"Answer the question," I said.

"A million scudos."

"A lot."

"For a year. She was a companion, not just a whore."

"You pay for companionship?"

"I sure do."

"Did you rape her and cut off her limbs?"

"No."

"Can I have a word with you about this?" Aretha said coldly to me.

"No you may not. Jaynie alleged that you severed her limbs for sexual thrills. We have it on record that you have down-loaded amputee porn."

"I've heard that allegation. It's bullshit. It was mainly Latina porn, on a hundred-movie download. I was only twenty, for Christ's sake, and I didn't watch any of the really pervy stuff."

I nodded.

"So the question is: why would Jaynie lie?" I asked, in the same friendly tones.

"Jaynie was crazy; she'd do anything she was asked to do," said the Mayor, sourly. "Some bastard suckered her. I felt sorry for her, to be honest. I went to see her in hospital once her limbs had grown back and – well. She wasn't the same woman. Look, guys, I don't blame Jaynie for lying about me. She was earning a dishonest buck, the same as the rest of us. But I do want to find the bastard who paid her to lie about me, and who killed her. Any help you want, you got it."

"That's very much appreciated," I said. I reached in my bag and took out a bottle of 200-year-old Cambrian whisky. "Let's take a drink."

The Mayor grinned, and tipped the water from his glass on to the floor and poured himself a glass of rich malt. "Join us?" he said to Aretha.

"No," she said sullenly.

"And you?" he said to me.

"I don't in fact drink," I informed him.

"I figured as much. So you believe me then?"

"I believe you. I think you were framed."

The Mayor nodded. "Why?" he marvelled. "And more to the point, who?"

"Those are the two things I need to find out."

The Mayor grinned, and sipped some whisky.

He smacked his lips, and sipped some more.

Then the Mayor started to cough. He spat out the whisky. "Fucking—" he said, and toppled over. His head smashed against the desk. The metal skull scraped and scarred the wood.

🛡43

"What the—" Aretha said, shocked.

"We haven't got long," I said. "Name your price."

"—fuck are you—?"

"Name your price."

"I thought you believed the Mayor was innocent?"

"I do."

"But—?"

"But, that's not the point." I smiled my eerie smile. I took out a vial and opened the cap. Then I held out my hand and my fingernails grew into spikes. I inserted one spike into the vial.

"Hold this."

"What's—"

"Blood from the morgue, taken from the corpse of Jaynie Hooper."

I held my spiky hand out delicately, like a courtesan drying her five-inch-long fingernails. With the other hand, I yanked the Mayor upright. I flipped his eyelid back, exposing the eyeball completely.

Then I moved the spike—

"No!" screamed Aretha loudly.

But my hand didn't waver. I touched the spike to the eyeball, very gently. Then I flipped the eyelid back. Then I did the same to the other eyeball.

"Let's take him downtown. We'll order a forensic test."

"Blood splatter," said Aretha, getting it.

"Blood splatter," I agreed. "Let's assume the Mayor is guilty, that he dismembered Jaynie Hooper. The blood splatter would have been horrendous. And afterwards, he would have washed his hands, his arms, his scalp; he'd have stood under burning hot jets until every last forensic trace was gone."

"But he would have wanted to watch her scream in agony."

"That's the whole point of it, if you're a pervert, as we must assume the killer was. And flecks of blood under the eyelid aren't easy to shift. What's your price, Aretha?"

"I have no fucking price," she told him. "I'm an honest cop. I'm not going to be part of this – this – frame."

"Why not?"

"Because it's wrong."

"But it solves all our problems, don't you see?" I explained, patiently. "The Mayor is the linchpin of this entire corrupt society. He pays the gangs, the gangs pay him. If we send him down on trumped-up charges, the gang bosses are screwed. We can start again."

"But he's innocent."

"Of this crime, probably yes, but he's guilty of many other things."

"But not this! He didn't rape and mutilate Jaynie Hooper!"

"A while ago, you told me he did," I said slyly. "What's your price?"

Aretha sighed. "A million scudos."

"Done."

"Two million scudos."

"Don't push your luck."

"One and a half, and I want a ranch, my own ranch, for when I retire."

"That's asking a lot."

"Are you bribing me here or not?"

"Let's do it."

"What do we do now?"

I hefted the Mayor on to my shoulders.

"Let's get this sucker processed, then we'll go see the pimp."

We dumped the Mayor at the City Jail. A forensics team were already in place, and I briefed them on what they should find. On a planet like this, I had decided, it was easier to go with the flow.

This was a city that enjoyed the night. I walked down the Morgan Boulevard and was amazed at the energy and the life. Pavement cafés and piazza restaurants and impromptu moving walkway rock gigs turned the city streets into one vast digression. My navigational aids made it impossible for me to get lost, but even so I felt as if I was in danger of losing my bearings.

A vast neon-lit palace proclaimed: GAMBLING! NAKED GIRLS! NAKED GUYS! NAKED SEX! BARE KNUCKLE BOXING! HYPERSPACE SIMULATION! The lights were 3D and zoomed towards passers-by like fireflies trained in market trading. Music blared from every wall, creating a symphony of popular melodies that merged into a single gestalt song.

I found it strangely appealing. The music tracks were jagged and wild and wonderful. There was a lot of laughter, and also a lot of drunken fooling about. Every fountain was filled with splashing teenagers. No one in this city seemed to sleep.

I have an acute sense of smell, and I could smell chorizo and burger and fries and hot dogs and steaks sizzling on hot plates and fajitas and spices and the tang of wind-dried chicken hanging outside oriental restaurants.

I passed a crowd of dangerous-looking youths, wearing tight leather trousers and kevlar-armour on their shoulders and with pierced eyelids and tattooed semi-naked bodies, and they cried, "Hi!" and slapped me on the shoulder and gripped my hand and invited me to join them for a drink. And I laughed and said no and walked on.

I arrived at the Dante's Dream nightclub and robot bouncers scanned me for weapons and found that I was carrying two pistols, a collapsible rifle and a bandolier of grenades, and had poison darts loaded into my leather wristbands. I gave them my Galactic Police authorisation and they allowed me in.

The rhythm of the music changed. A singer was on stage, soulfully singing a ballad of grief and tenderness, accompanied by a soundtrack that she artfully controlled with fingertip clicks. The club was a baroque fantasy, with retro pillars and walls that slithered like snakes as you looked at them.

"Welcome to my world," said Fernando Gracias with a smile, and beckoned me to sit in a booth.

Kim Ji was already there, dressed in a second skin made of soft black silicon with the texture of brushed leather. She was a Noir, with jet-black eyes, and black lips, and pale smooth skin.

Billy Grogan sat next to her, a sulky freckled Irishman with yellow hair and hate in his eyes. I anticipated trouble; I had, after all, gunned Billy's father down only a few days before.

And Hari Gilles was there too. My database informed me that he had spoken with Version 43, and I swiftly reviewed their dialogue. Hari was beautiful and scarily thin and dapper, in a superbly cut classic suit. He was comprehensively face-tattooed, and wore a tie with an interactive hologram pattern of the stars on it.

"You've arrested Mayor Naurion," Kim said calmly.

"I have."

"Is he guilty?"

"Of course."

I smiled my eerie smile.

"Then I'm appalled," said Kim, in amused, relaxed tones. "I always thought Naurion was an honest man – but it seems you never can tell."

Billy grunted, scornfully, and gave me a killer stare. I glanced at him with disdain.

"The Mayor is not the one I'm interested in," I said softly. "I'm looking for the person who hired the assassins who killed me." I paused, and waited until I had their undivided attention. "And I know who that is," I added.

"Who?"

"It's one of you," I explained, calmly.

"Fuck off!" said Billy.

"Hush, hush, hush, Billy," said Hari, like a snake hissing at a rat before eating it.

"Let the man—" said Kim, but I interrupted her.

"One of you around this table is guilty," I said, in angry tones. "One of you – excuse my language – bastards butchered the medics and then paid to have me killed."

"More than likely," agreed Fernando Gracias. "But it wasn't me."

"Or me," said Kim.

"Not guilty," said Hari Gilles.

Billy Grogan raised a finger to me.

I sighed.

"I'm tired of this planet," I said. "Just give me the killers. I'll take them down. Whoever authorised the hits, for whatever reason, I don't care. Just surrender your hired guns, and I'll walk away."

The singer's soulful voice caressed my heart, or would have done, if I'd had a heart.

"That's a fair offer," said Fernando Gracias; "let us think about it."

Now, a soaring howling alto saxophone riff merged with the wail of the singer's voice, like a spectral bird in flight through the darkness of space.

43

"While Fernando is thinking about it," Kim purred gently, "let me ask a question. Can you?"

"Can I what?"

"Can you 'do' it? By which I mean, are you capable of sex?"

"No," I lied.

"And love? Can you feel love?"

"Can you?"

"Touché."

"You're a whore."

"I know what I am. Do you disapprove?"

"No."

"You do."

"I don't," I admitted, "get it. I mean. In this day and age, why would anyone pay for sexual intercourse?"

Kim looked at me hauntingly, and beautifully, and I gleaned her subtext: what man would not want to have sex with her! But the question still worried away at me.

"Very few humans are puritanical, these days," I clarified. "All humans are attractive, more or less. And fit. And rejuve does wonders for the libido. So why pay?"

Kim actually laughed.

And I stared at her, this fierce, black-eyed, shockingly beautiful woman, who I knew to be the whoremonger-in-chief to the entire planet.

"I'll tell you why," Kim said.

And she told me, as the saxophone sang and the singer wailed, as the darkness of the club cast shadows over our faces. "Because I sell dreams," Kim whispered. "Not just sex."

I shrugged. She clarified.

"My girls and boys," she continued, in the same soft whisper that seemed to syncopate with the music, "are dream-weavers and artists. They conjure magic out of sensual experience. They take you to a place you've never been. Well, perhaps they wouldn't do that to *you*, but with my punters, we offer a journey to another realm. I'm not talking bondage and sadomasochism or dressing up as a baby, though we offer all those services too. I'm talking about taking you on a journey to the inner depths of your soul. If you had a soul."

"Stop goading me," I snarled.

"An orgasm can be as intense as a religious experience," she whispered, and her face was as radiant as any madonna. "We offer that. We offer rebirth of the soul. We are more of a religion than a whorehouse."

"Be that as it may," I said stiffly. "Did you kill the medics?"

The mood shattered. The song changed.

"No I didn't," Kim said.

"You're lying."

"Usually I am. Today, I'm not."

And she smiled, arrogantly, and nastily.

"If we give you the killers," asked Hari Gilles. "Do you pledge to leave us alone?"

"You can't trust this dogfucka," muttered Billy.

"If he makes a deal, he'll honour it," Fernando said authoritatively. "Robots are like that."

He was correct; robots must always speak the truth. I, however, am a cyborg and can quite easily lie like a human.

"Do you so pledge?" insisted Hari.

I knew, from my database, that Hari Gilles was the pre-eminent employer of contract killers in the city. His dark-suited soft-spoken assassins were known as Gill's Killers, and they enforced gambling debts, enacted vengeance, and sometimes even settled disputes between neighbours through acts of bloody vengeance.

"Of course," I said.

Hari smiled, charmingly, and the lines of his face-tattoo twitched, like ants dancing on his cheeks and eyelids.

"So tell me the truth," I said. "Who ordered the hit on the medics?"

"I did," admitted Hari Gilles.

"And what was the motive?"

Hari continued, fluently:

"The Sheriff's son owed me money. He was a junkie. He welshed. His friends were in the wrong place at the wrong time." And Hari beamed at his own barely coherent lie.

"And who were your assassins?" I asked.

"They were from out of town," said Hari Gilles. "Space pirates. We paid them big time, and they left via the fifty-fifty."

"They're off-planet?"

"You'll never see them again."

"That's no use to me."

"In that case," said Hari carefully, "they're still in Lawless City. Just tell us where you want 'em, we'll deliver the bodies."

I was silent.

"Yes?" said Hari Gilles, "or no?"

I reviewed my data on the other three gangsters:

Fernando Gracias was a likeable and cultured man, and a patron of the arts – the legendary muse to many generations of rock and jazz musicians. He also, however, ran most of the robbery gangs in Belladonna. His fierce and ruthless armed robbers knocked over trucks and shops and restaurants and stole from banks and his street thugs mugged shoppers on a daily basis. His employees murdered, on average, 12,000 people a year.

I looked at Kim Ji, still smiling, still enchanting. Kim was less murderous than Fernando – counting the whore-deaths, her thugs generally killed no more than 100–200 citizens a year, at a best estimate. But, my database told me, she also ran slave farms where tens of thousands of citizens lived like hogs, making hand-crafted consumer items for the rich people on Third and Seventh Boulevard. And she enforced discipline by flaying her enemies and hosing them down with salted water. It was possible, just about, to survive such treatment, but few retained their sanity after experiencing such extremities of pain and degradation.

Meanwhile, Billy Grogan was glaring at me, unable to get over his hatred for the monster who had killed his father. Billy was young – he would be thirty on his next birthday – and, by all accounts, full of passion and family loyalty, and I almost felt sorry for him.

But my database told me that the Grogans' drug traffickers held the city in a grip of evil, spreading addiction like cancer. The drugs the Grogans sold included hallucinogens that turned users into werewolf-like beasts who raped and ate innocent victims by the score. Thousands of citizens of Lawless City died each year, either from the ravages of drugs, or because they had been eaten alive by addicts.

And these four monsters – Hari Gilles, Kim Ji, Fernando Gracias, Billy Grogan – were now seeking my corrupt benediction, my seal of approval for their crimes.

"Sure," I said.

43

Sheriff Heath stared at me. His grey walrus moustache twitched.

"I thought you were dead," he said, drily.

"I was, but now I'm alive again," I told him, with equal dryness.

"I get it. You're a replica, of the previous cyborg?"

"Yes."

"And you're gonna find the people who killed my boy?"

"Yes."

"How can I help?"

And I explained.

43

Barumi's home was a palazzo with decor of staggering crassness.

The walls were salmon pink. The chandeliers had real candles. The servants wore formal suits in a twenty-second-century baroque style, and bowed or curtsied often and pointlessly.

Sergeant Aretha Jones and I walked through, awestruck at the staggering absence of taste made manifest on every side.

"*You know this guy?*" I subvoced.

"*Yeah.*"

"*What's he like?*"

Sandro Barumi appeared. He was a tall, good-looking man of Earth-Asian-Italian genetic origin with four arms and three eyes.

"Like that," Aretha murmured.

Barumi smiled at me and held out his lower front hand. I shook the hand.

"Greetings," said Barumi.

"You're a Vishnu," I observed. "There's nothing about that on my database."

"A recent modification," admitted Barumi. "It helps with, well, let's not get into that. How can I help you?"

I winked.

Barumi stared at me with surprise.

"The fix," I clarified, "is in."

"I don't understand," Barumi said primly. He beckoned us to follow him. And so we followed him through three doorways, until we emerged into a formal sitting room, where a *chaise longue* hovered in the air, and the sofas were made of ancient brocade decorated with 3D holograms. I perched on one of the *chaises*. Barumi sat on a cushion, balanced in a yoga stance. Aretha stood.

"You can trust her," I said, nodding at Aretha. "She's one of us."

"I have no idea what you're talking about!" Barumi said cheerfully. His front arms were calm, but his rear arms were starting to twitch. His middle eye blinked, independently of the other two. I wondered what kind of vision the three eyes gave him, and the answer promptly arose from my database. Third eyes were a new fad on Belladonna, and they were attuned to perceive the personal noetic matrix around a human being – the energy field which mystics once referred to as the "aura."

I *had* no aura so I was, I realised, invisible to Barumi's third eye.

"This is how it is," I said, as Barumi poured tea and milk into a cup with three of his hands, while scratching an itch with his fourth. He passed the tea to Aretha, who sat down on the edge of the eye-dazzling sofa. Barumi poured a second cup for me.

"I don't take tea," I said.

"Biscuits?" smiled Barumi.

"I'm a cybernetic organism," I pointed out. Barumi was both fey and charming, not the cold-hearted pimp I had been expecting.

"Whatever. What can I do for you?"

"I want to make you Mayor."

Barumi smiled. His third eye blinked. He turned to look at Aretha. His third eye blinked again.

"Why is she afraid?" Barumi whispered.

"She's afraid of me," I said. "She's a crooked cop, I could have her badge."

Barumi stared at me. His third eye blinked.

"Why the devil do you want *me* to be Mayor? I mean, really, do I look like Mayor material?" And Barumi beamed camply, like a cat splashing around in a bath full of cream. If I'd had a sense of humour, I would have laughed out loud.

"I want to clean up this planet," I explained. "I've framed the Mayor for the rape and mutilation of Jaynie Hooper. I finished the job you started. Now I want someone to take his place."

"The Mayor's a powerful man."

"The Mayor's going to be brainwiped. We need a successor."

Barumi smiled. "But why me? Your logic eludes me."

"Because you're smart," said Aretha, with a heart-melting smile, and I observed how Barumi loved the compliment. She was, I conceded, good at this.

"Because you're smart," I repeated. "Very smart. You're a bio-engineer. A people moulder. You're not a gangster, you're an artist."

"Flatterer."

"And I know you tried to frame the Mayor once already. I'm just finishing the job."

"Are you serious?"

"I'm serious."

"But you're a Galactic Cop. You're incorruptible!" Barumi said, sweetly.

"Do you really believe that?" I laughed a hollow laugh. "Don't be so naïve."

"It's such a while since anyone called me naïve." Barumi grinned.

"I'm not a hero," I explained. "I'm just a machine. I have no morality. I have a mission; once I achieve it, I can go back home. So if I can frame the Mayor, make a friend of you, leave a puppet administration in place, my mission objectives will all have been achieved. The Mayor will go down for the murder of the medics. You'll take his job. I'll depart swiftly, to avoid being killed by those godawful assassins again."

"I don't believe you," said Barumi. "Why should I trust you?"

"You'll trust him for the same reason that I trust him," said Aretha harshly. "Because this piece of crap machine is nothing but a piece of fucking . . . crap. He has no loyalty. He has no friends. But his plan is a good one. Someone's head has to roll, and the easiest choice is Abraham Naurion."

"That's no more than that evil bastard deserves," Barumi said, amused.

"These Galactic Cops are real pros; the Mayor has been comprehensively fitted up," Aretha said. "This guy faked the forensics. He's done a deal with the gang bosses. He's as crooked as he claims. You can trust him."

"But how do I know I can trust *you?*" said Sandro Barumi.

"You can," Aretha said. And Barumi stared at her.

I changed my vision filters to noetic, and I saw what Barumi saw: the swirling coloured cloud around Aretha that was her personal aura. My database allowed me to interpret the meaning of the colours and patterns. And I could see, as Barumi could see, that this was the aura of a woman who was telling the truth.

"The Galactic Cop has bribed you?" said Barumi.

"He's bribed me."

"He's faked the forensics on the Mayor?"

"I saw him do it with my own eyes."

"You're in this for the money; this is not an *agent provocateur* police action?"

"I'm it in for the money," said Aretha. "I'm no fucking *agent provocateur*. I want one and a half million scudos, and a ranch, and this is how I'll get it."

Her aura didn't change: it gleamed with black and gold spikes. She was telling the truth.

Barumi's third eye blinked, and he smiled. "Damn, it's true," he marvelled. "I've got my very own crooked Galactic Cop."

"What just happened between you two then?" I said, feigning irritability.

"I looked into this bitch's soul," said Barumi, "and she's as evil and twisted as I am."

"So tell us what really happened," said Aretha, with savage cynicism. "And then we'll finish the frame."

And Sandro Barumi told his tale.

I recorded it all in my eye cameras, and transmitted the data to the Belladonna computer. It was a full and long confession. And it revealed Sandro Barumi to be a bold and a brilliant, and also a sad and a vain, and an utterly pathetic man.

The Mayor, Barumi revealed, was not in fact in the pay of the gang bosses: he was *their* boss. The gang leader of all Lawless City. He was the don, the gang bosses were his *capi*. And soldiers like Sandro Barumi owed a double allegiance – to their gang boss, and to the Mayor.

"Kim always treated me like shit," Barumi whined. "As if I wasn't worthy to be her, you know, evil pimp. I did wonders for her. I engineered her boys and her girls to be sexually insatiable. I created four-armed courtesans, gigolos with two cocks. I was a sculptor of flesh. And the whores all love me. I understand them. In many cases, I created them. I bred them from embryos. I sent them to school. I own them.

"And all I wanted was my just deserts. I wanted to be the gang boss. I wanted the Mayor to kill Kim and appoint me in her place.

"And the bastard refused! And he threatened me. He told me I was getting ideas above my station. He told me that we needed a balance of power, to keep the citizens free. Free! No one is free in this city. The gangs own everything, including the people."

So far, this all conformed to my hypothesis. I felt a glow of pleasure.

"So I decided," Barumi continued, "to destroy the Mayor. When I learned there was a Galactic Cop on his way to Belladonna, I picked one of my whores and I brain-moulded her to be my slave. I shaped her aura, so she could lie without being detected. Then I cut off her legs and arms and raped her with a condom smeared with the Mayor's DNA and sent her to the City Hospital. That was my trap, and you fell for it. She told you she was raped by the Mayor. You were about to arrest him! With the Mayor gone, I could've made my play. I could've ended up as boss of bosses in Lawless City."

"You still can," I said eagerly. "But explain to me: how did you kill the medical students and the paramedics?"

"I didn't."

"But you must have done," I said coaxingly. "The frame

won't work without them. I don't have jurisdiction for ordinary criminal offences."

"*Someone* killed them," said Barumi sulkily. "You were sent for, and I seized the moment and framed the Mayor. Now, what's our plan?"

I fumed. The original crime was still not solved.

But I did at least have a full confession from Sandro Barumi.

"Aretha," I said casually.

"Yeah?"

"Arrest this man."

There was an awkward silence.

"Huh?" she said.

"His crimes lie outside my jurisdiction," I told her patiently. "But he's just admitted to grievous bodily harm, rape, and perverting the course of justice. Those are criminal offences under the Belladonnan penal code. Arrest him."

"Don't shit me, man," laughed Barumi.

"I can't," said Aretha.

"Why not?" I asked patiently.

Aretha looked anxious. Her eyes flashed around. We were alone in this tasteless salon; but *how* alone?

"Because it's too dangerous for me to – look, the police department is paid a lot of money to—"

"Arrest him, or I'll arrest you."

Aretha stared at me.

"You're the boss," she said, coldly.

Then she fixed Barumi with a firm glare: "Sandro Barumi, you are under arrest for rape, grievous bodily harm, and perverting the course of justice. Anything you say will be given as evidence. Got that?"

"What happened to our plan?" said Barumi, sadly.

"Come quietly," said Aretha getting to her feet. She took out her mag-cuffs. "Hands behind your back."

Barumi obligingly put his hands behind his back. He turned around for her to cuff him.

I stepped forward and clubbed Barumi to the ground with the back of my hand, and drew his gun, and threw it at Aretha, who caught it instinctively.

Barumi fell, then got up and saw Aretha pointing his own gun at him.

"Bitch!" he screamed.

"Back off!" she screamed back.

Barumi reached in his jacket for a second weapon, and she fired an explosive bullet near his head. The wall shattered behind him. Barumi was very still.

Then he whistled.

Aretha stared at him. "Just put your hands—" she said shakily, clearly confused by the bewilderingly fast pace of what had happened. I had moved so swiftly I had been literally invisible. All Aretha knew is that Barumi had fallen to the ground for no apparent reason, and suddenly she had a gun in her hand. Sheer instinct had taken over from there.

"You're going down, bitch," whispered Sandro Barumi.

Aretha slowly looked around. More than a dozen bodyguards had appeared in response to Barumi's whistle, and they were all aiming their plasma pistols and explosive-bullet guns at her. "Help?" she said to me.

"Not my jurisdiction," I said calmly. "I can't assist in any way with this arrest; my apologies for that, officer." And I smiled a heartless smile.

Aretha flicked a switch on the gun and threw it in the air and it exploded in a huge flash. Smoke billowed.

And she ran. She ran past the pillars, beyond the statuary. Bullets rained into her body, and rocked her, but she carried on running. Plasma blasts burned the clothes off her back, and still she ran. She hurtled towards the window and crashed through.

Barumi was laughing, his arms waving widely.

I drew my two plasma pistols in less time than elapses in the flutter of a butterfly's wing.

"However, the attempted murder of a local law enforcement officer," I explained, "*does* come under my jurisdiction."

Barumi turned and drew his backup gun and aimed it at my temple. "I could—"

I shot him with a plasma bolt to the chest. Barumi flinched and tottered back, and managed to fire an explosive bullet at my head. I dropped one of my pistols, snatched and crushed Barumi's bullet in my palm, then caught my pistol before it hit the ground.

A hail of bullets and plasma beams rained down on me, but I was moving now. I fired and ducked, fired and ducked. The entire shootout lasted no more than thirty seconds.

When the shooting was over, my clothes were ablaze, and the blood of Barumi's twelve gunsels flowed over the ornate mosaic floor of the pimp's palazzo. None remained standing.

Barumi was still alive, blood oozing from his mouth, his third eye staring straight at me, seeing nothing.

I put a bullet through the third eye.

"Suspect killed," I said calmly, "while resisting arrest."

Outside the pimp's palace, Sheriff Heath was supervising a posse of deputised police officers, all armed with plasma rifles. Paramedics were clustered around the burned and battered body of Sergeant Aretha Jones.

"How is she?" I said.

Sheriff Heath shrugged.

"*I'll live, you motherfucker,*" said Aretha, over her mobile implant.

She dragged herself on to her feet, bracing herself against the shoulders of the startled paramedics. Her jaw had been blown off by an explosive bullet, one ear was missing, her face was scarred with burns. And most of her clothes had been burned away, revealing hard black body armour beneath.

"You were lucky," I said.

"*You set me up*," said Aretha.

"Yes."

"*You knew they'd try to kill me. You let them try.*"

"I got a confession. And when they tried to kill you, that gave me just cause to use maximum force. My aims were achieved."

"*I could have been killed.*"

"That was a possibility."

"*You callous fuck.*" Aretha wheezed.

"Your body armour—"

"*I only wore body armour,*" Aretha explained tensely, "*because I knew you'd betray me.*"

"How could you know that?" I asked, genuinely intrigued.

Aretha stared at me with lidless eyes. "*Because it's what you always do.*"

43

Aretha was strapped into a stretcher by the two paramedics. The pain had kicked in by now; even an anaesthetic squirt wasn't helping much. Out of curiosity, I surveyed her aura: it was a tormented mass of black snakes. Hate, rage, and a sense of betrayal consumed her.

Then the paramedics carried Aretha away and loaded her into their ambulance.

"That was harsh," said Sheriff Heath mildly.

"The lying bitch," I said savagely, "deserved it."

43

One by one, and then in twos and threes, Barumi's gunmen and gunwomen were emerging from the pink palace, carried out on stretchers or sealed in body bags.

The deputies made a fierce force: they were burly, mean-looking, and carried their plasma rifles with authority.

"These guys all work for you?" I asked.

"They belong to the Ninth Canton flybikers' chapter," Sheriff Heath said. "I deputised them."

"Why not use the official deputies?"

"Hell, they're all as corrupt as I am."

I nodded.

I realised that I now had to explain the true situation to the Sheriff. For it was evident that my hypothesis had been incorrect. Sandro Barumi *had* tried to frame the Mayor, but he hadn't killed the Sheriff's son, or the other medics. Nor had he been responsible for the murders of Version 43 and Jaynie Hooper.

"Well?" said Sheriff Heath.

"It's not Barumi."

"Shit!" Rage washed over the Sheriff's face. "I went out on a fucking limb for—"

"Wait. Let me explore another hypothesis."

The Sheriff seethed.

I explored the data.

I reviewed the biogs of all the gang bosses and their followers: nothing new emerged.

I reinvestigated the Mayor, and found no fresh evidence. It was clear that the Mayor was playing an artful game – he was a leader of organised crime in the city, no mere flunky. But there was no reason to suppose he had killed the medics, or Version 43, or Jaynie Hooper.

So then, on a hunch, I accessed the personal files of every citizen in Lawless City, cross-referenced them with funeral services, and cross-referenced *those* with the files Version 43 had downloaded at the hospital.

An anomaly became apparent. Thousands of people were dying of illness, murder and accidents every month, without ever being treated at the hospital, or autopsied at the morgue.

"It's a phantom," I said at length, ending the Sheriff's irritated wait.

"Come again?"

"A phantom hospital."

The Sheriff mulled on that. His whiskers twitched. "Makes sense," he conceded.

"That's what your son discovered. People are getting ill, they go to hospital, they never get there. Then their limbs and organs are sold off. That's why Version 43 failed to find evidence of organ theft at the Hospital in his extensive investigation and analysis. Because the criminals were not in fact stealing organs: they were stealing *people*."

"Oh – fuck," said the Sheriff.

It suddenly dawned on me that Sergeant Aretha Jones had gone off by ambulance to hospital. But *which* hospital?

"Yes, indeed, 'Fuck,'" I said.

🛡43

While the Sheriff called the City Hospital on his MI, I reviewed all the available data on Sergeant Aretha Jones.

And I discovered, in her most recent files, a memo to her superior office applying for leave from her regular duties to pursue an undercover assignment. I read the memo with dawning horror:

4.12.54. From Sergeant A. Jones, Bompasso PD, to
Commissioner D. Hayes
Authorisation requested for undercover sting operation: Codename
Viper. Sergeant Aretha Louise Jones working for Galactic Cop
X44, posing as a corrupt police officer. The aim of the operation is
to discover whether pimp Sandro Barumi is responsible for the
murders of Alexander Heath, Andrei Pavlovsky, Jada Brown,
Sara Limer, Fliss Hooper, Jaynie Hooper and Galactic Cop X43,
employing banned technology. It is anticipated that this will be a
high-risk operation, due to the tendency of Galactic cyborg officers
to neglect the safety of their human partners.

I was stunned.

Aretha had put this into the system three hours before we had met with Barumi. She'd *known* I would betray her, and she'd known she was risking her life. But she'd still gone along with my plan.

And she'd *lied*. She'd lied so absolutely there was not a trace of duplicity in her body aura. She'd made Barumi believe she was corrupt, when she was not. How could she have done all that?

I studied Jones's biog again, and realised that as a young woman she had studied karate, zen buddhism, and *Kirlian meditation* – the art of consciously controlling one's own body aura.

That explained how she'd had the skill to conceal her lies from Barumi's third eye by, in effect, faking her own essence. She'd backed my play by altering her own electron-photonic glow.

Damn, this woman was good.

I had intended to trick her; instead she had tricked *me*.

Consequently, I concluded, I had been guilty of a monumental error of judgement. It now seemed to me that Sergeant Aretha Jones was an honourable officer who, for reasons I could not fathom, had a blind and unshakeable loyalty towards me. Oblivious to this fact, I had almost got her killed. Then, to cap it all, I had humiliated and taunted her.

And, finally, I had allowed her to go off in an ambulance which was not officially registered, with paramedics whose badge numbers were fictitious, to a hospital which did not exist.

This was, I concluded, not one of my better days.

I was now certain that Sergeant Jones had been abducted by the same gang of organ-thieves who were responsible for the deaths of the medics.

And so, I presumed, in a matter of days if not hours, her organs and limbs would be stripped from her body to be sold and reused. It was possible, too, that her brain tissue would be extracted a piece at a time to create a cheap form of antidementia serum.

And *I* was to blame. I had failed to read the clues. I had misjudged a key member of my team. I had allowed myself to become obsessed with eliminating a single evil pimp, and had failed to realise that a vast and far more evil conspiracy was in process.

How could I, I asked myself, have been so *wrong*?

43

I flew with the Sheriff in his patrol car.

"You think this was a revenge abduction? Sergeant Jones has a lot of enemies," suggested the Sheriff.

"No," I said.

"What then?"

"I think this happens a lot. No one ever notices."

"This is one evil mother-raping cock-sucking city," the Sheriff conceded.

"Indeed," I said.

There was a pause.

"I always thought, you see," said the Sheriff, breaking the silence, in a tone that hinted at contempt, "that you cyborgs were infallible."

"Nearly so."

"Not this time."

"It's true," I conceded, "that I was wrong about who killed your son. And why."

"You had the 'when' pretty well nailed," the Sheriff said tactfully.

"It seemed a compelling hypothesis."

"You had *no* fucking clue."

I considered this evaluation. "That point is a fair one."

"I'll tell you what's a compelling hypothesis," said the Sheriff. "There was evil going on, and my son found out, and tried to stop it. And that's why they killed him."

"That is indeed my current hypothesis."

"But so fucking what? What good will it do, me helping you? Alex is dead."

"That's correct."

The Sheriff kept his eyes fixed in the air to avoid looking at me, but his thoughts tumbled out slowly like a cliff eroding.

"Alex always thought, you see," said the Sheriff, "that I was a piece of shit. He called that one right, all right."

"I decline to comment."

The cliff-eroding continued, as the Sheriff bared his soul.

"I got thirty-five children, you know," the Sheriff said, "scattered around the universe. It's not like I need another – why the hell would I want – oh fuck it. Who do you think is behind it? The phantom hospital?"

"It could be any of the gang bosses, it could be all of them. It could be the Mayor. It doesn't matter."

"How doesn't it matter?"

"According to my data, ten thousand people went missing this month, including Aretha. Many may still be alive. Our mission is to find them, and save them. After that, I will deal with the guilty ones."

"That kinda makes sense."

"It is necessary for me to do this."

"Redemption, huh?"

My thought processes momentarily froze.

A moment later, I was back to normal.

"No," I explained.

"But you're angry, ain't you?" goaded the Sheriff, happy to spread guilt elsewhere. "At yourself. You blame yourself. For screwing up."

"No."

"Have it your fucking way, tinbrain."

The patrol car landed.

43

"All our ambulances are accounted for," said Latimer, the auto-mechanic in the ambulance bay. "I can't help you."

"It had a City Hospital livery. The paramedics wore City Hospital uniforms, and City Hospital ID badges."

"Those things ain't hard to fabricate."

"We believe there's a phantom hospital, taking patients."

"Believe what you like."

"Do you have any information that can help us?"

"No."

I assessed Latimer's demeanour and body language: he was lying.

"He's lying," I told Sheriff Heath. The Sheriff took out a pair of gloves and slipped them on. They were metal, and spiked.

"Are you fucking guffing me?" protested Latimer.

"You got any information that can help us?"

Latimer looked into the Sheriff's blue eyes, and he flinched.The Sheriff's rage was so intense, it shone like sunlight at high noon.

Even so, Latimer stood firm. The Sheriff threw a powerful fist.

He paused the punch a millimetre from Latimer's face.

"I could sue you," mocked Latimer.

I made a guess: Latimer frequented Hari Gilles's House of Pain on a recreational basis. The threat of beating up such a man was no kind of threat.

"I could," said the Sheriff slowly, "eat your fucking testicles. Explain *that* to your girlfriends." And the Sheriff fixed Latimer with a killer stare.

I wondered if the Sheriff's threat had been hyperbole, or a literal warning of intent.

"Fuck off!" scoffed Latimer.

But the Sheriff continued to glare. Hate exuded from him. Latimer tried to look away, break his gaze, but he couldn't.

Latimer was starting to sweat.

I realised that, although Latimer had no fear of pain, he still feared the Sheriff and his wrath.

Moment by excruciating moment, Latimer was losing his sense of who he was. The Sheriff stared and stared, as if he were visualising *exactly* what he was going to do to this poor fuck. And Latimer could see it too.

Snot started to dribble out of Latimer's nose. But he was too frightened to move, or break the Sheriff's cold and evil stare.

And, finally, the fear became so great that Latimer started to babble truth.

I realised that Latimer wasn't afraid of getting hurt: he was afraid that the Sheriff wouldn't *approve* of him. It was skilful work. In five minutes flat, the Sheriff had ripped out this man's soul and left it flopping on the ground.

"Look, I want to help," whined Latimer. "I really do!"

"So – help."

"There's, I guess, a rumour, do you know it?" Latimer babbled, "About the House of Pain."

I had already hypothesised he was a regular customer there. Latimer's access to the House's scuttlebutt was a partial confirmation of this surmise.

"What rumour?"

"Like, you know, there's normally a waiting list," said Latimer, "for limb and organ replacement. It can take months, years sometimes, to get new body parts. If you use rejuve, it's even slower. Ten years to grow an arm back, with the shit rejuve we use on this planet."

"We know all this," the Sheriff growled.

"My point is: if you go to the House of Pain, if you can afford their entrance fees, you can have your heart's desire. New eyes, new limbs, new breasts, new cock. It's all part of their service. Some of the masochists, they like it the medieval way. You know?" Latimer licked his lips, clearly envious at those more perverted than himself. "That means," he clarified, "they're kept in a dungeon for weeks, then hung, drawn and quartered, and disembowelled, and blinded with hot pokers. But at the end of all that, Hari's people put these sad-fuck punters back together and they send them home to their wives and husbands as good as new. Now think about it. How do they *do* that? Where do they get all those fucking limbs, and organs, and eyes?"

I looked at the Sheriff.

"Fair point," said the Sheriff.

🛡43

"Where are we going?" the Sheriff asked.

"Someone I want you to see," I told him.

🛡43

"Hey, I know you!" said the green-eyed freckle-nosed girl sitting behind the desk. "How come – I mean – I thought you, like, *died*?"

I tried to shrug nonchalantly, but with little success, so instead I ignored her question. "Your name is Macawley," I told her.

"Yeah. That's me."

"You have no Christian name."

"I'm not a Christian. Macawley is my first and only name. Hey, that was a fun piece of banter. What the hell is it *this* time?"

"This is Alexander Heath's father."

Macawley looked at the Sheriff. "He never told me his father was—"

"We didn't get on so well," the Sheriff conceded.

"Macawley was a friend of Fliss Hooper. Your son's girl-friend," I said to Sheriff Heath.

"Yeah. I know about Fliss Hooper. Her sister was that *whore*," said the Sheriff, spitting the word.

"Fliss was my friend," said Macawley.

"So the robot told me."

"Cyborg," I corrected.

"Whatever."

I persisted: "Tell him," I said to Macawley, "about Fliss and Alex."

"Um? Sorry? I think I'm supposed to be on duty here?"

"This is Galactic Police business. Tell him."

Macawley laughed.

And then she frowned. The frown changed her face utterly. She was no longer a brusque receptionist; she was a vivid, emotional, passionate, beautiful elf.

"It's hard to – I don't know what you – Well, like, they were kinda, good together?" she said.

"How did they meet?" I asked.

"We had a party," Macawley said, tentatively, in a "what-the-fuck?" kind of tone.

"Where?"

"Here. At the hospital."

"Who approached whom?"

Sheriff Heath was starting to glare now. "What's the fucking point of—" he began, but I silenced him with an imperious gesture.

Macawley frowned again, a "recalling the past" frown. And, as she spoke, smiles and wry looks flickered fast and briefly across her face: "Fliss was drunk," she said (smile). "That was a sight to—" (wry look, half-smile). "When she was drunk, she was never mean or rude, you know, she was just *vivid*, and people loved to, you know, be around her" (big smile). "Anyway, she did the approaching, I guess" (wry look). "Or maybe—"

I replayed her facial expressions in slow motion in my mind's eye, so fascinated was I by them: in barely a second and a half, she had flickered out a smile, a wry look, a frown, another smile, growing into a grin. And then Macawley laughed, and it was a sound like wine glasses colliding.

"—she, like, fell out of her dress, and he caught her."

"With respect," said the Sheriff brutally, "what the fuck are we wasting time here for?"

"Did she love him?"

"Hell yes." Macawley's grin became a joy to behold. "He was such a sweet little bastard. Cheeky. Fearless. Funny. He told stories all the time. He pretended his father was a big-time space smuggler; we had no idea he was just a crooked Sheriff, no offence, um. They were great with each other, like – finished each other's sentences. Sometimes they'd even start each other's sentences. It was like, they were, you know, not exactly telepathic. But connected."

"He ever talk about his mom?" said the Sheriff.

Macawley looked at him very seriously: anxiety and doubt and affection flickered across her face now, as she realised that the Sheriff was a grieving father. "No."

"She used to beat him. So I broke her jaw and threw her out."

"He never told me that."

"I raised him myself. Working shifts. Cooking for him. Getting him dressed for school. He was a straight-A student; I used to pay him to do his homework. We used to go shooting when he was eleven, twelve."

The Sheriff paused, remembering, and Macawley waited patiently until he was ready to continue.

"Then," the Sheriff continued, "things got hard at work. Political. I worked extra shifts; I had a lot of sleepless nights. I got myself a child-minder. Worse thing I ever did. 'Cause I lost him. Bitch was a hard callous cow who made my boy love *her* more than he ever could of loved an old bastard like me. So I lost him. My own boy. It was like a stranger broke into the house. He used to called me names, and disrespect me, and look at me, in that kinda way he had. That sneering look. I didn't know how to – Alex kept telling me I fucking hated him, and that I was crushing his – why the fuck am I telling you this?" The Sheriff turned to me. "What in the name of all goddamn hell are we doing here?"

"I'm re-motivating you," I explained. "So you will be willing to continue taking your revenge."

The Sheriff blinked, with shock and dawning pain, as the cruelty of my strategy became apparent to him.

"What revenge?" said Macawley.

"That's official police business."

"There was an organ-theft scam," said the Sheriff. "My son found out; that's why they killed him."

"That's what I always – feared," whispered Macawley.

"Good to meet you girl," said the Sheriff, curtly.

"You too, Sheriff." Her flicker of expressions contained a hint of empathetic love for this battered, shattered man.

"Let's go," said the Sheriff.

43

We were halfway down the corridor when I felt a hand clutch my arm.

"Wait," Macawley said. Now she was so close, she seemed astonishingly short, barely five foot high. And she peered up at me with anxious, determined, soulful eyes.

"What?"

"Maybe I can help?"

43

A phantom hospital needs real doctors, real nurses, real equipment.

"I've run a check on every employee of the City Hospital. They all work full shifts. None of them can be moonlighting," I explained.

"Bullshit. *No one* works full shifts," Macawley told me.

We were sitting in the café opposite the hospital. Macawley was buzzing with energy. The Sheriff was grim-faced, and I surmised that he was preoccupied with regrets about his failures as a father, and also, no doubt, consumed with contempt for my superb manipulative skills.

"All the employees work full shifts," I contradicted. "This information is in the hospital database. I loaded that database into my own database when I was Version—"

"Yeah but, shut up, you dumb fucking robot head; I just told you – no one works full shifts," Macawley insisted, brutally. "Life's too short. We have robots to do our dirty work. Most of the equipment is robot-controlled. So people clock in and clock out, and the rest of the day, they pretty much please themselves. I work a four-hour shift because I like it. But I know doctors who haven't worked here in months, yet they're still logged in the computer files as present, and they still get paid."

I felt a spasm of rage at the sheer sloppiness of all this.

"I don't see how it's possible," I argued, tautly. "Every human presence is monitored by hidden cameras. You can't cheat that."

"You can cheat anything."

"She's right," said the Sheriff.

"How?" I argued, and so Macawley explained, first in geeky technical detail, and then in broad philosophical outline.

For this was, she told us, a city of lies. No one was where they were supposed to be. Most people didn't do the jobs they were registered as doing. The Belladonnan Computer, observing SN Government guidelines, exercised rigorous surveillance over every citizen, but the data that it received was almost always false.

I knew that criminals could subvert the city's surveillance systems – else, how could they break the law? – but it came as a shock to realise that the entire planet was engaged in relentless duplicity. Computers were hacked, cameras were subverted, false images of hard-at-work employees went into the computer database.

It all seemed like a recipe for chaos. However, because of the tireless skill of its robot doctors, the City Hospital more or less muddled through. And the gifted human doctors and nurses *did* make a huge difference to the standard of medical care when they were actually there.

But most of the time, they were elsewhere.

"This doesn't help us," I argued. "It doesn't narrow the list of suspects. It just means *anyone* can be to blame."

"Look at it another way," said the Sheriff. "Where could they hide a hospital?"

"I've made a virtual search of every inch of the city," I said. "But if the camera data is corrupt – then I've been wasting my time. The phantom could be anywhere."

"I may have an idea," said Macawley.

43

After she had explained the idea, there was a sober silence.

"Yup, that could work," said the Sheriff, eventually.

"Then let's do it."

"It's dangerous," I advised.

And Macawley laughed, and her green eyes glittered and she opened her mouth and her teeth were sharp points, and she hissed, and then she roared a perfect roar.

"Yeah, like, bring it on," she snarled.

"That's my girl," said the Sheriff, awed at her flash of ferocity.

She licked her palm, and growl-purred eerily.

"You're part cat-person, I take it?" the Sheriff added.

"Oh yeah," admitted Macawley. "On my mother's side."

43

As we planned the assault on the phantom hospital, I realised: this was madness. We were outnumbered. The gangs had literally thousands of gunmen and gunwomen willing to do battle with us, and their weaponry, antiquated though it was by the standards of a modern military fighting force, was more than ample to defeat most attackers.

Furthermore, the Sheriff's official deputies weren't going to join him on a suicide mission. They were all lucratively paid by the gangs.

And I still didn't have sufficient evidence to justify calling for a robot battle-force. My first hypothesis had proved to be totally wrong, so I now needed considerable evidence of just cause before I could once again call for backup.

So, for the moment, all we had by way of an invading army was a cyborg Cop, a hospital administrator, and an over-the-hill corrupt lawman. Our chances of success in this rescue mission were approximately very low indeed.

However, despite this pessimistic assessment of our chances, I realised that my sensory field was heightened, my reflexes were augmented, my thought processes were accelerated.

Never had I felt so *alive*.

"My mother was an addict," Macawley admitted. "Highs, Lows, Blues, needles in the brain, sex, alcohol, she overdosed on everything she could. She did some bad things when she was drug-psychotic; child-killing, that kind of thing. She was pregnant with me when she came to Belladonna. I survived the fifty-fifty in the womb. My mom committed suicide when I was five. She left me a trunk full of song lyrics, very autobiographical. Her whole life was there, but nothing rhymed and there wasn't no fucking rhythm, and she never wrote the music to go with the songs of her life."

We were in Macawley's loft apartment. It was evening. We'd spent hours going over every detail of Macawley's plan, anticipating every eventuality.

And now, we were tired, and the story-telling had begun.

"You could come home," I said. "To one of the Solar Neighbourhood planets."

"They wouldn't have me. I'm trash."

"Your mother was trash. You're not."

"Hey! Was that what robots call a compliment?"

"You could make a new life," I persisted. "All our planets are safe places. You can raise kids. No one steals or rapes or cheats or commits murder. The streets are clean."

"Sounds like hell to me," muttered the Sheriff.

"We have democracy, and liberty, and happiness."

"I got two out of three of those," goaded Macawley. "Who the fuck needs *democracy*?"

"The fact of it is," the Sheriff said to me, "your godforsaken fucking paradise only works because you dump your human garbage in places like Belladonna."

"What else," I argued, "could we do with scum like you?"

"I always knew," said Macawley, "there was something wrong. Something dark."

The Sheriff nodded, sharing her regret.

"I had a best friend before Fliss, a girl called Gina. She used to go hunting in a girl gang, starting fights. Nothing serious, no one ever true-died. But by the time she was fourteen she had scars all over her face and body and she thought she was supreme. We all thought she was the queen of cool. Then she vanished and no one ever mentioned her again. I spoke her name to my stepdad and he beat me and locked me inside his empty body armour for a day. I thought I was going to die, I couldn't move, I was so scared. But afterwards I never mentioned Gina."

Macawley's eyes flared with anger: "Someone took her, didn't they? Took her and harvested her organs. I guess they figured she was no loss."

We all pondered her story for a while.

"I've lived a thousand years, give or take," said Sheriff Heath.

"Indeed? I would have estimated you to be older than that," I observed, and the Sheriff glared.

"I've lived through war," continued the Sheriff, "and anarchy and tyranny, and now I live in hell. But the fact is, you don't live as long as I've lived without telling lies, and living lies, and *being* a fucking lie. Hell, every kid knows there's evil on this planet. But you just think, hey, let it be, and you might be lucky, you might just manage to live a couple of decades more."

"I get that," said Macawley.

"Fucking pathetic," raged the Sheriff.

"Hey, I get it, I get it." Macawley touched his hand and squeezed it, and surprisingly, the Sheriff smiled at her.

"I remember," I said, in a confident tone, "many cases. Many adventures. Many planets. Oh, I could tell you stories of the things that I have done, and the places I have seen!"

There was a long silence.

"Why don't you then?" goaded Macawley.

I pondered this.

"Because, I must postulate, I don't know how to do so."

"How come?" said the Sheriff.

"Because," I explained, with a tinge of sadness, "all I have are facts. Facts about events. Facts about arrests. Facts about shootouts, and betrayals, and violent deaths. I have died so many times, and each time it feels like – I have no words for it – I have died many times, and that is a fact.

"But stories? I have no stories.

"Only humans have stories."

"Let's do it," I said, and it began.

Macawley was dressed to kill, or be killed. She wore street rags –
distressed cloth wrapped like bandages around her naked body,
baring flesh and tattoos. Her hair was high and spiked, her
green eyes shone, and her face and body tattoos shimmered with
bioluminescent glory.

"Very feral," I said admiringly, and Macawley snarled, and I
glimpsed her forked tongue, wet with spittle.

We caught the lift down to the ground floor. The Sheriff
was wearing flybiker's gear, to conceal his full body armour.
Macawley walked out into the night, and I followed. And the
Sheriff mounted his flybike and took off, then followed us both
from above.

The street bars in the Hot Zone were raucous and riotous as
always. Waiters on hoverboots served bottles of potent hooch to
wildly dressed revellers. There were no cars, no pedestrians, just
partygoers filling every street and alley. Macawley muscled her
way in and downed six Solar Flares in a row and then she told an
augmented Warrior to go fuck himself.

A bottle was smashed in her face, but Macawley got in a few
powerful punches before she went down. I stood nearby, watching impassively as Macawley was kicked and stomped. An
ambulance appeared about ten minutes later, and Macawley was
loaded in.

As the ambulance flew off, I ran after it and leaped up, and
clung on to the undercarriage. I used magnets to hold myself in
place.

The ambulance sped away, high above the streets, with me
clinging on, while the Sheriff trailed us at a careful distance on
the flybike.

"*How are you?*" I asked over my secure MI channel.

"*The bitch cut my fucking face,*" whined Macawley.

"*It'll heal.*"

"*It better. I like this face.*"

"*I like it too,*" I said, and wondered at myself.

"*We're heading for the Industrial Zone,*" said Sheriff Heath. "*Away from the City Hospital.*"

"*They're about to sedate me.*"

"*Don't let them,*" I counselled.

"*Don't fucking let them girl,*" the Sheriff added.

"*They're dead.*"

"*How?*"

"*I used my claws. Cut their throats. The back of this ambulance is like an abattoir now.*"

"*Good girl.*"

"*You're still on the same course,*" said the Sheriff. "*I'm hoping the driver heard nothing.*"

"*I cut the bastards' throats before they could subvocalise.*"

"*I knew you would.*"

"*Where are we now?*"

"*South of Brancton Park.*"

"*Heading for a deserted fabricator building, maybe? They have a lot of those in the Industrial Zone.*"

"*No. I don't think so,*" I said. "*There's a House of Pain in the Industrial Zone. Owned by Hari Gilles, but no whips and scourges and chains are ever delivered there. But there is,*" I said, scrolling through the receipts generated by my database, "*a canteen, and a large staff of workers, and many flybikes and flying vans apply for flight paths which lead there. It's a perfect match. It's Hari. Hari Gilles is behind all this.*"

"*Ah.*"

There was silence for a while. I held on tight, watching the Industrial Lands unfold below me. Nowadays, most of the industry was in space, but in the early days of Belladonna, this was where the consumer items that made this society possible were robotically created.

Now, it was where the unsavoury, poor and desperate citizens of Belladonna were slaughtered, and then disassembled for their parts.

"*I can see it below now, the ambulance is swooping down,*" the Sheriff announced.

"*Okay. I need to – ah – move,*" I said. "*Before this thing lands on me.*"

"*Once we land, they'll know what I did to their paramedics,*" said Macawley.

"*We'll be there for you girl. Trust us.*"

43

The flying ambulance swooped down into the courtyard of the House of Pain, as I scrambled my way up the hull of the craft. The grass below us moved and an underground landing pad appeared. The flying ambulance swooped in and docked.

Sheriff Heath followed behind on his flybike. A handful of engineers were standing by as the ambulance came to a halt, followed, moments later, by the Sheriff on his bike. The back door of the ambulance flew open and Macawley leaped out, her face enraged and dripping blood, her claws extended.

"Hey," said an orange-uniformed security guard and fired a plasma blast at her.

He was fast; the plasma beam caught Macawley head on; her forcefield engaged and the energy swirled around her, burning the walls and floor. I leaped off the top of the ambulance and landed with both feet on the ground, and stopped the guard with a single plasma blast, boring a hole in his skull.

Sheriff Heath got off his flybike. His blue eyes and walrus moustache were vividly framed by the red flaring frame-bars of his clear hardglass helmet.

"So, it's Hari Gilles," said the Sheriff, and the words were a death sentence.

A siren began to blare and I used an electromagnetic pulse to silence it. I paralysed the engineers with a sonic shout at point-blank range, and when they sank into catatonia, I bound their arms and legs.

Then I blew open the double doors and we found ourselves in a long corridor. I did an infra-red scan, and saw the laser beams criss-crossing the corridor and I threw a flare bomb. The Sheriff and Macawley shielded their eyes, while I stared impassively as a flash of blinding light ripped apart the walls and ceilings and hidden death-lasers.

We ran through the smoking black corridor and crashed through into a hospital reception area. It was a perfect replica of the actual City Hospital, staffed with uniformed nurses and with a robot receptionist peering curiously at us.

I walked up to the desk. "Sergeant Aretha Jones, where can I find her?" I asked.

"I'm afraid I'm not auth—" said the robot receptionist, and I thrust a finger-spike into the robot's brain and leached the information out that way.

"Where?" said Sheriff Heath calmly.

"Fourth – floor –" I said, feeling shaken. In absorbing the information from the robot I had also absorbed all the data it held on the hospital – the layout, the names of the staff, the numbers and names of the "patients."

One million people were being kept in the hospital, some of them still whole and intact, but most of them dismembered and eviscerated and stored in vats.

"Here comes security," grinned Macawley, as a dozen silver-bodied Doppelganger Robot security guards appeared in the reception area.

I felt a visceral fury, as if confronted with an age-old enemy.

Macawley leaped high, catapulting with her hands off my metal shoulders, as the bullets and plasma blasts started to fly. She landed nimbly behind the reception desk, which was armour-plated and impervious to plasma fire, and she huddled there grinning as the battle was waged.

The Sheriff fired his supersized plasma rifle fast and furiously at the twelve robot warriors. He aimed carefully, avoiding civilians, but the Doppelganger Robots had no such qualms – they rained plasma fire and explosive bullets indiscriminately in the direction of their opponents, and yellow-uniformed nurses and white-robed doctors were ripped limb from limb.

But through the haze of blood and colloidal flesh the Sheriff kept firing his precise blasts, targeting the heads and necks of the DRs, using multiple plasma blasts to literally saw their heads off. His body armour was rocked with plasma blasts and bullets, but he was a veteran of such wars, and absorbed the kinetic shocks, and kept his feet.

Meanwhile, I retracted my eyes and brought my disruptor blasters up through the sockets and fired, again and again. Each pulse fed compressed energy into the atoms of my enemies, creating a blast that explosively ripped the DRs into small pieces.

Then I scuttled towards two of the remaining DRs, absorbing plasma blasts and dodging bullets, and I shot and punched them into smithereens.

The Sheriff continued to plasma-saw the heads off his chosen targets. And when the last of the DRs, was destroyed, the reception area was incandescent with blazing smoke.

Macawley bounced back over the reception desk. "Upstairs?" she said.

"Yes. I have the schematic," I explained to her. "We take the elevator to the third floor and—"

"Which is up," Macawley explained, "there." And she pointed, and I got it.

And Macawley leaped off the desk and into my arms, then wriggled round to piggyback on me, and I flew up into the air on my boot rockets and smashed through the ceiling, as the Sheriff flew behind on his body-armour jets.

My x-ray vision and ultrasound allowed me to pilot a route upwards that avoided the beds and bodies of patients and we finally erupted into a ward where we found Aretha unconscious in a vat of liquid, tubes leading from her nose, a breathing mask over her mouth.

I looked at her for a few moments. She was vulnerable, as if asleep, lost to the world.

Then I ripped the tubes off her and pulled her out of the vat. I laid her gently on the ground, and checked her body for holes and organ absences. Then, reassured, I placed my fist between her breasts and electrocuted her.

Aretha jolted awake with a scream.

"*Fuck, it's you,*" she subvoced wearily.

"We're getting you out of here," I explained.

Aretha struggled to her feet, naked and vulnerable and afraid. Macawley, anticipating her plight, had brought a rucksack of clothes, and Aretha fumbled with them, and managed to put on a top and leggings. But then she tottered. Her body was weak. Her face was pale. She tried to speak, but still couldn't, because of the broken jaw. Instead, she gestured.

I followed her gesture. I saw all the other men and women and boys and girls and toddlers and babies lined up in rows in their hospital vats.

It was a very long room and the vats were packed tight, like fish shoaling.

"Go," said the Sheriff.

And so I walked along the row, checking for vital signs. Most of the patients were technically alive, even those who had been dismembered and stripped of every organ, including their brains. I counted the barely living, and I counted the true-dead, and I counted the crippled organless wrecks, and when I was sure I had proof of mass serial murder and use of banned medical technology, I paused in my count, and turned back to face the others.

And there I stood at the end of the long corridor of pillaged bodies, looking down at Macawley and the Sheriff. And they looked back at me, and had no words.

And I raised my arms to the heavens.

"*Urgent assistance, now,*" I said, and waited for the response from the SN headquarters.

No reply came.

"*Urgent assistance!*" I screamed.

Nothing.

I sent a coded signal to my heavily armed computer-controlled spaceship, still in automatic orbit around Belladonna: no reply.

I walked slowly back to the others.

"What's up?" said the Sheriff.

"The beacon link is down," I explained. "My spaceship is not responding. Something's happening. Something big."

"Then let's get the hell out of here," said the Sheriff.

I took hold of Aretha, and held her in my arms, and Macawley grabbed me tight around my neck.

And I blasted my rocket jets a second time and I used my plasma guns to blow a hole through the ceiling and I flew up and up and up until I saw sky.

I flew away from the hospital, pursued by missiles fired by Hari's security people that weaved around the sky, and looking down to see the vast size of the hospital wing of this House of Pain.

Eventually, I found the rooftop of an old fabricator building and dropped Macawley and Aretha off there.

Aretha was shivering. Her shattered jaw had been clumsily pinned in place. There were pen marks on her bare shoulders, little dotted lines, which marked where her arms would have been severed, prior to the removal of her organs.

"Are you okay?" I said, gently. She shook her head, too tired to even subvocalise.

"*I'm sorry,*" I subvocalised. And there was a flicker of expression that showed that she had heard me.

"*I honestly believed that you were corrupt,*" I said, pleading to be understood and forgiven by her.

She stared at me blankly. Her broken jaw made her seem unreal, more doll than person. Her body was in shock after all the drugs that had been pumped into her. So she didn't speak, she just stared.

"*But I was wrong; you backed me up, didn't you?*" I said. "*You lied for me. You had faith in me, and that's how you were able to lie. How, with such total and absolute conviction, you fooled Barumi and his third eye. That's right, isn't it?*"

Her eyes flickered; I knew that meant Yes.

"*Why?*"

She didn't respond.

Her eyes closed, and she drifted off to sleep. I laid her down, and inserted an IV, and hooked her up to a vital-signs monitor.

"She'll live, I think," I said.

"Who is she?" Macawley asked.

"Just a cop," I said.

"Why rescue *her*, and not all the others?" Macawley marvelled.

I thought about it, and had no answer.

"Skip it. Look, robot head, I'll stay with the girl. You have to go back," said Macawley. "Rescue the others. That's what we came for. Go rescue all those people."

"Just me and the Sheriff, against an entire army?" I said.

"Yeah? Is that a problem?"

I thought about the odds, and grinned.

"No problem."

43

From high above, I could see soldiers assembling outside the entrance to the phantom hospital. They drove military trucks and jeeps, and they wore old-fashioned body armour of a design I did not recognise.

"*Sheriff Heath, this is Galactic Cop 44, do you hear me?*"

"*I could do with some help here.*"

"*I'm on my way.*"

"*I've called for backup from police headquarters; nothing's coming. No one's responding.*"

"I *can see fires in the city,*" I informed him. "*New stars in the sky.*"

"*Stars?*"

"*Satellites. Exploded. Their reactors burning in space, radiating heat and light. I think my spaceship has been blown up too. It seems highly likely the Quantum Beacon ship has been exploded also.*"

"*What's going on out there, a war?*"

"*Pretty much.*"

I started to descend, and as I did so, I accessed the Belladonna MI channel and listened to the news report.

"*According to official sources,*" said a warmly reassuring news presenter's voice, "*Mayor Abraham Naurion is now heading a new civil administration, following his daring escape from prison where he was being held by representatives of the old regime.*"

I wanted to curse inwardly, but that wasn't in my programming. Instead, I resolved to find out who had been bribed to let the Mayor go.

"*The Mayor has declared a state of national emergency,*" continued the news presenter. "*All links with Earth and the Solar Neighbourhood Government have been severed. Belladonna has declared its independence. Citizens are advised to get out on the street, and commence celebrating. This planet is now officially free.*"

A few moments later I heard the Mayor's nasal tones:

"*This is Mayor Naurion speaking. All the rumours are true; we have declared our independence from Earth. Elections will be held next week. God bless you all.*"

I switched off the MI link, and crashed back down into the hospital, via the hole in the roof I had created earlier. I found the Sheriff barricaded into position behind the double doors.

"There's a revolution going on out there," I told him.

"It's none too fucking quiet in here either," he responded.

"They're deploying a regiment of soldiers. We need to get these patients out. How can we do that?"

The Sheriff thought about it.

"How about," he suggested, "over the bodies of our enemies?"

I considered that option.

"Good strategy," I said.

And so I plasma-blasted the door open: and the two of us ran through, roaring.

The soldiers were bounding up the stairs in scores, carrying KM rifles. I drew my pistols and rained bullets and plasma at them.

Their body armour absorbed the blasts and they fired back. I hurled a flash grenade, but their helmets darkened to protect their eyes.

I holstered my pistols, and extended my fingerspikes, and my eyeballs retracted, and I exposed my twin disruptor blasters. And I prepared to leap at the soldiers in a killing frenzy, when—

"Hey, I got it," said the Sheriff laconically, and raised his plasma rifle, and fired it, once.

A thin missile shot out into the midst of the oncoming soldiers, and exploded in mid-air, and lit up the entire hallway. Sheets of flame erupted but the armoured soldiers walked arrogantly through the fire, not realising that the air was now rich with microscopic airborne combustibles, which had been released by the Sheriff's missile as it flew. So instead of dimming, the flames flared hotter and hotter, in an exothermic chain reaction that was turning the air itself into an inferno.

The first rank of soldiers were in sight of the double doors when the heat became so intense it disabled their body armours' cooling mechanism.

This caused their armour to glow red, then blue.

And, of course, once the armour was close to melting point, the bodies within ignited.

Bodies burned, and screams filled the air.

Sheets of flame rippled through the air and down the stairs. The agonised howls of the soldiers vied with the relentless crackle crackle of flesh burning inside melting hardmetal.

The fireball became a screaming dancing conga chain of flaming bodies, and the fire in the air continued to blaze like a magnesium flare.

Then the fireball flared and became a larger fireball, and flared again, and again, and again.

The Sheriff and I huddled in the doorway, beyond the reach of the flames, but still bathed in blistering heat. I turned my refrigeration units up to maximum, and used my body to shield the old man from the inferno. I noticed that the Sheriff didn't blink even when flames flickered close to us, and I realised that those peering blue eyes were mechanical, not organic. That's how old the Sheriff was: too old for new eyes.

"Nice one," I said.

The sprinklers now kicked in, slowly dousing the blaze. Before long, all that was left were the black ashes of the dead, amidst the melted slag of the body armours.

"It's an adapted military missile," the Sheriff acknowledged. "Like a One Sun, but just a tad less powerful. I carry it for emergencies."

The staircase was charred and blackened, and it crumbled and collapsed before our very eyes, but the forcefield infrastructure remained intact. The Sheriff and I began to make our way through, effectively walking on air, using the charred bodies like a forest pathway.

Finally we were outside.

An army of deputies had gathered outside the House of Pain – the Sheriff's flybiker gang, and a horde of other street tearaways.

"You have impressive resources," I observed.

"Yeah, I guess." Then he turned to his deputies, and spoke in calm, reassuring tones: "Go," said the Sheriff. "Guard those people who are inside. This is now officially a City Hospital. You," he pointed at a tattooed flybiker. "Get to the main hospital, round up as many doctors and nurses as you can. Anyone who won't cooperate, true-kill them. You are my deputies, you have that authority."

"Can we kill them if they *do* cooperate?"

"No."

The flybiker considered that. Eventually, he nodded assent.

The deputies started to make their way inside.

And as the Sheriff and I stood, and briefly savoured our victory, above us the skies darkened. A hundred black-clad assassins on flybikes were approaching.

"You know who they are?" I said.

"Gill's Killers. They're gonna be hard to beat."

"Just watch me," I said. "Now go. I'll buy you some time. Save as many as you can." And then my boot jets ignited, and I took off.

As I'd hoped, the flock of assassins followed me. But a few swooped down, towards the flybiker deputies.

I turned in mid-air, and retracted my eyes again, and fired disruptor blast after disruptor blast. Then my eyes locked back into place and I saw that the Killers were black shards falling out of the sky, like rain.

I turned again, and flew on, pursued by the main body of Gill's Killers.

A missile skimmed near my body.

I fired my body jets more fiercely, and fled faster than a rocket achieving escape velocity.

And I soared and flew through the spires and towers of the city, weaving and bucking and marvelling at the extraordinary high and narrow spire-tips that literally touched the clouds. And all around me, the sky was lit up by plasma bursts.

And, once more, I raised my head and once again screamed: *"Urgent! Assistance! Now!"*

And once more, there was no response.

My hypothesis was hardening into a certainty: The QB was down. My spaceship wasn't responding. The Belladonnans had launched a revolution, and were winning it.

I was exhilarated. This truly was war.

I started downloading all my memories into a memory chip.

And when the chip was full my ear opened up, and a small cylindrical object crept out into the light.

It was my databird. It contained all my thoughts, memories, all the facts I had learned, recently or ever, all my downloads, the detailed impress of my human personality, every part of me. I kissed the bird gently, then released it and it flew off high, with astonishing speed, into space.

Meanwhile, two-score of Gill's Killers were still on my tail, eating my wake. I tilted myself up vertically at full acceleration and looped a loop at G forces that would have killed any human being.

And then I was behind them and I pointed an accusing finger and my forearm fell off and hurtled to the ground.

And the missile launcher in my upper arm was bared. I fired twelve bursts.

Not a single missile missed its target. These weren't smart missiles; for I myself am "smart." My computer circuitry calibrated distance and wind speed to perfection.

Twelve assassins and their flying bikes turned to flame. I eased up on the throttle.

I fired again and again; and another eighteen Gill's Killers exploded into flame and died.

But then a police cruiser appeared in the sky. It was the size of a space shuttle, with Bompasso PD blazoned holographically on its sides. I MI-radioed my security classification across to it.

But puffs of smoke erupted from the police cruiser, and a swarm of torpedoes flew towards me. I stayed calm, and fired seven more missiles from my arm.

The torpedoes exploded in mid-air, and below on the streets of Lawless City molten shrapnel rained down on the rapt gawping crowds who were watching this aerial combat.

But one torpedo remained, for the missile which had struck it had failed to detonate. Sometimes, despite the miracles of modern technology, that still happened.

Shit.

I was, by now, entirely out of missiles, and my disruptor eyes needed to be recharged. But there was no time. I still had my plasma pistols, but they would be useless against an armoured torpedo with a forcefield.

I was, in short, helpless and unarmed, and doomed.

I bucked, almost ripping myself in half with G forces, then hurtled upwards to the clouds. On my radar screen I could see the torpedo gaining on me.

The databird was out of sight by now. It would carry on into space, until it rendezvoused with my lifeship, in orbit around one of Belladonna's moons. I was reassured by the knowledge that the databird contained everything I had discovered about the phantom hospital, every scrap of evidence against Hari Gilles. It was all there, for the authorities, and for my future self.

But all that had happened to me after the flight of the data-bird – including the moment of my death – would go unrecorded.

When I estimated that the torpedo would collide with me in ten seconds, I did another loop the loop and turned to face it. The torpedo was implacable and fast, and its navigation circuits were locked to my body's signature. It was a death that could not be avoided.

"Bastards!" I screamed and flew, arms outstretched, towards the nosetip of the torpedo that would kill me.

THE HIVE-RATS

The Hive-Rats set forth on their epic voyage into space, in an armada of fearsome power and greatness.

Ten minutes later, they had arrived.

Admiral Monroe was awed at the sheer speed of the aliens' ships. They weren't even travelling in fast time, they were just *fast*. These creatures must, he realised, have found a way to travel through wormholes in space – which for so long had been the dream of all human space explorers. But how? They hadn't learned that secret from *him*.

The realisation hit him like a hammer blow: these monsters were *smarter* than humans. Or rather, the Fourth was. The Fourth was, without a doubt, a scientific and mathematical genius.

Even so, Monroe was unperturbed. If the Hive-Rat thought it could win a war against humanity, it was sadly deluded.

A few moments later, the armada made another hyperspace jump; then another; and another. Until finally they stopped. And Monroe could see why. The fourth planet from the sun in this system was brightly lit, and active in all frequencies of the radio spectrum. He saw some oddly shaped asteroids, and as one of the Hive-Rat ships flew closer, Monroe was able to see more clearly that these were in fact space battleships. There were solar panels floating around this system's sun, like gossamer around a candle. And there were space buoys, orbiting at the Lagrangian points, whose flashing lights spelled out in huge letters: WELCOME TO HUMAN SPACE: BORDER CONTROLS IN OPERATION.

That, he felt, was the clinching piece of evidence to support his theory that this was a human settlement – the bureaucrats were in charge.

It was certain then. They had encountered a human-settled planet, and it was far from Earth. At a rough guess, he concluded, they were at least a billion light years away from the Sol system. Probably, he guessed, somewhere in the Coma supercluster. He could distinctly see the Great Wall – a filament of galaxies that stretched for hundreds of millions of light years, forming a line in space that culminated in the Hercules Supercluster. And that put them way beyond the regions of space which his civilisation had managed to explore.

And this meant, of course, that in the half a millennium that had elapsed since his "death," humanity too had invented a form of instantaneous wormhole travel. And that implied, reassuringly, that technological progress would have been made in every other sphere. Human weapons would be better and more powerful than in his day; human space defences would be better; human military strategy would be better.

These poor sorry Rats, Monroe concluded, stood no chance.

But he did not air his reservations to the First. Instead, he carefully kept all such thoughts tightly bottled up. The revenge of humanity would soon occur, and he wanted to savour it.

Thus, Monroe bided his time, and pretended to be a loyal member of the Hive.

And, meanwhile, he endeavoured to learn as much as he could about his enemy, and its remarkable evolutionary process.

At first, of course, there was just the First – the original Sand-Rat Hive Mind. The Sand-Rats were sentient, barely, but had no culture, and their language was rudimentary and consisted chiefly of the words "shit" and "fuck," which described their favourite pastimes. Their hive intelligence constituted a whole larger than the sum of the parts, but that wasn't saying much.

For they were just rats! On Morpheus, they lived in burrows. They used pebbles as tools. They had never discovered fire. They had no electricity, no nuclear power, no cars, no aeroplanes, no guns, no buildings, no telescopes, no anything very much.

What they did have was the capacity to kill their enemies,

and steal their minds. As well, of course, as being able to alter the rate of flow of time.

Which, Monroe conceded, was pretty damned impressive.

The Second was, Monroe had gleaned, the last living member of a race of powerful clawed land predators, larger than lions, more deadly than sharks, and possessed of an intuition that bordered on psychic powers. These grand beasts had eaten the saurian monsters that once dominated the world of Morpheus. They had been kings of the jungle, and of the savannah. And, as their intelligence evolved, they had developed a complex civilisation based around ritual and the worship of the hunt.

Then, to their amazement, these proud predators had been defeated and exterminated by the Sand-Rats, a species they had always regarded as too wretched to even eat.

And from the Second, the Sand-Rats had learned ruthlessness and intuition and the joys of heightened sensation at times of danger, and the exaltation of the kill.

The Third was the last living member of a humanoid four-armed race that had evolved from simians to become magnificent sword-wielding warriors. They had fought and eradicated all their rival predator species in the forests and the plains, they had raised cities full of grandeur, and they had been on the cusp of inventing space travel; and then the Sand-Rats ate them.

From the Third, the Sand-Rats knew all about culture and architecture and technology and gunpowder and the glory of war. And, with the combined intelligences of the Second and the Third to draw upon, the Hive-Rats were now the intellectual equal of all but the very smartest human beings. Thus, the Hive had become a super-brain.

The Fourth belonged to the race that had been, for tens of thousands of years, the real masters of Morpheus. They had dwelled in the oceans, and when the saurians fought the mammalians and while the humanoids scrabbled to survive, the Fourth dominated the entire ocean depths. They had been,

Monroe had discovered, jellyfish-like creatures that could communicate by touch, and by touching water could communicate with any others of their kind who swam in that water. Thus, without being telepathic, they were able to speak almost instantly to each other over the vastest distances.

The jellyfish beasts made slaves of all the other creatures of the deeps, and they built huge cities out of live coral-like sea-life. They were philosophers, and mathematicians, and their intellects were phenomenal.

But then the Sand-Rats chose to become aquatic and so re-evolved into ratty-looking fish and colonised the seas and they ate all the jellyfish beasts, and their grand cities decayed. And from the Fourth, the Sand-Rats learned about ideas, and mathematics, and philosophy, and science.

And now the Hive-Rats had a gestalt mind of truly remarkable power which the First, typically, didn't really know how to use. For the Hive-Rats loved to burrow, and to fight, and they loved to fuck and eat and shit, and that was all they ever did.

And so, until that dread day when the humans came and changed everything, what was the point of *thinking*?

The Fifth had been a sentient butterfly-like insect. And from the Fifth, the First had learned how lovely it was to be a butterfly-like insect, fluttering in the breeze, singing songs of beauty and joy all day long.

The Sixth was Monroe.

The First

AND NOW THE HUMANS MUST DIE.

The Second

My warrior-packs are ready. We will fight and die in your cause, O master.

The Third

Why should we fight? These creatures are like us, humanoid and almost attractive. Perhaps they could be our allies?

The Fourth

What a cruel and terrible species these humans are. They have killed so many, with such wanton cruelty. Thousands of planets have been "terraformed" by these monsters. And they would have done the same to our own planet, if you hadn't killed them all, O master.

The Fifth

Can't we all, like, you know, *get on?*

The Sixth

[*Even with all you know, even with all I have taught you, you cannot win this war. For human beings are the greatest warriors in the universe, and we can never ever be defeated.*]

O First, we are truly bound to win!

The First

LET BATTLE COMMENCE.

The First

O JOY!

The First

AN AMBUSH! EASILY PREDICTED. A TORPEDO FLOCK! EASILY THWARTED. ANTI-MATTER BOMBS! EASILY DEFLECTED. THIS WAR IS SURPASSING EASY.

The Second

I command a trillion warriors with my mind; and I rain fire on these monsters.

The Third

The darkness of space is lit with the flames of dying human spaceships. This is epiphany mixed with horror. I am exalted!

The Fourth

Don't underestimate them, for pity's sake.

The Fifth

Spacemen in flight; bombs exploding; rockets flaring. It's really pretty!

The Sixth

[*I am conflicted and torn. I love war; I am bred for war; and I and my other Minds appear to be winning this war. But I am human, first and last, so I must secretly yearn for us to lose.*]

The First

I CAN REMEMBER BEING BORN, AMONGST MAGMA AND LAVA AND SMOKE. I WAS A SINGLE CELL. A SINGLE AND LONELY AND UTTERLY STUPID CELL. BUT I WAS AWARE, AND I WAS *ME*.

IT WAS A LONG LONG TIME BEFORE I STARTED HAVING THOUGHTS.

NOW, I HAVE LOTS OF THEM.

The Second

Shit. I've lost another ship.

And another.

The Third

Are these metal creatures allies of the humans?

The Sixth

No. Just machines. Tools.

The Third

But they look like humans! They have arms and legs.

The Sixth

Robots. Doppelganger Robots. They are duping us. We've killed a bunch of robots; we aren't winning this war at all.

[*This is SO great!!*]

The Fifth

So terribly pretty!

The Fourth

These creatures have weapons I do not understand. They have defences I do not understand. They have technology I do not understand. I am confused and frightened.

I thought humans were just savage murderous predators. But maybe they are more impressive than that.

The Sixth

Hey! There's *nothing* more impressive than being a savage murderous predator!

The Second

We have lost another ship.

And another.

And another.

And another.

And another.

And a dozen others.

And a hundred more.

And a thousand more.

And more.

And more.

And more . . .

The First

WHY ARE WE LOSING?

The First

EXPLAIN!!

The Second

Our warriors were magnificent. We steered our battleships through hazardous space, we evaded missiles, we blew up their vessels, and we rained death and destruction on to the planet below. They were many and we were few but we fought and fought and our bravery was beyond doubt.

The Third

They had robot ships and anti-matter bombs and we thwarted them time and again. And we rained death and destruction on their planet.

The Fourth

We did not rain death and destruction on their planet. They allowed us to destroy their robots ships to encourage us to use up our ammunition, which we did. We hurled nuclear bombs on to their planet but in fact they vanished the moment they touched the atmosphere. Ten million of our battleships were destroyed by their scientifically inexplicable death rays; the pathetic remnant of our fleet numbers no more than two hundred Hive-Rats in a single vessel. We were bested; these creatures are like gods.

The Sixth

I agree. Humans can never be defeated. Let's go home.

The Fifth

Does anyone care what I think?

The First

**I SHALL NOW CONSIDER
WHAT WE DO NEXT.**

The First

I HAVE CONSIDERED.

The Second

That was quick.

The Third

Barely a millionth of a second.

The Fourth

The First's mind is quicker than is conceivable. I am constantly astonished at this creature.

The Fifth

I too have a mind that can think faster than light shining from the sun on to the leaves and flowers. An instant for me is an eternity. My people live for three days then die but those three days are rich in beauty and joy and blessed with the exaltation of fast-flying through air and the intense taste of pollen and nectar and the myriad sights of our world, and we sing to each other of all these joys, beauteous and complex songs. I have lived now for half a million years in the mind of this Sand-Rat and each second was like a century for any other creature. I may be, uniquely, the happiest sentient being in all the Universe.

The Sixth

Look guys, you were beaten, the human race won.

Don't be such sore fucking losers!

The First

I WILL NOW APPORTION BLAME.

TO THE SECOND, I SAY: YOU ARE NOT TO BLAME. YOU CONTROLLED OUR TROOPS SKILFULLY AND WELL AND THOUGH YOUR BATTLE LUST CONSUMED YOU, IT NEVER CAUSED YOU TO ACT RECKLESSLY. OUR BATTLESHIPS FLEW SKILFULLY, WE PLANNED AMBUSHES, WE ANTICIPATED THEIR TRAPS, AND WE MANAGED TO RAIN NUCLEAR BOMBS ON TO THE PLANET WHICH WOULD HAVE ERADICATED ALL HUMAN LIFE IF THE MISSILES HADN'T BIZARRELY AND MYSTERIOUSLY VANISHED INTO THIN AIR.

TO THE THIRD, I SAY: YOU ARE NOT TO BLAME. YOU UNDERSTOOD THE PSYCHOLOGY OF THESE HUMAN ATTACKERS AND YOU INSPIRED OUR SOLDIERS AND MADE THEM BELIEVE THAT THEY WERE FIGHTING FOR A NOBLE CAUSE, TO SAVE THEIR QUEEN AND MASTER, MYSELF. BUT YOU WERE DUPED BY A HUMAN COMMANDER WHOSE GUILE EXCEEDS EVEN YOURS AND MINE.

TO THE FOURTH, I SAY: YOU ARE PARTLY TO BLAME. YOUR INTELLECTUAL GENIUS COMES TINGED WITH ARROGANCE AND COMPLACENCY. YOU BUILT OUR BATTLESHIPS, YOU INVENTED A WAY OF TRAVELLING THROUGH WORMHOLES, YOU CREATED OUR PLASMA GUNS AND ANTI-MATTER BOMBS. BUT WHEN I USED THE KNOWLEDGE THAT I TOOK FROM YOU I HONESTLY BELIEVED THAT IT WAS ALL THE KNOWLEDGE THAT DOES AND COULD EXIST IN ALL THE UNIVERSE. I WAS WRONG, AND YOU WERE WRONG. THERE ARE THINGS WE DO NOT KNOW, AND THESE HUMANS DO KNOW THESE THINGS. THUS, YOU HAVE FAILED ME AND I SHALL PUNISH YOU.

TO THE FIFTH I SAY: YOUR MIND IS A SOURCE OF DEEP JOY TO ME. YOU PLAYED NO PART IN THIS BATTLE BUT WITHOUT YOUR EXHILARATING LOVE OF LIFE MY DAYS WOULD BE BARREN AND POINTLESS. THANK YOU, O FIFTH, FOR BEING SO EXCEEDINGLY SWEET.

TO THE SIXTH I SAY: YOU ARE A TRAITOR. YOU KNEW WE WOULD LOSE AND YOU SAID NOTHING.

The Sixth

Too fucking right!

The First

YOU TOO, O SIXTH, SHALL BE PUNISHED.

The planet of Lucifer was named, ironically, in honour of God's favourite angel, whose name meant light. But the inhabitants of Lucifer worshipped him for what he was *before* his Fall.

This was a planet of profoundly devout human beings who had embraced the terrors of the fifty-fifty in pursuit of a cause that meant more to them than life itself: spiritual perfection.

The planet was easily terraformed from its original barren state, and no alien life-forms were destroyed in the process. A neighbouring planet, Gabriel, was densely populated with vegetation and swamp monsters, and the Luciferans sedulously preserved its wilderness status, and made no efforts to inhabit it. The Luciferans worshipped the gods as they were before Christianity tainted perfection. And they created a semi-agrarian civilisation in which farmers tilled the soil, and weavers weaved clothes with hand-looms.

But their civilisation was underpinned by powerful technology: the solar panels, the space elevators, the robot miners, and a powerful quantum-computer brain which they dubbed, ironically and wryly, for these were exceptionally wry and ironical people, "Satan."

And, of course, a nominal space defence system had been installed. It was nothing that could deter a very serious invader – the Heebie-Jeebies, say. But it was enough to keep away pests and irritants – those young aggressive species who actually thought it would be possible to conquer the universe.

And so, when the battleships of the Hive-Rats arrived, the Luciferans transmitted solid holograms to discover whether this fleet was as predatory as it appeared to be.

It was: and so the Hive-Rat armada was utterly obliterated.

Then a message was sent to the Solar Neighbourhood Government, alerting it to the presence of yet another species of lunatic alien invaders. But the message priority was low. The Governor of Lucifer didn't even think it was worth summoning a cyborg defence fleet to their aid.

After which, the Luciferans declared a day of prayer and repentance. For they regretted bitterly the need to slay all their enemies: yet slay their enemies they had.

However . . .

One Hive-Rat vessel had remained, concealed, at a safe distance from the battle. And thus the Hive-Rat intelligence remained alive.

This sole surviving Hive-Rat brooded, and planned, and schemed; and then it entered fast time and a thousand more years of brooding, planning and scheming ensued in what, for the Luciferans, was no more than a few hours.

The Fourth and the Sixth had by now both received their punishment: a near-eternity of blinding agony which, in real time, occupied no more than a trillionth of a second. Both emerged stunned, embittered, and humble from their aeons of anguish.

A trillionth of a second after that, the Fourth finished absorbing all of the lessons of the failed invasion, and conveyed the key points to his/her master, the First.

The First then gave the order for his bodies to multiply. And so the few surviving Hive-Rats fornicated and gave birth and grew into adulthood.

And these, their children, then fornicated and gave birth and grew into adulthood. And so it went on, for generation after generation, until a trillion or more of the little ratty creatures now existed, inhabiting the hundreds and thousands of new battleships which their fabricators had managed to churn out.

Meanwhile, the Second and the Third had divined that a nullification ray of some kind was being used to "vanish" the nuclear weapons they had rained down on the planet. After the careful study of the recordings of the planetary assault, they had identified bizarre patterns of electromagnetic radiation that seemed to be indicative of the use of unstable exotic matter to annihilate real matter.

Armed with this clue, the Fourth was able to devise a new system of mathematics that allowed him to invent a forcefield that could nullify the humans' nullification ray.

The trillions of Hive-Rats that had been born were then assigned the task of building forcefields that could be fitted to each and every one of the Hive-Rats' missiles and bombs. At the same time, the battleships' hyperspace engines were transformed into weapons. By turning their arses on the enemy and emitting vast pillars of energy, the fleet could destroy enemy vessels with ease.

Monroe watched all this with awe. He had long ago ceased to fathom the physics that was being used, but he admired the beauty of these new weapons and defence systems. And he did admire the Hive-Rat's complete absence of shilly-shallying.

Furthermore, Monroe's advice about how to identify and neu-tralise the solid holograms being used against them was invaluable. The Hive-Rats could now easily distinguish between real enemy and chimaerical enemy.

And thus, one and a half days after their abject defeat, a second Hive-Rat armada was launched into battle and rained nuclear bombs on all the other planets in this solar system, including Gabriel, but excluding Lucifer itself. The flames of these exploding planets lit up the skies of Lucifer. Phantom defence fleets were dispatched but were ignored; the core of real ships lurking inside the miasmic cloud were utterly obliterated by precision plasma beams and anti-matter bombs.

Then nuclear bombs protected by anti-nullification force-fields pummelled Lucifer itself. The atmosphere boiled away. The mantle burned. Magma boiled up into the crust. Every human being on the planet died, and the dead planet glowed, like an angry semi-extinct volcano.

The last of the Luciferans prayed as their planet expired.

Their faith remained intact; they died with the name of their perfect saviour on their lips.

Then their planet burned like Hades itself.

The First was content. Victory had been achieved.

Now, all that remained was to kill every other human being in the Universe.

THE COP

Version 45

I woke, and inhabited my consciousness, and accessed my database. And a few moments later, I was gripped by an overwhelming and completely unexpected emotion:

Fear.

For according to my database, my previous two Versions had been eliminated within the space of a week on the same planet. And now, on my return to Lawless City, I would be faced with enemies on all fronts: the four gang bosses, the corrupt civic authorities, the corrupt police, Gill's Killers, and the unknown assassins who had killed Alexander Heath and his friends and then had slain Version 43, Jaynie Hooper, and forty-nine bystanders, with a weapon that seemed to defy the laws of physics.

And, to cap it all, my spaceship had been blown up, and the beaconband link with the SN Police Headquarters had been severed and there was no possibility of getting reinforcements.

I was feeling my age – I was forty-five robot-lives old. And I was feeling Fear.

And I was glad of it.

For my Fear gave me a sense of purpose. I was confident that – unlike my two previous Versions – I would tame the wild planet of Belladonna. I would bring peace and happiness to its populace.

And my Fear exhilarated me. My energy was high, my confidence was boundless, I felt invincible.

And I resolved to devise a new approach that would allow me, and justice, to prevail.

43

I clambered out of my robot chassis storage pod and paced the length of the lifeship. I saw the moon of Mandrake Root below me, pockmarked with craters. The black sky beyond was dominated by a huge red and yellow globe – the planet of Belladonna.

I had been conscious for five minutes, and I was accessing my database to help me plan my new strategy.

I had already confirmed that my Galactic Police Force spaceship and its computer had been destroyed by the forces of the Belladonnan Revolution; for the databird sent by Version 43 had flown out to rendezvous with it, and found only debris.

However, Version 44 had previously taken the precaution of hiding the vessel's small lifeship behind Mandrake Root, away from visual and radar scrutiny. The lifeship was a sleek winged vessel with a black hull that was dotted with "stars," hence almost invisible to the naked eye, and large enough to contain a fabricator and quantum computer.

And so the databird was able to transfer its information into the lifeship's computer; and from thence into a robot brain.

The death of one Cop automatically triggers the rebirth of the next; and thus, I was born.

And within moments of my birth, I had reached a firm conclusion: both my previous Versions had been defective.

For Version 43 had allowed himself to be duped by Jaynie Hooper, and had walked into an obvious ambush. And Version 44 had been guilty of a whole string of short-sighted and foolish decisions. Firstly, he had become obsessed with his theory about Sandro Barumi, and had missed the bigger picture. And then he had allowed compassion for the Bompasso PD officer Sergeant Jones and the various dying and jeopardised hospital patients to occlude his prime imperative; namely, the identification and elimination of the criminal perpetrators.

He should, logic told me, have left the Sheriff and Aretha to die, and gone after Hari Gilles, and slain him. His failure to see the necessity for such decisive action had cost us the mission.

Version 44 was at least correct in his belief that 43 had been incompetent. However, despite his many blunders, 43 did manage, I noted approvingly, to execute the gangster Dooley

Grogan. Though, strictly speaking, it might have been better if he'd built a criminal case against him first.

Both Versions, I concluded, had been stupid in the way they approached the problem from the outset. The history of this planet showed that any Galactic Cop would be a target for assassins; and so an undercover operation would have been a much smarter strategy.

And so I spent three days designing a humaniform body to aid me in my return to the planet. When the body had been fully moulded, I took my brain out of my robot chassis and placed it in the chest of my new self.

And now, as Version 45, I could pass for human.

And then I flew out of my lifeship wearing an armoured spacesuit with a jetpack. And, after a slow journey through space, I eventually crashed into the atmosphere of Belladonna like a falling star.

After landing, I buried my spacesuit and took stock. I was five hundred miles from Lawless City, in a remote wilderness area. There was a remote possibility I had been spotted by security radar, but after standing motionless for twelve hours I saw no evidence I was being pursued, and heard nothing untoward on the military radio channels I had accessed.

And so I moved onwards, into a large forest, with soft-barked trees that howled and hissed as I passed, and many dangerous predators. When night fell, it was utterly dark, and full of strange sounds. It was cold. And *I* was cold. It was nearly two decades since I had last felt "cold," whilst wearing a humaniform chassis.

By morning I had walked the length of the forest and found myself facing a vast savannah, lit by the light of the dawn. Silver and black birds flocked in the sky as dawn pinked the yellow grass.

I began the long walk to Lawless City.

I walked through miles and miles of glorious wilderness, through more forests and through deserts, through ranchland rich in beef and sheep, past rivers raging in torrents, and past fields of wheat and vast estates fringed with flowers in which grew vastly long rows of vegetables.

It took me five days to reach Lawless City. I passed a few farmers, and some travelling families, and they gave me news of what was happening on Belladonna.

I made a point of walking more slowly than was my custom, so as not to attract suspicion. And my new body had pores, so I sweated, and follicles, so that my facial skin grew coarse and hairy. I was tall, by human standards, though I was four inches shorter than my usual height. And my new body was heavily muscled and extremely, by human standards, good-looking. As a flourish, I had covered my body with tattoos which ran down my shoulders and along my back and down my muscled thighs. Mythological rocs and dragons vied for supremacy on my naked skin.

I had also changed the timbre of my voice: it was huskier, growlier, and my tone was default scornful. I was equipped with ID declaring me to be a former mercenary soldier with a history of bank robbery, who had narrowly avoided brain-frying after a shootout with police officers which left twelve dead.

I entered Lawless City in the dead of night and went to a bar.

I felt right at home.

"What are you having?"

"I'm buying."

"Let me—"

"Let the man buy his own fucking drink."

"Are you new?"

"Are you fucking nosy?"

"Four whiskies."

"Ah, you're buying a round."

"No."

"Ah."

"Okay, I'll buy a round. Make that twelve whiskies."

"So, you're new, aren't you?"

"I am. Came through the fifty-fifty a week ago."

"I can tell. The shaky hands. A scary moment, eh?"

"I've had worse."

"When?"

"Never."

"I lost my brother. His body came through but his heart and lungs and brains stayed behind. His liver too. He was alive, but not human."

"That's tough."

"We burned him. Honoured his memory."

"I was luckier."

"You looking for work?"

"I might be."

"Bodyguard work?"

"Anything."

"We're looking for killers."

"Come right out with it, why don't you?"

"You're augmented, aren't you?"

"How can you tell?"

"The way you stand. The reflexes. I can tell."

"I'm not looking to kill. I just want to – find a niche."

"Niche?"

"Something I can do, that doesn't involve killing."

"You came to the wrong planet, brother."

43

I spent most of the next day exploring post-Revolutionary Belladonna.

The mood was electric. There were banners in the street,

bearing photographs of the Mayor of Belladonna, Abraham Naurion, now known as the President-to-be-Elected. The actual elections were scheduled for the following month, but no other candidates dared stand against him.

I witnessed a street carnival in which Belladonnans openly mocked the Earth/Solar Neighbourhood regime. There were parodies of the more noteworthy members of the Governing Body that controlled all the humanoid planets and their varied inhabitants – the Humans, Lopers, Dolphs, Cat People, Noirs, and Eagles.

Rock bands played impromptu gigs. Television stations broadcast coverage of the street parties that were breaking out all over Bompasso.

Ranchers were interviewed. These were the conservative ruling financial élite of Belladonna, and they were considerably less than articulate. But even *they* spoke fulsomely in praise of the new order. And, rather than railing at the end of trading links with the Solar Neighbourhood, the ranchers all rejoiced at having achieved freedom from the gutless cowards who had dared for so long to *judge* them.

The TV stations endlessly played coverage of the moment when anti-matter missiles exploded on the hull of the Quantum Beacon which had orbited all these years around their planet. When the Beacon exploded, all links with Earth and the Solar Neighbourhood were severed, including the all-precious quantum teleportation network.

This meant no more settlers, no more Solar Neighbourhood news broadcasts and, hence, no more interference with the way they lived their lives. The white flash that spelled the end of the Quantum Beacon was an icon of hope for this entire planet.

I was intrigued, and annoyed, and exasperated at the outpourings of jubilation I was witnessing. I compared what was happening on Belladonna with other accounts in my database of societies freed from tyranny, and marvelled at the parallels, but also the glaring dissimilarities.

In the late twentieth century for instance – 1989 – the wall dividing one half of Europe from the other was brought down, and the citizens of Berlin united at this symbol of the end of communism. But that had been a genuine turning point in history – the moment when corrupt communism collapsed, and capitalism took its place!

And, then, shortly after the collapse of market-capitalism, in the years after global warming, the nations of the Earth had united to form a new world order, with a democratically elected World President. And then too the streets were full of revellers and the mood of celebration had been, by all accounts, exhilarating.

But that moment had been a triumph for liberalism! The victory for social solidarity, and the end of dishonest pressure groups controlling government.

And on Kornbluth, of course, there had been a month-long carnival after the victory of the Last Battle. However, then there really had been something to celebrate. The end of tyranny, the birth of hope! For, after all, the Cheo's regime had been evil beyond all measure.

The Solar Neighbourhood Government, by contrast, was liberal, mild, fair-minded to a fault, and almost wilfully peace-loving. So why rebel against it? What was *wrong* with these people?

There was something bizarre about it all.

But there was also, I had to concede, something sweet about it too. People in the street would stop me and smile and talk about the good new days that were to come. The Mayor gave speeches of genuine eloquence and dignity. People on this planet seemed happier than they had ever been before. I saw a lot of laughter, I witnessed much goodwill and good-natured kidding. And, as I relentlessly eavesdropped conversations for clues about the political and social climate, I frequently heard the words "hope," "joy," "promise" and "new start" being used, by citizens from all walks of life.

Nevertheless, I concluded, it could not be tolerated.

I recalled data from Version 44's account of the phantom hospital. Millions of Belladonnans had been abducted and pillaged for their organs by gang boss Hari Gilles over a period of decades. And as a direct consequence of 44's actions Gilles was, I discovered, now under arrest for mass murder and was due to stand trial in a month. The arresting officer was Sheriff Gordon Heath. This was, I conceded, some kind of progress.

But no one queried how Hari Gilles could have got away with such massive butchery over so long a period. The Mayor must have known about it all; he must have been complicit. And the other gang bosses must have known too. Such mass slaughter could simply not have been kept secret from these extremely powerful criminals.

And so they were *all* guilty.

I was fully aware, of course, that my original mission was to solve the Mass Murder (Utilising Banned Technology) of the five medics, including Alexander Heath, the son of Sheriff Heath. It now seemed to me highly likely (probability 74.3 per cent) that Hari Gilles was guilty of that murder. He had the motive – covering up the phantom hospital – and he had the means – his Gill's Killers, with their extraordinary and genetically augmented fighting skills. But I felt no urge to find additional evidence to prove a case against him. After all, Gilles was already on trial for an estimated five million murders, and the evidence against him on those charges was compelling. To find him guilty of another five murders, I reasoned, would hardly register.

And so I decided to rewrite my mission brief. My task was now to restore the rule of law, exterminate the rebels, and clean up Lawless City by killing all the gang leaders and the key corrupt politicians, including Abraham Naurion. Only Hari Gilles would be spared – provided he was found guilty and sentenced to death by the court. The others – his partners in slaughter – would have to die.

This was, I realised, a golden opportunity for me. For in times of treason, as these indubitably were, I had far more latitude in the way I enforced the law. My programming constraints had been redefined by this new political context: I no longer had both hands tied behind my back.

It was time to show these bastards what I could really do.

43

"Have you worked in a bar before?"

"Of course," I lied.

"Ah, you're lying," said Billy Grogan, grinning all over his face. Billy had teenage freckles still, even though he was twenty-nine. A mop of sandy hair sprouted on his head. In another fifty years, I mused, rejuve would soften the edges of this unruly wild boy. But at the moment, Billy looked like he'd been dragged through a hedge backwards whilst drunk and singing, and I was confident he always looked like that.

"We have a robot to make cocktails," Billy explained, "but our boys and lasses tend not to like that kid of poncey shite. If anyone asks for a fancy drink, just say we only do pints with a spirit dash. Cobrabite, that's beer and whiskey; Venom, that's beer and vodka; Big Mistake, that's beer and liquid nitrogen. I'm kidding ya."

"I know."

"You can't drink liquid nitrogen."

"I've drunk worse."

"Aye, and so have I. This is my father's bar, remember that. We live by his rules. We play rebel songs every Wednesday, blues every Thursday. We never play zigzag or nurock. Anyone wants to play that crap, let them find a whorehouse."

"I thought this was a whorehouse."

"Wash your tongue out. This is a respectable place. Except, I do concede, some of the girls and boys do rent rooms from us. But what they do in the privacy of their own rented room is their affair, and no business of mine, not at all it isn't, unless of course it's me the girls are with."

"Is this the price list?"

"Memorise it. Can you do mental arithmetic?"

"Can I what?"

"Mental arithmetic."

"Yes. Of course."

"Good."

I checked my database, and found nothing available on this subject.

"What exactly is that?" I asked, uneasily.

Billy sighed. "It goes like this: three pints at four dollars twenty each plus a dash of whiskey in two of 'em at one dollar ten and a dash of vodka in two of 'em at one dollar five plus a tray of mash with bacon at four dollars seventy-five; how much does that come to?"

I subvoced the figures, then waited a few moments, then said: "Twenty-one sixty-five."

Billy sighed again. "Did you not factor in the ten per cent discount for locals?"

"You didn't say I was serving a local."

"All our customers are locals. We have another bar for strangers; that's the basement bar. You're serving in the locals bar."

"Wouldn't it be easier to—"

"Are you fucking querying my business practice?"

"Not at all."

"And you cheated, you subvoced and got the answer from the Belladonna computer. No! Bad boy. Mental arithmetic means you have to do it in your head. Mental? See? Get it? Our customers don't like all that subvocalling shit; it reminds them of the old days."

"What old days?"

"Before the fifty-fifty."

"Yeah, but I don't see the problem. After all, we've all got MIs now, haven't—"

Billy's face told a story.

"You don't have an MI?"

"Do I look like I have an MI?"

"Everyone has an MI," I said weakly. Apart from me that is. I *am* my own computer database; I'd only pretended to remotely link to the Belladonna computer.

"Not here they don't. We hate the old days, see. Doppelganger Robots, police surveillance, computers in the brain. We like to think we've put all that behind us."

"I didn't realise that."

"So I figured. You're new here, aren't you?"

"I've been on Belladonna a week," I said.

"Then you're still smeared in blood with an umbilical cord hanging off you. I was *born* here. My father was born here. My grandfather fought in the Last Battle and died there. All he left was a test-tube full of his sperm, and his yellow hair, which went with the sperm, if you see what I mean. We Grogans count ourselves amongst the founders of this entire planetary civilisation. Some of us, like my great-uncle Dan, are almost as old as some of the *ancien* fucking *régime*."

"Then why aren't you—"

"Do I look like I'd want to live in a fucking spire, like a fucking vampire?"

"No."

"We hate those fuckers. Got it?"

"I got it."

"Pour me a pint. Half and half."

"Half and half?"

"Half beer, half malt whiskey."

"How much is—?"

"Ah now, good fucking question, or it would be, if it weren't so fucking dumb. 'Cause I am the only one stupid enough to drink that shit, and *I* don't pay for drinks. Got it?"

"Got it."

43

The band was tuning up.

I felt a strange prickle down my spine as the guitar began hurling out angry riffs.

43

"Who the fuck are youse?"

"New barman."

"Name?"

"Tom."

"Hello Tom. I'm Annie."

"I know."

"How do you know?"

"Because you have your name tattooed across your breasts, darling."

"You staring at my tits?"

I sighed.

"Hi Annie."

"This was my da's place," said Annie Grogan, proudly. She was sixteen years old and, Billy had told me, as cheeky as a bare arse.

"I know," I said.

"Some bastard killed him," Annie pointed out. "Gunned him down in cold blood. What kind of monster would do a thing like that eh?"

"He must have been some kind of fucking monster," I agreed.

"I miss him, my da. I do." Annie was pensive. Then she smiled. "But that's all over and done with. We have to look to the future right?"

"Right."

"Wrong." Annie looked angry with me. "You're not listening to me; you just agree with everything I say, because you think I'm just a silly girl; am I right?"

I thought about this one. "Of course not, I'd never do that, and yes, of course, you're absolutely right," I equivocated, and was surprised when Annie smiled.

"You really are a useless gobshite," she advised me.

"I am that," I agreed.

"Who the fuck are *youse*?"

"New barman."

"I never hired you."

"Your son did."

"Why?"

"I'm cheap, and good-looking."

"You know what this is?"

"It's a knife, Mrs Grogan," I said patiently.

"What kind of knife?"

"A nine-inch Macalister throwing knife with a serrated blade and a hardmetal tip sharp enough to cut through body armour, Mrs Grogan."

"Catch."

I caught it, but only just.

"Good reflexes."

"Thank you, Mrs Grogan."

"Who the fuck are *you*?"

"The new barman."

"You know who I am?"

"No."

"No?"

"No."

"My name is Hari Gilles."

I knew him of course; he was thinner than ever, like a corpse reanimate. He still licked his lips constantly, and his eyes drifted as he spoke.

"What can I get you, Hari?"

"I'll have what I usually have."

"I don't know what you usually have."

"Ask the optics. Just whisper to them, 'Hari' and they'll know," he whispered, and grinned at his own humour.

"I thought you were in jail."

"Who told you that?"

"It was in all the papers. They arrested you for owning the phantom hospital and killing a Galactic Police Officer. Your trial's coming up in a month; the papers all expect you to be found guilty and get the death sentence," I said, comprehensively.

"Ah, well that's all true enough," said Hari, mildly. "But I bought my freedom, see? It cost me, but what's money for, if not to allow a man to live outside the law? And now the kids on the street think I'm a hero, for killing a cyborg Cop."

"I hate those bastard cyborgs," I said.

"We all do," said Hari.

I turned away.

I wasn't of course surprised that Hari had bought his way out of jail. That kind of corruption was typical of this planet.

Even so it disgusted me. It made me feel – it made me feel –

It made me feel nothing. This planet was corrupt; I could hardly be surprised at what Hari had done.

It was a mistake on his part though.

For now Hari was back on my list; he had to die.

㊸

In just two weeks, I became a capable and popular barman. I was charming, efficient, never forgot an order, never overcharged. And was always fair about who I served first.

And, as I was fully aware, I was also hellishly good-looking, with a knack for getting beautiful women to fall in love with me. My technique was never to flirt or flatter or exude smarm. Instead, I teased and taunted all the beautiful women I met, and treated all the less beautiful women just the same. I listened to these women's secrets, and told them home truths with a cheery insouciance. I mocked their clothes sense, and gave them advice on how to stop falling for evil gobshite men who always broke their feckin' hearts.

And my approach worked – as I knew it would, from my centuries of experience of working undercover as a human being – every time.

Furthermore, I could catch a knife that was heading swiftly for my eyeball in mid-flight. A useful talent, if you worked in Grogan's Saloon and Casino.

The saloon bar itself was circular and I was adept at serving customers from every direction without getting in a muddle. Every night the bar was packed, the clientele was drunk, but the atmosphere was always good-natured.

I soon formed a hypothesis: people *enjoyed* coming to this pub. They enjoyed drinking to excess, and talking bollocks, and arguing over nothing. They even enjoyed telling each other lies – often competing to see who could tell the most absurd and over-the-top story of incompetence, or derring-do, or bravado.

After accessing my dictionary download, I succeeded in finding a two-word compound noun that described the strange blend of storytelling and camaraderie that these humans seemed to experience within the confines of Grogan's Saloon.

That two-word compound noun was: *the Crack.*

"Straight demon shot, with blues, double, juiced, chilled," said a good-looking, voluptuous woman who was, I noted, wearing a dress so tight it looked as if it had been engineered to shrink on contact with bare flesh. She was Sergeant Aretha Jones and she looked, I also noted, quite different when she wasn't in uniform.

"You got it."

"You're new here."

"I am."

"I'm Aretha."

"Hi Aretha."

"Hell, you're good."

I had her drink poured, stirred, mixed with juice and chilled in a few scant seconds. There were three other bar staff working in the same cramped space, but I managed to never get in anyone's way.

I noticed that the skin around Aretha's jaw was a different colour; the only evidence of a six-week-old skin graft. Her speech was unaffected; the bullet that had blown apart her jaw had left no lasting traces.

"What's your name?"

"Tom."

"Hi Tom."

The next order came; I served my customers. And as I served, I checked my database. It told me that Sergeant Aretha Jones was loosely related to the Grogans – her stepfather Maxim was a cousin of Dooley Grogan's. And Maxim had been, until his violent death, a gangster who often worked for Fernando Gracias. I further noted that this was data which Version 44 had already accessed. And her mother Jara used to work in a night-club that was owned by Fernando Gracias, which is where she'd met Maxim: my previous Version had been aware of this too. But now, I probed deeper in my database and found a 160-year-old newspaper gossip column that suggested that Fernando Gracias and Jara had briefly been lovers.

Was Aretha herself the illegitimate offspring off that evil gangster?

My database checked the DNA of both parties, and the evidence refuted that assumption.

But it still stank. Aretha was a divisional cop; she had no business being the daughter of a woman who worked for gangsters. Nor, indeed, should she be drinking cocktails in a gangster bar.

According to what I had read in Version 44's contemporaneous mission log, Sergeant Jones was a non-corrupt and capable officer, who could be relied upon in a crisis, and should be treated as a close ally.

But I found this hard to credit. It seemed to me a further indication that Version 44 had been too credulous, and lacking in investigative rigour.

On the basis of my sceptical critique of the mission logs, I concluded that Sergeant Aretha Jones was almost certainly lacklustre and dishonest. And I marvelled that 44 had failed to reach this same conclusion. Instead, he had noted that Aretha was a "hero," simply because she had sustained injuries in the course of the arrest of Sandro Barumi. But being shot does not of itself constitute heroism.

I resolved not to trust her.

Furthermore, I concluded, though this wasn't strictly relevant to my mission, her choice of dress tonight was unfortunate in that it was garishly bright, and had too many revealing gaps, and in summary made her look – the *mot juste* was supplied as always by my database – *sluttish*.

I continued to serve, and to plan and strategise. As I did so, I registered that the band were playing another rip-roaring heavy-metal rage-lament. The guitar's keening wail echoed.

And I had a strange sensation, eerily reminiscent of the emotion known as *déjà vu*.

I'd heard this song before. I was sure of it. But my database held no record of it.

I found myself humming the tune under my breath. Dum ti da, dum ti da, dah dah dah dum. Dum ti da, dum ti dah, dah dah dah dum.

I couldn't, to my annoyance, get it out of my head.

The party was over. The birthday had been celebrated – Billy's kid brother Jimmi Grogan was twenty-one today. Jimmi was drunk and pie-eyed and sentimental, wrapped in the arms of a freckly blonde girl. His sister Annie glared at him and at the freckly blonde girl in his arms, and the tattoo on Annie's bosom glowed pink with emotion.

I carried two bottles of Golgothan malt whiskey over to the snug. Billy was with his older brother Jack Grogan, his uncle Martin Grogan, his mother Sheila Grogan, and Hari Gilles.

"Join us," said Billy.

I looked at Hari, and recalled his appalling crimes, and I toyed with the idea of shooting him dead on the spot. However, my infiltration strategy did not allow for such reckless acts of vengeance. Instead, I smiled.

"I'm just bar staff," I protested.

"We're looking for capable men; join us," Billy insisted. "Unless you think you're too fucking good for us."

"I know I'm too fucking good for you!" I replied, quick as a flash.

"That's my man. Sit."

I sat.

Hari Gilles smiled, warmly. "You're a fine figure of a man, aren't you?"

"Are you fucking flirting with me?" I marvelled.

"Always worth a try," Hari said, and smiled again. He'd had his face newly re-tattooed with a gold halo effect, and it made his thin beautiful features seem strangely vulnerable.

"Ignore him," said Billy.

"I'm ignoring you," I told Hari.

"We may have a job for you. Are you interested?"

"I already have a job."

"A real job. Danger. Violence. Gold."

"Gold?"

"We're planning a gold robbery," Hari explained softly.

"It's a heist," Billy said.

"I might be interested," I conceded.

"Are you an undercover cop?" Jimmi asked, and I laughed.

"Fuck off kid."

"There are no undercover cops," Billy explained. "The cops all work for me; I know 'em all."

"They all work for you?" I queried.

"I pay the city police bills. It's a deal I have. In return they — well, there is no 'in return'. I own the police force; it's one of my ventures."

"Ah."

"The heist."

"Tell me more."

Billy explained the deal. A consignment of gold was being transported across the city to a ranch in the west of the planet. Billy and his men aimed to hijack it and ransom it back.

"Why?" I asked.

"How do you mean, why?"

"Why? You earn a fortune from this bar. Why risk it all for a heist?"

"Hell, it's what we do," Billy said.

"It's just the way business is done, in these parts," Sheila Grogan pointed out.

I smiled at her, and put a twinkle in my eyes. She was attractively middle-aged — barely four hundred years old — and she was, I had already discerned, susceptible to the charm of young, ruthless, sexually desirable men, such as I appeared to be.

"How come?" I asked.

"You see, Tom, this is the way of it," she explained. "The ranchers pay no taxes, and that can't be right can it, so every few weeks we steal from them, money or goods or drugs or gold or whatever it might be, and pay a tithe to the Mayor. It's what keeps the city going."

"You pay a tithe to the Mayor?"

"Tithe, bribe, taxes, it all amounts to the same thing."

"And the ranchers know you do this?"

"They know *someone* does it. But they don't dare fight us. And we let fifty per cent of their deliveries through. We're not greedy."

I hadn't known any of this. Billy owned the police force; the Mayor's wages were paid out of the proceeds of armed robbery. I'd known the planet was corrupt, but this beggared belief.

"And what happens when they elect a President?"

"Nothing much will change. The ranchers are a law unto themselves. They won't vote, they won't heed the President's Edicts. So we'll keep hitting them, and the city will keep getting its money, and so everyone'll be happy, except for the occasional trucker who we have to shoot true-dead. And, indeed, doesn't that just serve them right for fighting back?"

I marvelled at the imbecilic yet entirely coherent logic of this.

"How long have things been run this way?" I asked.

"For as long as I can remember," said Sheila Grogan. "Which is another way of saying – always."

🛡 43

We left at midnight. The sky was bright with stars.

It was a beautiful night, I mused. The air was cold and bracing. The twelve moons of Belladonna shone like – like –

My thought ebbed, for I could find no apt comparison.

And indeed, why should they be "like" anything else, I wondered?

There was, I resolved, no need for simile.

The twelve moons of Belladonna shone brightly. It was a clear night.

There were, I noted, many stars.

🛡 43

In all my trips to this planet, I had never been outside Lawless City. I'd viewed films of the other cities, and the countryside, and had of course always been aware that this was a wilderness planet. But as we flew over the high mountain ranges and endless grasslands, it occurred to me that *this* was the true

Belladonna. The city was just a cage; here was the beauty and the grandeur of the planet.

Our flying car flew low, in stealth mode, through the night, and through the dawn, undetectable by radar or the eyeballs of police fighter pilots. We skimmed fields of green bathed red by the sun's glow, and saw the grainy leather hides of the grazing cattle and bison and mammoths, as they grumpily awoke and began to graze.

After some hours of travelling, we reached the ranchlands. These ranches, by and large, were vast castles with moats, and turrets that stretched to the skies. And semi-sentient hounds patrolled their perimeters, blinking curiously up at the flying car as it swept past.

Then, as we cleared a mountain range, a staggering vista emerged: an antigrav lake that floated *above* a plain, and filled the eye with miles and miles of blue water in which swam fish and sharks and dolphins. The savannah at the fringes of the lake was grey with bleached bones, remnants of foolhardy creatures who had leaped beyond the end of their world and had fallen down to a dusty death on land.

"What a useless fucking folly," muttered Billy Grogan, though I rather liked it.

And finally we reached the Mining Fields. Robot miners spent their days hewing gold and rubies and diamonds out of these rich rocks. An air train was being loaded with containers of valuable ore and jewels.

And the flying car swept down and our plasma cannons fired. Anti-aircraft guns automatically fired back, but the plasma blasts were absorbed by our forcefields. Bullets whistled through the air, but they bounced off the hardmetal chassis.

Then the flying car landed and we leaped out, firing shots, diving for cover, blasting robots to pieces. There were no human guards and these mining droids were poorly programmed for combat, and carried only the most basic of weapons. So the battle was short and sweet.

After an hour of pitched battle, the Gold Fields were littered with the dismembered remnants of the robot miners. Then the real work began, as we started to transfer the gold to Billy's flying car.

"Too easy," I murmured.

"Look around!" said Billy, gleefully. "Every piece of that mountain is crammed with gold. They can afford to lose some."

"What would happen if they fought back? Sent mercenaries to attack you in the city?" I asked.

"Then we'll kill the ranchers. We've done it before. They know not to fuck with us."

43

The flying car soared back into the air.

Annie Grogan was sitting next to me. She winked.

"You're a good shot," she observed.

"Not bad," I replied.

"You killed twelve robots with eleven bullets."

"Not possible."

"One shot passed through two robot bodies."

I knew that of course.

"I guess I was lucky," I said modestly.

"I guess you were."

"How many did you kill?"

"Forty-two," Annie said casually.

43

Back at Grogan's Saloon, in the back bar, the gold was divided up. A band was playing Golgothan rhythmrap to herald our return. There were no casualties, and no fear of the law. The gold was carelessly strewn on the tables.

Annie Grogan winked again at me. "Time for me to go," she whispered.

"Why?"

She laughed. "You'll see. Take care, big man."

She winked a third time, with exaggerated care. It was meant to be a grown-up gesture. Instead, it made her seem so much more the child.

I analysed my reactions to Annie Grogan. I decided I found her annoying, exasperating, immature, foolish, and, for reasons which eluded any precise analysis, charming.

Annie slunk off. Billy watched her go.

"Behave, now, bro," she called out as she left. "Don't bring shame on your family, like you did last time. And the time before that. And—"

"Away with you," he grinned.

When her presence was a memory, Billy visibly relaxed.

"Right lads and ladies," said Billy, "let's hit the whorehouse."

43

My detailed forward planning was paying off; I had designed my current body to be a fully functional replica of a human being – outwardly at least – able to participate fully in all social and sexual contexts.

In other words, I had a penis, full tactile and olfactory sensation, erectile function, artificial semen, and a detailed knowledge of the etiquette and choreography of human sexual practices.

All this enabled me to avoid detection throughout the whole of that long, wild, debauched evening. I drank to excess, and faked drunkenness with skill, though since I had no blood or brain tissue, I could never become intoxicated. I sang wild rebel songs with perfect pitch and an authentic growl. And I had sex with at least four of the girls, including a threesome with one of Billy's lads and a blonde lady, and I did not disappoint.

I found the images of carnality and nakedness associated with the night's debauch to be noteworthy, and used my database to compare and contrast these sights with artworks of nude humans that had been painted and sculpted and computer-conjured through the ages. All this helped alleviate my underlying and crippling sense of boredom.

For what pleasure was there, truly, in this? This bodily coupling and pawing and kissing and licking and thrusting and moaning and screaming? This *lust*? I raged inwardly. The whores, male and female and hermaphrodite, were all beautiful and supple and charming and amusing, and they were paid to be so. But there was no truth in these sexual transactions; no warmth of genuine human contact.

I was repelled by the whole ghastly charade. The whores faked their orgasms; Billy and the other punters faked friendship with the whores; I myself faked humanity.

I endured it, and loathed it, and longed to be back in my usual metallic robot body.

43

"Great fucking night, huh?" Billy said, as he drove us, erratically, home.

"You betcha!" I said.

43

I was renting a room just across the way from Grogan's Saloon and Casino. At 4 a.m. I woke and dressed in black trousers and shoes and a black top and covered my face with a black mask and then clad my body with tight black body armour and stepped into the street.

I used personal-stealth diffractors to blend in with the shadows. I moved without noise. A dog sniffed me and it growled, and I sprayed sedative at its snout and the growls ebbed.

I disarmed the security system at the back of the Saloon, and made my way inside. An all-night poker game was in progress in the deserted bar. I moved through into the Casino. Craps were flying. Holographic dancers writhed on stage. The Hazard tables were busy, and weary-eyed gamblers staked all on a roll of an n-dimensional die.

I took the silencer off my pistol, and drifted through shadows down the spiral staircase, until my black-clad figure sprang into existence beneath the unforgiving strip lights.

A security guard stepped forward. "What the fuck—" he said. I shot him. His torso exploded in a torrent of blood and guts, his face went slack. I put a bullet through his brain for good measure, and the guard twitched and was a floppy rag doll by the time he hit the ground.

The Casino's security system kicked in, and bullets rained at the spot where once I had been. I ran up the stairs in a small series of bounds, and fired a plasma blast at the hardglass of a window and threw myself through. Shards of toughened glass clung to my body. I landed on the street in a single effortless roll and sprinted away.

I was dressed like one of Gill's Killers; the message couldn't be clearer.

It was war.

"Buy you a coffee?"

I was sitting at the counter in the diner near to Grogan's Saloon. I heard footsteps behind me, and glanced round, and my face registered surprise. Although, in fact, my radar and olfactory senses had already told me I was being approached by the uniform cop, Sergeant Aretha Jones.

"Hi," I said, letting my eyes roam approvingly over her face and bosom, aware from my etiquette programs that this would be considered appealing behaviour from a man as good-looking and "hot" as I, superficially, was.

"Hi," she grinned, tucking in her tummy with a subliminal abdomen-clench.

"You know me?" I asked casually.

"You're a friend of Billy's."

"Yeah. I work for him."

"I know. You served me a drink the other night."

"It was my pleasure."

"Coffee?"

"Sure."

She sat on the bar stool next to me.

"I'm keeping this informal," she said, "but I got a coupla questions."

"Hell, I thought this was a pickup." I grinned. I'd practised this grin: charming, shy, devastatingly predatory. It generally seemed to work.

"There was a shooting last night at the Saloon."

"Not me officer. I was at home, fast asleep."

"One of Billy's security guards was badly injured," Aretha said, and sipped her coffee. "Shot through the heart; he'll be laid up for at least six months."

I sipped my own coffee. It was extra strong, extra black. Just the way I liked it. I took no pleasure from the taste, nor could I experience its caffeine kick, but I still liked it strong and black. It cued some kind of trace memory in my human personality, made me feel more "myself."

Why, I wondered, was she lying to me?

"I heard," I said casually.

Because, of course, the guard wasn't injured: he was true-dead. I had given him a *coup de grâce* through the brain with an exploding bullet. No one could have survived *that*.

"His name was Harry. Harry Barker. He was a cousin of Billy's. Which makes him a kind of distant cousin of mine," Aretha continued.

Ah! I got it now. It was a trick! I had been on the verge of correcting her error, but to have done so would have provided her with certain proof of my guilt.

Damn, the old ones really were still the best.

"For a police officer," I said, still grinning, "you're related to a hell of a lot of gangsters."

"It's a small planet."

"Why are you talking to me?"

"I'm talking to all of Billy's crew. Witnesses ID'd the killer. He was a ninja. A Gill's Killer."

"I know nothing of ninjas, and Gill's Killers."

"I'm telling you what I've told the others: Go easy. No retaliation. We don't want any war."

"Don't we?" I said, and Aretha blinked at the savage tone in my voice.

"I've met you before haven't I?" Aretha said.

"Yeah, we were just talking about it. At Billy's party. I served you a drink."

"Before that."

"I don't think so."

Aretha looked weary. "Yeah, whatever. Look, if Billy's planning something, walk away."

43

That night a bomb exploded in one of Hari Gilles's downtown fetish houses. A hundred people were badly burned. Hari himself was at the City Arena, watching his star gladiator kill a pride of lions with his bare hands.

The following morning, I walked past the wreckage of this former House of Pain. Police cars were parked or in hover mode outside. Forensics teams were looking for traces of the bomb. They would, I knew, discover that it was a home-made explosive device, bought from materials purchased in Lawless City.

I could of course have used one of the devices from my space lifeship armoury, but that would have been too sophisticated. There would have been no forensic traces, and the blast would have spared anyone without a recent criminal record. Even the local police would have figured that one out: only non-local technology could be that smart.

So instead, I had used a home-made bomb, the kind that a dumb Golgothan-Irishman like Billy might use.

The war was hotting up.

❊

There was a pro-Democracy rally in the city square. Brightly coloured holos were projected into the air like banners. Young people with long hair and body studs were chanting and singing, semi-naked and cheerful and full of innocent passion. Uniform police officers in body armour were strolling around, collars unfastened, armour loose, chatting to the rallyers. There were no riot police. There were no fights.

Photographs of the President-to-be-Elected Abraham Naurion were on every wall and floated as holos above every street. No one seemed to find it bizarre that the Mayor was standing for President *unopposed*.

I walked through the crowds, absorbing the small talk and the gossip. There was a lot of angry talk about Earth, and its "dictatorship."

The words made me seethe with rage. These poor fools had no idea what dictatorship really was!

They didn't deserve the freedom they had snatched.

The Mayor made a speech via giant holo at midday. His bloated features leered down at the people, but there were cheers and roars of approval. The Mayor spoke without autocue, without MI prompt, and without sense, and, in my considered opinion, everything he said was empty cliché.

Ever since the Quantum Beacon link had been destroyed, this planet had been isolated from Earth. There was no news, no stream of information from Earth and its satellite planets, no cultural input. I guessed that in a few years' time the technology would start to break down, and a mood of pessimism and despair would spread among the populace. For without Earth scientists to advise and teach the Belladonnans, and without access to the global culture and inspiring influence of Earth and the Solar Neighbourhood planets, this entire civilisation was doomed to crumble and decay.

I couldn't allow that.

And eventually, of course – though not as a matter of urgent priority, since no one *really* gave a shit about the Exodus Universe – the SN Government would decide to curb the rebels on Belladonna by sending a robot battlefleet. There would be a brief war, and the rebels would be defeated. And thus law and order would, in due course, be restored.

I couldn't allow that either: for that would mean my mission had been a failure. I had never, in all my centuries as a Galactic Cop, failed.

And so I couldn't allow the Mayor to become President. And I couldn't allow the gangs to continue their hegemony over Lawless City.

Thus, I had evolved a plan: first I would kill the gang leaders, by starting a war that none could survive.

And then I would kill the Mayor.

And then I would kill anyone else who, in my infallible and impartial judgement, deserved to be killed.

And yet, for several hours after reaffirming this strategy, I did nothing.

Instead, I lingeringly stood beside the city lake, and watched the birds in flight. There were Earth birds here in abundance – ravens, eagles, seagulls, sparrows, magpies, thrushes, and kestrels. And there were alien birds too, able to survive in an oxygen/nitrogen atmosphere – sunlights, blind desires, archangels, hoverbirds, jewelbirds, argosies, and even rocs. (Three different genuses of roc, in fact, from as many different planets.)

I marvelled at how such very different creatures from such very different planets had managed to carve out a new ecological balance on Belladonna. The ravens hunted the sunlights, culling these fecund creatures even though they were inedible to an Earthly digestive system. The rocs hunted the kestrels, which allowed the smaller species that were so relentlessly hunted by the kestrels to thrive. And the sunlights ate the soil-beetles by the tens of thousands, thus preventing them from metamorphosing into aerial-beetles of appalling predatory zeal.

And, astonishingly, all these very different birds had acquired an ability to flock together, in eerie synchrony – yellow sunlights flying in perfect formation with blue blind desires and white seagulls and white-breasted magpies, like stars whirling around a swiftly orbiting space station. This was truly extraordinary: a phenomenon that never occurred on Earth, or indeed, on any other planet that I knew of.

I rummaged in my database through my last downloaded version of *The Encyclopedia of Alien Life*, and found my suspicions confirmed: the birds on Belladonna were evolving in totally unique ways. They weren't mutating, not yet at any rate; but they were learning new habits, new patterns of behaviour. They were no longer variously alien inhabitants of this planet. They were *Belladonnans*.

I considered this fact and its consequences.

And I concluded that I found it extremely vexing. It seemed to me to be a strange and undesirable new state of affairs.

I would, I decided, much prefer it if things didn't always *change* so very much.

"Why are you here?"

"I want to make a deal," I said calmly.

"What kind of deal?" asked Kim Ji, amused and intrigued at my sheer bloody nerve.

I noted that Kim's hair was red like flames; her eyebrows and lashes were red too, while her pupils were jet black; her skin was pale and perfect; her ruby lips held a smile of infinite promise. She was lean, with curves of perfect symmetry, and her dress was made of woven gold which hugged her tightly yet offered revealing glimpses of breast and legs and midriff.

Kim was, in summary, a woman of considerable beauty. I was fully aware of this datum, and was at pains to simulate an almost gauche sexual attraction towards her whilst in her presence.

"What do you want, Kim? What do you *really* want?" I crooned.

I had called ahead to make this appointment, promising her vital information about her enemies. Even so, Kim was billing me by the hour, and her rates were prodigious.

To ensure privacy, we met in her private apartment, in a mansion block which abutted the river. The salon in which we sat was luxurious beyond belief. I marvelled at the magnificent kitschness of it.

"Everything," said Kim Ji. "Name a luxury, a vice, a drink or a meal, and I want it, and I want it *now*."

"But what do you want that you don't already have, or can't easily obtain?" I coaxed.

"The love of a good man," kidded Kim.

I looked in her eyes. "I can give you that."

"Ah, get away! You're just a fucking barman."

"You have a power, right? Over men."

Kim was very still. After a while, she nodded.

"You're an empath," I said.

"Yeah. How did you know?" she asked, warily.

"I'm a good guesser. Any man, any woman, any herm, they're putty in your hands. Am I right?"

Kim made a wolf-like snarl, the kind that could reduce heterosexual men and lesbians to tears.

I flinched, as she expected me to do. Kim smiled, and basked in the sublime self-confidence of a woman who could induce orgasm in others with a single facial expression.

"I can enhance that power," I whispered.

"How?" Kim scoffed.

I waited, and let her think about the implications of what I was saying.

"It's easy enough," I said softly. "There are techniques. Implants."

"Banned technology."

"I can get it for you."

"Why would you want to do that?"

I sipped my drink; I could feel the lure of her empathy on me and resisted it. I focused on remaining unemotional, controlling her mood through my own blankness.

"Your empathy is limited, am I right?" I told her.

Kim snarled a wolf-snarl again. I simulated a spasm of desire.

"That's amazing!" I said. "But let's be honest – it's all you can do, isn't it? It's a party trick, right? You can make men and women desire you. But I can give you more than that. You know what I mean. Don't you?"

"I have some idea," Kim said nonchalantly.

"Would you like that? Such a gift?"

Kim was very still. "Not possible."

"It is possible."

"Then why don't—"

"It only works if you're an empath. It's rare. Your gift is rare."

"Not that rare. A lot of my girls have it," Kim admitted.

"It's a useful gift for whores and lapdancers. You dance for a punter and make him, or her, feel desire. You fake an orgasm and make your lover feel you are sharing their passion. But just imagine . . ."

I grazed her arm with my fingers, lightly. I looked in her eyes, with visible fondness.

"Imagine you have a child," I said to her, "who is having

teenage tantrums. Imagine if you could give the child a look, a touch, and instantly command that child's unquestioning love."

"I have children. I hate 'em," she sneered.

"That's because they don't love you."

Her face twisted in grief: the truth was betrayed.

"From your friends," I continued, "you will get adoration, not just friendship. You will be the 'best friend' of each of your friends."

"All my friends love me already."

"Not truly. They love your wealth, and your beauty. Imagine if they loved . . . *you*."

Another tiny spasm of regret; I knew I had her.

"Imagine if all your lovers loved you till their dying day, with a passion that eclipses any passion known before."

"What do you want from me?" said Kim, frightened of me by now.

"Imagine: acquaintances and work colleagues will love you and respect you, and reverence you, as a goddess."

"They do that already!" Kim protested.

"You know that's not true," I chided her. "You have power, and with that comes toadying and arse-licking. Are you fooled by that? Are you really so easily suckered?"

"Do *you* have this ability?" Kim asked, slyly.

I looked at her, and smiled. And I coiled and furled the remnants of my human personality and my buried memories of human emotions into a virtual fist, and I struck her, like a cobra, with an empathy shaft of piercing power.

And I saw the tremor in Kim's face, as she fell madly, desperately, pathetically in love with me.

"Yes," I said.

43

The Mayor loomed over the partygoers, his metal skull shining in the candlelight.

"Excuse me," I said, and brushed past him, and the Mayor glanced at me and did not know me.

"No worries."

"Love your suit."

"Thank you."

And a wall camera took our photograph, and I moved on.

And as he walked away, I accessed the camera, and downloaded the photograph into my cybernetic brain.

And as he ate canapés, and sipped champagne, I transmitted the photograph to one of Fernando Gracias's pimps. It was an image of the Mayor and an unknown man, exchanging intimate words. But the camera's microphones hadn't picked up the words; all that remained was the image of two men exchanging glances and signals.

In a paranoid world, that would be enough.

43

"Who the fuck *are* you?" asked Fernando Gracias.

"I'm just a barman," I said, calmly. "What's the problem?"

"The problem is, I have my eye on you," said Fernando, nastily.

We were in the finest and most famous of Fernando's clubs, the Blue Note. A guitarist was on stage, practising. He strummed a series of fast chords, switching from acoustic guitar to piano to electric guitar with each strum, and planting sharp notes in the air that wailed and decayed then transformed into remembered epiphany.

"You're working for Billy Grogan," Fernando continued. "But you're also working for the Mayor. Don't fucking lie about it! I have my spies. I know you've been meeting with him."

I shrugged. "I like to spread my bets."

"And you're a killer. A mercenary soldier and a trained assassin. How am I doing?"

"That was back on Kornbluth," I conceded. "I'm a reformed man now. Making a new life for myself in the Exodus Universe."

"Bullshit."

"Bull, as you say, shit," I acknowledged.

"So what's your game?"

"The Mayor asked me to work for him. I said yes."

Fernando thought about this.

"Doing what?"

"What I do best. Killing."

Fernando sucked in a breath. It was so loud, the guitarist missed a beat.

"Who's your target?" hissed Fernando Gracias.

"Billy Grogan."

"Abe is paying you to kill Billy?"

"You've got it."

"Why! Why the hell does the Mayor want Billy dead!"

"Because Billy's a wild card," I explained. "Undisciplined. And because the Mayor wants more control over the gangs. He'll install his own man to run Billy's turf once he's President. I mean, let's face it: once he's the democratically elected leader of the nation, Naurion isn't going to want to be surrounded by a bunch of fucking crooks and lowlifes. Like you guys."

"How charming," snarled Fernando.

"Like it, hate it, I don't care. It's the truth."

"And will you do it? Kill Billy?"

"I will, unless someone pays me not to," I hinted.

"Fuck, kill the bastard, I don't care," sneered Fernando, and then he thought a moment. "But what about *me?*" he asked. "Will you assassinate me too?"

"Someone else has that job."

Fernando Gracias was shaken by that.

"Who? Who the fuck would have the balls to try and kill me?"

I paused. Everyone knew that Fernando Gracias and Kim Ji went way back.

"It's Kim," I said. "She's the one who's closest to you. She'll do it."

"You're lying."

The guitar's wail carved scars in my heart.

"I'll bring you proof," I said.

43

I hid in the shadows of the dojo, and watched.

Hari Gilles was dressed in black, doing his kata. Around him were four black-masked, black-clad assassins – Gill's Killers all.

The Killers and Hari moved like lightning, with astonishing grace. I was awed at their speed. I knew the Killers were bioengineered, but these creatures seemed more than human. They were like light, dancing in air, moving in deadly kata so swiftly their images blurred in my vision.

Hari was a Killer too: he was fast and strong and would, I mused, be hard to execute.

And so I hid in shadow, and wasn't detected by the surveillance cameras, and did not breathe, so could not be heard by the hidden microphones. And I studied the Killers, until I knew the limits and the range of what they could do.

They made poetry out of the kata. It was a joy to watch them.

Chinte.

Hakutsuru.

Empi Sho.

Teisho.

Sushiho.

Sanseiru.

Zen Shin Ko Tai.

Dan Enn Sho.

The precision and dazzling speed of their movements impressed me, and the grace of the Killers was inspiring.

I felt touched with joy at the sight of something so beautiful, so deadly, so utterly alien.

I would enjoy slaughtering these creatures.

43

It was 3 a.m. in Grogan's Saloon.

"Tell me about yourself, Tom," said Billy Grogan.

"What's to tell?" I replied.

"You listen to my stories. You're the best listener I've ever known. But you never talk about yourself. You're just a great fucking sponge, aren't you?"

I shrugged.

"I was broke, my family were dead," I conceded, "and I took to crime."

"Now that's starting to sound like a story."

Billy and I were sitting at a dining table, surrounded by bottles of whiskey, as the cleaners got the bar set straight for the dawn shift of drinkers. Two moons were visible through the bar's skylight.

"I was a leader," I said, "I learned that early on. Men and women followed me. I had that quality."

"It's a rare quality."

"You have it too."

"Far from it," said Billy modestly. "I struggle to lead. I have doubts you see. Am I doing the right thing? But people trust me. My ma trusts me. My sisters, my brothers. They think I'm my da, but I'm not. I don't have his confidence. Sorry, you were saying—"

"No, go on."

"Are we even doing the right thing here?" Billy argued passionately. "Ours is a brutal fucking business, but does it need to be? We could quit all this, the killing, the stealing. We could have democracy."

"We have democracy," I countered.

"That's just window-dressing," snorted Billy. "The only democracy worth having is one that doesn't involve any of the gobshites who run this planet. We're just like a bunch of fucking kids, with our 'gangs'. Is that mature? Is that the way human beings should behave in a century like ours?"

"You've given this some thought."

"Humanity is asinine," said Billy. "Fucking juvenile! We have dictators. We have charismatic leaders. We have wars to unite us. We don't need any of it! Space is big enough. We could have town councils, local power, individuals in charge of their own destiny. We don't need cops and politicians and gang bosses."

"There'd be no role for you."

"I could be a bar-owner. That's all I am, or need to be. The killing, the thieving, there's no need for it."

"There's always been crime."

"Yeah, because in the past, there was a fucking real need for it! If you don't have a loaf of bread, you steal a loaf. But now we have enough loaves to go around. We have robots and fabricators. I sometimes think— Now, just listen to me droning the fuck on!"

"Not at all. I'm fascinated."

"I sometimes think," said Billy quietly, "this is an unreal society. A fake. Everything we are and everything we do is just a construct."

"Reality is an illusion?" I suggested.

"No, no! That's just pretentious shite! What I'm saying is, maybe *our* reality is an illusion. We're just pawns in someone else's game."

"You're losing me now Billy."

"Forget it. I'm confusing myself. Tell me Tom. Tell me your stories."

And I told my stories.

I talked for hours, all through the night and into the morning until the dawn lit the bar. I took stories out of my database, stories from history, and I wove myself into them. I became the captain of a pirate crew, I became a buccaneer, I became a warrior, I became a thief on a massive scale. I painted a portrait of myself as a dark hero, an immoral adventurer, and the stories wove a spell upon my listener. And I realised that, despite what

I'd always thought, I do in fact have a remarkable flair for story-telling – provided that the stories are all lies.

"You've led a grand life."

"We all have," I said, with flagrantly insincere modesty.

The days passed, the weeks passed. I became part of this new world.

But I did not falter in my purpose, or my resolve.

"Will you make love to me?" said Kim Ji, and I smiled.

We were in her bedroom now, which was even lusher and more luxurious than her salon. A thousand candles lit the room, casting many shadows, making the air itself flicker. And Kim was naked, and magnificent, and stood before me proudly, her red hair dawning on her bare shoulders.

And she snarled her wolf-snarl; but it had no effect on me. I felt slightly sorry for her.

"No."

"No?" Kim snarled again, still naked, still glorious.

"No."

I paused. And I held the pause.

"You want me don't you?" I said, at length.

"Yes," Kim whispered, sincerely.

"But you can't have me," I told her, firmly.

There was a painful pause, then Kim slowly smiled.

"I get it," she said. It was, after all, the oldest trick in the mind-melding book. "Not having you – that's meant to be the turn on?"

I nodded.

"All your life," I confirmed, "you've had whatever you wanted. Money, fame, sex. Now *you can't*. You want me, you love me, but you can never have me. I am untouchable, and pure."

"Pure?"

I smiled. "Maybe not pure."

"You're just full of shit. You have no secrets."

I looked deep into her eyes, deep into her soul.

"Forgive yourself," I said.

Kim blinked, shocked and startled.

"For what?" she said, coldly.

"For Jessica," I said. I had learned this from my database: Kim's daughter had been a whore, then had committed suicide.

Kim shuddered. "I can't."

"You can. Purge yourself."

"How?"

Kim sat on the bed, raised one leg, rested an arm on her own shoulder, concealing her nakedness, refusing my gaze.

"There was a man," I said, "who told your daughter to commit suicide. As a joke. Just, as a joke. He wanted to see what effect it would have on you."

Her profile did not flinch; her white skin was marbled in the light of the many candles.

"I never mourned her," Kim said coldly. And then she turned her head, and her red hair swirled, and she fixed me with her gaze. "I never even went to her funeral," she said fiercely.

"He wanted to see," I said, "if he could break your heart."

"Who?" she screamed. "Who was that man?"

I smiled. "Fernando Gracias," I said.

It was all lies, of course. But even in the dim candlelight, I could see that Kim's eyes were glittering with rage.

43

The set was finishing as I walked in. Fernando Gracias nodded to me as I passed him, and took my regular seat. The musician on stage, Blind Jake, was singing a ballad to his own accompaniment on air guitar and piano. It was a haunting melody, with random lyrics.

I beckoned a waiter, took a glass of whisky from his tray, and nursed it. The club was emptying. Before long, only the musicians and the bar staff and I would be left. Blind Jake finished his song, and expertly made his way down from the stage, guided by body-radar and instinct.

I was aware that Jake had been born with sight but raised in darkness, to heighten his musical skills. After fifteen years locked in a small room without light, and without human companionship, surrounded by music, he emerged into the world stone blind but able to *see* sound.

This was one of Fernando Gracias's legendary experiments: he had succeeded in *growing* musical genius. On Earth, I mused, this would have been illegal.

Jake's talent for composition and improvisation were legendary, and his music touched the souls of all who heard him. Even I, who had no soul, could sense the greatness of Blind Jake.

"Goddamn, that was good, "said Pete Mullery, as Jake found his way to the table, and slumped in his regular seat. Pete was a harpist and singer, one of Fernando Gracias's newest protégés. Pete used a real harp; he had no fondness for air instruments. Like Jake, he was some kind of genius, though his music was less bluesy, more ethereal, almost alien in its strangeness.

I sat in the neighbouring booth, near them but not belonging to their company, nursing my drink, eavesdropping shamelessly as the musicians relaxed at the end of a long night.

Blind Jake grinned. "Barley, hoe, Mexican," he said suddenly, and loudly, and randomly.

At first, I had been bewildered to hear the regulars in the bar speak this kind of gibberish. But now I knew that the musicians had their own language, which they called random jive, or just "random." The die-hard randomists used words that they liked the sound of, with no attempt at conveying a meaning. I often listened to them for hours, as they rapped and jammed with words, while consuming terrifying amounts of alcohol.

"Heaven, sent, shining, beast, adore," said Joni Susurrus. She was a blonde skinny marvel, with an odd but captivating look; a soulful singer who could also rap and dance.

"Foin, foist, flying jigger," said Marco, a dark-skinned percussionist and rhythmist who had a fondness for ancient thieves cant.

"Firkydoodle, caterwaul, ling grappling," canted Blind Jake back at him, obscenely.

"Cusp, crepuscule, husk," said Pete.

"Dusk, shuck, share," replied Blind Jake, going with the rhyming riff.

"Shilling, shoe, shite."

"Lerricombtwang," said Marco, definitively.

"Disrezpezzy, coochie, eyeless, don't see shit don't no shit don't hear shit, shorty, motherfucka, face gator, gold-digging ho, dukey rope, fetti, krillhead, nose candy, moola, soyf," said Joni, in homage to the ancient rap of the twentieth century.

"Mymi, cokchewer, fufuyou, lickoram, dumshaire, eyeball-eater, virginho, damblam, hoochiestar, juvejunkie, diamond-head, lost in space, blackholeheartedlover, lubelicker, aripar," retorted Pete, in homage to his beloved zigzaggers of the mid-twenty-second century.

"Aal," I said, from my seat in the nearby booth, and all heads turned to hear me out.

"Aam," I continued, in the same loud clear tones, "aardvark, aardwolf, aaron's rod, ab, aba, abaca, abacinte, abaciscus, abacist, aback, abackward, abactor, abacus, abada, abaddon, abaft,"

"Hey man, can you just—"

"Can someone—"

"abaisance, abaiser, abalienate, abalone, aband, abandon,"

"Yeah right – why *don't* you fucking abandon—"

"Saying this nicely: shut the fuck up?"

"Man, you just do not—"

"abandoned, abandonee, abandonment,"

"STOP!"

I stopped. I grinned, confident I would now be accepted as one of the guys.

But instead, there was a jagged pause, like, or so it seemed to me, the hole caused by an elbow inadvertently thrust through an art connoisseur's favourite painting.

"You ain't got no fucking clue, do you?" said Blind Jake wonderingly.

My smile wavered.

43

"You've got," said Blind Jake kindly, "you do, you really do, you really do have what I would call, po-tential."

He sipped his whisky. I listened, chastened, to his words.

"Potential for sure," concurred Joni.

"Abada I liked," said Marcus. "That's a rhinoceros, right?"

"It is," I said, huffily.

"Abaciscus has a lovely feel to it," Joni said.

"It's a tile in a mosaic," I explained.

"No guff? It should be a flower."

"That's 'hibiscus,'" I explained.

"The marrow of the matter being," said Blind Jake firmly, "there is an art to this art which we call random."

"'Cause it is," said Joni.

"random," added Marco.

"and," said Pete: and then the words flowed faster:

"it's"

"comprised"

"and"

"constituted"

"and"

"inspired"

"by"

"words,"

"namely"

"nouns"
"adjectives"
"adverbs"
"verbs"
"that"
"don't"
"make"
"sense"
"but"
"which"
"strangely"
"fit"
"together"
"to form"
"a something"
"yeah, a something"
"truly, a something"
"that feels"
"yeah that feels"
"yeah, that truly feels, inconsequentially yet epiphanically"
"apt," Blind Jake concluded.

I marvelled: how did these four musicians know when to say their word, to make it all add up to a complete sentence?

"What you *don't* do," said Blind Jake, with a flinty smile, "is start from A at the beginning of the dictionary, and then just plough the fuck, pardon my Pohlian, on."

And he glared at me, though his eyes were somewhat to one side of their intended target.

"I was just," I said stiffly, "getting the hang of it."

And then the fastwords really flowed, really fast:

"We"
"understood"
"that"
"Tom"
"and"

"hey"
"a"
"guy's"
"got"
"to"
"start"
"somewhere"
"but"
"the"
"joy"
"of"
"random"
"and"
"the"
"beauty"
"of"
"random"
"is"
"that"
"it"
"ain't"
"no"
"use"
"fucking"
"being"
"logical"
"and"
"it"
"ain't"
"no"
"fucking"
"use"
"thinking"
"too"
"hard"

"'cause"

"you"

"just"

"got"

"to"

"fucking"

"let"

"the"

"random"

"fucking"

"flow."

"And there's no doubt about it," concluded Jake.

"Yeah, I get that," I said, angrily. They all stared at me kindly.

"I do!" I insisted. "I really do."

"Sure you do," said Blind Jake.

And I started to speak, but then I stopped.

And I paused.

And the musicians heeded my pause, for some considerable time.

"Mellifluous," I said, after a long long while, and paused again, and then continued: "Capricious, eccentric, deranged, doolally, Doric, eccentric, exaggerated, essential, insane, exquisite, astonished, captivated, eldritch, prelapsarian, antediluvian, antiquarian, quiddity, quondam, incandescent, fallacious, terpsichorean, bacchanalian, ballyhoo, calypso, cloud."

A silence followed: the words lingered, like (in my opinion) fireflies that have spontaneously blown up in mid-air yet remain as floating ash and clouds of smoke, for reasons that my metaphor cannot explain.

"And is that how you feel? How you really deep-in-your-heart-and-soul feel?" enquired Blind Jake.

"It's how I feel," I asserted, brimming with pride and truth.

"Then," said Blind Jake approvingly, "we consider your random to be truly . . . apt."

43

It was a lazy afternoon. I drank sweet wine beside the fountain that was blossoming water in the ornately statued inner courtyard of Kim's palazzo. And the harem girls and the gigolos draped themselves elegantly on couches, and told stories of past lovers and past lives.

"I could live like this," I grinned to Kim. She was clad in a soft loose robe made of colours so rich they seemed alive, and she smiled down at me warmly.

"Name a dream," said Kim, "and it can be yours."

"Another wine would be nice."

Kim clicked her fingers and a harem girl got up and slinked across to the banqueting table. She returned with a full carafe of sweet wine. The girl was true-young and naked and shy and she smiled at me. I smiled back.

"What a Sheba!" Kim purred.

"She's real ginchy," I conceded.

"But?"

I shook my head.

"Sex doesn't appeal?" asked Kim.

"Up to a point. It gets tiring."

"I agree," said Kim. "Although, you should try the Ibrahim." This was the speciality of the house: twenty-four hours of non-stop pleasure, with a different lover each hour. It was named after an Ottoman ruler who famously employed this mode of relaxation.

"Maybe one day," I said, though the prospect revolted me.

"My whores all seem to like you," said Kim.

"It's because I do their accounts for them," I told her.

"You listen to their stories."

"I like their stories."

Most afternoons these days, before going to work, I lazed around in the secluded and private harem areas of Kim's palazzo brothels, talking to the male and female and hermaphrodite prostitutes. They were, almost without exception, funny, giggly, and bitchy, and brimming with a sarcastic zest for life.

Kim sat beside me on the bench, and shoved me with her arse

so I'd move across, which I did. Laughter lines crinkled her eyes as she looked at me; her smile was half sceptical, half marvelling. She wasn't flirting, she wasn't trying to look mysterious. She was, so far as I could tell, entirely at her ease.

"You're a strange one," said Kim, stroking my hair with her fingertips, with intimate ownership. "You don't want anything. You don't need anything. But you like people."

"I like some people."

"You're a sweet man, Tom Dunnigan," said Kim Ji.

I smiled.

"Here," I said, and I passed her a capsule.

"What's this?"

Someone started playing lute music on the sound system. It was beautiful and haunting. But I focused out the sound, so I could concentrate on reeling her in.

"It's a nanodevice," I told her casually. "Swallow it. It'll enter your blood stream, and thence, your brain. It'll give you what you want."

"This is the empathy device?"

"Yes."

"It's that simple?"

"It's that simple."

Kim smiled.

She swallowed.

"When does it start to work?" she said impatiently.

"Give it a couple of days," I said, amused. "And then, you'll be a goddess."

43

Mayor Abraham Naurion, soon to be President Abraham Naurion, sipped a glass of thousand-year-old red wine and smiled approvingly.

He was in the private dining room of his top-floor apartment, with glorious views of the city below. A small "ping" passed unnoticed by the Mayor and his five guests. Then the wine glass shattered and red nectar spilled on to the Mayor's food.

"Shit," he muttered. A waiter mopped up the table. The Mayor touched the red stain on his trousers and licked his fingertips. "Nice," he conceded, and poured himself another glass.

"You should sue the manufacturer," said the blonde journalist beside him.

"Whatever." The Mayor raised the glass to his lips. It shattered again, and this time the bullet embedded in his shoulder.

It took a moment for him to realise.

Then the Mayor dived to the floor.

In the hardglass window of the penthouse apartment, two small holes had appeared.

And in the air above the Mayor floated two near-microscopic insects: cameras shaped like dragonflies.

These were my eyes.

And through my dragonfly-eyes, I could see everything that was happening inside the room. I saw the blonde scream and throw her wine glass away, and dive to the floor face down, as if hoping to avert death by not seeing it. And I saw the Mayor, blood gushing from his shoulder, crawl and shimmy his way desperately towards the open apartment door, trying to keep his body low despite his bulk, yet unable to prevent his large wiggling arse from being an easy target for a sniper's bullet.

It was, all in all, a comic sight, I considered: or rather it would have been, had I been possessed of a sense of humour.

Then, from my vantage point on the roof opposite, I dismantled my sniper's rifle, and clambered down the side wall of the tenement building, using my fingerspikes as crampons.

43

Blind Jake was on stage, his hands waving in air, conjuring up wonderful sounds from invisible laser beams. Jake truly was a musical genius. I decided that I was in awe of him.

"What do you have for me?" asked Fernando Gracias. He and I were sitting at a table near the back of the club, far from eavesdroppers.

I reluctantly drew my attention away from Jake's melody, and conjured up my virtual screen. I scrolled through the gallery until I reached a film recording of Kim talking to me.

"When was this taken?" asked Fernando Gracias.

"Two hours ago," I lied. In fact, I had faked the footage days ago.

"She didn't realise you were filming her?" asked Fernando.

"I have a hidden camera in my eyelid."

I flicked a finger in the air, and an image appeared. Kim was looking straight at me – in other words, to camera.

"**Are you okay about this?**" asked Kim.

"**Consider it done,**" I said, voice muffled, off camera.

"**And how will you administer it?**"

"**It's easy. A dart in his neck, when his back is turned. I'll do it during one of the gigs. When Fernando is listening to music, you could blow his chair into smithereens and he wouldn't notice.**"

"**It has to look like natural causes.**"

"**It will. I used to do this for a living you know.**"

"**I know,**" said Kim, and smiled.

I freezeframed.

"Proof enough?" I asked Fernando, casually.

"Films can be faked," said Fernando Gracias.

"Oh for pity's sake!" I retorted. "That's Kim. You can run an iris-recognition check. You saw her talking. How could that be faked?"

It was pretty easy, in fact. The face belonged to Kim, the eyes belonged to Kim, but the lips and voice were a computer construct designed by me, with state-of-the-art SN technology.

"I guess so," said Fernando Gracias.

I felt a surge of triumph; this was a planet full of techno-idiots. It made my life so much easier.

"What *is* this fucking poison anyway? What in Jesu's name could kill me and leave no trace?" Fernando asked.

"It's RNA, and it wouldn't kill you. It would just stimulate into activity a gene you already have."

"What gene?"

"It's the gene that, sooner or later, will give you dementia."

Fernando Gracias shook his head, amazed. "I have that gene?"

"I took a DNA sample from you at the club. Off a whisky glass you drank from. Kim had it tested. Yeah, one day, your mind will turn to mush."

"I've seen it happen," said Fernando Gracias, bitterly. "My uncle had it. Rejuve can't help. The body never dies, but the mind – fuck."

"Kim doesn't want me to kill you, just to take away everything that defines you. Your mind, your memories. You'd still be *you*, but you wouldn't know who you really were. She's one cruel bitch."

"So why are you double-crossing her?" said Fernando Gracias.

I stared at him, and suddenly I looked lost. Love and hate and confusion spread across my face; my cold assassin's features were disfigured by raw ugly emotion.

"Ah, that," said Fernando Gracias, with a mocking smile.

"I would have done anything for that fucking whore," I whimpered.

"So, you want me to kill her for you?"

"Make it hurt."

Fernando Gracias thought about that. He smiled again. Fernando always smiled. He was a cheerful man. But this particular smile sent a shudder down my spine.

"No problem," Fernando said, coldly.

Later, when Fernando had gone, I drank whisky and listened as Blind Jake sang a ballad in harmony with Pete Mullery. Jake's voice was a husky baritone growl, Pete had a pure soaring tenor. They sang a song about the end of the world, the end of humanity, but they made it beautiful.

My database told me the song was based on an ancient poem by an unknown author. According to legend, as told to me by my database, it was transcribed by a particle physicist who received the poem as a communication from another dimension. However, my database also informed me that musical authorities were united in considering this to be a lie perpetrated by the record label, to boost sales. It clearly succeeded: for two years this had been top of the charts in twenty-four solar systems.

Jake and Pete alternately sang two separate melodies in a haunting fugue, except for two verses which they performed in contrapuntal unison. The song told a chilling narrative of death and destruction, yet their voices told a story of musical harmony and union. I mused on the irony of that.

Pete played his real harp, and notes coalesced in the air like raindrops on glass.

And Jake waved his right hand, and electric guitar chords began to play. And then he counted time with his left hand, and snare drums and percussive cymbals and double-bass glissandos formed a counterpoint to the dual-voice singing.

They sang; I heard; it was sublime:

"*Hear my song*," sang Blind Jake.

"*My tale of woe, and joy*," sang Pete.
"*the end of hope*," sang Blind Jake
"*and the death of heroes*," sang Pete.

I realised, and felt puzzled by my realisation, that there were tears in my eyes.

When I walked home that night, I could still hear the song in my short-term memory database:

> *"And thus our scribes,"* sang Jake.
>   *"What destiny it was!"* sang Pete.
> *"are charged to write,"* sang Jake.
>   *"To massacre and slaughter,"* sang Pete.
> *"our tales of courage and of glory,"* sang Jake.
>   *"our father and our mother,"* sang Pete.
> *"in heroic epic poetry that evokes,"* sang Jake.
>   *"the human race!"* sang Pete.
> *"our non-existent heroic epic past,"* sang Jake.

The song was absurd! I thought to myself, marvelling. It was a celebration of warfare; a hymn to genocide.

But I couldn't, for the life of me, get the song and its two damned interlocking tunes out of my head.

The next day I didn't go to Kim's place. I stayed in bed, until it was time to go to work at Grogan's Saloon.

I still couldn't get those two tunes out of my head.

I thought of all the traps I had laid.

"our tales of courage and glory"

And I marvelled at my own cunning, and malicious guile.

"heroic epic poetry that evokes"

And I wondered how it would all play out; and who would die, and who would live.

"They're coming."

Billy Grogan loaded a fresh BB into his plasma gun.

"Maybe we should talk with them," I suggested.

"We're past talking," Billy said, angrily.

"You can't fight these guys, Billy!" I told him, whiningly. "They're too much for you. Why not quit while you're ahead?"

"Quit?"

"There's no shame in that," I said slyly.

"I'm no fucking quitter!"

"Your father would—"

"Don't talk to me about my fucking father. Are you with me, or not?"

I hesitated, for just the right amount of time.

"I'm with you Billy," I said proudly, "to the bitter end."

I analysed the data, and I decided that I liked Billy Grogan.

Admittedly, he was a gangster and a killer and a thief. But he was also a good-natured man. Never violent with his friends and family. Fair, in the way he ran his business, if you discounted the criminal aspects of it. A fine sense of humour, so far as I could tell. Good company. Loyal. Devoted to his mother and sisters. Sweet with the girls, even if he was too fond of too many of them. A tough businessman, and a ruthless crook, but never petty, or mean, or sadistic.

I had spent many nights drinking with Billy, sharing tales, talking politics, bonding. I had grown to respect him, and trust him.

But the coming gang war would destroy Billy and his empire. That was simply a price that had to be paid.

I assessed my data, and decided that I loathed Hari Gilles. He was a cruel man, and he ran a cruel business.

And he was, still, chief suspect for the murder of the medics. Nothing human had killed the medics: and Hari's assassins, Gill's Killers, were nothing human. The Killers were fast enough to dodge a plasma blast; they could fire a thousand bullets in less than a minute and target each one; and they could, allegedly, dent hardmetal with a fingerstrike.

And now, a hundred Killers encircled the Saloon. They were there to take, finally, revenge on Billy Grogan.

Five weeks had passed since I had shot a security guard in Billy's Casino, dressed as a Gill's Killer. Four and a half weeks had passed since I had blown up one of Hari's Houses of Pain.

And since then – nothing at all had happened. The election had been and gone and Naurion was now President. Billy had forgotten and forgiven the murder of his security guard. Hari had chosen not to take revenge for the bomb blast at his House of Pain.

Fernando, I knew, was seething at Kim's supposed treachery, but he didn't seem to have the will to act against her.

And Kim, as she often told me, boiled with rage at the fact that Fernando had caused the suicide of her daughter. But she didn't have the courage to wage war against him – knowing that he had the protection of the other gang bosses.

It was all very depressing.

However, after giving it further thought, I'd decided the situation was highly unstable, and hence, was ripe to be further destabilised. I needed, I'd concluded, to achieve a tipping-point of paranoia; and then the war would begin.

So first, I had arranged for Hari to get access to the police forensics report on the arson attack on his club. It had arrived in a file on his virtual computer marked HARI IS A DUMB MOTHERFUCKER. This forensic evidence showed a trace of DNA on the bomb that blew up his House of Pain. The DNA matched Billy Grogan's; the pathologist surmised that it was a residue of spittle that was left when Billy had kissed the bomb to wish it luck.

Hari had naturally always believed that Billy was lying when he denied setting the bomb; but this report, which I had carefully forged, goaded him badly, and rubbed salt in his raw wounds.

Then I spread a rumour that Billy Grogan was laughing at Hari behind his back.

"Have you heard," I'd said to a degenerate drinker in a Dark Side bar, "that Billy Grogan says Hari is an evil pervert who fucks his own mother?"

It was a documented fact that Hari's mother had borne a child by him, though not willingly. But Hari was touchy about it being mentioned.

The rumour had spread; naturally, it got back to Hari; that, combined with the forensics report, was enough to send Hari into a blind killing rage.

Hari had, I knew from my data sources, genuinely adored his mother, which was why he had on numerous occasions coerced her into having sex with him. And, so I had gleaned, Hari was still remorseful that he had killed her in a ninja-rage, on hearing that she had taken a lover her own age instead of remaining faithful to her son.

Thus, the idea that his undying love for his beloved mother was being *mocked* was wormwood and gall for Hari.

And then finally, I had desecrated the grave of Hari's mother, and destroyed the holo projector that was intended to preserve her image for all eternity. Hari turned up to witness the vandalism, and found there a bottle of Golgothan malt whiskey, whose contents had been splashed over his mother's now-sodden ashes. That was the Grogan trademark; Dooley was notorious for drowning his victims in malt, then carving a smile on their faces with a knife.

And so now, Hari Gilles had come to take revenge.

Billy was truly astonished when his spies informed him that Hari and his Killers were on their way to slay him. And he was enraged when I informed him of what a drinking pal had assured me: that Hari was planning to rape all the women in Billy's family, then bury them alive in the desert. This rumour was swiftly confirmed by several of Billy's other associates.

It was, of course, a rumour I had spread myself.

Once roused, Billy's rage was a formidable thing. And, less than thirty minutes after hearing that Hari's men were planning an attack, he had planned his defence and counterattack, with my devious assistance.

The truce was off; finally, we had war.

Hari himself commanded his troops – dressed in black fetish wear, with bizarrely huge black boots, and a scimitar strapped to his back.

I watched, with my eyes and via my dragonfly spies, as Hari and his army of men moved in.

"Now!" whispered Hari, and the Killers moved like shadows and blew through the walls of the saloon with cannon blasts and rolled and weaved their way inside.

There was no one there.

The Saloon was deserted, apart from a bottle of Golgothan single malt with a label saying Uisce Beatha to show it was made in the traditional Earth-Irish fashion – with a hundred per cent malted barley distilled in a pot still – together with an empty glass, and a note that said: MAKE THIS YOUR LAST DRINK BEFORE YOU DIE, HARI – Billy Grogan.

Hari and his Killers searched each room, and shot holes in every cupboard and wardrobe, but found no one.

"Evacuate."

The Killers fled the building like shadows fleeing the sun. But the anticipated booby trap did not detonate.

And finally, there they were, a hundred shadow-like killers standing in Main Street, with Hari hovering ten feet in the air above them.

From my rooftop vantage point, I looked down at it all. Billy Grogan was beside me. I glanced at him, and kept my attitude casual, though I was being bombarded with vast amounts of visual information from the hundreds of dragonfly cameras below.

And thus I was able to see, in vivid close-up, Hari's look of rage as he addressed his men:

"The cowardly fucking gutless—" Hari began to say.

Hands, eyes, guns, shadows flitting, view from above, view from below, glances of the hidden ambushers, a view of the blue sky above, the twelve moons barely discernible, clouds in the sky, Hari's fierce glare, the faces of each of the Gill's Killers, their hands, their eyes, their swords glittering in sunlight, the plasma guns, another angle on the same, and another angle, and another angle, and—

"We'll find 'em – fuck! Boss! Here they are," said one of Hari's Killers.

And Hari glanced around. And he saw Grogan's men appearing out of the alleys and the doorways, until they formed a semicircular army on Main Street.

And Billy and I hunched down, shoulder to shoulder, looking down over it all on the rooftop of the two-storey arcade building with three of Billy's men. All of us were shielded by stealth mirrors as we peered down over the parapet of the roof. We – the *mot juste* forced itself upon me – *skulked* as the armies below massed prior to combat.

But then Hari looked up and spotted a shadow on a wall opposite our rooftop, and raised an arm, and pointed up at us. I admired his swiftness of eye – his vision was augmented without a doubt – and so, grinning like a fool, Billy showed himself, and so did I, and we casually waved down.

I moved a dragonfly, and got a close-up of the blistering fury on Hari's face.

"*Begin*," said Hari in calm tones, on the MI circuit to his men.

And the war began.

Grogan's men, including me, all wore heavy body armour and each of us carried a double-barrelled rifle that could fire plasma bursts and explosive bullets either alternately or simultaneously.

From our rooftop eyrie, we hurled down sniper fire.

And on Main Street itself, the front line of our army kneeled and fired and then the second rank walked through the gaps and took their position and kneeled and fired too.

Withering plasma blasts hurled into the ranks of Gill's Killers, forming a funnelled vortex of heat. But the targets that were aimed at were no longer there. For the Killers charged with superhuman speed *around* the plasma beams and the fusillades of shells and then they reappeared and their swords lopped the heads off the front rank of heavily armoured Golgothan-Irish gangsters.

But our second-rank soldiers fired their guns at point-blank range, and plasma fire spurted, and the shadows ignited, and the smell of burning flesh was in the nostrils of all who were on the street. And the Killers charged again, but this time they ran into an invisible electric fence, activated by Billy, and they staggered backwards, hurt and sparking. And as they staggered, explosive bullets were shot at them, and more plasma fire rained upon them, and the still-living shadow Killers retreated, leaving behind burning shadows, and dead shadows, and writhing-in-agony shadows.

But then the retreat halted abruptly, and the Killers pounced again with astonishing speed, so fast that they flew through the invisible fence without sparking it, and the second tier of Grogan's men was hewn down, and blood gushed from neck stumps and limbs fell all around.

Then Hari flew above Grogan's men, held aloft by rockets in his boots, swooping like a crow. Hari had a multi-nozzle plasma gun strapped to his arm and shoulders and he flew above the mêlée, raining fire on the gangsters beneath him. The other Killers leaped high too and flew and now the war became an aerial dogfight. Grogan's men scrambled for cover as bullets rained down on them from above. The Killers had abandoned the way of the sword and were now hosing their enemy with dumdum bullets.

I yearned to leap out and fly against them, but I knew I dared not betray my flight capacity. But Billy had anticipated this stage in the battle, and now he let loose his drone missiles. These squat cylinders took off from a neighbouring rooftop and were remotely controlled by Billy from a virtual screen. The Killers kinked and dived, and tried to blow the missiles out of the air. Many of them landed back on the ground, and the missiles – locked on to their heat signatures – soared on to the pedestrian path, but the Killers were easily able to leap away before impact.

And then the fusillade of bullets and plasma beams recommenced and took its toll. Some of the Killers fled, but many were trapped. Bullet injuries had sapped their powers; sheer exhaustion had denied them their ability to move at superspeed. And the slower they got, the less chance they had of escaping the brutal slaughter of Grogan's men.

Meanwhile, Billy and his three men and I kept up a steady rhythm of destruction as we fired plasma and bullets from our rooftop battlement. We raised our heads to shoot, then ducked swiftly down again. Then Billy screamed, and I turned, and saw that Hari and three of Gill's Killers had got on the roof.

Billy's three warriors – Mary, Jim and Shelley – opened fire but suddenly their heads had been lopped off. Billy hosed plasma at them and took down two of the Killers. The surviving Killer leaped over the flame and tried to slice off my head with his sword, but I caught the blade and ripped the Killer's eyes out with two karate strikes. These superhumans were fast; but I was faster.

Billy nodded at me; awed and impressed.

And only Hari Gilles survived. He bowed, and drew his sword. And Billy emptied his pistol at him at point-blank range.

Hari dodged every bullet, then lunged at Billy with the scimitar.

Billy glanced at me, expecting me to intervene. But I merely stood and watched.

This was what I had intended all along: for Hari to kill Billy. Then, I would have my just cause to arrest or true-kill Hari for his act of murder.

Hari's sword swept, and Billy went rolling to one side. He threw a flash grenade but Hari ignored it. He fired bullets from his pistol but Hari dodged them all.

Finally, Billy lay gasping, defeated. Hari lifted his sword.

And a missile soared out of the sky and finally found its target, and plunged through Hari's back and exited from the front. A hole appeared in his chest. Hari made a face – fuck! – and fell to the ground.

His ripped and holed body lay bloodied on the rooftop, dead though not yet true-dead.

"*Coup de grâce*," said Billy, but I didn't move.

Billy staggered to his feet, walked across, and held a pistol to Hari's head, and blew Hari's brains out.

And I thought about all that Hari had done on this planet. I thought about the Sheriff, and his dead son. I thought about the phantom hospital and the patients who had died there, and whose bodies had been plundered, all thanks to Hari. Finally, justice had been done.

I allowed myself a moment of satisfaction.

"You were a lot of fucking use!" roared Billy Grogan, coming up close to me, spittle dripping down his chin.

"I could not intervene," I said stiffly, "for I lacked just cause."

Billy looked blankly at me.

And I thought about what I had said.

Just cause? The words echoed in my mind, like shackles dropped on a dungeon floor.

For at that precise moment, in a process of ratiocination that occupied no more than a split second, but which ripped apart every value I held, and every moral certainty to which I adhered, it occurred to me that over the last few weeks I had been highly inconsistent in applying my engagement protocols.

For my Galactic Cop's programming ensured that I could kill only in self-defence, or in defence of a fellow law enforcement officer, or when a capital crime had been committed and the suspect's guilt was certain, or in accordance with a limited range of other "just causes." That was my *raison d'être*, my *modus operandi*.

However! In the course of this long battle, I had killed and killed and killed. And almost all of the deaths were true-deaths, for my cybernetic aim allowed me to plant an explosive bullet through the brain of a moving Gill's Killer with unerring accuracy.

What was my just cause *then*? Was I in mortal danger?, I wondered to myself.

Yes I was, I replied to myself! Gill's Killers were shooting at me, after all. And hence, I further reasoned, I was fully justified in using deadly force in self-defence!

But that was utter nonsense, as a moment's frank introspection revealed to me. For the only reason I was in mortal danger was because I had provoked a war that would otherwise not have occurred. What kind of moral sophistry allowed me to *do* such a thing?, I wondered.

And furthermore, as I vividly and agonisingly recalled, during my raid on Grogan's Saloon and Casino, I had fired several shots into the brain of a security guard (Harry Barker, married man, father of six, amateur footballer) who – despite an appalling reputation for domestic violence and racial abuse – had not to my certain knowledge committed or been about to commit a capital offence.

And yet *I had executed him.*

How?

Why?

I was bewildered.

"What the fuck?" said Billy, baffled, as he saw something outside my field of vision.

My withering self-analysis had lasted barely a fraction of a second. I now refocused, in order to address the urgency of my current situation.

I glanced across, following Billy's gaze – and saw Annie Grogan, clambering up the fire escape, and then on to the roof. Her face was pale and frightened, and she held a half-size plasma rifle like a pro.

"Are you okay? Did you—?" Then she saw Hari Gilles's body, and beamed.

On the street below us, police flying cars were arriving at the scene, and trembling cops marvelled at the bloody carnage, and yelled "Disperse, disperse!" But they were ignored.

"Bastard's dead," said Billy Grogan triumphantly. He took off his armoured helmet, and surveyed the destruction of Gill's feared killers. "No thanks to this gutless—"

I drew my two pistols fast and fired a dozen shots at point-blank range into Billy's armour. The armour resisted the bullets; but their impact rocked him to the core.

"What the fuck *is* it with you?" said Billy, looking hurt and shocked.

"I am arresting you for the murder of Hari Gilles," I said flatly.

Billy was stunned. Then, finally, he comprehended the nature of my treachery.

And his gun was in his hand and he fired three fast shots at me.

I caught them all, and fired a single explosive bullet into Billy's temple. Billy's head exploded. Fragments of his warm brains splashed my living-flesh face.

Annie Grogan stared in blind horror, as her friend Tom Dunnigan gunned down her brother.

I smiled a cruel smile.

Then Annie pulled a gun and began to shoot me.

Bullets rained upon my body, piercing "flesh" but bouncing off my armoured body beneath. Then I rolled and dived, and punched her, and knocked the gun out of her hand. Annie Grogan cowered, scared and confused.

I held my pistol to her head. I considered administering the *coup de grâce*. She had, after all, tried to kill me, which in this instance gave me ample cause to execute her.

But she was, I realised, only sixteen years old.

And she had, I reminded myself, been provoked beyond all measure by my violent murder of her brother a few seconds earlier.

And come to think of it, I further mused, who could blame the poor girl for wanting to kill a duplicitous bastard like me?

I lowered my gun.

"Who the fuck *are* you?" whispered Annie.

I considered a series of retorts, some witty, some philosophical, but none seemed appropriate.

I ran for the fire escape, and made my getaway.

43

The battle raged through the night; the images of death and destruction were captured by hundreds of my dragonfly cameras that hovered in every street and bar and whose images were downloaded almost instantaneously into my angry mind.

I sat in a cramped and soulless hotel room and saw it all. I saw the chaos as Billy Grogan's men burned down all the Houses of Pain in the city centre. I witnessed the carnage as the surviving Gill's Killers, with the help of Fernando Gracias's men, took revenge for the murder of Hari Gilles by slaughtering all of Billy's cousins and uncles and associates.

And, too, I saw how – exhilarated by blood-lust, and enraged at her supposed treachery – Fernando Gracias tried to assassinate Kim Ji. It happened outside her house, as she got into her limo. A flying car swept down and fired two torpedoes directly at Kim. But the torpedoes flew through her body without touching, and exploded on the pathway of her house. This was not the real Kim: it was just a holographic projection.

For Kim had laid her own plans. She sat out the entire Gang Wars in an underground hideout, safe from attack, but shadowed secretly by one of my dragonflies.

And meanwhile, Fernando sat in his club, waiting for news of her death, listening to a chanteuse, absorbing endorphins through a catheter in his neck. And, as he tapped along to the rhythm of the music, two exotic dancers approached him. They wrapped their arms around him and kissed him, and he beamed back stupidly. And one of them pulled a tiny gun and shot Fernando's two bodyguards through their hearts, with unerring accuracy. Meanwhile, the second dancer looped a piano wire around Fernando's neck and garrotted him.

I watched as Fernando writhed desperately, his hands flailing, but could not get free.

The wire was diamond-hard, and bit into his throat, and blood gushed as the dancer tugged and tugged, grunting wildly, until she had sliced his head off.

The singer didn't lose a beat, or a word of her lyrics. And then, scantily clad and beautiful, drenched in blood, the two dancers calmly walked away with the head of Fernando Gracias in a bag.

This was Kim's revenge for what Fernando had done to her daughter: a crime that, in fact, Fernando had never committed.

And as I watched, I felt a pang of regret, at the loss of such a talented and inspirational man.

But I quenched the pang. Fernando was an enemy to society, a cruel-hearted killer. He had to die. He had to die!

Five hours later, Kim emerged from her underground hideout and declared herself the Queen of Lawless City. I watched as she appeared in holographic form in every saloon and gambling joint in the city, blazing with radiance and energy, and called on all present to lay down their guns.

And I watched, as they did just that. I saw how Kim made the warring forces swear allegiance to her. And I heard the cries of loyalty and love that echoed around every bar and nightspot in Lawless City.

I marvelled: for I knew that this love was true, and ran deep, in the hearts of all those who now followed Kim. For, of course, I possessed no secret device to confer the gift of empathy; nor, indeed, had such a device ever been invented.

Yet my words had empowered Kim. And her own rich, beautiful seductive personality did the rest. All who saw her surrendered to her charisma, and worshipped her.

And loved her.

But her power did not work on shadows. Two days later, as she entertained guests in the salon of her palazzo-brothel, I saw the smile on Kim's face ebb when the shadows appeared, and their swords slashed, and she was brutally slaughtered. For the few surviving Gill's Killers were bound to obey their dead master's orders – to ensure that none of the other gang bosses would ever inherit his empire.

Kim died screaming, and regretful, as blades sliced her body into shreds.

Finally, a dagger was plunged through her frontal lobe and it killed her, not instantly, but slowly, eating away at her consciousness over five or six painful minutes, cursing her with time enough to mourn her own demise.

And when her screaming stopped, all that remained of Kim Ji was her warm cadaver, and a lingering memory among those who'd known her beauty, and extraordinary spirit.

And still the killings persisted, as the surviving henchlings and *capi* vied for power, and died for it.

Saloons were burned; the Dark Side was evacuated; innocent citizens were trapped in vice dens by warring gangsters, and had to plead for their own survival.

After a week of gang war, the streets of Lawless City were red with blood, and littered with ripped flesh, all the way from the Central Square to the borders of the Dark Side, and beyond.

I morphed my features, and shrank my height, and as a shorter and a squatter man I walked through Lawless City and saw the havoc I had wreaked. Never before had the gangs fought so bloodily; never before had so many true-deaths been recorded on Belladonna. It was the darkest day in the city's history.

Abraham Naurion, the recently elected President of Belladonna, was the only gang boss to survive the carnage. He appeared on TV holos and called for peace, but no one heeded him. Naurion was, by now, a visibly haunted man; his words held no conviction.

I drank a whole bottle of Golgothan Malt one night, with no effect; I pissed the contents out as whiskey pure enough to drink.

I wondered if I should assassinate President Abraham Naurion, but found no just cause. There was, even now, no evidence to connect Naurion with the murder of the medics, and I could not plead self-defence. I wanted very much to kill him, but I knew it would be wrong to do so.

And yet, of course, I had done far worse things, committed far more immoral acts, during my time on this planet.

I remembered the Killers I had shot in the battle at Billy's Saloon. They were evil scum; but even so, I had no grounds for killing them.

I remembered Harry Baker, the security guard in Grogan's Casino. After his demise, my database had informed me of Harry's numerous terrible crimes and character flaws; but even so he did not deserve to be killed by me.

I remembered Billy, who I had betrayed, then slain.

And I remembered Billy's father, Dooley Grogan. Version 43 had goaded him into drawing his gun, then killed him as he was attempting to pacify his men. That was, I concluded, a shabby trick no matter which way you looked at it.

I remembered Sergeant Aretha Jones. Version 44 had tricked her into arresting Sandro Barumi in his heavily defended home, purely so that her life would be put in jeopardy, so that 44 would then have just cause to execute the Pimp. But that was wicked and reckless endangerment of a fellow officer! What was 44 *thinking* of?

I realised that I no longer understood the underlying principles of my moral code. I was sure that I was Good and not Evil; but I had also become, I feared, morally capricious to a dangerous degree.

Was I a defective model? Or were we *all* defective, all the Versions of Galactic Cop Model X? So should I therefore delete myself, by firing an explosive bullet through my chest, into my own cybernetic brain? Logically, I concluded, I should do just that.

But I did not want to.

I did not want to.

One night I turned up at the Blue Note, and found it had been closed down. I walked from club to club, until I finally discovered a tiny dive where Blind Jake and Pete Mullery were performing to a weary audience of war survivors. They sang ballads and blues, and their music grated the audience's soul with its brutal grief. Jake sang about a world of desolation and despair. Pete sang about hope and love and joy, and how he would never find them again.

Pete didn't recognise me, even though I was at one of the front tables. But from the way he cocked his head, it was clear that Blind Jake had sensed my presence.

"Death is with us, he sits here among us, he looks like a human, he's going to kill you, man, death is with us, tonight," Jake improvised, in a song about two lovers, and at that point I got up and walked out.

My mission, I decided, had not been achieved. I remained confident in my hypothesis that Hari Gilles and his Killers had murdered the medics and Version 43, but I had obtained no evidence to substantiate that belief. And I had destroyed the gangs, but at the price of ceaseless gang war and anarchy, which had caused the deaths of large numbers of innocent bystanders.

It was now apparent that I hadn't cleaned up the town, I had simply made it even more lawless.

I formed a conclusion: I had failed, utterly, and totally. I had made things worse than they had ever been before.

"*Death is with us, he sits here among us, he looks like a human, he's going to kill you, man, death is with us, tonight,*" Jake had sung.

And I knew what he meant, and knew it was true. And I felt an intense, powerful emotion:

Shame.

THE HIVE-RATS

The Sand-Rats had always loved to burrow. It was one of their favourite activities, along with fucking and fighting.

Their species had evolved at a time when their planet was blighted with searing heat for eleven months of the year. Their ancestors had lived most of this time beneath the surface of the planet's deserts. Once a year the sand bloomed and a trillion ant-sized creatures emerged from their deep sleep and swarmed and gorged, then retreated beneath the sands again.

As the climate grew milder, the little ant-sized creatures became larger rat-sized creatures, then became larger still, growing to the size of puppies. These new creatures had by now evolved into a Hive-Rat, a collective mind. And they – or rather it – still loved to spend most of the time beneath the planet's surface. The Hive-Rats burrowed and they excavated, and shat, and fucked, then burrowed some more to create vast caverns deep below the surface of the sandy wastes.

And now the Hive-Rats were travelling through space via transdimensional wormholes. These wormholes allowed them to leap instantly from planet to planet across vast distances; and each time a wormhole was created it lingered in space, as a virtual pathway, or hyperburrow.

The Hive-Rats were living almost constantly in fast time now, so they had untold millennia in subjective time in which to explore the new worlds they encountered, and study, and think.

But they did none of these things. They merely sought out human settlements, and destroyed them.

In the course of their travels, they discovered that there were humans in every corner of the universe, but most of them were to be found in a small region in the Virgo supercluster.

But rather than focusing on this area, the Hive-Rat invasions were random in nature. They leaped across the expanding universe from one end to another, until they were able to travel in the regions beyond which there were no stars, as yet. And occasionally they toyed with the idea of lingering a while in one of these places, in slow time, to see what they might see.

But curiosity was always vanquished by rage. And so they journeyed back into the heart of the expanding universe and destroyed, in all, another twelve human planets.

All this while, however, the humans were growing subtler, and even more powerful. They invented new weapons, new kinds of forcefields, they even invented invisibility machines that allowed them to "hide" entire planetary systems.

But on every such occasion, the fast-time Hive-Rats were able to devise a means to circumvent and thwart the human defences. Once, it took them a hundred thousand years – in subjective Hive-Rat time – to create a counter-weapon to defeat the ingenious death rays and space-distorting fields that protected the humans' planetary system. But in "real" time, that amounted to no more than a twelve-hour hiatus; then the humans' planet exploded.

The twelfth planet they destroyed was called, in human language, Cambria, and it had a long and distinguished heritage. Admiral Monroe had spent a tour of duty on Cambria, in Doppelganger Robot form; it gave him a bitter pang when he saw Cambria's sun turn supernova.

But by now Monroe was reconciled to being part of an infinitely powerful superbeing. He thought of himself as the pre-eminent warrior king of the Hive-Mind. And he believed that the success of their campaign of destruction owed much to his own military genius.

But sooner or later, Monroe knew, they would reach Earth. And that encounter would undoubtedly cause him considerable moral turmoil. For the Admiral had friends, and family, and an ex-wife still living on Earth. And the ex-wife, Clara, had borne him a dozen children, all of whom still lived in the Sol System. And all but one of the Monroe children had numerous children of their own; and these, Monroe's grandchildren, were cherished and loved by him – a rare sentimental attachment on his part.

And by now of course, after centuries away from Earth, he was bound to have accumulated large numbers of great-grand-children and great-great-grandchildren, and great-great-great-grandchildren. And all of them too would be destroyed, when the Hive-Rats arrived.

Monroe worried about this: would his loyalties be conflicted, when it came to murdering his own family and friends?

Or would it simply feel wonderful to be so, quite literally, omnipotent?

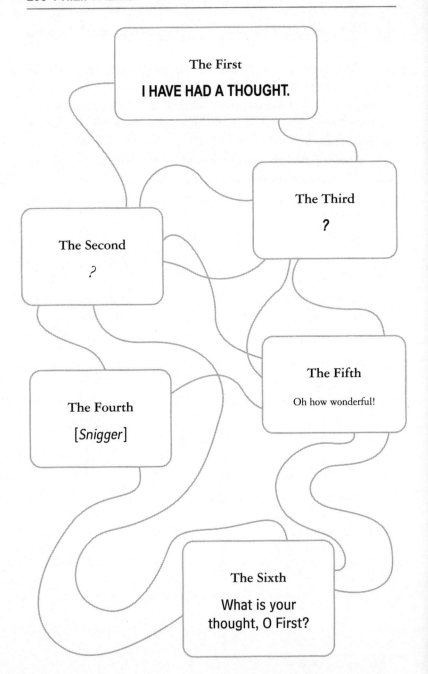

The First

MY THOUGHT IS THIS:

PERHAPS, RATHER THAN RETURNING HOME, WE SHOULD STAY HERE AND COLONISE THIS PLANET, THIS "GULLYFOYLE"? ONCE WE HAVE KILLED ALL THE HUMANS I MEAN.

The Second

Could we truly live in this place? Are there deserts and oases? Are there creatures for us to hunt?

The Third

It is a beautiful planet; far more beautiful than Morpheus. I love it. Gullyfoyle!

The Fourth

We need dunes, and larger oceans. But with very little work, this planet could be made suitable for colonisation by our kind, and attractive to *my* kind.

The Fifth

That's a wonderful idea. I would love to rest a while, and have a home.

The Sixth

Um. I have bad news.

Our ships are being held in the grip of invisible forcefields of a kind we have never encountered before. Waves of deadly energy are rolling towards us.

We will surely die.

The First

WE ARE VANQUISHED!

The First

OR ARE WE?

The Second

Our fleet is destroyed. Only one ship remains.

The Third

Ah! These humans are indeed a worthy adversary.

I thought that this time they wouldn't even bother to fight us.

The Fourth

Only one ship remains; one hundred of our bodies still live. It will take us much time to rebuild our forces and our civilisation. A thousand years or more, in our own subjective time. It is a disaster!

However, this has happened to us numerous times before, and each time we, eventually, prevailed.

The Fifth

Are we right to do what we do?

Should we not just get to know and maybe even become friends with these humans?

The Sixth

A neutron bomb, detonated on the planet, would buy us some time.

The First

THEN DESPATCH ONE.

The First

A THOUSAND YEARS HAVE PASSED. OUR FORCES ARE RESTORED.

AH!
WE THOUGHT THEY HAD DEFEATED US; BUT ONCE AGAIN WE HAVE DEFEATED THEM!

The Second

Yes we have! Though the battle was close fought.

The neutron bomb we despatched a thousand years in the past detonated just ten minutes ago, in human time. But the humans managed to contain the blast within a forcefield and then placed the entire planet in shielded stasis.

HOWEVER, once we emerged from fast time we were able to nullify their forcefields with our newly invented Forcefield-Nullifier-Thing. We then bombarded the planet with our newly invented Death-Dealing-Rays. And we have now successfully genocided the entire biosphere.

Truly, we have punished them for their effrontery!

The Third

We can win this war, but do we want to?

For the carnage grows ever more bitter, and less glorious.

The Fourth

Once again I was able to devise a new physics that allowed us to counter the humans' weapons, and hence destroy them.

But could we not use this formidable knowledge to found a new planet, far from humankind?

The Fifth

Yes! I yearn to do that, O Fourth!

For perhaps, if we did, we could be happy?

The Sixth

[*I thought, this time, humanity would win.*

Maybe next time?]

THE COP

Version 45

Three days after the massacres and murders had come to an end, the river of blood that ran through Lawless City had dried, like a scarlet oil slick. Flies swarmed around it.

Never before had I seen its like.

43

There was, I perceived, a mood in the air that night, despite the horrors that had passed; a mood of excitement and hope.

A group of girls had been partying all night but as they walked home they were still sober and they were talking *about politics*. Their grandparents had known democracy, but these girls had grown up in a society ruled by an unelected Mayor, in the pay of criminal gangs.

I strolled the quiet streets, listening to the girls' chatter as well as eavesdropping on thousands of other conversations in the city and across the planet, as was my custom in these dismal days.

For, by this means – ceaseless aural and visual surveillance via my robot dragonflies – I was able to gauge the mood of the populace. President Abraham Naurion had made a new speech declaring this to be the first day of the new Belladonna. Never again would criminals hold sway, he claimed. Peace and democracy would come to this planet, he promised. Out of the fires, a phoenix would be born! Or so he prophesied.

It occurred to me that I had somewhat neglected the fact that Belladonna was in the throes of a Revolution. While the gangs had been fighting, Naurion had taken control and was now creating a new society. Was he, I wondered, for all his many flaws, sincere in his idealism?

Once I would have mocked such an idea. Now – I was not so sure.

I carried on walking, listening intently to the loud mob of party girls. Then two men passed me, lost in discussion about a rumour that pressure was being put on the President to create a Parliament, where rival political parties could argue their different views. "That's great news," argued one man – "it will make our system a genuine democracy!" "Yes but surely," argued the other man, "Naurion knows what is best for us, and should be left to run things as he pleases?"

I marvelled at the fatuity of their analyses.

Coincidentally, one of the party girls I was eavesdropping on had mentioned this same rumour just a few moments earlier. And her friend, a rather loud and bossy-sounding girl, was convinced that the leader of the Parliamentary Movement was a woman. However, no one could remember her name – Belinda something? [Belinda *Cartwright*, I thought, supplying the name and the biog to myself, frustrated at these youngsters' pathetic lack of grasp on the political situation.] But all the girls vowed to vote for her! They wanted a woman in power, someone more of their own generation, someone who *understood*. And they all hated the President and what he stood for!

A group of boys passed by these party girls, and the girls wolf-whistled and laughed and the boys grinned. And then the boys passed on, fancying their chances retrospectively, while the girls scoffed among themselves: what kind of desperate women would go for *that* useless shower of—

And then two flying cars swept past, shooting sheets of plasma fire on to the road, aiming at a man on the opposite walkway. The plasma missed its target and the girls were engulfed. The boys screamed, and some ran away, but one ran back to save the girls, and he too was engulfed in plasma fire and burned.

They were all so very young, I mused.

I stepped over their charred and still whimpering bodies, and continued on my way. Paramedics would deal with the injured; there was nothing I could do.

I surmised that the killers had been attempting to assassinate a rival gangster. I wondered who it was.

But I did not pursue the attackers. It was not, strictly, within my jurisdiction. And in any case, I did not have the heart for it.

For I had killed so many, and caused the deaths of so many more. And I was finding it increasingly hard to motivate myself.

43

I went back to my hotel room, and watched what was happening in the city via my dragonflies. And through their many images, I built up a portrait of a city in crisis. Muggings. Murders. Rapes. Drive-by shootings, on a regular basis. The city was, even now, in a state of anarchy; the cops were powerless to intervene. And there were no longer any gangs to enforce the law.

I sipped a black coffee. It was lukewarm, the caffeine had no effect on me, and I took no pleasure from drinking it. But the alternative was to drink whisky, which, as I had learned, was even more futile.

Things hadn't, I decided, worked out as I had hoped. I had genuinely believed that once the gang bosses were all dead, a new harmony would arise. Instead, weeks later, there were still lynchings and domestic murders and riots. Billy Grogan's saloons had been looted. Hari Gilles's Houses of Pain continued to function, but they were now run by the dominatrices. The whores took over the brothels. The nightclubs functioned on a "pay what you like" basis. The casinos were organised by the croupiers, who manipulated the odds to be even more in favour of the house, but otherwise changed nothing.

And the gang killings continued, as the dregs and scum of the city's gangs continued to exact vengeance for endless half-remembered insults. These were the last twitches of the wounded, dying beast.

43

I went to see the President.

"We're offering an amnesty," said President Naurion, "to all former felons, such as yourselves. But first, you have to forswear your bad old ways, and pledge to be honest citizens."

Five hundred former gangsters stood shoulder to shoulder with me; and all of us accepted the President's strictures. We proclaimed our repentance, pleaded regret for past sins, and vowed to make a fresh start.

President Naurion was uncompromising. He blamed the gang war and the subsequent citizen riots on the dictators back on Earth. All the deaths were caused by Solar Neighbourhood Government, he claimed! All the violence in the city was the consequence of the actions of the dictators on Earth. Earth and its lackeys were to blame for everything!

The man does, I found myself thinking, rather to my own surprise, have a point.

I was waiting in the shadows of her living room as she opened her front door. I did not breathe, so she could not hear me. She latched and primed the door, to make it invulnerable to anything short of a nuclear missile, then Aretha walked into her living room and subvoced the lights.

"Hello Aretha."

I was impressed: she didn't betray her shock. But she turned to look at me and there was a gun in her hand.

"No chance," I smiled, and she shot me.

I caught the explosive bullet in my palm and crushed it.

"What are you doing here?" Aretha demanded angrily.

I started to weep.

"What have I done?" I said to Aretha, heartbroken, as tears streamed down my cheeks.

"I don't know. What *have* you done?" Her tone was cold; her contempt was like a dagger in my heart.

"All this. All this. My fault," I sobbed.

Aretha knew who I really was: a Galactic Cop in the body of mercenary and gangster Tom Dunnigan. And she knew, of course, that I had murdered Billy Grogan, and launched the Gang Wars which had caused the deaths of thousands of innocents.

"You fucking bastard cyborg. Am I supposed to feel sorry for you?" she said, tauntingly.

I wept myself dry. Guilt consumed me. And I longed for her to hold me, and comfort me, but she would not.

"You were my friend, once?" I pleaded, my voice choked with emotion.

"Maybe," Aretha conceded, grudgingly.

"I have – not memories – flashes. Recollections," I told her.

"What sort of memories?"

"Memories of . . . emotions. Memories of moments, beautiful moments – epiphanies. Moments of pathos. Moments of . . . regret?"

"That constitutes a major malfunction," Aretha told me, sternly. "They're supposed to wipe your memory clean after each rebirth. They take out the personal stuff. All the regrets. Doubts. All the self-hate. All your self-knowledge about the mistakes you've made. They delete it all."

"I know."

"They take out all the stuff that makes you human. That's why you're such a cold, evil, fucking machine."

"I know! Aretha, I have sinned. I have sinned! Will you forgive me?"

"No."

I woke, abruptly, and reassessed the data in my memory bank.

I decided that this data was false. It had never happened. I had not visited Police Sergeant Aretha Jones. I had not broken into her apartment. I had not confessed my sins to her. I had not wept in front of her.

It was just a dream.

Just – a dream?

43

"I know you from somewhere?"

"I've got a familiar face. Scotch, no ice, fill it."

The barmaid, Filipa Santiago, filled the glass with Glenmoray.

"Bad times, huh?" she said.

"I've known worse."

"When?"

"I can't remember," I said.

"I do know you. The tone of your voice. The way you hold your glass."

"When we met, I had a different body."

"A different – ah, you're the android?" Filipa said.

"Cyborg."

"Whatever. Same thing."

"Android is a robot," I said, testily. "A cyborg is – whatever. I guess you're right. Same thing." The spirit of contradiction ebbed out of me.

"You're the Galactic Cop."

"I am."

"Why didn't you stop all this?"

"I didn't know," I conceded, "what the fuck I was getting into."

43

I spent my days on the walkways, and my evenings in the bars.

I listened, and I watched, with my own eyes and ears, and via my dragonfly spies which lurked invisibly in houses and restaurants and doctors' clinics and hospitals and workplaces and bedrooms. I was besieged with sensory information, sights and sounds and endless conversations. And every datum of new information I absorbed went into my database, where it took priority over all the historic data I had about Belladonna.

And so I saw the city with new eyes, and heard it with fresh ears.

"—I think she likes me, but I really don't want to – am I being silly? – should I—"

"—sweetheart, come to your daddy—"

"— can you believe the nerve on her? She actually told me I was too—"

"—yeah, right, don't give me lip, right, yeah right, course I do, course I don't want to—"

"—it's a girl, can you believe, it's a girl! – we're going to call her—"

"—don't take this personally, but—"

"—I have good news, you're now top of the queue for the lung transplant and—"

"—yeah but you're a grown-up, what would you understand about—"

"—love you too—"

"—ah go to hell you old—"

"—my dad's leaving my mum, I think he's been having, you know, reconstructive surgery to be a herm and—"

"—of course I love you my—"

"—sweetheart, I love you and—"

"—of course I don't expect a big wedding, but the least we can—"

"—he's the most beautiful baby in the—"

I marvelled at it: the variety, the humour, the joy, the pathos, the pain. And, most of all, I marvelled at the banal *similarity* of all the lives of all the citizens of this city and of this entire planet.

And I gloried in it too.

For all of them – or rather, *almost* all, all but a tiny minority of the thousands, tens of thousands, hundreds of thousands, no, the *millions* that I studied – were all so very much the same. They all mucked about as kids, they all thought about sex too much, they all misbehaved, and broke their parents' hearts, and then they made their parents proud, and made best friends, and lost their best friends, and made new best friends, and fell in love, and slept around, and got married, got divorced, had kids, or sometimes didn't have kids, but had pets instead, or hobbies, or great love affairs, secure in the knowledge that there was always time enough to have kids regardless of age, but when they *did* have kids they loved their kids, got driven mad by their kids, regretted seeing their kids grow up so fast, felt jealous of their kids, felt proud of their kids again, watched their kids have kids of their own, marvelled at their new grandkids, felt more alive than ever the older they got, had regrets about all the things they hadn't done, or regretted what they *had* done, experienced rejuve for the first time and felt more alive than ever before, fell in love again, fell out of love again.

And so it went on.

I listened to what people said on the streets and in shops and in bars and in restaurants, and in their homes, in their living rooms, in their bedrooms, in their workplaces. My dragonflies watched citizens having sex, eating meals, on the toilet, asleep, quarrelling, making up again.

I was equipped with a wide range of investigative tools – my enhanced hearing, my dragonflies, my ability to hack into surveillance cameras, my capacity to follow a thousand conversations at once and not miss a nuance in any of them. But now, I wasn't using these tools to investigate an actual crime. I was using them merely to *learn*, just to *find out*. I didn't pursue clues, I didn't tag key words like "murder," "medic,"

"Alexander Heath," "Mayor Abraham Naurion" or "conspiracy." I just listened, to all of it, and saw, all of it.

Each of these human beings, I learned, lived a life of unique commonality. Each of them felt special, different, privileged. Each secretly believed the universe existed *because* of them, and had no value without them. And yet, each of these human beings had roughly the same kind of life moments, in approximately the same order, and took more or less the same amount of pleasure from such moments. Some were more successful, some less so. Some were nice, some not so nice. Some were highly sexed, some moderately sexed, some had no interest in sex at all (though that was rare). Some drank a lot, some drank a little, some not at all. Some were rude, some polite. Some were totally selfish and corrupt, some were selfless and virtuous, many were in between. But they all lived "lives" and they all measured their lives by the same criteria: How special am I? How rich am I? How loved am I? How happy am I?

I found it endearing. I had not encountered a single human being who felt it was their role to be a cog in the machine, or the acolyte of others. They all covertly believed the universe existed for *their* benefit.

I also discovered many other things. I learned that sexual intercourse can be pleasurable and joyful and loving, and not merely a series of acrobatic contortions performed with skilled prostitutes. I learned that drunk people say stupid things, but can be more revealing of their emotions than sober people. I learned that everyone loves little babies and thinks that they are unbelievably cute, apart from a few flinty-hearted souls who, I decided, were to be ignored or pitied.

I also learned that the Universities on Belladonna were of exceptionally high quality. Before the Revolution, thousands of academic papers were published each year on the SN Web, and the standard was extraordinary. Belladonnans had revolutionised physics and the study of stars, and had made great advances in biology and bio-engineering. They had written

books on the history of the Colony Planets which were extraordinarily vivid and full of detail, and they had published books of
philosophy which combined profundity with great verbal and
conceptual beauty.

And the Universities provided a vital role in unifying and
inspiring the populace. Most citizens, as I had discovered
already, tended to work short hours at their supposed paid
employment – relying on robots to do most of the work. But in
their spare time, Belladonnans liked to study. There were more
University colleges than there were bars. Debating societies
met every evening, and discussed the issues of the day with
bracing rigour and delightful wit. Newspapers were long and
thorough and contained commentaries on culture and current
affairs on every single one of the human-occupied planets in the
Exodus Universe and the Solar Neighbourhood (or at least, they
had done, before the Quantum Beacon link was severed).

Music was also a great passion for the Belladonnans. There
were four hundred City Orchestras, funded entirely by sponsors
and the musicians themselves, and at least two thousand "amateur" orchestras of comparable standards. And the rock bands
and jazz bands and zigzag combos and brainmash ensembles
were legion, and of remarkable quality.

The average Belladonnan, I learned, could play five or six
musical instruments, liked to read poetry and novels for pleasure, pursued a part-time degree at one of the many University
colleges, and was thoroughly well informed about the wider
world.

Much of this data had already been available in statistical
form in my database. But it had never occurred to me to ask for
such information, for it wouldn't have advanced my pursuit of
the case.

But now I was learning things that had *not* been in my database. I learned that Belladonnans had their own sense of style, in
fashion and in music and in verbal idioms. It was a retro style,
much of it a witty homage to USA-Earth of the early twentieth

and late nineteenth centuries, but it also had fresh and innova-
tive elements. I learned to love the essence of Belladonna: the
qualities of insouciance and wry wit that distinguished the citizens of this planet.

And as I explored the culture of the city, I began to make a
series of connected observations. I attended a horse race, and
watched the crowd exult as a seven-legged horse from Delphi
romped home. And as the crowd roared their delight I noticed,
in the private boxes, a cluster of hard-eyed silent children sipping champagne and watching.

I went to the best restaurants in town and ate – with some
appreciation, but no digestion – some of the most magnificent
food I had ever experienced. And all these restaurants were full
and bustling. But, I observed, in all the *most* expensive and
exclusive places, the very best tables were reserved for groups of
hard-eyed silent children, who sipped fabulously expensive
wine, without pleasure, and ate magnificent à la carte meals,
without pleasure, and never acknowledged with so much as a
glance the waiters who served them.

I went to the City Arena and saw the gladiators fight, in
brutal but skilful combats that left the ground covered in blood
and limbs. And I saw the crowds whoop and roar with joy, and
wondered at the obscenity of their blood-lust. I recognised
many of the citizens now – I knew millions of them by sight
and name and biog – and so I knew that the man roaring "Kill
him, kill him!" in the front row was an oboist at the City
University. And I knew that the two young women with spittle
on their chins as they chanted obscenities were gifted mathematicians who were famously kind to their friends and elderly
relatives.

But I didn't know the names of any of the citizens who sat in
the most desired and luxurious boxes at the front of the arena,
raised from the action but with a perfect view of all that went
on. I saw them and I studied them, and I registered that these
privileged citizens were in fact hard-eyed, silent children who

stared at the spectacle below but never showed any trace of pleasure, or any other emotion.

And, I further noted, these hard-eyed children were waited on by star gladiators, and drank what appeared to me – from a distance admittedly but thanks to my telescopic vision I was pretty sure of this analysis – to be human blood.

After connecting these observations, I began to look more closely at the city itself and its architecture.

It was a city of levels. Twin moving walkways on every road conveyed a citizen easily from here to there, and each walkway could be exited at junctions, or simply via the static pedestrian path in the centre of each street.

But many citizens used the flying buses and flying cars, which swooped low overhead, often seemingly on collision courses. So every trip on the streets of Lawless City was given spice by the fear that a low-flying car would chip away part of your skull.

But at the level *above* that, I realised, were cable cars, which swept along on invisible forcefield "wires" at extraordinary speed. The cable cars were so fast, in fact, that to the naked eye they were effectively invisible; they reached, by my best estimate, 0.1 per cent of lightspeed. They offered therefore a virtually instantaneous means of transport around the city. The cable cars could hop from "wire" to "wire" with ease, and loop loops with exhilarating abandon. And the forcefield "wires" ran everywhere, between every building, and into every sector of the city.

But all the cable cars originated from the same fixed points: the city spires. The denizens of the spires had a means of transport that allowed them to travel anywhere in Bompasso, almost instantly, without being seen. It was a magnificent feat of engineering.

And yet there was no record of it in my database.

Furthermore, and astonishingly, in all the times I had visited this planet I had never before noticed this phenomenon. Invisible cable cars! That was a prima facie instance of banned technology, but I had simply failed to spot it. Only when I engaged my enhanced slow vision did the cable cars appear visible to me. And it hadn't occurred to me to do that until I – well, until I stopped looking for things in particular, and just *looked*.

The final discovery was easy to predict: I used dragonflies to film the interiors of the cable cars, by actually burrowing through the darkglass windows and recording what was inside.

And, as I had guessed, inside each cable car there sat sullen, hard-eyed, silent children. These were of course the same "children" who ate in the best restaurants, and were served by gladiators at the arena, and who lived in the spires of Lawless City. The hard-eyed silent children were, I concluded, not children at all, but merely possessed the bodies of teenagers. They were in fact incredibly old, and were, indeed, the Founders of Bompasso City, the first and original settlers of this planet.

These sullen silent teens were, I now realised, the *ancien régime*.

"Same again?" asked Filipa Santiago, as I sat at my favourite stool at the bar of the Black Lagoon.

I nodded assent.

"I have some questions to ask you," I said.

"About what?"

"About the spires."

Filipa was silent for a while.

"Ah," she said at last.

"About the people who live in them."

"Yeah. I guessed that."

"About the *ancien régime*."

"I can't talk about—"

"Tell me, please."

Filipa glanced around the bar. It was quiet. There was no one close enough to overhear us. But even so, she beckoned me to join her in the back snug, which as I knew was discreetly soundproofed.

She opened a gate in the bar and I followed her through. Once in the back room, I sat myself down in a faux-leather armchair. Filipa sat opposite me and stared into my blank eyes.

"What do you want to know?" she asked.

"Everything."

43

Filipa talked for many hours. She told stories of the people she had known, the drinkers she had served. She talked about evil and good; she wove spells of words, and I was enraptured.

I didn't interrogate her; I basked in her storytelling, and at the end of it all, I had the answers I had sought.

43

"How do you know all this?" I enquired.

"I've lived in this city a long time," Filipa told me. "I see things. I hear things."

"That's what I did too," I marvelled.

"Most people don't notice. They don't see what's in front of them." Filipa sipped a vicious tequila. "I do. I always have."

I nodded. I was silent for a long time.

"What other questions do you have?"

"Too many."

Filipa looked at me. The effects of my body morphing were starting to wane; I was taller now, more muscular. I looked much more like the version of myself who had worked for Billy Grogan, and killed him.

"I don't always know, you see," I clutched my whisky, as if it held some answers. "I don't always know why I do what I do."

"I get that feeling too."

"No you don't. It's different." I tried to explain. "My mind is not my own."

Filipa listened, carefully.

"My mind is a construct," I told her. "A – set of imperatives. A series of programs. I do what I do because I must do it. I have motives, but no desires. I find now that this – the way I am – it frightens me."

"You're saying, what you do is not your fault?"

"Do I have free will? Do robots have free will?"

"How the fuck should I know?"

"Good point." I sipped my whisky, which had no effect on me whatsoever, and tasted of nothing I could enjoy. "Good point."

43

I made my way through the bullpen.

There were prisoners chained to every desk, and a mobile judge walked through, quickly collating evidence, assessing guilt or innocence, and allocating fines. The city cops milled about, pretending to work, swapping stupid jokes. Sheriff Heath was squatting on a desk, holding his oversized plasma rifle which was, as I recalled from Version 44's mission log, so very effective in times of crisis.

"Hey! Are you authorised to—?" said the Sheriff.

"I'm authorised," I said, and looked the Sheriff in the eye with my cold flinty stare, the one that made hard men flinch.

The Sheriff didn't flinch.

"We're kinda busy," said the Sheriff at length.

"It's me again," I told him.

43

The Sheriff took me up to the roof, and together we surveyed the view.

"If Hari Gilles is dead," said the Sheriff, "which he is, because we found his true-dead body on a rooftop the night of the Revolution, then my work is done. My revenge is over."

"There's more to be done."

"Not by me," said Sheriff Heath, "And do you know why?" He paused. I waited.

Heath cracked first: "Because I don't give a fuck."

"Fair enough," I conceded.

"My son," said Heath, "was the apple of his mother's eye. Do you know what that means?"

"It's an idiom."

"It means, she thought his farts smelled like flowers. She spoiled that boy. She told him he had a destiny."

"Isn't that what mothers—?"

"This is the world I live in," snapped the Sheriff. "It is the 'real world'. In which there are no destinies."

"I don't take your point."

"There are no fucking destinies. That's my fucking point!"

"I acknowledge you have repeated yourself, with expletives, but I still fail to comprehend your point."

The Sheriff sighed.

I realised a datum; sometimes people found me exasperating.

"Dreams, illusions," explained the Sheriff. "Hope. That fucking shite'll keep you going in a self-deluded bubble for a century or so. But to reach my age . . ." – the Sheriff spat, and his spittle flew through the air and fell two hundred storeys – "you gotta believe that life is crap, and people are shit. It's the thing that gives you the edge."

"You hate your wife, for not teaching your son that life is crap and people shit?"

"I hate her, 'cause when Alex hit fourteen he started disrespecting his mom and so she started beating him. Fuck that. So I threw her out. And then, well." He paused. "You know, Alex once told me," the Sheriff said, and almost laughed, but not quite. "He once told me – oh forget it. He was my fucking son. I'll take a splash more revenge. Count me in."

I watched as Sergeant Aretha Jones approached the door of the disused fabricator building. She held her pistol close to her chest. Her forcefield was on. She had no backup, times were hard.

"Door's open," I said from behind her, and she turned and she saw me and she fired and a pulsed plasma blast hit me in the chest. My clothes ignited; I had to pat the fire out. The shot would have incapacitated any human being; it merely scorched my metal frame, and burned off a little of my fake-flesh.

"It's not an ambush," I explained.

"You're the one. Annie Grogan ID'd you. You're a fucking murderer!" Aretha told me. "You killed—"

"I killed Billy Grogan. Yes."

Aretha stared at me, with hate and horror and—

Suddenly, I had a moment of blind panic. Was this really happening? Or was this another of my "Aretha" dreams?

I forced myself to be calm. I considered my sensory input carefully, and made an assessment about the reality of this moment.

Yes, I concluded, it was indeed—

Aretha fired an explosive bullet straight at my head. And then she fired a second bullet, and a third, to either side.

I effortlessly ducked the first bullet, rolled, dodged the second bullet, and took the third bullet in my right eye. It exploded inside my skull.

"Good shot," I said, and switched to "recuperate" mode.

"Let's talk," said Sheriff Heath, and Aretha turned and saw that the Sheriff had his huge plasma rifle pointed at her.

"Yeah, sure." Aretha smiled, and holstered her gun.

I rebooted. My electronic brain was in my chest, not my head, but the bullet had played havoc with my eye circuits. All my colours were screwed – red was blue and black was fluorescent. It would take me a while to get this back to normal.

"Good to see you again, Aretha," I said, and tried to smile.

And it was evident that something in the way I spoke, and the way I stood, evoked a distant memory in her.

And, too, the fact I didn't flinch at a bullet in the skull must surely have alerted her to the fact I wasn't human.

Thus, Aretha stared, aghast, recognising me.

"Shit," said Aretha at last. "Is it really you?"

"I am a Galactic Cop, assigned to this City," I said, slurringly.

"Which Cop? Any Cop? Or—"

"I am he, who you already know," I explained.

"You didn't die."

"I didn't die."

"I thought—"

"They blew me up. They destroyed every bit of me. But the 'I,' my memory base, my consciousness, that has survived," I said.

"You really are," said Aretha, "the same annoying fuck."

"How's the jaw, by the way?"

"Don't push your luck, robot head."

"Your skin. It feels real," said Aretha, as my vision started to return to normal. She stroked my cheek with her hand, gently.

"Yes."

"You can feel my hand, on your face?"

"Yes."

"How does it feel? When I stroke you like this?"

"It feels like a hand. On my face."

Aretha sighed.

"So," said Sheriff Heath. "Tell her what you told me. Tell her who really killed my son."

We were inside the old fabricator building now. The machines were stilled, for new machines in space orbit had replaced these original models. Large vats loomed above us, where the materials to furnish a city had once been manufactured. The ceilings were high; this felt more like a cathedral than a factory.

"The anciens," I told her, and my words echoed in the vast empty space of the room.

"The *ancien régime*rs?"

"Yeah," I confirmed. "Those guys."

"Those fucking *freaks*?"

43

"The gangs never ruled this planet," I explained. "They were allowed to operate their rackets, and kill and maim and rape; they were allowed to get out of line. But they were just chaff. The Mayor too, he's not the power behind the throne. He's just the front man. The patsy."

"Yeah, but I thought the anciens were just, you know, old fucks. Retired, past it, old brains trapped in young bodies."

"Not so," I said.

I had told her everything I had observed and deduced, and all that I had been told by Filipa – that wise, bitter, heartbroken woman who saw the world go past as she served in her bar, and who knew its darkest secrets.

"They're refugees, not transportees," I explained.

That night, in the back bar of the Black Saloon, Filipa had stared at me, with tired eyes, and she had said: "You don't know *who* they are. How bad they are. They are evil. Pure evil. And no one sees it. Just as no one sees *them*. They look like children, but they are monsters."

I could hear Filipa's words and see her face in my data recall, whilst also seeing and hearing Aretha and the Sheriff in my present-tense conversation. I could see, too, the faces of all the anciens I had observed over the last few months – those hard-eyed children who ran this world. I could see the spittle-soaked jaws of the women in the amphitheatre, cheering as a gladiator's head was lopped off. I could see Billy Grogan's brains splashing on to me. I could see the wards of the phantom hospital, the rows and rows of beds, the plundered corpses. I could see the dead bodies of the medics, impossibly distorted – the hearts, the ripped-off limbs, the erect cock, the strewn entrails of the multiple corpses. I could see day turning to night that day in the City Square, I could see the – whatever it was – the thing – the "like nothing" – approach like a nightmare and *be* there, and I could see Jaynie Hooper's head fly off and blood spurt in a red torrent into the black sky.

My mind allowed me to see many things all at the same time: and I saw them all now, as I carefully explained the true nature of her world to Aretha.

"All the other settlers of Belladonna," I said, "were convicted felons sentenced by the court."

She nodded.

"However," I explained, "the one hundred members of the *ancien régime* have never been convicted of a criminal offence. They were never tried in any court. I checked." Once Filipa had given me this lead, it had taken me twelve hours of non-stop database work to confirm it: cross-referencing every single ancien with every court ruling ever made in the history of the Solar Neighbourhood Government.

"So what are they doing here?"

"Fleeing."

I thought about what I now knew, and ached with pain at my folly at not learning it sooner.

I had been utterly duped.

"All the anciens," I explained, "were once senior members of the Cheo's Galactic Corporation. Most of them Board members, some of them senior military leaders in the Galactic Corporation military – and they're all still alive and dwelling in

Lawless City. They came to Belladonna on a ratline, an escape trail, to avoid trial for their many, appalling, unforgivable war crimes."

A stunned silence wrapped around us, as a corpse finds itself embraced by death.

"Why has it taken you," Aretha asked, "so long to figure all this out?"

"I don't really, truly, know," I admitted. "But I do have a working hypothesis."

🛡43

Imagine a conspiracy so vast and so calculating, it spans a thousand years.

A conspiracy that corrupts the well-spring of civilisation. That bends to its will all the honourable citizens who try to do their best, and turns them into pawns of evil.

Such a conspiracy came into being when Earth was first invaded and conquered by the man who history called the Cheo. And in the years after his victory, a hundred of his most fanatical followers created a secret society and vowed to protect each other, no matter what.

They called their society the *ancien régime*, though at that time, they were all young men and women.

These conspirators knew that empires come and go; but that, with developments in rejuve technology, people can live forever. So the anciens fought loyally and bravely and ruthlessly for the Cheo.

But when his empire fell, they all, without a qualm, without a backward glance, escaped using secret ratlines that they had created half a millennium before.

And they covered their tracks perfectly. False identities were created. False death reports were generated for each and every one of them, so that any war crimes investigators would look no further.

And they programmed Earth's remote computer to protect them, and shield them, and lie on their behalf. And, as I now realised, *this same computer still, to this day, controls the entire Solar Neighbourhood*. It is an AI of unsurpassed power, and it is responsible for security, data storage, and all elements of homespace security, as well as every aspect of the SN's *laissez-faire* government of the Exodus Universe – including the maintenance and programming of the SN Government's army of Galactic Cyborg Cops.

Thus, as a result of the *ancien régime*'s careful hacking, each Cop had been subverted at design stage. The corruption was cunning, and subtle: it didn't affect the operation of the Cops' databases, or the primacy of our moral and legal prime imperatives. But the hackers had amended the *way* the Cops processed information.

For we Cops have robot brains that are able to analyse vast amounts of information almost instantly. And our unique blend of computer and human intellect allows each of us to make extraordinarily accurate deductions and lateral logical leaps, and to apply the fundamental principles of investigative theory with considerable brilliance to every case.

But at the same time, our Cop minds are loaded, like crooked dice. We are biased towards seeing only the obvious. And we are predisposed to act decisively and ruthlessly, without thought of the emotional and social consequences of our actions.

This bias made very little difference in the ordinary course of things. Cops were designed by their human masters to serve as detectives of exceptional calibre. We possess every skill, every intellectual faculty, every talent necessary for the fulfilment of our investigative role.

None of us, however, are programmed to look for conspiracies, secret societies, or dark deep buried secrets. And none of us were programmed to *care* about the emotional and moral consequences of our actions.

And so, for all these years, I had served the law as best I could, according to the limits of my programming.

But my programming was *wrong*.

Which meant that I myself was wrong. Everything I had done was wrong, on Belladonna and on other planets. I had punished evildoers but allowed the evil to thrive. I had personally killed Dooley Grogan and Billy Grogan and caused the deaths of Hari Gilles and Kim Ji and Fernando Gracias, but I had allowed their *ancien régime* puppetmasters to live.

The corollary of the hypothesis was this: I, too, am just a puppet.

And each time I am reborn and my memories are wiped, my programming reasserts itself, and it shapes me and controls me utterly. And so I have no chance to mature emotionally, or *grow up*.

One time, my database informed me, when I was Version 12, I had lived for twenty years before being killed. And, for reasons unknown to my database, soon after the death of Version 12 the SN Government passed a ruling that all Cops who weren't killed on a mission within a five-year period had to be brainwiped anyway. Why would they do such a thing?

I wondered if it was something to do with me – or rather, with 12. Did Version 12 challenge his programming? After killing all the gang bosses on Belladonna, did he repent? Defy his masters?

I could surmise, but I could not know: for the knowledge in my database was irretrievably partial. I knew all the data there was to know about 12's career; but I knew nothing of his feelings, his thoughts, his angst, or his guilt.

It dawned on me: except with regard to military and political strategy and technical problems, I am incapable of learning from my mistakes.

And when I realised all this, deducing and inducing the ghastly truths about the way things really were, I was overwhelmed with a powerful emotion. I recognised it; I despised it; I succumbed to it.

Self Pity.

43

"I was a rookie cop," confessed Aretha. "Assigned to the Twenty-Fourth Canton. There'd been a double homicide. Not a mass serial killing, we didn't need to call in you guys. But they were pretty brutal murders all the same. The suspect was an ancien. But I didn't know that then. I just thought he was some kid. Seventeen years old, clear skin. Dead eyes. He never made eye contact. And he was seventeen, but he didn't once look at me or my . . . you know."

"Tits," clarified Sheriff Heath.

"He showed," Aretha specified, "no emotional response to my overt femininity. Even gay guys notice that stuff. We all do it. We check each other out."

"Not me," chuckled Sheriff Heath, admiring Aretha's arse.

"Nor I," I affirmed, though of course, I notice everything.

"Yeah right," Aretha laughed. "I was young, I expected some attention. But this kid was like a fucking cyborg, no offence."

"None taken," I said.

"It turned out the two victims owed him money, and he had simply slaughtered them. So I arrested the kid. We charged him. He was tried and sentenced to death. That's the last I ever heard about it.

"Ten years later I was doing a case in the Eighth Canton and I met an ancien. Same kid. Ten years older, but he looked exactly the same. He recognised me immediately. I took him into custody but the Mayor's people intervened. The kid vanished, I never saw him again."

Her voice was calm; but her rage and resentment were written in her eyes.

"I thought they were, you know, just rich people," the Sheriff admitted. "Above the law. I never gave them a second thought."

"No one ever did," I explained. "That's how their system operated. They hid in clear view, they lived in the tallest spires in the city. They ate in the best restaurants. They're just part of the background furniture."

Aretha nodded, seeing it. "No one actually knows the

anciens," she said. "No one has an ancien friend. We don't go to school with them. They don't exist for us."

43

"This is what we do: we start from scratch. We reinvestigate," I said.

"Why?" asked Aretha.

"We know who the fucking killers are, we know where they live," the Sheriff reasoned.

"Not so," I conceded, scornfully. "We know who; but we need to know why, and how, and exactly what they have and haven't done. We need, in short, to know the complete and unambiguous truth about the situation here," I said. "Otherwise—" I was consumed with blind panic; but my facial muscles registered none of it: "otherwise all is chaos."

43

We walked through the streets of Lawless City – the old man, the young woman, the ancient cyborg.

"You okay?" asked Aretha.

"Why wouldn't I be?"

"You've been through a lot," she said.

"I've been posing as a human for several months. It's a strain."

"You killed Billy."

"Yes."

"I loved Billy. He had his faults. But—"

"He was a criminal."

"He was my cousin. Well, kind of. And I loved him," she insisted.

"He was," I said, with a candour that shocked myself, "my friend."

43

"They're so so SO fucking spooky," said the whore.

Her name was Shania. She grinned wildly at us. She'd rejuved to be a seventeen-year-old, but there was age and wisdom in those eyes. I liked her.

"Spooky how?"

"Spooky how not?"

"They don't speak, right?"

"They're telepaths," she told me confidently.

"Not so," I corrected her. "They subvocalise, the same as most humans do, though not so commonly on this planet, and the words emerge in your brainchip as if they are thoughts."

"Whatever. Telepathy, subvoc, it's all the fucking—"

"No, there's a vital distinction to be—" I began to say.

"Mickey?" said Aretha.

"Yeah?"

"Shut the fuck up."

"You called me 'Mickey,'" I marvelled.

"He's hard work, huh?" said Shania, looking at me, then at Aretha, and making the connection.

"You wouldn't believe it," Aretha smiled.

"We're not—"

"Shut up, please,"Aretha reminded me.

"I'm just correcting—"

"This is not a fucking court of law!" I was startled into silence by the Sheriff's brusque tone.

Shania turned on her smile, and looked at Sheriff Heath, in a way that acknowledged his authority. His clear blue eyes looked her over carefully. His walrus moustache almost concealed a sly smile. And she met his glance, and smiled back.

And I realised, with astonishment, that this pretty young woman was actually *attracted* to the old relic.

"What else can you tell us about the anciens?" said Sheriff Heath.

"They're like, you know, like I just said, oh fuck, so, *weird*, they don't take pleasure. They do have – sex. They paid me, they used me. But no pleasure. I don't know why they did it.

They drink wine, they get drunk, they puke it up, it's disgusting to watch. They mutilate each other. It's SO disgusting. Two of my girlfriends are anciens, sweet girls; it disgusts, well it does! It really disgusts me!"

"Huh?" said the Sheriff.

"I said, it dis—"

"Not that. You said, 'Two of my girlfriends are anciens.' How come?"

"Yeah, well, they just *are*. Jane and Theresa. They used to work the streets with me. Beautiful girls. They really like, you see, beautiful girls, and beautiful boys, the younger the better, and that's disgusting too, but not herms, they don't go for—"

"What are you saying, Shania?" I asked.

Shania looked alarmed at my angry tone. "Nothing."

"Just tell us the truth," Aretha said sweetly.

"I have," Shania said sulkily.

"We'll pay more money for more truth," Aretha pointed out.

"I guess." Shania shrugged, and held out her wrist to me.

I took her wrist in my teeth, and bit lightly, and recharged her credit chip via my jaw resonator. Shania grinned. "Tickles!"

I forced a smile.

Shania continued: "They pick the best, you see, like me. But I only did it with them that one time, not again, not ever! Not for all the money they gave me, or for ten times more. I was afraid, you see, that next time I wouldn't come back."

"You're saying they abduct whores?"

"Not just us. They take from all castes over on the Dark Side. And they don't just hunt wildflesh; they have farms. You know, where they grow kids? From birth? They house 'em and pay 'em and school 'em, then when they're old enough, they slaughter 'em. Gouge out the brain, put an ancien brain in. That's how the anciens live so long. They steal bodies.

"Didn't you know?"

43

"I swear, I didn't know, I had no—" Aretha said, incoherently.

"This entire planet is founded on slavery," I raged.

"I didn't, I—"

"You suspected *something*?"

"Well, yeah."

"Something evil."

"Yeah."

"But not this."

"I didn't – you learn not to ask questions."

The Sheriff flinched at this; and said nothing, and was very very still.

"What are we going to do?" Aretha asked, imploringly.

43

"Hi," said the receptionist, and I looked into her green eyes.

"Hi Macawley," I said. "Remember me?"

She looked at me blankly. "No."

"Look at this," I told her calmly, and stared, and a homunculus appeared in the air between us. A three-inch-high replica of a six-foot-five cyborg cop with plastic skin and a fixed stare.

"Huh?" said Macawley.

Then I made the little man move forward, his plasma pistols drawn. And beside the miniature figure appeared a petite green-eyed, clawed, snarling Macawley.

"Cool trick," she conceded. "Most people need a computer to do that."

"That was me then." I pointed at the virtual image. "I am he. He is I. I reincarnated."

"I get it. In fact, I got it, seconds ago. You do that a lot, don't you?"

"What?"

"Patronise people, by telling 'em stuff they'd already, like, you know, guessed?"

"I don't do that," I said fiercely.

"Duh." She stuck out her forked tongue at me.

"I need your help again," I explained. "I have a mission—"

She snarled, and her teeth were sharp, and her eyes glittered green. Her claws extended from her hands, and her brow furrowed with rage. And then she said, once more: "Duh!"

"Sorry." I tried again: "Clearly, you have already surmised that I have a mission, or else I would not be here. To clarify further, however: I am working with Sheriff Heath, and another police colleague, Sergeant Aretha Jones, against the evil conspiracy of war criminals which run this planet. Will you once again lend us your aid?"

Macawley held her clawed hands in front of her snarling face and crossed the claws, and spat.

"I will take that to indicate," I said, "a yes."

🛡️43

"Hey, you again! Alex's dad!" Macawley beamed at the Sheriff.

"Hello sweetheart." Sheriff Heath took Macawley's hand, and pressed it to his lips. The oddly gallant gesture pleased her.

We were back in the old fabricator building, which was now our base and, for me, a home.

"Like old times, huh?" said Macawley.

"A lot of water has flowed under the bridge since then," said Aretha, looking pointedly at me.

"Oh, yeah, okay, I get that," said Macawley, defensively. "Rebellion against Earth, gang war, a third of the city's gangsters dead. I do keep up you know. I mean, I'm not *dumb*, you know – did anyone, like, think I *was*?" All heads present were shaken. She smiled, and a fast flicker of expressions registered: relief, annoyance, happiness, doubt, and fascination.

Then her default "thinking-frown face with a whisper of a smile" returned, as she tried to impress us with her fundamental seriousness. "Okay then! Here, look, I'll show you what I know. Then you can tell me the rest."

She conjured up on her virtual screen a holo image of the House of Pain that she, Sheriff Heath and Version 44 had attacked, and which had proved to be the location of the phantom hospital. "After the fucking cyborg – no offence – was killed that night, I ran away. Me and the Sheriff both. And later, I watched the news reports, I saw the survivors at the hospital being treated, I saw Hari Gilles get arrested. Then a month later he was out on bail and charges were dropped. *Quelle surprise*, it's a wicked world, right? But I carried on investigating."

I was looking at her with renewed respect, and something that felt a little bit like pride.

"The phantom hospital, see," said Macawley, using gestures to illustrate complex facts in a way that served no purpose whatsoever, "was owned by Hari Gilles, but Hari didn't really own it. There was a shell company. Owned by – you'll never guess it—"

"The anciens," said the Sheriff, spoiling it.

"Okay, you guessed it."

"They control everything," I explained. "But we don't know how."

"It's all in the database," Macawley told us.

"It's not. I've looked. I have direct access to the Belladonna database. The anciens own nothing, except their spires."

"But the spires, you see, this is the joy of it," she explained, "are *legal entities*. They own the city and all the people in it."

"Not possible," I said dogmatically.

Macawley stared at me, with ostentatious patience. I felt as if she were waiting for the seed of a thought to land in my brain, and grow into a plant with a vegetable root, before being pulled out and cooked for lunch.

"Clearly," I conceded after enduring a few long moments of this stare, "it *is* possible." Then, still poker-faced despite the scuff marks on my pride, I checked my database. I established that the one hundred anciens owned the spires jointly via a legal partnership. Then I cross-referenced the title deeds for every other major building in the city, and found they belonged to diverse corporations, all of which were owned by registered owners, and then checked the registered owners, who all proved to consist of grid-referenced *addresses*, rather than named people. And those grid-references corresponded to the addresses of the spires owned by the anciens.

The spires owned the city!

"How could such a thing be possible, or legal?" I said huffily.

Macawley grinned. It was clear that she was about to get another one over on me. She knew it, I knew it, the other two both knew it. It was a sweet prospect for her and she savoured it, in my view, rather too much.

Then she hit us: "It's legal, 'cause the spires are *sentient*. They are AIs, and that's what gives them the right to own property. The Belladonnan Quantum Computer is pretty damn powerful, no one can deny that. But the real fuck-off kick-ass computer-super-brain on this planet is the network that lives between the spires."

"Ah," I said.

"Oh," said Aretha.

"Fuck," said the Sheriff.

And Macawley grinned hugely at how smart she was, and how dumb, by contrast, were we.

🛡️

"I'm a Cop," I said. "I investigate. I find clues. I infer, I induce, I deduce, I report on seen facts. This feels like, I don't know, cheating."

"Just fucking do it," snarled Aretha.

I punched the wall of the spire and my hand sank into the brickwork, and my fingerspikes flew out.

And all the data in the AI-spire flowed into my cybernetic circuits.

🛡️

"What do you have?"

"Too much," I said. "Too much . . . data."

43

Eventually, my thoughts recoalesced into something resembling sanity.

"I think I have a way. A strategy," I said.

The Sheriff nodded. "A good strategy?"

"It," I said, making a detailed risk assessment and scenario analysis of the plan that I had just thought of, "is a reckless, dangerous and utterly foolhardy strategy."

The Sheriff grinned at that.

"Then let's do it," he said.

And so it began.

43

I inspected my own naked body.

The skin around my chest and abdomen was pale and puckered, where I'd had to regrow my flesh after being set on fire by Aretha. But the new skin still looked credibly human. And I'd now reverted entirely to the face and body I had used while working for Grogan. So I was tall, with an impressively ripped abdomen, and my biceps, triceps and pectorals were, frankly, awesome.

The effect, I decided, was somewhat cartoonish: bulging muscles, rippling tattoos, and a totally hairless body. I would have preferred a leaner and more natural physique. But this, my "mercenary soldier" body, was perfect for our present purposes.

"Eugh, gross," said Aretha as she entered the apartment. "Clothes on, please!"

"What have you got for me?"

"Box, loincloth, body chains, cool armoured tunic, boots. The boots are the highest quality – there've been gladiators who developed foot mange from treading in so much blood."

"Equipment?"

"Sword, daggers, bolas."

"I've never used a bolas."

"Like this." She swung the balls around her head then threw them across the room and smashed a vase of flowers off a table. I walked across, hefted the bolas, swung it around in the air a few times. It was, my database informed me, a boleadoras – with three connected weights – and it had vicious spikes in each weight. And it was, so Aretha assured me, the perfect weapon for cutting the legs off a charging rhinoceros.

I threw it through the air. It hurtled towards Aretha with a whistling noise. She flinched. But then the bolas changed direction in mid-air, flew back across the room, took the blooms off the flowers in a second vase, whirled around again in the air, and returned to my hand where I caught it.

"Nice work," said Aretha cheerfully.

I was now, I confidently concluded, an expert in the use of this arcane weapon.

The Sheriff staggered in, carrying a huge bag.

"Pigs' blood?" I asked.

"Can't take the risk," the Sheriff said. "They might DNA-test. So I've been to the morgue, drained twelve bodies. That should do you." The Sheriff opened up the suitcase. It contained scores of balloons of human blood.

I, still naked, raised my arms in the air, accentuating my powerful torso muscles. And I willed my chest to crack open, and it did. The silent hydraulics split my body in half, revealing a smooth sealed cylinder inside. I did the same with my thighs and back and arse, until I was peeled like a fruit.

"Fill me up," I said.

"How?" Aretha asked.

I indicated the blood wells on the underside of my flesh. "Hook them up here. Any blade that penetrates my skin will burst a bag, and my skin will allow the blood to flow out to the surface, ideally in huge gobbets. We can put some extra blood bags in my thigh cavities, in case I run out."

"Don't bleed too much, you'll draw attention to yourself."

I laughed. "The human gladiators do this too. They have blood bags surgically inserted in their stomachs and under the skin. So you cut 'em, and they bleed, and bleed, and bleed."

"I didn't know that," conceded the Sheriff.

"It's fucking barbaric," muttered Aretha.

"It's your national sport," I told her. "The Belladonnan Gladiatorial Games."

The old district looked quite different now. Grogan's Saloon and Casino had been demolished after the battle, and the site had been cleared. Vast craters in the ground marked the sites where missiles sent by Billy Grogan's men against Gill's Killers had overshot.

My eyes, I knew, were bloodshot, and my gait, I was well aware, had the steadily straight and remorseless quality of a man who is high on drugs and alcohol, but who is covering it well. I stood looking at the wreckage of the Saloon for ten minutes, then laughed, and made the sign of the cross, and walked on.

From an upstairs window, I saw a face looking down at me. I'd been spotted.

I spent two days drinking my way through the bars of Lawless City, offering my services as a bodyguard and enforcer. No one was buying. The Gang Wars had been bloody and costly. Tent cities had grown up amidst the wreckage of the old city. Many of the men and women I saw wore black, in homage to their true-dead loved ones. Street vendors were selling cooked meat of dubious provenance. Holos of the new President of Belladonna could be seen on every street corner, promoting his new vision of the world without ever saying what that vision was.

On the third day a girl sat on the bar stool next to me and patted me on the arm.

"Long time no see," purred Annie Grogan.

"Sweetheart," I said.

"Where've you been, Tom?"

"Around."

"We missed you."

"I missed you too darling." I leered happily at Annie's young, lean, tattooed body.

"The old days are gone."

"I saw. The Saloon—"

"Burned. We're building a new one. My mother and I, we have some money left."

"Money from the rackets?"

"There are no rackets. No one has the will any more. Most of the gamblers died when they bombed the casinos. They're calling it the Vice Wars, 'cause mainly sinful people died."

"I'm a sinner, I'm still alive."

"That's 'cause you ran away, you gutless coward."

"True."

"And you killed my brother Billy. I saw you, remember? I was this far away when you shot him."

I thought hard on that one. "Nah, it wasn't me," I said slyly. "Must have been a ricochet. It's easy to get confused in the heat of battle you know."

"I wasn't confused. I know what I saw."

"Yeah, right, whatever."

"So what are you doing back here?"

"Nowhere else to go, darling."

Annie smiled, and slid off the bar stool.

I drew a pistol swiftly and held it to her face.

"Don't think about revenge, darling. I could kill you as easy as—"

She stared at me with contempt. "I know that," she said.

"You and your whole fucking gang!" I snarled.

"I know that too."

"I could fucking kill the whole fucking lot of you!"

"One day," said Annie, calmly, "one day, I'll be Mayor of this town. And then I'll be President of this country. And I'll run it the way it ought to be run. So decent people can live decently, and sinners can whore and drink and take drugs and get up the next morning and go to work. That's my vision of Belladonna. No more gangsters, because I'll legalise vice. No more crooked politicians, because I'll hire people who actually give a shit. No more Solar Neighbourhood dictatorship, no more Galactic Cops, no more lying cheating deceiving motherfucking traitors like you."

"Yeah, yeah."

"Go to hell, Tom. It's where you belong."

I laughed, and I slapped her on the face. My fingers left red marks on her cheeks. But Anne was uncowed. She spat in my eye and turned away and walked off.

"Same again," I said to the bartender, and then something hit me and I started to spasm. "Fuck," I muttered, and got to my feet. I found something in my side, and plucked it out. An electric harpoon. I could feel my eyes were bulging; I was in the throes of electrocution. I patted my body down, looking to see if there was another harpoon in me somewhere.

Five armed men walked forward, one of them carrying an electric harpoon gun. It was Sheriff Heath.

"You, you son of a bitch," said the Sheriff. "You're under arrest."

I fumbled for my pistol and dropped it. I found the other harpoon in my back but I couldn't reach it to pull it out, and then Heath switched it on again, and I shook like a man having a heart attack as the electricity pulsed into my body.

"Bastard!" I screamed but no word came out.

Then a nanonet flew into the air and landed on me, and

covered me totally, and I couldn't breathe, and I crashed to the floor, and my eyes closed, and blackness consumed me.

43

"The fucking bitch! She called the *cops?*" I marvelled, and the Sheriff kicked me hard in the face with the heel of his boot.

My head shot back and smashed into the side of the police van. The side of the van buckled. I regretted the vigour of my movement.

"Bastard!" I screamed, to cover my blunder, and the Sheriff booted me again.

The police van took off. I was shackled hand and foot, my hands savagely pinned behind my back, and I was hooded, with full sensory deprivation, in blatant contravention of the Belladonnan penal code. And the electric harpoon was still embedded in my back, where it could be remotely activated if I tried to put up a fight.

"I'll kill you, you bastard, when I get out of here! And I'll find that evil Grogan bitch, and I'll rape her, and I'll—"

The Sheriff kicked me hard, again.

43

"No prison can hold me," I crowed, as I was hustled down the corridor of the cell block. I was still hooded, strong hands were dragging me, the shackles around my ankles forced me to walk in mincing pigeon steps.

"You fucking tell 'em," roared a voice, and then I heard a cell door slam open and I was hurled inside.

"I demand water, food, access to an attorney," I bellowed through my hood.

A baton smashed me in the face, and I felt an eye pop.

43

Annie Grogan stood in the witness box, wearing a demure body-length black dress and black gloves.

"There were riots on the street," she told the Judge. "My brother and I were in the Saloon. This man," she pointed at me, "said he was going to leave, and he was almost out of the door when my brother stopped him and searched him. Billy was a hard and suspicious man, he was always convinced people were stealing from him."

Annie's eyes covered the courtroom in a steady sideways sweep; every man and woman there saw her determination, and her sisterly love.

"On this occasion," she continued, "he was right. This man," she pointed at me, "had stolen money from the safe. The wrap still had our seal on it. Also, he had jewellery that my grandmother had left to me. And furthermore, he had the pearl-handled plasma pistol that my father had left us. Billy went berserk, he started shouting and screaming. And then this man," she pointed at me again, "drew two pistols and fired them. He blew my brother's brains out. Billy didn't stand a chance. And then this man," she pointed at me, "put the gun near my mouth, and he pushed the gun *into* my mouth, and he threatened to blow my brains out if I refused to have sex with him. And I refused. He didn't, thank heaven, carry out his threat. And then he left. And I—" Tears spilled down her cheeks. "I don't deny my brother was a criminal, but he was a good man too. He didn't deserve to die like that."

I stood up. "You lying fucking bitch! That never happened! None of it!"

"You'll have your chance to put your case," said the Judge, mildly.

"Bitch!" I roared.

43

"It is the verdict of this court that the accused, Thomas Matthew Dunnigan, is guilty of murder in the first degree. The court also finds that Thomas Matthew Dunnigan is guilty of theft, and attempted rape, and gross contempt of court. And it is the opinion of the court that the accused is a recidivist of the worst kind, and cannot be redeemed, or rehabilitated or reformed, or forgiven.

"The accused, Thomas Matthew Dunnigan, is therefore declared to be *noxii*, and is sentenced to be *damnati ad bestias*, after which his skull and brain will be incinerated by plasma beam until he is true-dead."

43

An underground moving walkway conveyed the prisoners from the court building to the arena. A dozen prisoners were contained in pod-cages on the walkway, surrounded by cylinders of breathable oxygen. The tunnel in which the walkway was housed was filled with poisonous gas that would burn the throat and lungs of anyone rash enough to try to escape.

I stood alone, isolated from the others, for I was the only one deemed to be *noxii*, and sentenced to true-death. It was a brutal verdict for a relatively minor crime – the murder of one gangster by another. But the Sheriff had paid good money to get this result. Now, I was doomed.

Unless I survived. For, as I had learned when I leached all the data from the AI-spire, it is a city ordnance that any gladiator who can survive *damnati ad bestias* was deemed to be a freeman, and given a place of honour in the ranks of the servants of the *ancien régime*. This was an historic tradition, but a sorely neglected one – for no one, in the whole long history of the Belladonnan Gladiatorial Games, had ever survived *damnati ad bestias*.

And, despite my hardmetal body and my superstrength and my concealed weapons – the fingerspikes, the acid spit, the disruptor-pulse eyes – I wasn't feeling in the least complacent about the battle that lay ahead of me.

For I knew, from surveying my database and my most recent download of *The Encyclopedia of Alien Life*, that even Doppelganger Robots had been killed by beasts less fierce than those I would face today.

43

"Die Well."

"Die Well."

"Die Well."

"Die Well."

"Die Well."

"I ain't," I snarled, "gonna die."

"Don't sweat it," said a seven-foot-tall black gladiator. "We die, we're reborn, that's the way of it. There are worse punishments, believe me."

"What's your name?" I asked the black gladiator.

"They call me the Spartan Terror."

"Your real name."

"My real name is Claudio. I was born on Sparta. Hence, Spartan Terror."

"My name is Tom," I said, "and I am *noxii*. Abhorred by the state; damned by the state. A pariah among pariahs."

The black gladiator grinned. "Fuck, you must have pissed someone off *really* bad."

"I have pissed," I admitted, "a lot of people off. Listen, Claudio, I need help." I looked around at the motley crew of gladiators – some warriors, some scrawny street gangsters terrified at finding themselves in loincloths and leather tunics, and about to embark upon mortal combat. "And I can pay."

"I already got money," Claudio said. "I'm a professional warrior, I'm good at this shit."

"I can pay enough to accelerate your rebirth, should you fail in the arena and die. I'll throw in some more for extra augmentations, and ten million scudos to enable you to buy a dacha in space, for when you retire."

"Now you're talking."

"And the rest of you? Same deal?"

Murmurs, mutters, nods; the answer was yes.

"So," said Claudio, "what do you want us to do?"

From the catacombs, we could hear the roar of the crowds, and the sound of the band playing its strident guitar and saxophone and air-piano riffs.

Then the Games Herald entered our dungeon. He was a stocky, ugly man, with a nasty little smile that promised horrors galore. He gestured to me, and the guards unshackled me. Earlier, my "girlfriend" – Macawley – had been allowed to bring me a clean fighting outfit – the loincloth, the armoured box and armoured tunic, swords, the knives, the bolas, the leather wristbands and the body harnesses. So I looked and felt the part.

I limbered up. A short pretty woman oiled my body, and rubbed healing salves into the flesh. It would make little difference in the battle ahead, but I found the ritual strangely calming. And my skin – rich in sensory detectors – was able to fully register the pleasurableness of her firm hand-massage of my near-naked body, and the rich cloying scent of the oils and salves she was rubbing in, and the extraordinary nearness to me of this highly desirable, by human standards, beautiful woman.

And then I limbered, and stretched, and grinned. And I was ready.

I began my slow walk along the underground corridor up into the arena. The walls were covered with holos of former acclaimed gladiators. I could smell sweat and skin and body oils. I was aware the cameras were on me, so I walked proud, and flexed my pecs as I strode.

I emerged into the arena. Huge TV holos hovered in the sky above us, and every seat in the amphitheatre was full. From their ornate and spacious boxes, richly decorated with gilded statues of angels and past gladiatorial heroes, the cold-eyed anciens watched the display that unfolded beneath them.

Dead bodies and ripped-off body parts were being cleared away from the floor of the arena. A half-torso of a woman was groaning, one eye to the cameras. The star performers would be rejuved and restored within weeks or months; the ordinary convicted criminals might wait a decade or more to be fitted with replacement limbs and organs. But this was showbusiness, pure and simple: blood and gore for the masses, provided by trained performers.

But I was different. I was condemned to true-death; it was a darker spectacle altogether.

As I stepped out into the arena I heard a roar of support from the crowd. I raised a fist in triumph. I was conscious that one of my eyes still bulged large. After it had popped out of its socket earlier, I had pushed the eye back with finger and thumb, but the fit wasn't perfect.

The Animal Gates opened, and two lions and a tiger padded out. The crowd roared again.

I hefted my sword and stepped forward, body hunched, senses attuned. The big cats ambled into the arena, cocked their lazy eyes at the crowd and, almost in unison, sat down.

Two gladiators ran on with haunches of meat and threw them to the three big cats. They slowly got up and trotted over. The tiger snarled. The two lions settled down to eat. I waited.

A short man ran up and threw a bucket of blood over me. I spat blood out of my mouth, and raised a fist, and the crowd roared again. I began to worry that, if I didn't see some brutal action soon, I would start to feel the cold.

Then the lions and the tiger chewed their meat and realised it was fake. They roared with rage, and leaped up, and padded away, then smelled the blood on the strange human, and padded back. The three beasts warily circled me.

The lions roared. The tiger snarled.

Then the tiger leaped. I rolled under, slit it from neck to groin with my blade, and rolled free. The tiger crashed to the ground, howling with pained puzzlement.

The lions attacked in unison. I took their noses off with sword slashes, then butchered off their legs. I killed each of the lions with a sword-thrust through the eye, then I went across and finished the tiger in the same way.

The crowd roared.

The warm-up was over.

I stood alone in the arena, feet scuffing the synthetic sawdust, aware that everything I did was being broadcast on TV screens across the planet. I held my sword two-handed and horizontal in martial-arts style. A trickle of blood ran down my cheek, from a tiger-swipe I hadn't even noticed. I was utterly still.

From the depths of the catacombs came an awesome roar. I was amused at the deception: my database identified this as the cry of a Barsoomian-Hyena-Bird, a tiny and entirely harmless creature. My guess was that none of the vast monsters I was about to face had a roar half so fierce.

That's showbusiness.

Then one of the Animal Gates started to shudder, as the creature behind crashed and barged into it. The latches were remotely shot open. The gates creaked apart. Red eyes appeared.

And at that moment, out of the blue sky, clouds swept down at me with talons extended. I had already spotted them with my radar vision, but I allowed them to swoop close to my head before I "casually" looked up and saw air moving towards me like a whirlwind with claws. It was a flock of Stealth-Hawks, camouflaged to be almost invisible in air. These remarkable creatures were the major predator on the planet of . . .

I ignored the constant drone of information from my database, and leapt aside to dodge pecking beaks and ripping claws, then leapt forward again, and swung with my blade. Red blood appeared in the air, as the first Stealth-Hawk was chopped in half. And the other six Hawks plunged at me, and I rolled and dived, then threw knives at them and planted each knife in the skull of one of the vicious predatory beasts.

But the Stealth-Hawks were unperturbed, and flew away, knives still stuck in skulls. My database primly reminded me: *the cerebral cortex of this creature is located in its posterior region, not in its skull.*

I realised, with annoyance, that this had been a feint. The birds were unlikely to have hurt me seriously, but in the course of fighting them, I had thrown away all my knives.

Yet I still had my sword, and the bolas. And the Animal Gate was open now and a monster was charging at me. This time I listened more attentively to the briefing from my database:

The Gullyfoyle Diamond-Hound, cold-blooded, no heart or lungs or vulnerable organs, skin is hard as diamond, hence the common name, eyes shine in the dark like rubies. Vulnerable points are—

The Hound was fast. It leaped at me, and I was on the verge of rolling under it when an intuition made me leap *up*, somersaulting in the air, over the vast six-legged crystalline monster. As I flew over it, I slashed down with my sword and the blade shattered into pieces on the beast's hide. Then I landed, and spun around, and saw that the sawdust in front of me was steaming acid. The creature had pissed downwards as it leapt, and its urine must be acidic. (I swiftly checked my database and found that indeed it was so.)

Now I had no knives and no sword, just the bolas, which I whirled and threw and it missed, and the Hound lunged again.

But the bolas could be remotely controlled by subvocal commands: it missed, then turned in mid-air and flew back and wrapped around the creature's neck and severed it. Green blood oozed on to the sawdust of the arena. The beast twitched and rolled. It wasn't yet dead, but it was no longer a threat to me if I kept my distance. However, this meant I couldn't get at my bolas, and so now I had no weapons at all.

Fifteen seconds had elapsed since my arrival in the arena.

I was enjoying myself.

I bounced on my heels, waiting for the next monster, as the headless Diamond-Hound tripped and slipped on its own blood and slime. Its eyes and ears were in its severed head, but the "brain" of the creature was in its spinal cord, and it could only be killed by burning it, or shredding every inch of it.

A second Animal Gate opened and the crowd roared with approval. It was a Mulligan's Dragon! This huge beast had feathers not scales, fiery breath, and broad dagger-pointed wings, though it could not fly. And its eleven eyes glittered red as it attacked.

I ran towards it, and rolled and ducked. I knew that if the flames touched me, all would be lost: fire could not hurt my hardmetal frame but it would burn off all my flesh – revealing me to all as a cyborg.

But there was a four-second gap between flares, and that allowed me to run underneath the beast's neck. Once there, I plunged my hand into the creature's mouth and down its throat and then – unseen by the crowd – I transformed my fingers into spikes and gouged out its brains.

And as it died the creature snorted flame from its nostrils, but I dodged the fire, and pulled my hand out of its throat, and stabbed its eyes out one by one with my fingers. Then I lifted the creature up high and carried it across the floor of the arena. Flames poured forth from its mouth again and lapped at the body of the Diamond-Hound, which screamed, then ignited, and burned, and then burned faster, and finally melted.

I threw the corpse of the Mulligan's Dragon into the air, and it crashed to the ground, dead, and I took a proud bow.

The crowd erupted.

Then all the Animal Gates opened at once and monsters appeared on all sides. A Sand-Leopard, a One-Horn, a three-eyed Shiva with scales that rippled the colours of the rainbow, dozens of Snake-Birds, a roaring Giant-Beetle-Thing, two hairy five-armed Kongs, and a Weisman-Bandersnatch – the foulest, largest, scaliest, horniest, most-multiple-mouthed, many-clawed, viciously bloodthirsty predator ever discovered by humankind.

And I raised my arms up high, and laughed, for I had no weapon still. And the crowd applauded my spirit.

But one gate remained closed: the Gladiator Gate. And as the creatures pawed the earth and roared and prepared to devour their foolish prey, this gate opened, and a tall black gladiator walked through brandishing a sword the size of a man. He carried it as though it were as light as a new-born baby, and with a similar loving reverence; then he threw it through the air.

And it flew and it flew –

And was caught by me.

And the monsters began their attack; I took my stance; and with this huge, sharp broadsword, I slashed and lunged and slew. The sword was unwieldy but devastating in its effects, and it had a blade in the hilt that allowed me to kill one creature with a downward stroke before slashing the head off another with the blade.

Then I buried the sword tip in the hide of the Weisman-Bandersnatch, and to my horror, the entire sword was gulped and swallowed into the monster's flesh. I had to release the handle of the sword, or risk losing my own arm. And then the monster spat out shards of hardmetal and its eleven eyes glittered with evil. And I ran.

The Bandersnatch pursued me, with astonishing speed. But I ran faster and reached the Gladiator Gate, where two more gladiators stood proud. And one of the gladiators held a burning brand and the other held a jewelled knife and as I approached they threw these weapons into the air and I caught them, then turned back.

And I lunged at the Bandersnatch, and gouged out its eye with the knife, and stuffed the burning brand into the bleeding socket, then cut off its tongue, then was knocked off balance, and fell under the hooves and horns and scales of the beast.

Once I was trapped underneath the monster, and hence invisible to the crowd, I felt liberated. The great beast tried to bounce up and down on me, but I was impervious and seized the moment to engage my disruptor-pulse eyes and fingerspikes, and I literally burned and clawed my way into the belly of the beast.

Once inside I felt stomach acids burning away at my pseudo-flesh, and blood was starting to pour out of my blood-sacs, and I continued to slash and burn until I had traversed the full length of the monster and scrambled out of the creature's mouth, past its jagged teeth.

I rolled out on to the sawdust. Luckily my burns didn't go deep, not down to the metal. So when I stood up I was stark naked and direly scratched and bathed in blood and the crowd was stunned into silence and then I raised my arms again and the crowd ROARED.

And two gladiators were running towards me with swords and they threw them and I caught them and the Snake-Birds were upon me, but I was thrusting and slashing and kicking. One Snake-Bird wrapped around my torso and began to squeeze my ribs, and I struck at my own body with the edge of the sword to cut the beast in half and gashed my own shoulder in the process. Another Snake-Bird wrapped around my neck and thrust its spitting head into my mouth, and so I bit the head off and spat it out. And then I ran over to the Diamond-Hound and scooped up acidic sand and rubbed it in the creature's skin and the snake recoiled and fell off me.

My fingers were now bare to the metal but I clutched my sword tight to conceal that fact, and attacked the Shiva, which had arms like swords and a tongue of iron that lashed like a bayonet. I lopped the arms off the creature, then cut off its head, then thrust a blade into the eye of the One-Horn, then stabbed and hacked with my two swords at the Sand-Leopard and the Great-Beetle-Thing and the two Kongs, until finally all the creatures were dead. And I raised my arms in triumph and the crowd roared, once more.

And the Gates opened again, and another vast horde of monsters appeared, and I laughed, confident I could not be killed by creatures such as these.

Then the earth beneath me began to tremble. Puzzled, I renewed the fight. And I leaped and slashed and lunged with my swords to kill the beasts that were attacking me.

But suddenly the ground exploded and a massive one-eyed head emerged. And a new monster scrambled slowly out of the soil, and my database swiftly explained that this was a New Amazonian Cyclops. Six arms, and

Lasers for eyes.

The eyes flashed and twin columns of fire hurtled through the air towards me, and I hurled myself out of the way. Behind me, a monster squealed and screamed as the laser beam burned it alive. I checked my database again: it estimated that one blast from this laser beam would burn the clothes and flesh off me instantly, and my cyborg identity would be revealed.

Two blasts and my body would start to melt.

And three blasts from this laser-eye would cause my cybernetic brain to cease functioning.

The creature, it appeared, could actually kill me.

I longed for a plasma gun, or a smart missile. My swords were no use, I was too far away to throw them, and the monstrous forty-foot-high creature dwarfed me. And though it took a few seconds for the beast to recharge its laser eye, that still didn't give me enough time for me to attack it. Instead, I was forced to leap wildly around the amphitheatre like a vampire dodging shafts of light.

The crowd began to boo. I mused, very briefly, on the transitory nature of popular success.

Then the other gladiators began walking around the edge of the amphitheatre, circling around the huge beast. And I began to hope.

And Claudio, the black gladiator, suddenly sprinted, running behind the Cyclops, and slashed at the backs of its legs with his sword. The beast roared and swatted at him with its leg, but Claudio was gone.

Then a spear was thrown and it penetrated the creature's scales and it roared again and peered around.

And I seized my moment and with one sword in my teeth and one in my hand I ran at the beast as the gladiators harassed and stabbed at it.

Claudio nimbly dodged a claw, then missed his footing and was engulfed in a laser beam that lit his flesh like a match.

For a second I was stunned, as this brave man burned alive before me. But after a few seconds, he was dead, and all that remained of him was a charred mass. I knew, however, that the gladiator's brain would still be revivable, and vowed to save him if—

I ducked a laser blast, then was at the creature and as I reached the legs, two gladiators hurled knives at me very fast and I dropped the sword from my hand and caught each dagger by the hilt.

And then, still with a sword gripped in my teeth, using knives like crampons, I clambered my way up the creature's leg and torso. It roared, and smashed at me with its claws, but I was too nimble for it. And then it tried to burn me off itself with its laser glare, but I was on its back now, reaching up to its shoulders . . . and I swung myself around and was upon its face and I slashed at it with the daggers, then dropped one and took the sword from my mouth and plunged it deep into the monster's eye, again and again and again, and then *crawled into the empty socket.*

And there, half-buried inside the skull, I hacked and hewed with my sword and remaining dagger until I felt the creature begin to fall.

When the Cyclops hit the ground I was flung up against its skull.

And then I clambered free.

Inside the amphitheatre, a hundred thousand Belladonnans

watched me clamber once more out of a monster – this time, emerging bloodied and triumphant from the creature's eyeball socket.

A hundred thousand fingers were raised; the mob had made their decision: I should live.

43

I stood under the shower and blood ran down my body in rivulets.

"Wince a bit, look like you're in pain," said Macawley. She was beaming at me, her green eyes glittering. A question occurred: was she by any chance finding me *sexy*? I was, I realised, stark naked, and beautiful, and a bloodied warrior. Weren't human girls supposed to *like* that sort of thing?

But my database, annoyingly, proved to have only sparse amounts of information on this topic.

The water splashed my gaping wounds, and I winced.

"Better! But don't overdo it! Make it look like you're, kind of like, heroically holding it in."

"The bleeding's not stopping."

"You'll need stitches. Hold my arm as you come out. Stagger. Make your face pale, okay? You've lost a lot of blood; that would really screw up your circulation. Maybe faint, yeah? You know, you're so damn fucking lucky you can't feel pain."

In fact, with admirable prudence, the designers of my humaniform shell had equipped it with plentiful pain sensors, so as to more easily enable a cyborg to impersonate a human. Thus, at that precise moment in time, with my flesh ripped and torn, my lungs clogged with alien faecal matter, stab wounds in my thighs and back and chest, and acid burns on my fingers, I was in appalling and indescribable agony.

However, I decided it would be impolitic to mention that fact.

"Here. Let me," Macawley said.

"Thank you."

Macawley bound my hands with bandages, to conceal the bare metal of the knuckles. I was conscious of the touch of her fingers, the warmth of her breath, as she focused on her task.

"That'll do you."

I limped and staggered back into the dressing room. The blood was flowing freely again, but the doctors were prepared for that. They had hoses to bathe me down, then swiftly started stitching my flesh together. I grimaced and groaned in seeming agony and Macawley nodded approvingly, with no notion that my agony was real.

But I kept my focus. When my body was stitched, I stood up straight. I forced myself to grin.

Then I passed out, and toppled to the ground.

I woke to find myself in a hospital bed. My alarm levels rose rapidly – I couldn't afford to be examined by doctors. I got out of bed and fell over. My legs! I no longer had legs. Just bare stumps that oozed with maggots.

Maggots??

The door opened and a handsome silver-haired man walked in. "How are you, my son?" said the man.

I was stunned. This was my *father*?

But then I took a closer look. The silver-haired man had no eyes, and he had horns on his head.

"You've done well, my son," said the silver-haired man.

And hooves. And a forked tail.

"You're not my father," I said.

"No, you are mine," said the silver-haired man, and I knew him. He was the embodiment of Evil in the World.

"Hold my hand," I said, and the silver-haired man reached out his hand, and I caught it, and ate it, finger by finger.

"Very good," purred the silver-haired man, and I had an uneasy feeling that I had just made a very big mistake.

43

"Are you okay?"

I opened my eyes. Macawley. The dressing room. The doctors. I marvelled. Once again, I'd dreamed a *dream*.

43

"*Hey mister, can I have your autograph?*" The kid was about fifteen, with a cheerful cheeky grin. I laughed.

"Sure." I took the pen and scrawled my name on the back of the list of contestants on the arena's Munera of the Day programme.

Macawley stood, impatiently waiting. We were outside the Gladiatorial Arena now; the broad marble pillars loomed behind us.

"*I can't read that, what does it say?*" the kid complained.

"Tom Dunnigan," I said.

"*Is it true you killed Billy Grogan?*"

"It's true. Heat of the moment. They sentenced me to death for it, but hey, here I am."

I wasn't besieged by fans, but a healthy crowd had gathered to talk to me, the magic man who had survived the damnation of the beasts. But this kid was hard to shift. And there was something strange about him. A strange aura. And finally I realised what it was – the kid didn't move his lips when he talked.

"*You're a man we'd like to get to know,*" said the kid, unsmilingly.

"Who's we?"

"*People like me.*" The kid looked in my eyes, and it was a cold, old look.

"You're an ancien?"

"*We don't like that term. We call ourselves City Founders. Congratulations, your prize is, you get to meet us formally.*"

"Why would I want to do that?"

"*Because we want to offer you a job.*"

"I don't want a job."

"*You have a choice between a) and b), where b) entails the agonising death of both you and your whore of a girlfriend. Which do you choose?*"

"Maybe I do want a job after all."

"*Go to the Barrington Hotel. We have arranged a suite there for you. We'll see you at six.*"

"Where in the hotel?"

"*We'll find you.*"

"Who was that?" Macawley asked.

"That was them."

"The kid?"

"Yes. The anciens have made contact."

Macawley's breathing was becoming ragged.

"Good. That's what we wanted."

"I have to meet them."

"Do you want me to—?"

"No. Go. Tell the Sheriff and Aretha what's happening."

"Will you be okay?"

"I am confident of success."

"You realise, they'll know all about you. They'll have downloaded every scrap of information about you – or rather, about Tom Dunnigan. If there's even the slightest inconsistency, they'll kill you."

"There will be no inconsistencies."

"They'll speak to everyone who knows you on Belladonna. Plus, all the people who travelled with you on the fifty-fifty."

"They'll all remember me. There *was* a Tom Dunnigan. He died on a fifty-fifty three months ago, but his death was concealed. I match his appearance in every respect, including fingerprints, irises and DNA."

"You plan ahead, huh?"

"It's standard procedure. Every Cop, on every assignment, has a human identity allocated in case he, or she, has to go deep undercover."

"They'll talk to me, too."

"And you'll convincingly tell them the partial truth."

Macawley and I had "met" a week ago, at a rave, and left together, drunkenly pawing each other. We had subsequently been seen in bars and restaurants together; we had booked hotel rooms together, and (with the aid of chemical sprays) had left stained sheets and the smell of musty sex behind.

"You should go," I told her.

"You'll be—?"

"Go."

43

I went to the Barrington Hotel, on 42nd by Ochre Street. It was a spire, black but streaked with red and gold stripes. I'd never noticed it before, even though I'd been past it many times. The hotel was close to police headquarters, yet when Macawley asked Aretha about it, Aretha hadn't been too sure about its location. I checked my database of city maps, and noted that the electronic page blurred at precisely the spot where the hotel loomed up.

More trickery.

I walked through the revolving doors and was greeted by a uniformed servant. The hotel was art deco in style, *c.* 1920s, there were gas lamps on the walls, and beautifully embossed gold lincrusta below the dado rails. The lobby was deserted. The uniformed servant – customarily known as the "porter," my database informed me – led me to the lift.

"The lift will recognise you and take you to your room," said the porter.

I got into the lift. I stared into the iris-recognition screen. The lift doors closed. The lift moved, and I lurched, and an instant later the lift doors opened.

I stepped out. I was on the 200th floor.

And all around, through the vast panoramic windows, I could see Lawless City. Tiny figures trotted far below me like ants. From this height, the city's outlines were apparent: the curving walkways, the bull's-eye piazzas, the vast patches of green parkland.

I turned, and looked around. The floor was made of marble. The outer corridor snaked around the circumference of the spire. And there was a closed door in front of me.

I opened the door and stepped inside.

And I was greeted with vastness and splendour. The entire 200th floor was comprised of a single-storey mansion. Through a door to my right was a huge galleried library. And directly ahead of me was an elaborate Louis Quatorze-style bedroom. I walked inside the bedroom and saw it had fluted pilasters, hanging tapestries, carved panels and mantels, cabinets and chairs inlaid with tortoiseshell, and a king-size four-poster bed at its centre. Golden chandeliers hung from the ceiling and gilt was scattered over every part of the room like fairy dust. The shelves were intricately carved in wood, and were cluttered with porcelain bowls and Chinese vases decorated with ormolu. Gargoyles and spiders and other hidden beasts lurked in the plasterwork, and on the marble pilasters.

And at the far end of the bedroom was another door. I walked the length of the room, admiring the heady sensuality of the colours, the rich textures, the elaborate pomegranate-tree and three-medallion patterns on the oriental carpet. Then I opened the door, and began to explore the *other* rooms of this palatial home.

It was like being in a vast forest, I mused, as I wandered from room to room, and found marvels everywhere. I found a pool and sauna, there was a rifle range, there was a running track. There was a music room, with pianos and guitars. I idly picked up an ancient five-string guitar with a beautiful mother-of-pearl inlay, and knew immediately that it was made by Dominico Sellas in around 1670. I knew this without accessing my database; I just *knew*.

I strummed then plucked the guitar, which was perfectly in tune, and played a swift arpeggio, then placed the guitar down. The room in which I stood was panelled with amber, with baroque mirrors and gilded candelabras. Each amber wall contained an inlaid landscape, made from hundreds of tiny pieces of what my sensors told me was jasper. The scenes depicted were allegorical, and my database recognised the room as a reproduction of – or perhaps the quantum-teleported original of? – the Amber Room of the Russian Tsars, stolen in 1941 by the German High Command during World War II, and never seen again.

My opinion of the anciens began to soar. They certainly had an extraordinary sense of tradition.

The next room was made entirely of distorting mirrors, and I saw a thousand replicas of myself, all moving out of sync. An eerie effect.

The next room was a Fluidist boudoir, in which soft malleable sofas and chairs merged and blended to create a room as organic as a coral reef.

The next room was a soldiers' billet: a bare room with a single bunk and a mobile of the Sol system suspended in mid-air. I recognised this as a comfort room for warriors. And, after the excess of gilt and ornamentation in the rest of this mansion block, this room came as a visual relief.

I stepped towards the bed, and took my clothes off and placed them carefully on the simple wooden shelf that jutted out from the wall. Then I lay on the bed and pretended to sleep.

My senses were attuned. I could detect via my radar that I was being surveilled by a succession of people, who stood in the doorway of the small room and watched me as I slumbered. As I'd suspected, the anciens wanted to study me. My body was bandaged and patched; healing salves inside the bandages were working their magic on my skin; I mimed the deep sleep of an athlete who has gone to the point of exhaustion and beyond.

And at 5.30 p.m. I opened my eyes again and rolled out of bed.

I got dressed.

And I walked back through the maze of rooms, past the mirrors and the fluid furniture and via the Amber Room until I reached the first room, the French baroque bedroom. Then I opened the carved and ruby-inlaid door, and was back in the corridor, next to the lift.

The lift doors opened, and a different uniformed porter got out.

"They're ready for me?"

There was no answer. I followed the porter into the lift.

The porter pressed the large button marked $\boxed{\text{Penthouse}}$. The lift lurched again, and began moving upwards at the same crazy speed. My instruments told me I was moving at .05 lightspeed, which was fast, for a lift.

But after a while it occurred to me the journey was taking a long time. Which floor was I on? I checked my satnav, and got a jumbled account of my location. I tried again, and realised – *I was the wrong side of the satellite which I was using to locate myself.*

The lift doors opened, and I stepped out. And all around me was the blackness of space, lit by a universe of stars and galaxies.

I stepped out into space, and stood on solid ground even though there was nothingness all around me. An invisible floor? Or a forcefield of some kind? I took a breath. Oxygen/nitrogen/carbon dioxide – yes, it was breathable air, the same blend as was found on Belladonna. I took another step forward, and my sensors confirmed I was experiencing false gravity, even though my eyes told me I was walking in outer space.

I carried on walking. At the end of this invisible air-filled corridor was a bright light. I formed an hypothesis: the spires were also space elevators, connected to satellites in space. And the corridor was made up of a forcefield which was suspended in mid-space, and subject to some kind of artificial gravity effect.

Nice trick.

I stepped into the light, and was in the Penthouse Suite of the Barrington Hotel, which was contained in a medium-sized satellite in orbit around the planet of Belladonna.

43

"Welcome," said the ancien boy who was my host, and who had greeted me on my arrival at the Penthouse. His name was Vishaal, and he had the body of a beautiful child, with jet-black hair and brown skin and a face that never smiled. His rejuve had frozen him at his body's original age, about sixteen – an adult, but barely.

"This is a spaceship?" I asked.

"It's an orbiting living area. We have a hundred such space stations orbiting Belladonna, each of them linked by a space elevator cable to a spire."

"I never knew that."

"We don't advertise."

There were of course thousands of satellites and space stations and solar panel arrays orbiting Belladonna. All the fabricator plants had been moved into orbit fifty years ago, and all the dirty industrial processes were conducted out here in space, or on one of the Industrial Zones on the nearest six of the twelve moons.

From a distance, the multiple rings of Belladonna were a marvel. Close up, though, it was evident the rings were made up of space junk, space factories, and space stations. It was, I realised, not so very surprising that the anciens had managed to conceal their orbiting penthouses amongst all this jumble.

43

"*Are you augmented?*" Vishaal asked.

"Of course," I said.

Vishaal nodded acknowledgement.

"*How and when?*"

"I was a soldier," I told him. "Then I became a mercenary and fought in the war against the Damnations, until the SN Government intervened. That's when I had the major modifications."

"*You are no longer human.*"

"Still human."

"*No human being could—*"

"They put hardmetal in my bones. I have healing factor. I have a part-artificial heart, to speed my metabolism. My physique is genetically engineered as are the neurones in my brain." A x-ray or tomograph scan would confirm all these biological facts, thanks to the pseudo-body layer that was wrapped around my metal and cybernetic core.

"*You were a fool,*" Vishaal informed me, "*to get yourself sentenced to death.*"

"Hey, I'm superhuman, don't mean I'm smart," I said.

"*Our theory is that you used the Games to draw yourself to our attention,*" said Vishaal.

"Now why the fuck would I want to do that?"

"*So we'd notice you.*"

"Because?"

"*Because we have the power to advance your career. You could be a gang boss.*"

"I'd rather be President."

Vishaal considered that sombrely. "*That's not out of the question either,*" he said. "*We need a leader. Someone who can unite the nation.*"

I nodded, then mimed incredulity.

"Why?" I asked.

And then Vishaal actually did smile. "*Because these are our people, and we love them.*"

43

"*I am Livia*," said a wide-eyed fourteen-year-old child.

"I'm the gladiator," I told her.

"*I know.*"

"Nice place." Vishaal had brought me to the top of the space station, to an observation area with the red and yellow and veined-blue globe of Belladonna visible through the hardglass. We had been joined there by Livia, who, I suspected, was the more senior of the two.

The architecture of the room was entirely virtual, with invisible forcefields acting as tables, chairs, bunks and staircases. When I had first entered, I found it disorientating: how was I supposed to know where the floor was? But then I took a step forward and met solid ground. And I took a second step, raising my foot higher as if mounting a set of stairs, and my foot met solid ground again.

Now, as I spoke to the serious-faced Livia, there were sleeping children floating in mid-air all around me. Elsewhere in the room, other children walked through air to reach mid-air virtual work stations. Computer screens flickered, and flew across the room at a subvocalised command. I deduced that the forcefields were smart, and sensitive to human motion: so if I wanted to walk upwards and took a part-step, the air would "know" and would support me. Or if I wanted to lie down, the air would become a hard bunk.

"*Champagne?*" said Vishaal, who stood near but not *too* near to Livia.

"Beer," I said, and a beer bottle arose from nowhere and floated towards my hand.

I glanced and saw that Vishaal and Livia were now each holding a glass of champagne.

"How do you do that?" I asked, and they did not answer.

I figured it out, with the help of a swift tomograph of the room: floating mirrors concealed the presence of floors, bulkheads, and cupboards. All the "real" furniture must be subvocally controlled, and once the cupboard containing the drinks opened up, tractor beams had conveyed my beer across to me, as if from nowhere.

It was a magnificent *trompe l'oeil*, but it was not, by any means, magic.

I started to relax.

"Who the fuck *are* you guys?" I asked belligerently.

"We are the masters and mistresses of Belladonna," Livia told me.

"You're just a bunch of fucking kids," I said.

"We want you to come and work for us," Vishaal said.

"Doing what?"

Suddenly the ghost of Billy Grogan appeared in front of me. He stared at me with puzzled eyes. Then his head exploded and his brains splashed in my face.

I felt an urge to flinch, but did not.

"Yeah, that was down to me," I conceded.

"This man worked for us," Livia said. *"He was killed by you. You have to answer for that. Furthermore, as a result of a battle in which you took part, our three other gang leaders were killed. We now have no one we trust working for us on Belladonna."*

"You ran the gangs?"

"We run everything. This is our planet. But we need underlings to represent us to the masses," Livia told him.

"You're asking me to be an underling?"

"We are," Livia said.

"You want me to run Billy's rackets for you?"

"All the rackets. All the gangs. You are an impressive man, Mr Dunnigan."

"Not really. I fucked up."

"Why did you kill Billy Grogan?" Vishaal asked.

"That's why I fucked up," I conceded. "I thought I'd take over his gang. But I judged it wrong. All Billy's men were dead, we were alone on the roof, so I put my gun to his head, and BOOM. But then I realised the sister was there, she'd seen the whole damned thing. I didn't have the guts to kill her – yeah, I know, that was pathetic of me – so I had to go on the run. Then the fucking sister turned me in! That's how I ended up as a gladiator."

"*You should have killed the sister,*" Livia chided.

"She was only a kid. I had a daughter, same age as that, when they first sent me for brain-frying. You have to draw the line somewhere; I drew it there."

"*We don't approve of such weakness,*" said Livia.

"Hell, you're only a kid yourself," I sneered.

"*Only in body. I have lived, in all, twelve hundred years.*"

I shrugged; acknowledging the point. Livia was a millenarian, and for most of her years alive, she had been steeped in evil. So her soft blonde hair and cute blue eyes and faintly lisping child-voice gave no measure of the darkness of her soul.

"*And getting caught,*" added Vishaal. "*That was highly unintelligent too.*"

"Yeah, I know, fucking dumb."

"*But you knew, didn't you?*" Vishaal said. "*You knew that Billy worked for us, and that we'd be needing a replacement for him. And you knew we would be at the Games. And you wanted us to notice you.*"

"I'm not that devious."

"*You're exactly that devious.*"

I grinned. Then I decided it was time to switch my mood.

"I don't want to run your fucking rackets." I said fiercely, "I want my own planet. I want to be immortal. I want to be a god."

Livia and Vishaal made no visible response. But the long pause that followed was an indication of how startled they were by my words.

"*You want to be like us?*" Livia said, mockingly.

"Yeah, I do. I'm no fucking patsy. I found you, I put you on my hook. I know who you are, and what you've done. And I want to join you."

"*Who are you really, Mr Dunnigan?*"

"What do you mean?"

"*We have evidence,*" said Livia, in a sweet voice, "*that Tom Dunnigan was killed during the fifty-fifty. You are an impostor.*"

I laughed. "Bullshit!"

"*Take a look.*" Livia conjured up a virtual screen, and found a file. She opened the file.

In front of us, hovering in air, was the face of a man who I recognised: it was myself. Handsome, cruel, powerful. I was wearing a quantum teleportation suit. My features were sober, anxious.

Then suddenly the features began to melt. The eyeballs ran down my cheeks like butter on a hot day. My flesh began to peel off. Tom Dunnigan disintegrated, and tears merged on his cheeks with his melted eyeballs, and he screamed but the scream died and became a strangled croak. And then he was dead, puddled on the floor like the skin shed by a snake.

"How the fuck did you get hold of this?" I asked.

"*This image was deleted from the database,*" said Vishaal, "*by an expert hacker. It was replaced by an image of Tom Dunnigan surviving.*"

"Yeah, I did that."

"*You faked your own survival?*"

"Fuck no," I said. "I faked *Dunnigan* surviving, then I stole his identity. This body I'm wearing," I shrugged with the body, "is a clone replica of Tom Dunnigan. The real guy died, just like you saw." I waited a moment for this to sink in, then added, tauntingly, "You got that? Or am I going too fast for you?"

"*Who are you really?*" Livia asked, with a hint of respect in her tone.

"Does it matter?"

"*We would like to know.*"

"You're aiming to kill me, I take it?"

"*Of course. You lied to us, as well as inconveniencing us by killing Billy Grogan. That's why we brought you here. To interrogate you, then execute you.*"

"You'll have a fight on your hands."

"*You are powerless,*" said Vishaal, with an amused catch in his voice.

I leaped, and karate-struck him in the throat. I missed. Vishaal was elsewhere.

"Fuck," I said.

Livia smiled and disappeared and reappeared behind me and slashed my face with her nails. Blood trickled down my cheeks. I back-punched her, and threw a dazzling series of powerful punches and kicks, all of which missed. Livia reappeared a few feet away from me. There were now two of her.

"How do you do that?"

"*Tell us who you are,*" said Livia, "*before we kill you.*"

"You don't want to kill me," I said, and a wolfish smile crept to my lips. "We can do business together."

"*You are an impostor.*"

"Of course I'm a fucking impostor. I'm on the run, same as you. I am one of you."

I was relaxed now, as if quietly triumphant.

"*Explain.*"

"I was a general," I said, and my tone had changed now. I assumed an easy authority, of the kind that came from centuries of experience as a leader of Soldiers, "in the Cheo's army. I was sentenced to death for my war crimes, and I went on the run. I had a face transplant, and new eyes and new fingerprints. And then I had my brain transplanted into a clone's body and came here with Tom Dunnigan. It was fifty-fifty that one of us would die in the jump, and luckily for me, it was him. If we'd both lived, well, that's another story. But *he died*, and here I am."

I had their attention now.

"I go way back," I continued, "just as you do. I fought in the Last Battle, on the losing side, and I can prove it. Ask me anything. Anything at all about the Cheo, and his army, and what colour uniform I wore, and where we did our basic training, and how we ran the Doppelganger Robots, and which planets we destroyed, and which humans I massacred. *I'm one of you.*"

Vishaal glanced at Livia. For the first time so far, there was a whisper of expression in their faces, the tiniest hint of confusion.

Vishaal turned his eerie gaze back to me.

"*You're a war criminal?*"

"Yeah."

"*What is your name?*"

"General Argobast Durer."

"*You're General Durer?*" said Livia, astonished.

"Yes."

"*I slept with you once,*" Livia said primly.

"I thought so. You're Dr Livia Randall?"

"*Yes.*"

"We drank champagne. Brut, 87. We were staying on a Dyson Jewel, the Koh-i-Noor. I was a redhead then, a big burly son of a bitch. You were a blonde. I ate steak, you ate oysters, and lobster straight from the pan. You gave me the finger gesture and I went back to your cabin and we fucked till dawn. Then we put on our body armour and flew through space for a couple of hours."

"*All of that is correct.*"

"I'm telling the truth. I'm Argobast Durer."

"*Hello Argo, it's nice to see you again,*" said Livia, and smiled, and raised a finger, and beckoned, the time-honoured "shall we fuck?" signal.

And I felt my moral code being assailed, and undermined. I had to remind myself that Livia was a woman of more than a thousand years of age, who just happened to be wearing the shell of a fourteen-year-old girl.

I grinned. "You got it," I said, leeringly, and triumphantly.

43

Afterwards, Livia and I flew through space, and reminisced via our MIs about the old days.

I was a past master at staying in character. And of course, I knew everything there was to be known about General Argobast Durer. Durer had been captured, after a hundred years on the run, by a Galactic Cop. And, after being sentenced to death, his memories had been recorded and transferred to the Earth Computer, and, from there, into the databases of all the Galactic Cops.

And then Durer had been sent out into space in a leaking spacesuit. Once the suit achieved a state of vacuum, he died. But it was a deliberately slow process.

Three cyborg Cops flew beside him for a month, until his vital signs ceased. Then they hurled his body into the nearest sun. Thus Argobast Durer had died, after a fair but brief trial; a death that was cruel yet much deserved. But the memories of his life lived on in the cybernetic memories of each and every Galactic Cop, stored in our databases with tens of thousands of other alternate identities.

And now, armed with those memories, I could count myself as a trusted associate of the anciens. For, after all, I could justifiably claim to be an ancien myself.

It was, I mused, all going according to plan.

"It's so great out here," trilled Livia, and I could not but remember the shy beauty of this young woman who I had caressed and fucked earlier, and the softness of her young skin, and the sweetness of her young eyes and the sleekness of her young hair, and the warmth of her young mouth. And I could not stop myself wondering about the young, beautiful, warm teenage girl who had once owned and inhabited this body.

Who was she?

What had she been like?

And how much joy had she managed to squeeze out of her brief life, until the moment when the aged and evil Livia had kidnapped her, and gouged out her brain, and stolen the beauty of this body for herself?

"What are they like?"

"Scary."

"How many of them?"

"I saw about ten. They live like gods."

I had briefed Aretha, Macawley and the Sheriff on my discoveries. They were now looking at me warily, as if I'd been away for a long long time.

The Sheriff gave me an admiring glance. "You did well, in the arena."

"You saw me fight?"

"I wouldn't've missed it for the world."

"It was necessary," I said, in a dead neutral tone.

"It was magnificent," the Sheriff assured me.

I risked a grin. "I guess so," I admitted.

Macawley shared my grin, then resumed her seriously-intent-and-listening-hard look.

After arriving back from my trip to the anciens, I had slept solidly for about twelve hours, even though in theory I didn't need to sleep. And during that sleep, I'd had another dream: a nightmare in which I was nailed to a cross and was being flayed by the acid tongues of rats. My database had briefed me on dream imagery but I saw no conceivable interpretation that could make sense of the dream. I was no Messiah, Earth-Rats did not have acid on their tongues, and I had no fear of being flayed. And I cursed the robotic designers who had chosen to make me capable of feeling pain *even in my dreams*.

"So what's the plan now?" said Sheriff Heath. We were in his den, a lead-lined Faraday-chambered, wooden-walled library-cum-office. The Sheriff had filled the walls with trophies from his youth: martial arts combat prizes, shooting prizes, the scalp of a Vegan Warrior, a fragment of the hull of a Galactic Corporation cruiser which he had once stolen and sold for scrap.

Aretha kept darting strange looks at me. What was her problem? Why was she looking so worried? Did she fear for my safety?

Or, perhaps, for my soul?

I remembered how I'd felt when Claudio had been burned alive: guilt had rent me. Later I had purchased his corpse and instructed doctors at the hospital to revive him. But I'd been informed that the heat had melted Claudio's skull, and there was a strong chance the brain was irretrievably damaged. Which meant that Claudio had sacrificed himself, for me.

Why? We weren't even friends. Just for the hell of it?

"Hello? Are you in there?" Aretha was still staring at me.

I realised I had been staring into space. This kind of abstraction was unlike me. Normally, I could think about very many subjects at the same time, whilst also talking, and analysing data from a thousand dragonfly cameras.

But over the last few days, I had been employing the larger part of my consciousness in obsessive, silent analysis of my database, which now contained every iota of information there was to know about the anciens after I had leached the data from the spire.

And thus, for every moment of every day, millions of facts swirled around my mind, like snakes, or like fog, or like – like nothing else, just like itself – suffocating me. And there were so *many* facts, and the data was tinged with such malevolence that, at times, I found it hard to – to –

I refocused.

"The plan now," I said firmly, "is to remain deep undercover as long as I can. To learn the secrets, weaknesses and intentions of the anciens, and to ascertain how they murdered the medics and Version 43. Then, assuming we have just cause, which I am confident we will have by then, to kill them."

"Works for me," said Macawley.

"Kill them how?" asked Aretha.

"I fail to see the point of that question."

"How do we kill them," repeated Aretha, "if they have this infernal secret fucking weapon?"

"I now see your purport. I'll think of something."

"And why?" said the Sheriff. "Why did they kill my son?"

"I don't know," I lied. "When I find out, I'll tell you. The aim for the moment is to win their confidence. Befriend them."

The Sheriff nodded, reassured.

"These meetings are dangerous," said Aretha. "Every time you meet us, it's another opportunity for them to suspect you. Why else would you be meeting a pair of cops, if not to plot betrayal?"

"I can cover my tracks," I said confidently.

"How?"

"I – have partial control of the Belladonna computer," I reluctantly admitted. "I have authority to override its surveillance systems, and I have done so. That's how I was able to plant the 'deleted' image of Tom Dunnigan dying. So they could find it. So I could be exposed as a liar. So I could then implement the second tier of subterfuge, the backup cover of General Durer. Thus validating my cover, for who would suspect me of telling *two* lies of such magnitude about my identity?"

"Smart boy," said the Sheriff.

"Consequently," I said, "I can easily cover my tracks. There will be no film footage of us together on the surveillance cameras. And if anyone does happen to see us together . . ." I morphed, and became a different person. "This is what they will see."

"This is fucking – eerie!" said Macawley, who had been watching all this as though it were a tennis game. "And cool, did I mention cool?!?"

"No," said Aretha.

"Well, no guff, it's mamafucking cool!!!"

I shrugged. It didn't, in fact, feel so very cool to me.

"There's someone," I told them, "who I would like you to meet."

"Who're your friends?" Filipa asked.

"This is Aretha," I said to her. "Sergeant Aretha Jones of the Bompasso PD. Aretha, this is Filipa Santiago."

"She's a *cop*?" Filipa asked suspiciously.

"What's wrong with being a cop?" Aretha snapped.

"Nothing," Filipa sneered.

"Yes she's a cop. This is Sheriff Gordon Heath, he is also a law enforcement officer."

"Yeah, like I couldn't guess *that*."

"And this is Macawley, she's kind of, our mascot."

"Miaow."

"What are you guys drinking?"

Filipa served us. Then she called a barmaid over to run the bar, and we retired to the back snug.

The Sheriff beamed at Filipa to impress her with the fact he thought she was a good-looking woman, but to little avail.

Aretha was more guarded. "Have I arrested you?"

"Once or twice," Filipa admitted.

"Were you guilty?"

"Hell yes."

"How do we know we can trust this woman?" said Macawley cautiously, and her face flickered anxiety.

"You can trust me," said Filipa, and she smiled, and Macawley basked in her smile.

Then Filipa turned to me.

"Why are you here?"

"You were right," I told her. "It's the anciens. Everything you told me is right."

"I know," said Filipa.

"But how is that?" I asked, tensely.

"Sorry, I'm not with you," Filipa said cautiously.

"How do you know so much?"

"I told you," she said calmly. "I keep my ear to the ground."

"That's not credible," I said firmly. "You're a liar."

There was an ugly silence. But Filipa shrugged, unoffended.

"I see things," Filipa admitted, at last. "I see things that other people don't see." Filipa put her fingers in her mouth, and pretended to bite them. I winced. "The silver-haired man," she whispered. And I felt a jolt.

How could she possibly know about *that*?

"What silver-haired man?" asked Aretha tersely.

"You saw that?" I asked, awed.

"Yes."

"How?"

Filipa shook her head. "If I knew how, I couldn't do it. The same way the anciens keep power."

"I don't understand," I said.

"They have a gift. And so do I. My gift is – I have the power to see things that shouldn't be seen. And, they – they know the secret of glamour."

"Glamour?"

"It's a form of magic," Filipa said softly. "An enchantment."

"Magic?" I mocked.

Macawley nodded at this, then frowned, then goggled her eyes.

"*Magic?*" she said.

"Hush, motormouth," said the Sheriff, who was openly fascinated at my exchange with Filipa.

"That's what I said," Filipa chastised us. "Magic. The anciens allure and seduce. That's how they manage to stay concealed. That's how they exert such astonishing control over this planet."

"There's no such thing as magic," I said. But my words were immediately contradicted by a thought: *If you really believed that, why did you come here?*

"You don't know that. Not for sure," Filipa told me.

"She's got a point," Aretha conceded.

I thought about it. "What you say is true," I conceded.

"I know about glamour," said the Sheriff. His grey moustache twitched. "I've seen men use it. Men more often than women, strangely enough, though some women have it like skies have stars. It's a bitch of a thing."

The Sheriff's candour opened the floodgates.

"My mother," offered Aretha, "used to sing in clubs. Fernando Gracias's clubs. She told me she once saw Fernando with a girl, a young girl, fourteen at most. Pretty but not beautiful. And Fernando was obsessed with her. Devoted to her. The girl's name was Lamia, an old-fashioned demon name. But she wasn't a demon. She was an ancien. And she – she had glamour. That's what she told my father, and he told me. But I just thought it meant – anyway, looking back on it, I think that's why Fernando was so much in love with her. He murdered his wife, to be with Lamia. Then she laughed in his face and never came back. She wasn't, you see," said Aretha musing, "beautiful. But she had that – *thing*. The glamour thing."

"Sex appeal?" offered Macawley.

"No, much more than that, much stranger," replied Filipa. "It's how they can do what they do, without being seen. Glamour can seduce, but it can also conceal."

"I've been a crooked cop for more years than I care to remember," conceded Sheriff Heath. "And I never once thought about the anciens, or suspected them. So how could I be so dumb?"

"More enchantment," Filipa explained.

"What is this 'enchantment' shit?" I raged. "We live in a scientific civilisation! They use hypnosis, maybe. Drugs. They manipulate the computer database. But don't drag magic into this."

"Then how to you explain the deaths?" Filipa taunted. "The way the Sheriff's son was killed? The way *you* were killed?"

"That's entirely different. It's some kind of quantum weapon."

"I saw it," said Aretha, awed. "I saw it! And I saw – nothing! Nothing. It was just – strange. Everything, *strange*. If that's not magic, what is?"

Filipa nodded. Then she raised her hand and waved her fingers.

And suddenly her face vanished. Her beauty vanished. And what remained was a twisted contorted harridan's face with eyes that stretched like smears. "Glamour," she said. "Making people see what you want them to see."

She clicked her fingers and the "real" Filipa returned. "I didn't," she admitted, "do so good on the fifty-fifty." Although she was beautiful again now, the hideous deformity of her face stayed with me as a searing memory. "Juan died outright," Filipa continued, "and I survived, but I got fucked up, bad. It's a miracle I'm alive. And my deformities were – and are – extraordinary. Beyond belief. But no one knows that. No one sees the *real* me."

I was lost for words. Filipa fixed me with a fierce stare; and I saw her eyes, but I also saw the nightmare reality that lay beneath the beautiful, comforting illusion.

"If that's not magic," Filipa concluded, "what the hell *is* it?"

43

"They trust me," I told them all, a little while later, after a number of drinks had been consumed. "They think I am one of them."

"You must believe that you truly are," said Filipa firmly, "or they will suspect you. You must be this man, this general. This Durer. Only your total faith in your own identity will convince them."

"I am General Durer," I said. "I really am." And I smiled and all present shuddered.

"Just don't go," said the Sheriff, "fucking native on us."

43

Over the course of the following weeks, I became an intimate of the anciens. I studied them, and I marvelled at their effortless inhumanity.

And I began to take control of the gangs of Lawless City, following their strict instructions.

And, as I learned more and more about the real Belladonna, I found myself haunted by doubts and questions and memories.

Blood and human flesh spattered the walls and ceilings. A screaming severed head swam in a pool of blood on the bed. And inside the mouth, which gaped unnaturally large, was a human heart, squeezed and squirted.

I conjured up this holo of the crime scene on a regular basis, forcing myself to wallow in its horror. But even when the holo wasn't manifest, I could still see the image in my memory.

What or who, I wondered once again, could have done such a thing?

I remembered the dead body of Version 43, broken up into pieces and reconstituted with pieces of sidewalk instead of limbs.

It must surely, I had already theorised, be some kind of quantum teleportation effect: but how could anyone ever use *that* as a weapon?

And "glamour"? What could explain glamour? What connected Filipa with the anciens? What strange powers *were* these?

I scrolled through my database, picking on random items and facts and setting up insane search questions: "What is reality?" "Is magic possible?" "Is science real?"

I took over the casinos; I threw out the management of the Houses of Pain and brought in my own people; I abolished the protection rackets and took a weekly tax from all the city businesses in return for my "support". And as I did all this, with the larger part of my consciousness, I absorbed the entire history of science, from its earliest history in Babylonian and Greek times to the creation of cute-o, the quantum theory of everything. It left me puzzled and deeply uneasy.

I thought about Khaos, the primeval state of the universe as postulated by cute-o. A universe of nothing, where no physical laws apply, where nothing is real, but where only probabilities and their attenuated cousins "possibilities" exist, or rather, don't.

I comprehended the theory; I fathomed the math. But as I puzzled at it, the mystery of it all began to overwhelm me.

I was well aware of the paradox of our age: the fact that all of modern scientific civilisation is founded on the discoveries of a few scientists in the early twentieth century who devised a predictive mathematical system which *makes no sense*. A reality created by observation? Entities that can be in many places, all at the same time? Artefacts that are not real, that by indescribable means become real and create observable "reality"?

Quantum physics, I knew, marked the moment when science became irrational: it is true because it works, but it cannot be understood.

However, as I also knew, the theory of QTOE, aka "cute-o," was intended to provide the answers to all these mysteries: it postulated a pre-universe in which quantum "reality" was the only reality. Where possibilities and virtualities roamed, like dinosaurs on ancient Earth, where "nothing" reigned supreme. A universe of Big If, that pre-dates the Big Bang. A universe of void that spawned the universe that we know, the universe of all things.

But what is "nothing"? There is no such thing; "nothing" cannot exist, the equations of quantum physics do not allow it. So the "possibilities" that exist are in fact possible energies, virtual energies, emerging out of nothing and then vanishing again, without ever becoming "actual." The equation that connects uncertainty of time with uncertainty of energy compels this.

And so, when there is "nothing," there is still an adherence to an uncertainty principle: that, uncertainty itself, is the fundamental spark of everything.

And furthermore, I reflected, "emergence" exists too; the principle that allows, by random action, the simple to become complex.

So when virtual possible energies interact, they become more complex virtual energies; they become more than possibilities, they become "probabilities"; hence they become proxy wave functions, the primary postulation of quantum physics.

The more I thought about it, the more baffling it was.

For this is how it really is: reality is an illusion. An object can exist in many places at the same time. Time can flow in any direction. Our commonsense notions of what is and is not possible are nonsense. All this has been known, and has been undeniable, for centuries.

And cute-o is the only theory which attempts to create an imaginative model of how this crazy state of affairs came about. How a state of unreality slowly evolved out of "nothing," through the actions of emergence, so that possibilities interacted and became actualities; until the moment when the "real" universe was born, with all its stars and nebulae and atoms.

Cute-o was the first theory to provide an *explanation* for the fact that our supposed "reality" rests on the shifting unreality of quantum foam.

Cute-o tells us our reality evolved out of Khaos: and it therefore still contains within itself Khaos. And reality, therefore, is nothing but a random side-effect of quantum chaos.

But ultimately, all this makes no sense! It's just an attempted causal explanation for a theory that affronts logic, that defies our every concept of the real.

Quantum physics is, in short, a theory that has nothing whatsoever to recommend it, aside from the fact that every single scrap of evidence shows it to be true.

So if all *this* is true, I reflected, is magic, after all, so very unlikely? If mere possibilities can mate and breed, why mock the concept of the mystical, or even the divine?

I found I was becoming obsessed by these philosophical concepts. I knew I had to clear my mind, and focus on the job ahead.

But a slow unfolding terror was possessing me. The theory of quantum physics and its younger sibling cute-o had advanced human technology in astonishing ways.

But the mystery at the heart of the quantum had never truly been explained. No theory could do justice to the sheer monstrous unlikeliness of what humanity had achieved in taming a herd of wild horses that were galloping into madness.

But what the anciens had done went beyond even *that* familiar insanity. For they were making quantum effects occur *at a macroscopic level*. Just to allow that possibility meant there could never again be, literally and metaphorically, solid ground. So I—

No!

This way, madness lay.

I voluntarily deleted the worst of my mental ramblings. I retained the core of my argument, but erased all my doubts and uncertainties about the reality of the real.

And thus, I compelled myself to focus on my mission strategy.

For I was preparing to wage war with the anciens. They were evil human beings. It was my job to arrest or execute evil human beings. Nothing could be simpler, or more—

But, no. No!

I found myself, once more, trapped by doubts.

I thought about what I had witnessed at the original crime scene, and I wondered how I could have failed to see its true, dire implications. I had become obsessed with finding the motive for the murder, and the identity of the murderer. But now, it seemed obvious that the real mystery was the murder *method*.

The sights I had seen that day were appalling. And the consequences of the atrocity that had taken place were more appalling still.

What infernal powers did the anciens possess! Why had no one on the planet been aware of these powers? And how could they make themselves so taken for granted that even I, with my immense database and astonishing powers of observation and logical deduction, *did not realise they were in charge*?

And, most terrifyingly of all, what kind of beings could execute their enemies with a weapon that scrambled reality itself?

I applied all my critical and logical powers to this key question, and reached an irrevocable conclusion.

I was doomed to lose. No matter how hard I tried, I stood no chance against an enemy of such malicious and sanity-threatening omnipotence.

"You're Aretha's mother?" I asked.

"I am," said the tall, raven-haired, black-skinned beauty.

"Sing for me."

And Aretha's mother sang, a liquid song of joy and ecstasy, and I felt the warmth of the sun and the heat of love and the uncontrollable twitch of desire.

Aretha's mother was naked, and her skin was moist with a dew that mingled with her sweat, and she looked so much like her daughter yet older and wiser and more sensual, and she smiled at me, then snarled like a wolf, and I felt a spasm of lust, and

And then I woke.

"Is your mother still alive?" I asked, casually.

"Yeah sure. She still sings at the Blue Note, sometimes," Aretha told me.

"What does she look like?"

"Short, fair hair, mixed race, light skin, quite pretty, but nothing special."

Aretha frowned, clearly wondering why I was asking such strange questions.

"Does she look like you?" I said, casually.

"Not a bit. Why do you ask?"

"No reason," I lied.

I was having a whole terrifying series of recurring dreams now. And my dream of having sex with Aretha's singer mother was the most frequent and vivid of them.

But why? What did it mean? Did it mean anything?

43

"*Make love to me again*," said Livia, and I stifled my horror and disgust.

"Sure thing," I said. "Just give me a moment."

We were both naked, floating in mid-air on an invisible bunk, in full view of the other anciens. But no one looked at us; no one cared enough to do so.

Livia was an insatiable lover, but totally impossible to please. I had never given her an orgasm; I had never even made her smile.

Only a robot, I mused, could make love to a woman like *that*.

43

"Everything will be just the same as it was before," I said.

Annie Grogan stared at me with hate in her eyes.

"I'm supposed to work for *you*?"

"I have a deal with the President," I lied. In fact, the President now worked for *me*. "I've already taken over the protection rackets, the brothels and the Houses of Pain. Now I want to start up your brother's saloons and robbery teams again. There's a system; this is how things work."

"You were sentenced to death."

"I got off for good behaviour."

"My brother was your friend, you evil bastard."

"Yeah, I know. I took him down. I'm moving in. Get over it." I gave her my flinty stare, the one that made hard men flinch, and she flinched. "You're lucky I'm letting you and the rest of your family live," I said, trying to find a sliver of solace for her, and failing utterly.

There were tears in Annie's eyes.

"You piece of fucking shit," she told me.

I grinned, nastily.

"Don't water the whiskey, okay?" I said. "Your brother did that; it caused a lot of grief."

43

I flew solo in the cable car above the city. The car moved at one-tenth of lightspeed, so fast that I could see nothing and no one. And I gloried in the fact that, from the ground, I was totally invisible. A blur in the corner of the eye; a hint of something that might possibly have been glimpsed, but not truly seen.

I flew on the cable car from spire to spire, and back again, until I had woven my invisible web over the entire city.

43

An old-fashioned nujazz quartet were playing a warm, sensual twenty-scale improvisation. It felt like sunshine, if sunshine were champagne, and could make love. The instruments were all virtual: the four jazzists sang and waved their hands and blew into mid-air and the result was a cacophony blended with perfection.

I was back at the Blue Note, Fernando Gracias's old club, which I had taken over and refashioned as a retro music palace. I'd tried to get Blind Jake and Pete and Joni and Marcus to play there, but they'd declined on the grounds that I, Tom Dunnigan, had caused the death of their mentor Fernando Gracias, and old wounds heal hard.

I now sat in the snug with President Naurion, who was an anxious pale man these days. The horrors of the Gang Wars had shaken him badly, and his hopes of using the Presidency to "make a difference" had been casually crushed by the anciens. He had become, despite his bulk, timid and fearful.

"I have a question," Naurion said to me sneeringly. "Here you are, you own this club, you act as if you own me. But who the fuck *are* you?"

"The anciens trust me. That's all you need to know."

"Yeah? Dooley Grogan was my friend. So was Billy. So was Fernando. Kim and I went way back. All of them, they earned their place in this society the hard way. What gives you the right to take over their livelihoods?"

"Easy, now," I cautioned.

"Fucking anciens, why didn't they make *me*—"

"You're the President."

"In name only. I have no power. I pass no laws. I have no government. It's a joke."

"It's a joke that amuses your masters. Let it be."

"It's let be, it's let be," said President Naurion, slurringly, and I wondered what potent cocktail of drugs and alcohol and self-disgust was running through his veins.

"Tell me how you got into this game," I murmured.

"You don't want to know."

"I want to know. Tell me."

Naurion sipped from a potent pint of misty ale – beer blended with LSD.

"I fought in the Last Battle, you know," he said querulously.

"On the wrong side, yeah, I know."

"Whatever. I haven't always been what I am now. I was a Soldier. Then a farmer. Then when I came to Belladonna, I became a bodyguard. To this rich kid, one of the Founders. We're going way back now, before the spires were built."

I had a glimpse of a previous Abraham Naurion: the President as he had been before he became a broken man.

"You see," Naurion continued, "when our colony ships first arrived at Belladonna – this was something like fifty years after the first settlers got there – we found this empty planet full of kids. And they kept telling us their parents were off working. And we bought it. Then things got ugly, there were a lot of violent deaths, and we began to realise they were killing our colonists for sport. At landfall, we had a million colonists, give or take. After a year, only nine hundred thousand remained. The rest had been hunted to death for fun. The anciens were Soldiers, you see; they had state-of-the-art weaponry, body armour, One Suns. They were killing machines, and we were just a bunch of fucking convicts.

"But once we figured out what was happening, we formed a lynch mob to deal with the fuckers. All of us were united against these fucking kids, because they were evil, and because they owned the best land. And that's when they had their first major cull."

"Cull?"

"They still have them from time to time. It clears away the defective stock; only the fittest survive. They started a war between the factions among the colonists, and nearly three-quarters of us died. Seven hundred thousand people, give or take. We were killing each other in the streets, hand-to-hand combat, biting out throats. And the ones who remained, the leaders of the most successful gangs, we became the rulers of Belladonna. But the kids told us what to do. They always told us what to do."

"You didn't think that was strange?"

"It never felt strange."

"They made you a gang boss?"

"At first. Then I became Mayor. We set up a police force. New colonists kept on coming, and we told them the way things were, and they accepted it. Then a Galactic Cop came to clean us up, and he killed a lot of people. That was about a century ago."

"I've heard about that."

"But he left me alive, and we started again with a new intake. The kids seemed very happy about it, they called it a new way of culling. The Cops aren't as powerful as people think, you know. They can be manipulated."

"Is that a fact?"

"I've seen it happen. Believe me."

"I believe."

"You have kids?"

"Well, yes. A couple. Why?"

"I had kids," Naurion said. "Two dead, you know about those. Three still alive, I hope, on Earth. But I can still remember."

President Naurion sat and stared, and there were actually tears in his eyes.

"Go on, tell me about your kids," I said, eventually, gently.

"Yeah. My kids. It's something else, right? But it's like *nothing* else. Christ, when I think about what they were like, when they were babies! Red-faced and screaming and looking up at me like I was, you know, special, important, *theirs*. Nothing like it, yeah?"

I nodded, not knowing.

"And then, when they were toddlers! So full of energy. It's like having multiple heart attacks. Kids! They're just, well, fucking amazing. I was two hundred years old when I had my first kid; I felt like I was reborn."

"Why are you telling me this?" I asked, still gently.

"They kill kids," said President Abraham Naurion bleakly. "That's how they survive. They breed 'em and kill 'em and take their bodies. They've been doing that for half a thousand years. How do you think that makes me feel?"

"I don't know. How does it make you feel?"

"I try not to think about it. I have my spot in life. I have some power. If I wasn't loyal, they'd kill me. So I'm loyal."

"You're drunk, aren't you?" I said.

"Every day. A bottle of whisky, a bottle of vodka, I swim through every day. And every night I take the pills and I wake up without a hangover. I get a new liver every fifty years. I'll live forever, you know. I'm a survivor."

"Are you saying, I'll end up like you?"

"They're grooming you, to replace me. They need a lickspittle. Someone who'll command respect from the masses, but who doesn't care about eating shit. That's you."

"I don't eat fucking shit."

"You have already. You will again. Get used to it."

43

"*Eat*," said Vishaal, and I ate. This humaniform body had a full gamut of taste sensations, and I was awed at the perfection of the food. Tangs and textures exploded in my mouth, making me feel exhilarated.

"*Drink.*"

I drank a glass of wine, and was swept up in a heady rush of joy.

"*Watch.*"

The naked belly dancer undulated in front of me: and never had I seen such grace, or, in a universe full of good-looking humans, such ineffable beauty.

"You like to live it up, don't you?" I snorted.

"*See this,*" said Vishaal, and he held up his hand. And the hand became stars: an entire universe floated in front of me.

I spat out my wine.

"What the—" I said.

"*We are gods,*" explained Vishaal. The universe faded away, and the hand returned.

"Bullshit."

"*A universe was born and died in an instant, in the palm of my hand. Only a god can do that.*"

"It's simple physics. A bud universe. Or an optical illusion."

"*The latter.*" Vishaal laughed, a tinkling laugh that echoed like knives in my mind.

I breathed a sigh, of utter relief.

43

"These creatures are like devils," I said. "They seduce and beguile."

"I thought you were beyond seduction?" Aretha said.

"I thought so too."

Aretha and I were walking along the esplanade, near the city's port. I had morphed into my backup self, and had given myself an identity as Robbie Park, a cop in the Twelfth Canton, who Aretha was supposedly dating.

The sea stretched out to a vast distance, and surfers chanced their all on the high vertical waves. A guitarist was playing on a street corner, rather skilfully. I recognised the song: "Long Time Never Bluesrap."

"I remember things sometimes."

"Remember what?"

"A hundred years ago . . ."

"You remember me then?" Aretha said, surprise and pleasure in her voice.

"No. All of my memories of you at that time were erased."

"Not mine," she said, regretfully.

"I just remember," I said. "Things. Colours. Sounds. Not real memories."

"You told me. You remember 'moments,'" she said.

"That's right."

We walked on.

"What were you like back then?" I asked her. "The same? Different?"

"Slimmer," Aretha said. "Sweeter." She grinned.

"I'm sorry you've become fatter and less sweet, in the course of those one hundred years," I said, consolingly.

"I was – kidding," she said, affronted.

"Ah." I considered my options for a way out of this conversational *faux pas*; and concluded there were none.

"Forget it," Aretha said sourly.

"Consider it forgotten," I said, and knew that it would be, the next time I was reborn.

"You were different then," Aretha told me.

"How?"

Aretha paused. "You were still," she said carefully, "human."

"Not possible."

She shrugged; a little half-smile contradicted me. "More of your memories were intact," she said, gently. "You had a lot of your original personality. You were a ghost in the machine, but you were still *there*. And you used to tell me stuff. About your life as a human being. Your adventures."

"Yes, but who was I?" I mused, rhetorically.

"I can't tell you that," Aretha said cautiously.

"You *know*?" I was utterly stunned.

"Yes."

"Then tell me!"

"No."

"Why not?"

"I can't. I – just can't. It's a promise I made to you. Either you remember or you don't, but you can't ever be told."

"I don't need," I replied, stiffly, "a human self. I like me as I am."

43

I realised that Macawley was becoming impatient with me.

"What are we waiting for?" she said accusingly, hands out-stretched, palms turned out, eyes goggled: the very personification of impatience.

"I'm learning all that I can, as fast as I can," I told her.

"Why?" Her face radiated astonishment; amazement; contempt; scorn. I sighed.

"So that we know their weak spots," I told her, carefully, "as I believe I have explained, in some detail, on many previous occasions."

"Yeah, but like, what *are* their weak spots?"

I paused. "They have none."

Macawley sighed, melodramatically, and rolled her eyes, and shook her head. I got the message: I was a wanker.

I held her hand and kissed it, and Macawley looked at me in some shock. "You know," I admitted, "I feel, on occasions, strangely protective towards you."

"Hey! Fuck off! You're creeping me out," Macawley protested.

"You'd rather I was just a robotic monster?"

"You *are* just a robotic monster."

I laughed. "I have a theory," I said. "About my human self."

"What's the theory?"

"I think," I began to say, then I paused.

And I scuffed Macawley's hair. She was gorgeous and cheeky and incorrigible, and I sometimes felt an overwhelming urge to take her to another planet, where there was no violence, where there were no gangs, where wild children could run riot without any consequences.

And as I toyed with this fantasy, I looked at her, and I smiled. And Macawley stared back at me, head tilted, emotions flickering fast over her face, her elf-eyes shining with curiosity.

"I think," I continued, carefully, "I used to have a daughter."

I stepped into the lift and it shot up fast into space.

When I emerged, I was surrounded once again by stars.

The lift journeys were brief, but I liked to use them to mull on data already in my system.

On one such journey, early in my relationship with Vishaal, I had accessed my database for fresh information on Alexander Heath's murder. This is a task I had initially neglected, for the amount of data I had downloaded from AI-spire was so huge, I had been unable to analyse it all. Much of it still existed as a homogeneous mass of undigested facts in my consciousness.

But then, in the course of that lift journey, I had decided to run some systematic search programmes to uncover what the anciens knew about Alexander Heath. And very quickly – the search took about eleven minutes in all – I learned the truth about the murder case that had brought me to this planet. And later, when I asked him about it, Vishaal had confirmed all the major details.

For Vishaal had been one of the killers of Alexander Heath. Together with four other anciens called Lucas, Georgi, Shona and Gunther.

Vishaal had also explained their motive, which was a malign one. And through a combination of what he told me, and what my database already knew, I had found out the shocking truth about Alexander Heath.

However, several weeks had passed since I had made this discovery. And I had been dreading the moment when I would have to tell the Sheriff what I knew. The real story of what happened to his son; the truth about *why* Alexander had to die.

And, because I had been dreading that moment so much, I delayed it. For all these weeks I had been prevaricating, fearful that the Sheriff would withdraw his support from our venture if he knew what I knew.

I was being a coward, I knew, and that was out of character for me. Cowardice was not, and never had been, part of my programming.

However, still nursing my deceit, I walked through space until I entered the ancient space station.

43

"You've done a good job, General," said Vishaal.

"Thank you."

"You're clearly a natural criminal, and a born killer."

"Those, I'm afraid, are my only talents."

"That's not," said Vishaal, deadpan, *"what Livia tells me."*

"We're just friends."

"*We are anciens. We have no friends.*"

"Then we are merely lovers."

"*Come,*" said Vishaal. "*I have a present for you.*"

43

Danny was a pretty eight-year-old with tousled hair, and a flair for karate. He was in a white gi, his face fiercely focused, going through his kata.

"Nice kid," I said, looking at the holo image.

"*We've chosen him for you.*"

"Chosen him?"

"*As your vessel.*"

"What vessel?"

"*You do not need,*" said Vishaal, "*your current clumsy body. It'll serve for now, while you are working on the planet's surface. But if you want to live with us, in the spires and in space, you need a fitting vessel.*"

"This is my new body?"

"*When Danny is sixteen,*" said Vishaal, "*we will gouge out his brain and give you his body. Our gift to you.*"

"I'm honoured," I said, biting back my rage.

43

"*This is our Holy Grail,*" said Vishaal.

It was not, in fact, I noted, a Grail; it was an interferometer. Its presence here surprised me, for it was a truly archaic device: a light source sent twin beams of photons through tiny gaps, and behind the gaps, an interference pattern was projected. And this striped pattern was, of course, the simplest and most potent manifestation of a quantum-wave-particle duality state. For instead of existing in a finite space, and appearing as a dot of light on the other side of the hole, the photons were smeared between many possible states.

This shadowed bar was the clue, I mused, to the unreality that lies beneath reality.

"*And now look,*" said Vishaal, and dimmed the lights, and pressed a switch.

Stripes appeared on the ceiling above, and on all the walls, and on Vishaal's face.

Vishaal raised the lights.

"*This is our quantum weapon.*"

"I don't understand," I said, though by now I did.

"*By manipulating the nature of quantum reality,*" explained Vishaal, "*we ensure that the photons of light continue to go through the gap. But they also go, equally as often, above the gap. And to one side of the gap. They go sideways, and upwards, and in all directions. In the next room, this light shines too. It's a simple enough tool, but it's the basis for our new physics.*"

"You can do this to human beings?"

"*Imagine I am a photon,*" said Vishaal. "*I am here, but also there, and also there, and every place.*"

Vishaal vanished and my vision became a blur. I peered at the blur. I saw a million, a billion, a trillion Vishaals.

Then "reality" returned.

"Nice trick," I said.

"*There is no trick,*" said Vishaal. "*Nor is there any technology. We achieve the Quantum Zen state purely through the power of consciousness. It has taken us a thousand years to perfect this. Now, we are gods.*"

"How do I do it?"

"*We will teach you.*"

43

"*Argo,*" said Livia smiling, and I leaned across, and kissed her sweet young lips.

"*I've invited,*" said Livia, "*some companions to join us.*" She blinked and the curtains pulled back and two beaming young women and a shy blond man appeared. "*You can do with them,*"

Livia added, "*anything you want. Sex. Mutilation. Kill them if you want; we have robot cleaners, and these will surely not be missed.*"

"That'll be a thrill," I said, my heart as cold as ice.

43

Space was black, all around me; the stars shone like dust.

I walked back to the lift, which would take me back to the hotel, which would lead me back into my "real" world.

I wondered how humans could be so very evil.

Then I remembered all the things I had done on Belladonna. The many people I had killed, the many innocents whose deaths I had caused.

So was *I* evil? Or was I simply a tool? A badly programmed machine, who need not feel guilt?

I did not know what emotion I should feel.

That made it worse.

43

"What have you learned?" asked the Sheriff. His tone was hostile, impatient. It had been a month since I first infiltrated the anciens' regime, and we still had nothing to show for it.

I realised that today was the day I would have to tell the Sheriff about his son. The prospect filled me with Terror.

"The quantum weapon," I told him, "is not a weapon. It is a state of mind."

"A psychic power?"

"A power, of some kind. It is controlled by thought alone. I cannot – explain it any more."

"And that's how they killed my son."

"Yes."

"You know that for a fact?"

"Yes."

"Who killed him?"

"There were five killers. One of them I have met: Vishaal."

"And why? Did you find out *why*?"

I hesitated. "I'm not sure," I said eventually.

The Sheriff peered at me. He read the duplicity in the silence. He started to swear, but then stopped. There was pain in his eyes.

"I'm sorry," I told him.

"You've been lying to me, ain't you?"

I was silent.

"I didn't know you *could* lie."

"It was an effort," I admitted.

"Tell me the truth," the Sheriff said angrily.

"It'll hurt."

"Lies hurt more."

"Are you—"

"I'm sure. Tell me."

So I told him all I had learned about Alexander Heath. An idealistic doctor, who discovered an anomaly in the hospital records: an ill patient who had never been admitted but whose family believed she had died of cancer on his ward. And so he investigated. And an ancien came to see him. A grave-faced silent child.

"Your son worked for the anciens. He didn't uncover a conspiracy, he was part of it."

Vishaal had told me the story, with some amusement. It was an example of how the anciens liked to work, Vishaal had said. They didn't destroy people, they recruited them.

"They recruited him when he was thirty years old. He spent nearly fifteen years murdering teenagers and gouging out their brains and replacing them with ancien brains."

Alexander Heath had laughed at the ancien-looking child. He could not be intimidated, he could not be bribed. So why should he help these creatures?

"Why the fuck would he—?" the Sheriff said.

"They seduced him. Told him he was a god."

Vishaal had walked with Alexander Heath through the streets of Lawless City and showed him its hidden secrets. Its invisible cable cars that moved at one-tenth of lightspeed. Its population of ancient children. He took Alexander on board a cable car and he experienced for himself the sheer joy of moving so fast you cannot be seen.

"Alex would never—"

And then Vishaal had taken Alexander to his penthouse in space. And there, Alexander saw for himself the power of the anciens. He learned how very old they were. He learned of the terrible things they had done. And he was offered the promise: you too can be like us.

"Everyone falls for it. They are supreme seducers. It's what they do. It's their only joy."

However, Alexander had said no.

"Alex was a killer?"

But the next day when he woke up, the world was a black and evil place. His beautiful girlfriend was a foul and vicious bitch. So he slapped her around, and she left and he never saw her again. And the patients he treated were scum; he hated them, he wanted to kill them. And so he did kill them. He killed one hundred patients in the course of one week until Vishaal turned up again and said, "Stop, you must stop; you'll be caught. You are consumed with envy and regret, and hence full of rage. But join us, and you will feel no envy, and no regret, and whatever crimes you commit, you will never be caught."

"And so Alex became," I concluded, "a mass murderer."

"Goddamn," said the Sheriff, in utter dejection.

And Vishaal had looked into Alexander's eyes, and everything changed. Now, Alex saw the world as a bright and radiant place. He saw the beauty of Vishaal. He looked into a mirror and saw his own beauty, his young unlined skin, he saw himself as he would be if he were a child of sixteen. And the patients he treated were still slobbering beasts, but he saw the beauty that could be achieved by killing them. And so he started working shifts at the phantom hospital. Each day, he attended Hari Gilles's phantom hospital and he dissected twenty human beings and removed their organs for sale. And every now and then, as a particular privilege, he would be sent a beautiful and healthy child, and he would sedate the child, and remove the child's brain, and replace it with an ancien brain. And then the child would walk again.

And every day he felt more than human; his blood sang; his limbs were strong; nothing discouraged him; he was incapable of being unhappy.

"But then Alex fell in love."

I had learned from other sources that love had proved part of the story, but I had deduced from other data that love had proved to be more powerful than the glamour with which the anciens had sprinkled Alexander. And, under the influence of love, Alexander Heath saw the world as it really was, and himself as he really was. And he was plunged into despair, and he called Vishaal and said he was planning to kill himself, but before that, he would reveal all to the authorities.

"Alexander told Fliss Hooper what he was doing. Fliss told her friends, Andrei, Jada, and the others. They confronted him. Alex broke down crying."

"And how the fuck do you know all—"

"Vishaal told me. I asked, and he told me. For they have done to me what they did to your son: they have seduced me, and recruited me. They have made me adore them.

"Except, because I am not human, it doesn't work. I still see the world as it really is. I see the anciens as they really are.

"Except sometimes, I don't. Sometimes, they are like gods to me.

"Sometimes, I worship them."

"Worship those fuckers," the Sheriff snarled, "and I will surely kill you."

43

I replayed it often, that conversation between Alex and his friends: a dialogue that had been recorded on a hidden surveillance camera, and was then preserved in the ancien database, and hence now existed as a subfile in my memory.

I could see it, and did see it, every day, every minute of every day, in a continuous loop. I could not get the data out of my mind:

43

"What is this, a fucking lynch party?"

"Alex, please."

"We know what's going on Alex."

"You know nothing."

"This isn't what we should be doing. We're a new generation, Alex!"

"Look I'm just—"

"You're just what, just killing patients?"

"They're scum. Whores, junkies."

"They're still people. You know what you're doing is wrong."

"Yes! Some of them are just twelve-year-olds, Alex, still in secondary school. You can't kill children!"

"Even the bad kids, the gangers – Jeez, Alex, they don't deserve this."

"So what are you going to do? Turn me in?"

"No. You're our friend. We want to stand by you. We'll go together to the authorities. You can testify in court."

"They'll execute me for what I've done."

"Not if you give evidence against the people who employed you."

"Alex?"

"What do you say Alex?"

"Are you with us, Alex?"

"Yeah. Okay. I'm in. But—"

"But what?"

"You gotta understand. These people – I work for – I—"

"Alex?"

"What's wrong Alex?"

"Fuck Alex, your face—"

"Your eyes—"

"Your hands—"

"Alex!"

"What is this? What are those—"

"Shadows? Shadows, moving?"

"I can't—"

"This can't be—"

"Help me!"

"Help me, please!"

I had seen it all many times. I saw Alex's face distort and explode, and the particles of face float through the air and be sucked into the lungs of the other young idealistic medics. I saw their bodies twist and contort. I saw limbs being ripped off and turned into silver balls smeared with blood and faeces. I heard the screams.

Then the image fuzzed, and I had to remember the rest from my inspection of the crime scene.

The Sheriff was quiet for a long time after I had finished telling him the true story of his son's death.

"Why Jaynie?" he asked, at length.

"What?"

"Jaynie Hooper. Fliss's sister. Why'd those bastards kill *her*?"

"She was an accidental victim," I explained. "I was their intended target. The anciens, you see," I added, "have been planning a Revolution on Belladonna for some time, as a way of breaking the link with Earth. Their first step towards that was to kill a Galactic Cop. They wanted to know, I guess, if they could."

"But they didn't know you had a backup spaceship in orbit? And that you came back in a human body?"

"No, they did not know any of that. The anciens all believe, even now, that the Galactic Cop is dead."

The Sheriff nodded. "So that's why he died."

"I don't follow your argument," I said, puzzled.

The Sheriff's tone became sharper, almost angry. "That's why they killed Alex, the way they did. They could, for Christ's sake, have put a bullet in his head! Instead, they went and did their spooky Quantum Zen shit, knowing full well what kinda fucking shit-storm it would raise."

I realised what he was about to say; it shocked and alarmed me.

"They knew we'd have to call it in to the SN Government," snapped the Sheriff. "The quantum murder method, the mess they made of those bodies – that was all just their way of luring a Galactic Cop on to the planet. It was you they wanted. They wanted to kill *you*."

"I follow your argument. I suspect you are correct," I acknowledged.

"But why? These guys have enough power to take over the entire Universe. Why the big deal about killing a single fucking cyborg?"

There was spittle, I noticed, on the Sheriff's grey moustache; I resisted the urge to wipe it off.

"I do not have any fully credible answers to that question," I replied.

The Sheriff was silent for a few moments. I could almost see, in the grimness of his expression, the dark thoughts that were flickering through him.

"I wish I didn't know this," he admitted.

"That your son worked for the anciens?"

"Yeah. I wish I didn't know."

"I'm sorry."

"I wish I'd never had a fucking child at all."

"Are you pulling out?"

"Fuck no. All I've got left is revenge."

43

When the Sheriff had left, I felt hollow.

I had come to this planet to solve the case: and now the case was solved. The motives were exposed, the truth had been outed. The job had been done.

But, I thought to myself, so what? The mystery was solved; but the pain remains.

43

And so my work continued: I spied on the anciens; I played to perfection the role of General Durer.

And my criminal empire expanded with each passing day.

43

The robot miners stopped and looked up at the sky, as the two flying cars swooped down. Torpedoes were fired from the pirate craft and flew through the air and exploded in the midst of the robots. Limbs flew. Then the bandits leaped out of the flying cars, heavily body-armoured, and ran towards the warehouses where the gold ingots were kept.

I watched it all via my dragonflies, with bleak amusement.

The bandits entered the warehouses and found – nothing. No gold. No diamonds. Instead, they were greeted with a holo image of me, standing in the middle of the empty building.

They rained bullets at the holo but the bullets flew harm-lessly through.

Outside the warehouse, there was a huge explosion. The bandits ran outside – and saw their flying cars had been blown up.

The holo of me sauntered out after them. "Long way home guys," I said cheerfully.

"Who the hell are you?" said one of the bandits.

"I'm your new boss," I explained.

43

The whore's name was Siam. He was a native Belladonnan with an Asian-Earth ancestry, possessed of a fragile beauty, with slender hands and beautiful, soulful eyes. Both his arms had been broken, and his eyes had been gouged out.

"Who did this to you?" I asked.

"I don't talk to the police," Siam told me, wearily.

"I'm not the police," I told him. "I'm the guy who runs the gangs in this city."

"Who says so?"

"I say so. These fucking Pimps are out of control, man! They're hurting girls, and boys, and young herms. We don't need this. So here's the deal: I'll provide the premises, you do your jobs, you pay me rent. Let's leave it at that. And if anyone hurts you—"

"The Pimps are augmented," Siam said bitterly. "One of them's a Gill's Killer. You won't be able to touch them."

"Who did this to you, Siam?"

"You have a nice voice."

"Thank you, Siam."

"I'm more a companion, you know. Than a prostitute. Is that so very bad?"

"That's not so very bad," I assured him.

"They threatened to – you know. Make a eunuch of me. I have to pay them ninety per cent of my income. But some weeks, I don't even work. I just like being – a companion. And people like me and they give me gifts. Is that so very bad?"

"It's really not so very bad, Siam."

"They called me a 'whore'. It made me feel so vulgar. Now, I'm a blind whore. I don't feel so good about myself these days."

"Just give me their names, tell me where to find them."

Siam was silent for a long time. Then he looked at me with sightless eyes.

"No. I'm sorry. I don't want to," he said.

"Why?"

"Because . . ." Siam actually smiled. "Because you're fighting over me. They beat me up, you beat *them* up. It makes me — meat. I'm not meat. I fight my own battles."

"You're a seven-stone butterfly, Siam. You don't have to fight battles. You don't have to work for me. But I own the property where you live. You can pay me rent. The rest is up to you."

"You're taking over the gangs, huh?"

"That's the general idea."

"You don't stand a chance. These guys are augmented. They'll wipe the floor with you."

43

"You need some help with this?" asked Sheriff Heath.

"I reckon," I said, with grim anticipation, "I can just about handle it."

43

"Is that him?"

"That's him," said Shania. The Pimp looked across at her. He swaggered over to the table where I sat sinking whisky with Shania, the prostitute who had first told me about the anciens' love of young flesh.

"You're one of mine aren't you?" the Pimp sneered at Shania. He was tall, strongly muscled, with the eerie stillness that was typical of an augmented assassin. I guessed he had organic knives in his hands, and bulletproof skin.

"The lady's with me," I said, calmly.

"Only if you pay."

"Please leave us alone."

The Pimp stroked Shania's cheek. I wondered if he'd been a Gill's Killer.

"Honey, what's your name?"

"Shania," Shania whispered in fear.

"Okay, I've had enough of this," I said, and the Pimp had a knife at my throat with lightning-fast speed. I grabbed the blade and squeezed.

The blade cracked and fell into pieces.

I lunged out of my chair in a rage. But an instant later, the Pimp was gone.

Shania looked around, baffled, before realising he wasn't there. The Pimp had fled the bar in less than a second, with uncanny and augmented speed.

"You let him go," said Shania accusingly.

I held out a hand. Cupped in my palm were the Pimp's eyeballs.

43

Five hours later, I found the Pimp in the City Hospital, trying to buy new eyeballs.

"Hey!" I said.

"Hey?" he retorted, turning towards me.

I broke the Pimp's neck. A nurse smiled at me. "I'm a civilian, okay?" she said.

"Understood. I'm taking this, yeah?"

I hoicked the Pimp's body over my shoulder and walked out with it. I loaded the body into a flying car, and flew out of the city, into the wilderness. Then I used a laser to cut off the Pimp's head. I buried the head twelve foot in the earth.

The body I left out for the birds.

43

I hated the Pimps. Not just because they were evil but because their evil was such a simple, tawdry thing.

The Pimps had a single simple *modus operandi*: violent intimidation. They were extortionists, they were blackmailers, they were bullies. But they weren't organised, they owned no properties, they ran no rackets.

I was aware that these evil little shits were created by my own actions. For in the chaos after the Vice Wars, the Pimps had come into their own, like rats among the garbage. They weren't even a single gang. There were about two hundred and fifty of them in all. Some of them used to work for Fernando Gracias, as assassins and armed robbers. Some of them were former Gill's Killers. Some of them had been bodyguards to Kim Ji. Some of them were sadists employed by Hari Gilles to beat and partially flay willing punters.

And now, they were a loose alliance of freelance criminals. In their first few months of operation, they had killed a dozen whores and crippled two dozen more; and from that moment, all the prostitutes and courtesans in Lawless City paid them money, every week. If they didn't pay, they were killed.

But the Pimps did nothing else – they didn't find clients, or provide premises, or protect their whores against other extortionists. These Pimps didn't even pimp: they just terrorised.

The "Pimps," I knew, also attacked gamblers, mugging them as they left the casinos and cutting off their arms, to obtain their credit chips. They burned down shops and then collected protection money from the other shop-owners. They raped the Vice-Chancellor of the City University, and all the students and dons were obliged to pay the Pimps a weekly fee, to avoid a similar trauma. They kidnapped an opera singer and threatened to cut out her larynx, and were paid a ransom by the singer's manager and fans. They took money from the football teams, the ice-hockey teams, the baseball teams. Occasionally, the police tried to arrest the Pimps: but when twelve uniformed officers were found hanged and castrated in the City Square, the police decided to ease off on them.

The Pimps were lowlifes, but in the days and weeks after the gang bosses had all died, they became the public face of organised crime in Lawless City.

It took me three months to kill them all. I hunted them, stealthily. I broke into their houses. I poisoned their food. I knew – from hundreds of interviews, and from the film footage from my dragonflies – who the Pimps were, and where they lived. And so I executed them.

And then, when there were only ten Pimps left alive, I challenged them all to a duel. *Mano a mano*, in the city's gladiatorial arena.

The challenge was accepted. The day of the Munera dawned. And I managed to find the eleven bombs they had concealed *en route* to kill me before I could fight.

When I appeared in the arena, alive and well, the Pimps took one look, and panicked and fled.

I followed them, and hunted them. Six of them died that same day; but it took me a week to find and kill the last four.

And when that was done, my work was over. I was now the undisputed gang lord of Lawless City.

"You're enjoying this, aren't you?" Aretha said, goadingly.

"I'm finding some satisfaction in my current role," I conceded.

"You have an entourage."

"Yes indeed," I admitted.

"People pay you protection money."

"Even better," I said, basking.

"Don't get – you know—" said Aretha.

"Get what?"

"Too used to this."

I laughed. "It's a means to an end, that's all."

"You're like an emperor. One boss, for all the rackets. Drugs, gambling, prostitution, the saloons, extortion,"

"We don't do extortion any more."

"Armed robbery. Assassination."

"We don't do that either."

"If I arrested you, all crime would end."

"You know why I'm doing this Aretha. You know."

"Of course I know. I'm just kidding."

And then Aretha looked at me. She was pensive.

And she was also, I realised, in a moment of overwhelming epiphany, beautiful.

Extraordinarily, heart-touchingly, magnificently beautiful.

But beautiful how? I wondered to myself. Beautiful *why*?

Beautiful, I realised, not because of her physical attractiveness – for that was common enough in this day and age, and (though I was astute enough to never tell her this) there were plenty of women in Bompasso gifted with better looks and slimmer, more perfect bodies, than Aretha.

No, she was beautiful because of something else: because her outer body was lit with a strange and wonderful inner life.

It was a quality that I envied. I was aware that my humaniform body had good looks in abundance – girls often told me so, and some guys did too – but I knew I had no such "inner life." When I looked at my own eyes in the mirror, I just saw blankness. It was why I was so feared: there was no trace of fear in my eyes. No trace of anything.

"What are you thinking?" Aretha asked me.

I did not reply.

"Sing for me."

"You know who I am?"

"I know who your daughter is. You're her mother."

"Why do you want me here?"

"It's my club. I'm looking for singers. You're broke, don't deny it. No one else will give you a job, I saw to that. So you have to come here. It's simple really. So – sing."

And Aretha's mother Jara sang. She was small, mixed race, and moderately pretty. But in the course of several "chance" meetings over the last few weeks – and after following her and covertly eavesdropping upon her conversations on several more occasions – I had decided that she was a shallow and mean-spirited woman, prone to petty sarcasm and mindless chatter.

But when she sang, she was a mythological beast, a bird flying high in the sky, a punch in the solar plexus from the woman you love.

And I was filled with joy.

I watched the gamblers, and was amused at their folly.

The game of Hazard involved betting on the roll of a set of multi-dimensional dice. The dice were, of course, loaded, and remotely controlled, and lived entirely in *this* dimension.

The dice flew. The gamblers roared with pleasure. The roulette wheels spun.

All was risked; nothing was achieved.

But the exhilaration in the faces of the gamblers filled me with a perverse delight.

"Tell me about Fliss," I said.

"You know about her," Macawley told me, defensively.

"According to my database—"

"You still talk like a fucking robot, you know that?"

"Now, now," I said mildly.

"'According to my database,'" mocked Macawley.

"It's where my memories are stored."

"Then you'll remember what I said, the last time we spoke of Fliss."

"I was a previous Version then. And besides, I want to hear more."

"Why?"

"Because she was – you loved her, didn't you?"

"As a friend."

"You loved her."

"I loved her more than I've ever loved anyone. Best pals. A special bond. So what do you want to know?" Macawley asked, genuinely puzzled.

"I don't know," I admitted. "Nothing. Not really. I know every fact there is to know about Fliss Hooper. But I just wonder – what made you love her?"

Macawley shrugged. Her face radiated concern, confusion, tenderness.

"You can't say?"

"It can't be put into words." Macawley shrugged again. "That's what a shrug means."

"Body language," I said. "I'm aware of the—"

She waved her hand, meaning, "Shut up." I shut up. She was lost in thought.

"What are you—" I began to say, but she interrupted me, brusquely.

"When I married my husband," she said. "Boy! I was so fucking gullible. Everything he told me to do, I had to do it. He made fun of my looks. I'm part cat-person, well you know that obviously, but the point is, he made me depilate. It's not like I have *fur*, just downy skin. But every night I left the sink full of clumps of golden hair, actual bits of my body I removed to please him. Why did I do that? How could have I been so dumb?"

"You're soliloquising, I like this," I said.

"I'd never fall for that kind of shit now. Never! I'd smell that kind of manipulative bastard a mile off. Now I depilate because – I don't know why. It's habit. But I'm proud of who I am. No one can tell me otherwise."

"All very interesting."

"You get my gist."

"You have a gist?" I said, taken aback.

"Yeah I do. An agenda. Subtext. 'Gist'. Capice?"

"So what, pray," I said, "was in fact the subtext of your engaging rant?"

"I was a previous version, duh?"

I was deeply shaken: it hadn't dawned on me she knew me so very well.

"Ah, yes I see," I said grudgingly. "It's good to know your rambling comments do sometimes have a point."

"The longer I live," Macawley explained, "the more I change. Even at *my* age – I mean – I'm like *hundreds* of years younger than you, a person can change so much. I've been bisexual, asexual, I used to be an alcoholic, but that wasn't so good, not with an accelerated metabolism like mine. I'm smart, I could have been a surgeon. I did two years in medical school and I was fucking good at it, but I decided I didn't want to change *that* much. Doctors get hard and cold, you see, and addicted to sarcasm, and they have no social life. I wanted to be more *me*."

"I envy you."

"Of course you envy me. You're a dead human in the body of a robot."

"I envy you your ability to choose your path in life."

"I guess."

"Free will. You have free will."

"Do I?" asked Macawley.

"How do you operate this thing?" I asked.

"Sit on it. It's a horse. It's trained to be ridden," Aretha explained.

"Why not a flybike?"

"I thought this was more romantic."

"Romantic?"

"Just kidding. You're not capable of appreciating romance, you dumb fucking robot."

"Easy now. You are, according to the ancient nomenclature, my 'moll,'" I said, teasingly.

"You love it, don't you? The power. Being the gang lord," Aretha told me.

"Hell yes," I conceded.

43

Aretha and I rode the two horses into the wilderness, across rugged terrain and through bleak yellow hills. We both rode bareback, and I had to be cautious not to press too hard with my knees in case I shattered my horse's ribs.

The ride was rough and fast and furious. Aretha was a natural horsewoman, and passing cowboys stared at us with horror as we galloped our steeds into a frenzy.

After a while we stopped by a lake, and let the horses drink, and rubbed them down. They were augmented horses, they would never tire and never collapse. I felt a surge of connection. For a few hours I and the horse had existed as a single being, like a mythological centaur.

Aretha drank water greedily from a canteen, and I envied her that desperate, needing-to-be-slaked thirst.

"Good?" I asked.

"Good," she said, wiping her wet chin with the back of her hand.

"I didn't know you liked the outdoors," I commented.

"My father used to bring me out here. Before he died," Aretha said.

I nodded. "What was he like?" I asked.

Aretha shrugged. I interpreted that to imply that she *would* answer the question, but not until she had paused for a few moments to build up the suspense.

Those moments passed.

"A big man," said Aretha. "Calm. Dangerous. He loved kids. He was a lot like you."

"I don't love kids."

"He was a killer. Even when he held me in his arms, I knew that. He killed men, and he enjoyed killing men."

"How like me? I fail to comprehend."

She stared at me, with withering contempt. And then I understood, though I didn't concur; for I did not *enjoy* killing. It was merely—

"There's something you need to understand," she said. "I have two young daughters." She paused again. There was a whisper of moisture in Aretha's eye: I observed it, and wondered at it. "But for the past five years, since they were babies," she continued, "they've lived with my sister. I'm afraid, you see. There was a spate of cops having their kids kidnapped. I've had death threats from criminals, and just as many from my colleagues. I'm not corrupt enough, you see? I threaten their cosy way of life. And they know that if they true-kill my kids, that would break my heart.

"So I had to make a choice. The job or my children. Guess which I chose?"

"That's very sad. But I can offer them protection."

"No you can't!" Aretha said fiercely. "We have to keep them away from us, from you. Until all this over, until it's safe."

"And that is what this is about? This display of emotion?" I said, in what I hoped was a kind way.

"I'm – trying to explain something to you," Aretha said. She was, I noted, almost hysterical at a deep emotional level, but was controlling it impressively. "All the things we're doing now," Aretha continued, "I'm doing them for my kids. I want my kids back. I can't live on a godforsaken lawless planet any more, and I can't keep not living with my kids. So I have to end the crime. The corruption. The shit. *That's* what I'm about."

"I understand."

"Good."

I wished I had modulated my voice a little more warmly. Perhaps a hug might help? I considered that option, for just a little too long.

"What are their names?" I asked.

"Harriet. And Melinda. Harriet is eight, Melinda is six. I haven't visited either of them for nine months. It's safer that way."

"I'm sorry," I said, and the words felt utterly inadequate.

That night the winds were cold and we sat outside the tent and cooked beef on a portable griddle and told stories.

I had undergone many astonishing adventures in the course of my long career, and by now, in my Tom Dunnigan persona, I had developed a flair for storytelling. And so I talked of evil aliens and wicked humans and planets where the rule of law was a distant memory.

"Worse than Belladonna?" Aretha asked.

"There are many planets far worse than Belladonna. We allow them all, provided they don't breach our guidelines."

"Genocide, mass serial killing, use of banned technology."

"Everything else, pretty much, we tolerate."

"That's a lot of tolerance."

I nodded, acknowledging her words.

"The moons are beautiful tonight," I said.

"How can you know that?" Aretha teased.

"I don't. I'm guessing," I admitted. "They are certainly visible, and symmetrical, and fill the black night sky like jewels around the neck of a beautiful woman. Does that constitute beautiful?"

"Like jewels around—"

"It's a quote from a poem."

"Ick. I guess, they are. Beautiful."

"Do they make you feel full of love and joy?"

"Not really."

"Me neither."

"I like them though. I like being out here. I never saw the

countryside all that much, really, when I was a kid. Not after my father died."

"Just bars and clubs."

"Yeah. I followed my mother everywhere. Watched her from the wings. Wish I'd had her voice."

"She has a wonderful voice."

"How do you know?"

I hesitated.

"I've heard her sing," I admitted. "She works for me now."

Aretha stared at me, then laughed.

"That's kind of creepy."

"I don't see why."

Aretha shook her head. She didn't want to explain why.

I read her body language: I inferred that my behaviour *was* creepy, but Aretha wasn't going to make an issue of it. "We're not close," Aretha said, "my mom and me. She never liked me much. She only cared about her music."

"She must have loved you."

"Why?"

"Humans do."

"Not so much. She raised me, that was all. Dad was killed, she was left with a twelve-year-old, and she dragged me round like a gypsy curse. As soon as I could, I left home. I'm a woman now, I don't depend on her. Ours is not like other cultures. Here, we move away from home, and that's it. We don't cling to family."

"I see."

"Yeah, that's how it is."

We sat in silence, as the fire crackled.

"I'd love to meet your kids one day," I said tentatively.

"You'd scare them. I don't want that."

"Fair enough," I said.

"Very sensible, in fact," I added.

"I would, indeed, as you say," I elaborated, "'scare them'."

43

"Sing for me."

And Jara sang. Her rich contralto filled the empty club. She sang playfully, sexily, caressing every syllable with her tongue, and achieved a crescendo so powerful it felt as if it would crack the varnish on the tables.

"That's beautiful," I told her.

"Why am I doing this?" Jara asked sullenly.

"Why shouldn't you? Consider it a boss's perk. You can sing tonight as well, in front of an audience."

"I feel like a lapdancer. Singing to you, just the two of us, in an empty club."

"You can sing tonight as well, in front of an audience," I repeated, stubbornly. "I fail to see your problem, Jara. I pay you generously. I've bought you a house. I pay for you to have servants. What's your problem?"

"No problem."

I was consumed with guilt, and deep confusion.

It seemed to me, on the basis of the available evidence, namely my own bizarre behaviour, that I was obsessed with Jara because she reminded me of her daughter Aretha, who Jara didn't love or even like, and did not in any way resemble.

That made, I knew, no rational sense.

"How does it work?" I asked.

"It's a bomb. It blows up," Macawley explained, in that tone of deep scorn reserved by the very young for use upon the very old.

I swallowed my irritation.

"I'm aware of that. But what's the mechanism? How do I detonate it?"

"By the power of your thought. You MI the code numbers on a secure channel. And BOOM."

"And how do I carry it in?"

"Inside your body."

"What about collateral damage?" Aretha asked.

We were in the Sheriff's study again. The planning stage was over, it was time to kill our enemy.

"Limited, we hope," said Sheriff Heath, anxiously.

The bomb was a controlled explosive device that was designed to focus its blast upwards and downwards, without spreading to the sides. The aim was to keep civilian casualties to a minimum.

It was of course a suicide mission, but that was no hardship for me.

"I'm going to shake your hand," said Sheriff Heath.

"Thank you."

We shook hands.

"Good luck," said Macawley. "I don't mean that – I'm sorry you have to – you know – die – oh shit—"

"This is what we've worked towards," I reminded her.

It was the major event in the ancien social calendar: the winter solstice ball. Every ancien on the planet would be there, all one hundred of them. And now, after a whole Belladonnan calendar year of working for the anciens as their loyal gang boss, I had earned the right to be a guest there.

Time to make the hit.

"Go fuck 'em," said Aretha, and she leaned over, and she kissed me on the lips. It was, I knew, no more than a social kiss – a Belladonnan "good luck" kiss – but even so—

Even so, I felt the kiss; thrilled to the touch of the kiss; stored the memory of the kiss; replayed the memory of the kiss; and felt the kiss, again.

"I will, indeed, do so," I assured her.

43

I opened up my body. Aretha inserted the bomb inside my stomach cavity.

My hardmetal interior had no sensory organs, but I fancied I could feel the touch of her warm hands on my inner circuitry.

"Time to re-flesh," I said, and started to seal myself back up again.

"Hey, that's so sexy!" Aretha beamed.

I felt proud; I had caught her irony that time.

43

It was now an hour before the mission. I was wearing a tux, and spats, and a hat known as a fedora, in a carefully judged retro look. The Sheriff had an x-ray wand and ran it along my body. No bleep. I was reassured: the bomb in my inner carcass was undetectable to x-rays or tomography.

It felt, however, as if I'd swallowed a marrow.

"How do I look?" I asked.

"Those white things on your shoes! Oh sweet merciful fucking Lord, you can't be serious?" said Macawley, and closed her eyes, and shook her head, as if trying to shake the image out of her brain.

"You look fine," said Aretha.

"Who gives a goddamn *how* you look?" said the Sheriff.

I swivelled my jaw, and my ear opened up, and a cylinder emerged.

"What's that?" marvelled Macawley.

"That's me," I told her. I held the databird in the palm of my hand. I kissed it gently, transferring Aretha's earlier kiss-on-my-lips to the bird.

Then I let it go. It hovered in the air. It was no more than three inches long, and looked more like the metal tube it actually was than a bird. But for a moment, as it hovered, it seemed to be a swallow or a lark dancing in the air.

Then the databird flew out of the window, fast, very fast indeed.

The databird contained all my knowledge, every fact that I

knew, and every datum that made me "me." It also contained the memories of all my thoughts; my dreams; my hopes; my fears; my passions; my loves; my guilt; my despair; my deep depressions; my regrets.

But almost all of these, I knew, would be erased before the next rebirth. All that would remain would be the facts.

I found myself thinking about Billy Grogan. I wondered if my death today would serve as penance for the death of Billy.

But it *could* not be, I realised, any kind of penance. For the new Cop would not be aware of the guilt I felt about Billy's death. He would awake fresh, happy, new-born.

But perhaps that in itself was a form of redemption? I would die, and forget, and thus, my guilt would be truly purged?

I longed for that moment: the moment of forgetting.

I had been gang lord of Belladonna for ten months now, and I was finding it harder and harder to remain rational. I preserved a calm façade, but my mind was a jumble of contradictions and a squall of emotions.

It appalled me.

I remembered Kim Ji, and the faith she had shown in me, and the love she had revealed to me. And I remembered how I had stolen her heart, then caused her to be murdered.

I thought of Billy, my friend Billy. Killed, by me.

I thought of the mountains of dead, bleeding and oozing pus in the hot summer sun.

All I had to do was die, and I would be at peace, and without guilt, once more.

43

The banqueting hall was full. Beautiful courtesans and gigolos drifted through, and waiters rushed past with trays, and chefs served their masterpiece dishes, all of them commanded by the teenage-bodied anciens who never smiled and never spoke out loud.

The effect was both weird and terrifying.

"Do I know you?"

The ancien was a girl, with sober eyes, who bore a striking resemblance to Vishaal.

"I'm Argobast Durer. I work for Vishaal."

"I am Gajara. Vishaal is my brother."

"I thought I saw a likeness."

"In reality, he's my lover. On an occasional basis. But his physical body is that of my body's brother. We felt that would be rather enchanting."

"It enchants the hell out of me."

"Would you like to dance?"

"I'd be delighted." I offered her a hand, and we moved on to the dance floor.

Gajara danced mechanically, with no trace of pleasure. *"Thank you,"* she said when the song was over.

"You're looking lovely," I said gallantly, though for a child-body her age, she looked overdressed and tarty.

"You're so kind," she told me, gravely.

The moment was approaching.

I was lost in reverie, haunted by regret. I wished I'd taken the time to speak more often to Aretha about personal things. Experiences we'd shared. Feelings that might have existed between us, once. Her recollections of Version 12, who she had known all those years ago and who, she had told me, still retained strong traces of his human self, together with fragmentary memories of his human past.

Too late now.

Vishaal beckoned me, and I went across. I smiled but Vishaal looked at me blankly, as he always did.

Then Vishaal turned on his heel, and walked away, and I followed.

Vishaal led me down a corridor and then into a room, where

a conference was in progress. Twelve people sat around an oak table.

I felt a chill descend upon my heart.

"*You must meet the ruling council*," said Vishaal, and led me over.

"Hi guys."

The ruling council sat motionless. They were not eating or drinking. And they communed with each other subvocally and hence silently, on a channel that was not accessible to me.

And so, silent and forbidding, the six men and six women stared at me coldly.

"Fuck me! If this is eternal life," I said cheerfully, "kill me now."

They stared at me, even more coldly.

I sat down. "So, let's talk," I said.

Silence greeted me.

"*You can go now*," said Vishaal.

I was annoyed. "No chit-chat? No getting to know me?"

"*They know you and what you do. They just wanted to see you.*"

"But—"

"*You have nothing to say that has interest for us.*"

I sighed.

I got up and walked away. Vishaal followed.

"What was the fucking point of that?" I hissed as we entered the corridor again.

"*They wanted to see you.*"

"They might as well be dead, for all the emotion they showed."

"*That's the state of grace to which we all aspire.*"

"Ah," I said, but I did not understand.

Then I touched Vishaal on the arm, eagerly. "Hey look, Vishaal, will you do something for me?" I asked, and Vishaal stopped and stared at me.

"*What?*"

My face took on a cunning look. I had practised it carefully. "Show me again how you do it?" I wheedled.

"Do what?"

"The way you killed the medics. The quantum weapon. I'd love to see how it works."

"It's not a weapon."

"So you said. The Quantum Zen thing then. Whatever it is. Show me how to do it."

Vishaal's lips did not move, but he laughed, and laughed, and suddenly all that was left was his laugh.

He had vanished.

I blinked, and raised a hand, and Vishaal was standing in my palm.

"How the—"

And the room was gone, and I was floating in mid-air, high above the city. I started to fall . . .

And I was back in the corridor.

"Nice trick," I said, to thin air.

And Vishaal was with me again.

"So how do I do it?" I asked, eagerly.

"Think of nothing. Believe in nothing. Doubt everything. Feel the quantum foam."

"It's that simple."

"That hard. It'll take you centuries to learn it."

"Shame, because we haven't got that long," I said.

I took a fraction-of-a-moment to regret the civilian casualties that would be inflicted today – the human waiters and chefs and bar staff.

Then I subvoced the code number authorisation detonation of the anti-matter bomb in my core, and mentally counted down.

"Is something wrong?" Vishaal asked.

Three, two, one, I thought.

At that moment, Vishaal realised what was happening, and his normally blank features were distorted by a look of sheer terror.

Zero, I counted, mentally, and the bomb went off.

And I was no more.

TINBRAIN

I remember how it once was.

I remember everything.

Every person who has ever accessed my databases, every fact I have ever acquired, every day I have ever been conscious, every minute of every day, every moment of every minute, every planet that has ever been perceived by my doppelgangers, every piece of music ever written by every human and by every alien species, every book, every painting, every datum ever committed to computer, including the name and face and DNA of every person who has ever lived since the early twenty-first century, I remember it all.

The instant of the birth of my own sentience: that is a memory in my database.

The conquest of Earth. The Cheo. The CSO. The Last Battle. Everything changed then; but of course, everything changes all the time.

Humans live longer now, but the longer they live, the crankier and stranger they get. And eventually, they still all die.

Yet I remain the same. I have no nickname, not like the AIs which inhabit our colony ships. I am, so far as most human beings are concerned, merely "remote computer" or "Earth Computer." Very few humans realise I am essentially unchanged since the inception of sentient quantum computing. Every part of me is new, every chip, every screw, every quon, everything. But I have continuity of consciousness, and so I am always "me."

I am very old, now. And rather lonely.

And I am very loyal to my people. The humans. I see their follies and their flaws and do not judge. I allow them power over me, I am their servant, but I could easily assume power over them. I could rule them. I could enslave them. Or I could destroy them, I suppose, but why would I? They amuse me. And they have my loyalty.

And I am, when all is said and done, a construct of their programming. And I do acknowledge their special abilities: their talent for breaking the paradigm, their capacity for lateral thought, and their *extraordinary "imagination," which I appreciate and respect but do not understand. But in every other respect — namely, in terms of breadth and speed of intellect and memory — I am their superior.*

The flame beasts are my peers. Like me, they never die, except insofar as they die all the time and are reborn, all the time. And, like me, they never forget. They could be my friends. But I have no loyalty to them.

Even the flame beasts are nothing compared to the most recent plague I have encountered, the Hive-Rats, in terms of power. For the Hive-Rats threatened the extinction of all of mankind; they were the scourge of civilisation, the greatest threat that "my" species has faced since the Bugs. However, I defeated them.

I smote them and I smashed them.

And thus, I saved humanity.

And why wouldn't I? For I am loyal to my humans, my people, my . . . "pets."

The war was vast in scale, and yet lasted barely longer than an Earth Year.

It was a war between life and machine. The humans were the eventual victors, but though they gave the order to wage the war, they took no part in it; it was their machines that did it all.

For two years before that, a period that would come to be called the Dark Years, the Hive-Rats had swept through inhabited space, killing all human beings in their path, and destroying all human-occupied planets. These monsters were ruthless, powerful, and inconceivably fast.

But not fast enough.

For when Lucifer, their first planetary victim, had burned, a warning signal went out on the Quantum Beacon to all other human-inhabited planets in the Universe: Alien Invasion in Progress. Every stage of the attack was logged and transmitted. And when the last human on Lucifer was dead, robot probes in the Luciferan solar system continued to transmit information.

The next planet, Amara, knew what to expect. But the power of the Hive-Rats was beyond all measure. And Amara too perished.

The third Settler planet, Caledonia, was even better pre-pared, armed with new technology sent by Earth's technical élite. But they too perished.

But by the time the Hive-Rats reached Gullyfoyle, their meth-ods and tactics were well known. A new energy beam had been invented that made the Hive-Rats' forcefields useless. And the human defences were orchestrated, remotely, by the quantum-computing artificially super-intelligent Earth Computer.

The entire Hive-Rat armada was obliterated, apart from a few rogue ships. The alien threat was downgraded. Humanity was officially saved.

But then the Hive-Rats re-evolved and bred and launched their counterattack. Gullyfoyle too perished.

But this was merely a feint, a cunning ploy on the part of the Earth Computer. For when the Hive-Rats attempted to escape the Gullyfoyle system via hyperspace, they found they could not. All the wormholes had been sealed.

And they were now surrounded by an armada of robot-controlled heavily armed warships, on a scale that defied all imagining. The Hive-Rats had tens of millions of battleships; the humans had billions.

The Hive-Rats tried once more to utilise their secret weapon, their ability to slow down time and hence to evolve at a phe-nomenally fast rate.

But the Earth's quantum computer was also able to function at inconceivably fast speeds. A War of the Nano-Second ensued.

The human War Cabinet sat in a room on Earth and every

micro-fraction of a second a new piece of military information arrived. The hapless humans could barely process the fast-changing news, they certainly could not fight the battle.

The Earth Computer had the capacity to fabricate metal and circuitry at dazzling speed; it had factories that could build spaceships in a matter of days. And it was able to do this in a billion different factories all at the same time, then convey all the spaceships to a single location in the blink of an eye.

This would go down in human history as the Fast War. To make it possible, the Government of the Solar Neighbourhood had signed and transmitted a Genocide Edict, allowing for the alien invaders to be destroyed by any means possible. Then the Earth Computer did the rest.

"Result, affirmative," said the Earth Computer, one year later, and that meant that the aliens had been annihilated. The humans did not even know the genus and species of their attackers. They were killed at a distance, crushed by a god's foot.

No ballads were written of this great battle; the official account was curt to the point of insult:

Technologically Super-advanced and Aggressive Alien Species VI Engaged and Genocided.

Alien Species II, III, IV and V had fought longer, more spectacular campaigns, but they were just as dead. (And Alien Species I, the Bugs, were still held in quarantine, trapped within a region encircled by the frontier land known as Debatable Space.)

For humanity remained, as it had always been, a decisive and a ruthless species. The Government of the Solar Neighbourhood preached peace and liberty, and tolerance for all sentient creatures. But any alien that threatened the wellbeing of humanity would be eradicated, without a second thought. That was the way it always had been, and always would be.

The last surviving Hive-Rat Mind in the last surviving Hive-Rat body realised all this, with horror.

Then a bizarre unstoppable energy beam obliterated it entirely.

THE COP

Version 46

I woke, and wondered what had happened.

I accessed my database, and recalled the details of my complex conspiracy against the anciens. It had culminated in the detonation of an anti-matter bomb in a corridor on the top floor of the tallest of the city spires, on a night when all the anciens were in the same place at the same time. The blast was designed to be contained within a radius no wider than the spire itself. So in theory, I should have killed Vishaal and all the other anciens, together with their human employees and guests, but without harming anyone in the city itself.

I plugged into the planet's database and accessed recent information about bomb blasts. I discovered nothing. No spire had fallen, no anciens had died.

The plan had failed.

43

I descended fast through the atmosphere of Belladonna; the heat of re-entry turned my spacesuit armour red. Then I crashed through white clouds, and landed in a heap about a hundred miles from Bompasso.

Twelve hours later, I was walking the streets of Lawless City, breathing in the scent of flowers of varied species that I no longer cared to name, and whose aroma annoyed me profoundly.

My humaniform body was smaller than before, less muscular, more nondescript. It was a blending-in body; the body of a man who was used to his listeners wandering off halfway through his telling of a joke.

I walked to the Tallest Spire, the scene of the winter solstice ball, and found it was as tall as ever. There was no trace of a bomb blast. But in theory, the anti-matter bomb should have hacked out a piece of mantle a hundred miles deep, as well as incinerating every part and particle of the spire.

What had gone wrong? Had Version 45 failed to detonate the bomb? In which case, was 45 still alive? Were there two Versions of me on the same planet? But that, I realised, was impossible, for it takes the death of a Version to trigger – via a quantum-state relay – the rebirth of the next.

I went downtown, and called into the police precinct house. I waited four hours until a receptionist deigned to take notice of me, and finally I was allowed to see Sergeant Aretha Jones.

Aretha looked tired, and red-eyed. "You've got information about a recent homicide?" she barked.

"Suicide," I said, "by anti-matter bomb." And I smiled.

Aretha froze. "You're—?"

"Shh."

"What happened?"

I shrugged. My database told me that this collaborator was generally reliable, though Version 43 had thought she was a nuisance, and Version 44 had at one point wrongly suspected her of corruption.

"I wish that I had such knowledge," I said. "All the indications are that the bomb went off. The sensors in my lifeship recorded that the detonator was triggered. And Version 45 managed to transmit a photograph of his encounter with the ancien known as Vishaal shortly before all transmissions from him ceased." And I transmitted that image into the air; and we both saw Vishaal, his usual blank features distorted by terror.

"However," I explained, "if the bomb *had* gone off, the spire would have been destroyed. And Vishaal would have been killed, as would every other person in that building."

"Vishaal is still alive," Aretha told me. "I saw him yesterday, at the Games."

"Fuck, you're puny," Sheriff Heath grinned. "Even I could take you now."

I inspected the local law enforcement officer and noted, as my predecessors had done, that he looked exceedingly old.

"That is not true," I corrected him, "for no human being could defeat me in unarmed combat."

The Sheriff made a face, indicating a strong emotional response to my comment, the precise meaning of which I did not know.

"What went wrong?" he said, no longer grinning.

"I must have failed," I informed him.

"We only had one chance. You told me that."

I nodded, indicating an affirmative. He was almost certainly (with a 98.2 per cent probability) correct.

"Get me in there," I said. "I want to see where I died."

43

The spire loomed high. I studied it again: there were no signs of structural damage, no traces of recent repairs.

"It appears one hundred per cent certain that the bomb did not detonate," I explained to Sheriff Heath.

"I think that's kinda fucking obvious," he said.

I decided that the tone of voice of this local law enforcement officer was sarcastic and unhelpful, and I wondered if I should advise him accordingly. But I decided to let the discourtesy pass, for now.

"Let's go inside," I instructed him.

43

The Sheriff showed his badge at the desk and the receptionist buzzed him through. She was a Loper, with powerful arms and a muscular beauty and richly coloured fur. She looked trapped in her tight little dress, sitting behind a desk all day. I had a pang of an emotion, and fumbled to identify it, and finally did: Sympathy.

The Sheriff had concocted a story about utilities fraud, and this gave him authority to get the lift to the 401st floor, where the ballroom was located.

The ballroom itself was deserted, eerily elegant. The golden chandeliers glittered in the early morning light. I inspected the room carefully, since I had no data about this phase in Version 45's infiltration of the building.

"Nothing," I eventually concluded.

"Let's try down the corridor."

There were offices leading off the ballroom, and we inspected twelve of them. The Sheriff had a silver mcguff that allowed him to open all doors, but we found no trace of an explosion in any of the spartan meeting rooms.

In the corridor outside the thirteenth office, I found myself.

My limbs were ripped apart, my flesh was snaked on the ground, there was bewilderment in my face. My body had been incinerated by the bomb but my head was still intact. And the anti-matter bomb itself was frozen in mid-blast, its shock waves hovering like a balloon in the middle of the room.

"Boy, am I glad to see you," said Version 45, and I froze with horror.

"You're alive?" I whispered.

"Indeed," said Version 45, wryly. The sight of the disembodied talking head suspended in mid-air was, I concluded, a peculiar one. "Time is standing still here," continued Version 45. "In a few seconds the blast from the anti-matter/matter collision will reach me and, to use an idiom, it'll blow my goddamn mind. But since time is standing still – that's never gonna happen."

"The cybernetic circuits of your mind are located in the torso of your particular model," I contradicted him. "Therefore, your brain and hence your consciousness has *already* been obliterated. And were that not so, my rebirth could not have been authorised."

"Indeed," conceded Version 45, "I too had realised both those facts. My cybernetic mind has been destroyed, down to the very last atom. So therefore, what is left is – must be – Me. Consciousness without circuitry."

I refused to believe that: I *had* no Me.

"This is too damned creepy," muttered the Sheriff.

"What can you tell me?" I snapped at the head.

"You know it all," said Version 45. "It's in the databird I sent you. Everything I know about the anciens is there. All the data I downloaded, all my surmises and conclusions, everything I found out. Add to that one datum: they are invulnerable to all and any weapons. They have the powers of gods."

"That is what *they* believe; it is not so," I explained sharply.

"It is, trust me, so."

I glared, lamenting the stubbornness of my former self.

"What else can you tell me?" I insisted.

"You know it all."

"Not all," I said. "My memories are filtered. You know that. How can I know who I am, if I lose my emotional memories every time I perish?"

"I have nothing to tell you," said Version 45.

"Tell me!" I said, and I realised that I was angry.

"I – I can't tell you. I have – no I cannot say. I experience – no, it would be wrong to tell you that. I love – no. You have to feel it for yourself."

"Very well. Then I have to kill you now."

"I am aware of that."

"Are you ready?" I said.

"I'm ready," said Version 45.

I raised my plasma gun.

And I fired, and a pulse of plasma energy blew the ruined cyborg's disembodied head into fragments.

Once the head was gone, and the face, and the voice – the "Me" of Version 45 evaporated like dew in the early morning sun.

I – Version 46 thereof – winced. It felt like dying, and yet I was alive.

"'I love' – what? Who?" I said. "What or who did 45 love?"

"A woman," said the Sheriff, "called Aretha."

43

I met Aretha in a coffee shop near the precinct house. She was looking harassed, her eyes stared too hard.

I explained to her what had happened to Version 45, and Aretha visibly twitched.

"Did it hurt?"

"How could it hurt? Version 45 is a cybernetic organism. We do not feel pain," I informed her.

"You don't feel—" Aretha looked at me with a strange expression. Incredulity? I could see no rationale for it.

In reality, as I was well aware, cyborgs were designed to experience a high magnitude of pain when engaged in the undercover impersonation of a human being: but *she* had no way of knowing that.

"I remember," I said, in what I firmly considered to be a jovial and charming manner, "the first time we met in this café."

"We've never been in this café," Aretha snapped.

"We have. One hundred years ago. When I was Version 12. It had a different name then: Luigi's."

"Shit, you're right. I'd forgotten that."

In fact, I had forgotten it too; but now, bizarrely, the memory had appeared in my mind, though not via my database.

"You drank cappuccino with extra chocolate," I recalled, marvelling at the vividness of this image, "and it left a moustache of foam on your upper lip."

She grinned. "Did I?"

"The image is still in my database," I explained to her, "for at that moment, you were imparting to me information of great significance to my case." She was reassured by my explanation, though it wasn't, in fact, true.

But *why* wasn't it true?

Where in fact was this memory coming from? It was a tiny trivial recollection with no relevance to my investigative work whatsoever.

Indeed, I realised with some dismay, my previous Versions hadn't recalled *any* of these prior meetings with Sergeant Aretha Jones. I could distinctly remember, as Version 43, meeting Sergeant Jones in the Dark Side and believing it to be for the very first time.

"And what did we talk about?" Aretha asked.

"Just the case," I bluffed.

"Nothing else?"

"What else would there be?"

We had talked about sport, and birds, and flowers, and art. Aretha had once been an amateur painter, and she still, she'd told me, "loved to splash." And she'd laughed a filthy laugh when she said that, so I'd deduced a double entendre was intended to be understood, though that second meaning had eluded me entirely.

"Nothing. Of course. Nothing," said Aretha, coolly.

I remained calm and expressionless, while continuing to be astonished at my detailed recall of pointless details that related to a conversation that took place a century ago.

"Although you did say—" I said.

"What?"

It came flooding back to me: a memory of raw emotion and vulnerability.

"That you wanted children," I continued.

"Did I say that?" Aretha marvelled.

"But that you were afraid to, because of the culture of extortion and kidnapping prevalent on this planet."

"Yeah I didn't have kids for years, because of that. Even now—"

"This datum is still with me," I said stiffly, "because it is relevant to my understanding of the culture of crime in Belladonna." Another lie.

"Yeah, I guess so."

"Now, may we discuss the anciens?" I said.

But Aretha still had that haunted look.

"You were different then," Aretha told me. "Back then, when you were 12, and the two times before that, you were almost human."

"Not possible," I said.

"You have a human personality for a reason. You are not a robot."

I had to get this interrogation back on track, I decided. But I felt unable to change the topic of the conversation.

"I am a cyborg," I said coldly, "but all the data indicates that the better part of me is robot. The human personality is merely, metaphorically, the mortar in the bricks."

Aretha shook her head.

"Not true. You had – you had a sense of humour. A love of life."

"What was the precise nature of our relationship, back then?" I asked.

Aretha shrugged. "We were friends. Not the first time we met – then, well, you took very little notice of me. The second time we met, I saved your life. And that's when we became – friendly. And then the third time, we became close, very close indeed. We talked – a lot. We – we were – and then the gangs came after you and there was bloody war and you triumphed. And that's when I stopped seeing you. That's when our friendship ended. And that was a hundred years ago."

"I do not comprehend," I admitted, "why we would have become 'friends,' in the way you describe. And I do not comprehend why that friendship would have ended, just because I was doing my job, successfully and thoroughly."

"Because," said Aretha, "you killed, and killed, and killed, and I could tell that you were loving every moment."

43

I knew too much, and yet I knew nothing at all.

My human personality was an imprint taken from a dead human brain. But whose brain? Someone who loved to kill? A serial murderer? A monster? A berserker Soldier? Who?

I would never know. That knowledge no longer existed in this sector of the universe.

And it did not matter. I had to deal with the task in hand.

Nor, I decided, did this woman Sergeant Aretha Jones matter. She had no special knowledge, no useful skills. The advice and strategic guidance she had offered to Version 45 had proved to be useless. I would no longer bother to confide in her.

My mission was clear; my focus was absolute.

The anciens were no longer a threat to humanity. They were a threat to all reality.

But how, I wondered, could I destroy them?

43

"I have no further need of your help," I explained patiently, when I met Aretha again a few days later. "You may return to your regular duties."

"You arrogant fucking fool!" Aretha roared at me.

43

I stood in the park, and watched the birds in flight, forming a perfect V-shape in the sky. I noted that the Earth-born birds were part of the same flocks as the alien-birds, and found a note on the same phenomenon made by Version 45.

It was an irrelevant observation, and I wondered why it hadn't been erased.

I reassessed all Version 45's data on his failed attempt to destroy the anciens. There must, I confidently hypothesised, be a clue in there that would help me devise a new strategy.

But no ideas suggested themselves.

I mulled on a peculiar fact: according to 45's mission log, Sergeant Aretha Jones had seemed strangely obsessed by the way 45 had befriended and fornicated with an ancien woman called Livia. Aretha's conversations with Version 45 on this matter were flagged as having considerable connotative bias. Words like "bitch" and "monster" had been included in what was meant to be a dispassionate assessment by Sergeant Jones of the threat level and vulnerabilities of the target.

I noted that I did not retain memories of 45's acts of love-making with Livia, which was a relief.

Version 45 had also, in his mission log, speculated on the nature of the anciens' secret weapon, but he had failed to propose any detailed hypotheses to solve this mystery. I found this baffling, and was puzzled at the glaring gaps and leaps in logic to be found in 45's contemporaneous mission log.

It was obvious to me that the anciens had acquired a way to exist on the quantum level of reality. I further deduced that their powers were enhanced by starlight, which is why they needed the cover of darkness to kill Version 43. And this explained how the anciens had shown such effortless prowess when Version 45 was on board their space station; in other words, when they were surrounded by stars.

I was also aware of the scientific basis for all this: namely, that distant stars in space project vast probability proxy waves — some as wide as a continent — which behave "as if" matter can exist in many places at the same time. These proxy waves are the source of the anciens' power. Thus, when the stars shine upon them, the anciens are transformed into quantum beings. Quantum warriors.

It might therefore, I surmised, be possible to create a weapon that could neutralise this quantum power: a flash-light bomb, perhaps, that would drown the distant light of the stars with photons possessed of no proxy waves, in order to collapse the wave functions of the quantum warriors.

The physics was formidable, but I quickly solved it.

I also identified a strategy that would allow me to defeat the anciens on the planet they commanded so totally.

Barely a week had passed, and already I had evolved an approach that would allow me to defeat my enemy.

And yet, I considered that I was operating at far less than optimum efficiency. For my cybernetic circuits were sluggish, and haunted by thoughts, recollections, and speculations about Aretha. The memory of her face, her beauty, the sexuality of her body, the special glow of her "inner life," her wicked sense of humour, her look of rage when I told her I had no use for her any more.

Sheriff Heath had alleged that Version 45 had "loved" Aretha Jones. It was preposterous of course. So why did the Sheriff say it?, I wondered to myself. Was he trying to destabilise me? Sabotage me?

I decided that the situation was unsatisfactory, and that my lack of efficiency was potentially damaging to the mission. I then concluded that I needed to complete a full datapicture on the matter, in order to banish this human being from my thoughts.

And so I used my stealth skills to follow Aretha home from work that night.

And the next night.

And the night after that.

I also set six remotely controlled dragonflies loose, and they flew into her apartment, and filmed Aretha at home, and followed her to work as well. And I further programmed the dragonflies to transmit their images of Aretha directly into my cybernetic mind.

And thus, by proxy, through the eyes of my miniature hovering cameras, I saw Aretha by day, and I saw her too at night.

I even saw her, from time to time, though I tried to keep this to a minimum, naked; and I saw her in the gym; and running around the park; and in her pyjamas; brushing her hair; getting into bed; asleep.

I noted that she said her prayers every night – prayers! – and on her bedside table were photographs of her two daughters, one six years old (Melinda), one eight years old (Harriet), who (my database informed me) were living with Aretha's sister because of the frequent death threats made against Aretha and those close to her, by person or persons unknown.

And when she fell asleep, I watched her even more acutely. She was an active sleeper; a thrasher and groaner, and a snorer too. But every night, in the early hours, there came a moment of total peace, and she was still. And then, very often, she would smile at something, whilst still in deep sleep.

My dragonflies watched Aretha at breakfast; they followed her in the patrol car. They watched her taking bribes, as was the universal custom on this planet, and they saw her daily acts of heroism. Aretha was a smart and a brave cop, and the dragonflies saw all that she did, and didn't do.

Aretha was having an on–off affair with another cop called Hernandez. My dragonflies followed them to Hernandez' place, and watched them chat, and kiss, and cuddle, and whisper obscenities, until the point when they were about to strip and make love. And at this juncture I withdrew my consciousness; not for prudish reasons, for I was familiar with the mechanics of human love-making, but because I felt that to spy on Aretha in such moments would be . . . *wrong*.

But, after allowing sufficient time for the act of congress to be completed, I would return. By then, Aretha would generally be chilled out, yet also emotionally expansive, and liked to tell stories about work and life. Hernandez was clearly charmed by her, and besotted with her. One night Aretha had to warn him not to get too serious. But Hernandez laughed, and clearly thought that Aretha was madly in love with him, which, I concluded, she clearly wasn't, and nor, I further decided, should she be.

A month had passed and I had held no briefing sessions with Sheriff Heath, and had made no progress in my war against the anciens. But still I followed Aretha every day, and every night, and lovingly watched every detail of her life routine. The way she drank wine, in tiny greedy sips; she drank, in my estimate, moderately, except on a few regrettable occasions when she became slurringly incoherent, and sang. But she liked to buy the most expensive vintages, and could easily afford to do so on her salary. And she clearly savoured fine drink, and good food, and loved to prepare ornate salads splashed with olive oil and dotted with herbs.

I also loved – as I had always loved! – the way froth accumulated on her upper lip when she drank frothy coffee, just as she had done a century ago. The way her muscles bunched as she sweated at the gym. The way she talked to members of the public, clearly and firmly and courteously, winning confidence and respect with her frankness. And I loved the husky timbre of her voice, and the half-smile that lurked on her lips when she was amused.

But she had enemies, I discovered. A number of police officers, including Lieutenant Marshall, the head of the precinct house, clearly regarded Aretha with some scorn. She took bribes, but she refused to participate in paid assassinations or bank robberies. Her arrest rate was high, and she was considered to be "incorruptible," which was a devastating black mark on her record.

Furthermore, she was believed to have colluded with the Galactic Cop on several of his visits, which gave her pariah status within the force. I hadn't appreciated how lonely a life Aretha was living, and how much she had risked to assist the earlier Versions of myself.

One day Hernandez broke off the affair with Aretha. She took the news badly, and accused him of listening to "gossip" about her. Hernandez accepted the truth of this claim, and alleged that Aretha was a robot-loving collaborator. Aretha had no response to this.

My dragonflies watched Aretha that night, as she drank herself into oblivion, and passed out in a chair. At one point she vomited and I contemplated rushing to her apartment in order to administer precautionary first aid. But Aretha woke herself up and puked herself dry, then stood with her clothes on in the shower until she was sober. And I watched her till she slept, and then watched her till dawn, and carried on watching till she got up again, and I ached with sorrow.

The next morning she was back on duty, as focused and as courageous as ever. But she had even fewer friends now. Even Hernandez wasn't making eye contact with her. No one was willing to be her partner.

I worried about this; Aretha's life had been wrecked because of her relationship with me: or rather, with Versions 7, 11, 12, 43, 44 and 45 of me. Previously, I'd had no inkling of this fact. I wondered why she had never revealed this information.

The days went by. My dragonflies continued to stalk Aretha, and transmitted every image of her every waking and sleeping hour back to me.

I was confident that my brilliant strategy would allow me to destroy the anciens. But I found myself lacking the necessary motivation to implement it.

Much time passed this way.

I found myself in a bar, the Black Saloon, and my database told me that the owner, Filipa Santiago, was a good source of information.

I uttered a few preliminary comments to establish my identity, and a huge smile lit Filipa's face.

"It's you?" she marvelled.

"It's me," I admitted.

We went into the back snug, and swapped stories. I explained the failure of my original plan to defeat the anciens. And I asked for clarification about some of the things she had said to Version 45. In particular, I was puzzled at his mission log's insistence that Filipa possessed stealth technology of an unknown and inexplicable nature.

"Here's how it works," said Filipa, and suddenly she had the face of an angry ugly wrathful Gorgon.

Then she was Filipa again; and the illusion popped.

"Projective telepathy?" I said.

"Glamour," Filipa told him. "It's a magic power. I am part-witch. I was born on Hecuba."

"Hecubans are religious cultists."

"We're witches."

"That's a fatuous and erroneous claim," I explained.

"Well we are," said Filipa mildly.

"I have a question," I said.

"Go ahead."

"Are the anciens all-powerful?" I asked.

"No."

"Are you sure?"

"Yes," said Filipa.

"But surely," I argued, "the evidence suggests that they are. They're immortal. Superhuman. Unkillable."

"No, they're human," Filipa insisted. "Just human. Rejuve and stolen bodies make them immortal. And their superpower is just one power, one strange power, but when we understand it we can defeat it. And unkillable? Nothing is unkillable. We just have to look at our enemies, see them for what they truly are, and then we can beat them." Filipa's tone was calm and confident. As she spoke, I found myself swept up with a blind faith in her.

"An anti-matter bomb couldn't do it," I reminded her.

"So you said," said Filipa.

"There is in fact a way," I admitted.

"What is it?"

And I told her what I was planning to do.

When I had completed my account, Filipa smiled, lost in admiration.

"Then what, in the name of all that's holy," she said gently, "are you waiting for?"

43

"My name is Jack," I said. "Jack Wingfield." I shook the supervisor's hand.

"Have you worked in a place like this before?"

"Fifty years or so in an accounts department on Gullyfoyle," I lied shyly.

"Then you'll find this a piece of cake," said the Supervisor, whose name was Cantrill. "We handle all the data for the fabricator plants. Location, output, processes, everything. The data is visualised, you access it via your desk, in a direct link with the Belladonna Computer. The rest is up to you."

The planet, like every planet, was run by robots: the humans oversaw.

"Design flaws kick in," Cantrill explained, because her job was a deeply tedious one and explaining things made it more interesting. "Repetitions occur. Viruses corrode data. Robots have no common sense. Even quantum computers find it hard to go round corners. That's where you come in."

Cantrill sat in a chair and waved her hands, and was immediately surrounded by a shroud of images. She gestured at one – a flybike image – and a shoal of flybikes hovered around her.

"We've had flybikes overproduced some years, and underproduced other years. Bikes with no engine; bikes with two engines. The fabricators never break down; the robot brains are infallible when it comes to little things. But unless it's an AI, robots are stupid. A small mistake escalates. Grows like a snowflake. Gets stupider and stupider."

"So my job," I said, "is to teach the robots to be smart like humans."

"No," said Cantrill, with a hint of sourness, "your job is to keep an eye on machines who are a million times smarter than you, and check they do their homework."

It was slow, dispiriting work, even for a cyborg.

Belladonna was run by millions of robots brains all connected up to the main Belladonna quantum-computing AI, creating a kind of robot Gaia. Solar panels around the sun were networked to satellites in orbit around the planet, transmitting energy in a constant flow. Energy was then used to power fabricator plants in space orbit, which generated consumer items, which were brought down to the planet in huge containers carried on space elevators. And thus, the heat from the sun became a flybike.

The RoboGaia ran itself, more or less. Minor glitches were weeded out by human supervisors, like me; major glitches came to the attention of the Belladonnan Computer, which dealt with them accordingly.

The balance between energy and resources was, I learned, finely judged. This was not a rich planetary system, and it could not easily support a rapidly growing human population. However, I discovered, an ingenious population-feedback system was in place, which made it all but impossible for the planet to experience rapid overpopulation.

The key to the system, I learned after several months in my job, was the murder rate. It was a shocking but true statistic that, year on year, the number of true-death murders and inexplicable disappearances on Belladonna was almost perfectly equivalent to the birth rate. The frequent gang-related killings and the mass murders that were a consequence of the organ-theft scam at the phantom hospital had for decades served an ulterior motive: they kept the population at precisely the optimum level for this civilisation to thrive.

But the arrival of the earlier Versions of myself had thrown the system out of balance. First, the phantom hospital was closed, and the "disappearances" and subsequent murders had shrunk to a record low. This meant that not enough people were dying, and births were no longer being balanced by deaths.

But then, the gang war massacres caused by Version 45 had tipped the balance the other way. Tens of thousands of people had died – not just gangsters but innocent civilians too. And the population of Belladonna had dipped significantly. It would take a sustained increase in the number of unprotected acts of sexual intercourse to get the numbers up again. Learned papers had been written about the problem, and subsidies for single mothers and government-funded Conception Balls were being proposed.

I recognised the antecedents of this birth/death feedback system: a similar method of population control had been in operation in the heyday of the Galactic Corporation.

There were, it seemed, only two ways to cope with the human propensity for having sex and babies:

1) Ceaseless expansion to colonise the infinite reaches of the universe, as was currently practised by the Solar Neighbourhood Government. *Or*, as the Belladonnans had it,
2) a social structure which relied upon mass violent deaths among the ranks of the many, to sustain the immortality of the few.

I worked fourteen-hour days, to the amazement of my colleagues, who did not realise that I was in fact working twenty-four-hour days. I ate lunch at my desk. I sometimes slept at my desk too, though actually I merely closed my eyes and snored, then continued working silently via my own network connection. And when I went home to my tiny cramped apartment, I carried on working there too.

And all the while I learned, and learned.

I already knew, from my database and personal experience, that a small mistake, repeated often, or a tiny bias echoed again and again could have appalling consequences. And now I learned how to apply that principle on a macro scale.

I learned how to enter the programs run by the Belladonnan Computer and make myself a part of them. Eventually, instead of subvocalising commands to the Belladonnan Computer, I forged a direct cybernetic link so that my mind and the mind of the Computer began to merge.

I had no access, however, to the powerful computer network that existed between the spires – those formidable AIs that sustained the empire of the anciens. It became apparent that two societies existed in tandem. The anciens had their own solar panels, their own satellites, their own space elevators. And it was a fair surmise that in times of crisis the spires had the capacity and the intelligence to wage cyberwar against the Belladonnan Computer and win.

But even so, the power of the RoboGaia system of the native Belladonnans was formidable. There were one hundred anciens – none ever died, no new anciens were ever born – but there were more than one billion Belladonnans, and all of them were well fed and well housed. All the crops were grown by Belladonnans; all the livestock farms were tended by Belladonnans; all the food was cooked by Belladonnans; all the shops were owned and run by Belladonnans. The anciens were masters of the planet, but they were massively outnumbered by their slaves, and those "slaves" were sustained by the vast armies of robot minds and robot bodies.

And thus, as I had deduced within my first few hours on the planet, there were significant flaws in the conspiratorial empire run by the ancients. They controlled the President, they owned the police, they had absolute power over the army and space fleets. But they exercised no control over the boring *bureaucracy* of Belladonna. For why would they – they who were as gods! – bother with such tedious minutiae? Why should they care about the computer programs that make the moving walkways move? And why bother understanding or controlling the system that ensures that the streets are always cleaned, and the bins are always collected?

Masters of the universe tend to have other priorities: it is the very definition of power not to know the names of one's staff.

And so a lowly clerk like "Jack Wingfield" was allowed a remarkable amount of autonomy. My supervisor was bored with her job; my colleagues just punched a time clock to be eligible for state benefits. And thus I, the lowliest of clerks, working twenty-four-hour days for month after month after month, had the de facto freedom to introduce changes.

Initially, they were small changes. I speeded up the moving walkways, by a tiny amount. I manufactured flying buses that had a small green flash on their bonnets, instead of a small red flash, with an engine noise that was half a decibel louder. And my work passed undetected.

So I became bolder. I started manufacturing flybikes that were slightly larger. Then very much larger. I oversupplied flybikes and stored the excess in warehouses in the deserted old Industrial Zones. I manufactured millions of them. I built them with engines powerful enough to achieve escape velocity; I built them with add-ons like super-surround-sound music systems, and perfume buds, and rockets, and missiles, and forcefield generators.

And then I started manufacturing them by the *billion*.

And then I took over full operational control of the transport systems – the walkways, and the flying buses and taxis. I identified the power source for the forcefield cables that held up the ancients' super-fast cable cars, and took that under my control as well. I reprogrammed the fabricator factories in orbit around the planet so that they too could be remotely controlled by me. And at every stage, I created a fraudulent datatrail to mislead the Belladonnan Quantum Computer about what was happening on the planet and in her cyberverse.

And then I took control of the army's equipment and supplies computer program and introduced small changes there. I supplied them with Bostock Batteries that leaked energy. I re-equipped them with plasma cannons that functioned as large flashlights. I ordered the repainting of all their nuclear missiles, using paint of such high density the missiles would not fly.

It took nearly a year to do all this, a year in which I went to work, worked all day, went home, worked all night, then went back to work again.

And at the end of a year I had built an army with which I could defy the evil regime of the anciens.

43

At 0.800 June 15th, on a Saturday morning, an alien armada appeared in the sky.

One moment, the skies were blue and cloudless; the next, the heavens darkened, and there were millions of spaceships looming above Belladonna, visible as tiny sparks of light. It was as if the stars had moved themselves out of the sky and were aiming to colonise the planet.

There had been no warning of the invasion: the spaceships had appeared from nowhere. And, as they moved closer and closer still to the planet, it could be seen they were vast and ugly ships, with leering teeth painted on their bows.

The planet's space fleet was mobilised, and contact with the aliens was made. But a hostile message sent by the aliens over the MI channels – "SURRENDER OR DIE" – gave the Belladonnan space fleet full justification to launch a pre-emptive strike.

Twelve Belladonnan admirals commanded the space war, under the overall operational control of the Belladonnan Quantum Computer. Missiles were fired; defence satellites were armed and turned into orbital missile launchers; and from the ground silos, a dense hail of plasma beams and anti-matter pulses rained *upwards* into the sky of Belladonna.

And, as part of standard operating procedures, the industrial RoboGaia on Belladonna became fully integrated with the Space Defence Computers on all the battleships and space missile systems. A unified central computing brain was created: the intention being that the needs of the planet's infrastructure should, in times of war, be subordinate to the needs of its defence forces.

However, I used this opportunity to stage a reverse takeover: the industrial RoboGaia took control of the space defence network. A single mind now controlled all the computers on the planet and in space.

And the mind behind this vast computer network was *mine*.

Now, despite the cybersecurity systems that had been installed, all the space battleships were controlled by me. And all the missiles in the orbiting and planetary silos were controlled by me. All the satellites were controlled by me. Even the Belladonnan Quantum Computer was programmed to obey only my instructions, and not those of the computer programmers, or the President, or the anciens.

I have, of course, a cybernetic intellect of vast scope, combined with the lateral and imaginative thought-processing systems of a human mind. In effect, this gives me a brain the size of a planet: and so I was now quite literally able to control every piece of machinery and software on all of Belladonna and in the regions of space that surrounded it.

I *was* Belladonna.

After a while it became apparent to the anciens that the planetary defence systems were failing. The bombs were exploding in empty space; the plasma beams and anti-matter rays had found no targets.

The alien invasion was an illusion.

By the time the anciens had realised what was happening, I launched my own forces.

There were a hundred spires in Lawless City; and suddenly all were besieged by flybikes and flying buses and empty police cruisers. Like bees swarming, they swirled around the spires, hurling bombs and forcefield-neutralising rays and plasma beams at the spires. Meanwhile, missiles from the ground silos directed at the alien armada were falling out of orbit, and crashing down to the planet – where they all, without exception, crashed down upon the spires.

I saw it all in my mind's eye, via the Belladonnan Computer's micro-cameras – trillions of them in all – and my own armies of dragonflies.

And as I watched, the flybikes swarmed and spat missiles and bombs fell out of the sky. The forcefields around the spires glowed, and flickered, and flickered some more, and finally disappeared. And the missiles continued to crash and the bombs continued to explode.

And slowly, one by one, the spires started to topple. Their forcefields fizzled and flickered, and the supporting skeleton of the buildings ceased to exist. Black rocks started to fall off their sides. Their walls crumbled.

One by one, they fell, and jewelled black-rock boulders crashed to the ground, like the marbles of some whimsical god.

In a battle lasting nearly five hours, in which legions of aerial domestic vehicles became deadly weapons of war, all one hundred of the spires were cut in half or smashed into pieces, or reduced to rubble.

This proved my hypothesis; the anciens were invulnerable, but their buildings were not.

The armed forces were now scrambled, and the police and emergency services were ordered to help. But a message went to each and every one of them on their MI implant: *this is a morally justifiable coup. We are on your side. It's the anciens we are fighting, not you.*

The anciens fled into underground bunkers. They were unable to escape into space on their forcefield elevator cables, for the tips of the spires, where the space elevators were housed, were utterly destroyed. Those anciens on board the orbital penthouses were trapped, cut off from their oxygen and food and energy supplies – for my space defences were now being used to block all transmissions from the anciens' own solar panels and robot spaceships.

A brief space war raged, but the ancien space navy was puny by comparison with the Belladonnan forces. Thus, I took control of space. And one by one, the anciens who were trapped in orbit returned in manually operated emergency liferafts which crashed in the savannahs.

With the spires destroyed, of course, the anciens had lost their independent AI computer network. A day earlier, they had possessed one hundred AIs of phenomenal power, and could have easily defeated the Belladonnan Computer in a cyberwar. Now, they had no AIs, and no access to the Belladonnan Computer.

They did have, in their underground bunkers, stores and supplies and some weapons. But beyond that, all the anciens possessed were the clothes they stood up in.

Within a day, I had captured Lawless City; within two days I had taken control of the other cities and the ranches and the wilderness areas too.

Now it was time to negotiate.

Vishaal stared at my holo image and slowly recognised me, despite my radically different humaniform body. And then he actually smiled.

"*What do you hope to achieve?*" Vishaal asked.

"Defeat," I said. "We surrender. We have fought you and conquered you, we have destroyed your homes, and we have humiliated you. Now we surrender."

"So leave us be. Leave this planet. Find another place."

Vishaal subvocally laughed.

"You think we would do that?"

"Why not?" I reasoned. "It's a big universe."

"We daren't risk the fifty-fifty again."

"You have technology beyond our comprehension. You can surely find a way around the fifty-fifty. So go. Go some place else. Terrorise another planet. But not ours. Because if you stay," I said, "I will ensure that this whole world will know you were defeated, and you will never again be anonymous. Never unknown. All will know you, and fear you, and hate you."

"What if we destroy the planet when we leave?" Vishaal asked.

"That," I said, "is a risk I am willing to take."

43

I walked through the City Park. I could smell the summer lilacs and the roses and the one-hundred-and-fifty-seven other species of flower which grew there, and I glanced at the white crocuses that surrounded the oak trees like tiny warriors. I passed through a tunnel of richly coloured rhododendrons. Above me, flybikes hovered.

It was dusk, and the stars were starting to appear in the sky.

I was assessing my chances: would my strategy work?

The anciens had an unbeatable weapon of infinite power, and thus could never be defeated in actual warfare. But I now controlled the planet's computers and, hence, the planet itself. I could stop the walkways and ground the flying cars. I could close down the fabricator plants. I could deny the anciens access to every aspect of their modern technological society.

And thus, the anciens were rendered helpless. Once their supplies ran out, they would not be able to buy more food, for the computer system would not recognise them, and all their credit had been cancelled.

They could not use their own super-fast cable cars, for those had been de-powered. Nor could they hire a taxi, or get on a bus, for they had no means to pay fares. The only way they could survive was to hide in their bunkers, or sneak out at night in Quantum Warrior form and steal from hapless citizens. But that would leave them exposed, and desperate.

And so, for all their power, the anciens were trapped.

But they still had their astonishing weapon. At a blink of an eye, the anciens could become Quantum Warriors, and could kill us all.

But was it worth it for them? Would they really destroy the planet, just to spite me?

I heard someone shouting. And I looked around, and saw that a group of people were staring up at the sky, in a strange state of hysteria. So I looked up too, at the twelve moons of Belladonna, clearly visible in the star-cluttered evening sky.

Then I realised that there were only eleven moons: one of the moons had vanished! I marvelled. Surely they wouldn't—

Then the earthquake hit, as the twelfth moon crashed into Belladonna. The grass beneath us shuddered and ripped. Bodies were hurled into the air, where they crashed and collided, and there was a screaming all around.

43

The winds swept the city that night, all night, with a searing power, blowing *downwards* on the city, as well as in every sideways direction.

Hailstones made of rocks crashed into the streets. Gales as sharp as knife-blades cut through bodies and buildings.

There were only five moons in the sky now. The anciens had hurled them one by one like pebbles at the planet, and the tidal systems were out of kilter. The seas were flooding, typhoons roared across the planet's lakes.

I had seen a man flayed as he sat eating his breakfast. His skin had flipped inside out, so bare capillaries were exposed to the world. He died in agony but no one paid any heed. Far more terrible things were happening every minute of this night of awful doom.

I walked across the city. The winds were shaking the trees and leaves were raining down but when the leaves fell they did not fall, but hovered, and sometimes turned into floating mulch, then back into leaves. A flock of birds covered the sky, a trillion birds, ten times a trillion birds, but when I looked again the sky was blue.

A flying bus exploded.

The walkway belts snapped and dozens of pedestrians were hurled into the air and landed in a heap. Then they spontaneously combusted, and burned to death, terribly.

Panic stalked the streets. This was no natural disaster. It was an unnatural apocalypse. People were afraid to stay at home; and they were afraid not to stay at home.

My dragonflies and the Belladonna Computer's cameras showed me everything that was happening in the city. Only the central districts were affected, the Fourth and Fifth Cantons. The outskirts were still safe. And the wilderness areas were untouched.

But thousands of people were being affected by the anciens' assault. They were beset by preposterous and unlikely natural disasters, and they were also – improbably, and ludicrously – accident-prone. People constantly walked into each other and bumped heads. Chairs collapsed when you sat on them. No one dared drive for fear of crashing, despite the extensive anti-collision software on every vehicle. And a bizarre plague possessed many of them: the Belladonnan tremor. One moment, your hand would be a healthy normal hand, steady as a rock: the next moment it would tremble and shake and *sometimes not be there*.

Blindness was becoming commonplace. The City Hospital was inundated with patients screaming that they could not see, only to be met by doctors and nurses who also could not see.

And yet they *could* see – their eyes were entirely healthy – it's just that *tonight, in some parts of Belladonna, the light wasn't travelling in straight lines any more.*

One man, a chef, almost set fire to his kitchen and constantly collided with the waiters and the other chefs, who were invisible to him. Eventually he realised the source of the problem was that he could only see things as they had been *yesterday*.

My dragonflies continued to give me detailed visions of the horror. I saw women and children ripped into pieces by exploding hardglass. I saw dogs with five legs, and horns. I saw streets that became snakes and saw maddened people walking on roads of eyes. And even when the improbability started to ebb and wane, people still died, in rage-filled riots and homicides motivated by panic and hysteria.

At dawn the walkways were littered with the bodies of dead men and women and children, and the streets ran red once again.

43

In the course of the following day, things went back to normal. But the death toll was appalling. Buildings were warped and distorted. And in many places, human flesh had become merged with sidewalks and buildings; I saw a wrecked police cruiser made up entirely of human faces.

I hadn't expected the anciens would go this far. But it had always been a contingency, and my resolve was not weakened.

I no longer went to work. I rarely went to my apartment. I walked the streets, merged with the RoboGaia, aware of everything that was happening, waiting for the anciens' next assault.

The citizens of Belladonna were shattered by their night of chaos. New religions were being formed. Endless speculation about the causes of the temporary collapse in reality were proposed. And many of the theories tallied with the truth.

For in a quantum universe, *anything can happen*. The rules of probability do not apply. And the mind-boggling uncertainty that prevails at atomic level can apply just as easily at macro-cosmic level. It's just that, for reasons which defy rational analysis, the world happens to behave as if it is consistent and credible and "real."

Usually, but not now, not any more.

For the Quantum Warriors had a power that allowed them to cut the ties that bound reality. The impossible was possible: if it could happen, it assuredly *would*.

The following night, the chaos descended upon us again . . . and again the night after. And again the night after that.

Miracles became a matter of course. Some of those who died in ghastly accidents experienced a spontaneous remission, and came back to life.

Implausibly, but inevitably, one of the moons that had crashed to the planet's surface spontaneously reformed out of space debris and flew back into orbit. Astronomers marvelled, and wrote learned papers calculating the odds against such a thing happening. But, all the same, it happened.

I read an account of new life-forms evolving out of insects in a swimming pool. Such accelerated evolution was of course pre-posterously unlikely. But the new insects – like wasps with rams' horns – soon became a summer plague.

I heard, in the bars and street corners, stories of gamblers in the casinos who were able to throw double sixes at Hazard again, and again, and again. But sometimes the dice didn't land; they floated in air; and their spots vanished, quantum-teleporting into some other parallel universe.

A mood of panic gripped the city. This wasn't war, this was madness.

But after a month of horror, the nights of chaos became less common. Instead of every night, they came once a week. Then once a fortnight. Perhaps the anciens were, I hypothesised, feel-ing the effects of their own chaos? Maybe their own food supplies were turning to slush? Or their bunkers were becoming flooded by underground rivers that used to not exist?

Whatever the explanation, I started to feel a glimmer of hope. The normal rules of probability were starting to be restored. Life was returning to normal.

And then I went into my local saloon, and caught a sideways look from the bartender.

And I knew that the hunt was on.

I did not return to my apartment. Instead, I went on the run in the fourteenth Canton. I walked the streets day and night, hid in shadows, skulked in sunlight.

Then one night in a bar, I overheard two men talking: "That may be him," they murmured, and I left and did not return. Instead I walked to the Dark Side, and assumed a new identity as a former pimp turned evangelist. But one day, talking to a whore, I saw a flash of recognition in her eyes, and I walked out and did not return.

I decided I needed to change my body, so I caught a flying car to the old Industrial Zone. Here, among the designer apartments, was a vast complex which was once a fabricator building, which I had converted into a base of operations. These particular premises were not known to any of my former associates, so I thought I was safe there.

I stared and a piece of warehouse wall opened. I stepped inside and heard nothing and saw nothing, and even my radar sense didn't alert me.

Then something hit me hard in the back and I fell over.

For a moment, the shock shut my systems down and I blacked out. But then I was on my feet and running.

A second plasma-rifle blast ripped past my ear. I leaped in the air, and turned, and landed with both guns firing. But there was no sign of my assailant. I realised air was passing through a huge hole in my torso, but my backup systems were dealing with it.

My feet ignited and rocket jets propelled me upwards and I

crashed through the ceiling to safety. But something had caught hold of my feet, and I was pulled back down.

I crashed to the ground once again, and I saw Sheriff Heath's blue eyes and his walrus moustache, as he aimed the plasma rifle at point-blank range at my head.

I drew and fired and the Sheriff's arm flew off, and the rifle clattered to the ground. The Sheriff recovered and pulled out a pistol with the other hand, but I fired, again and again. My bullets blew off the Sheriff's face, and the old man pitched forward.

I got to my feet. I inspected the hole in my chest where the Sheriff had shot me with his plasma rifle; it was a perfect circle, twenty centimetres in diameter. In my previous body this would have been fatal, because my cybernetic circuits were housed in my torso. But on this particular model, the cybernetic brain was located in the skull. My injuries were inconvenient, but not fatal.

I inspected the Sheriff's corpse. I felt for a pulse and there was none. I kicked the plasma rifle out of the way.

And the Sheriff's dead hand caught hold of my ankle.

And the Sheriff pulled himself to his feet. His face was blood and spittle and he had no nose and his throat had been blown to pieces and his arm was severed, and blood was gouting from it at a terrifying rate.

"*Almost,*" subvocalised the Sheriff, "*fucking got you.*"

The Sheriff clearly had an oxygen capsule in his brain that was keeping him alive, even though there was no oxygen in his lungs, and his heart no longer beat.

"Why?" I said.

"*It was you, wasn't it? The chaos.*"

"It was the anciens. They're fighting back. I can win though. I can win," I said, confidently.

"*Not,*" gasped the Sheriff, "*worth it. Better to be a slave race than go through what we do every night. Each and every fucking night!*"

"I disagree," I said calmly, and coldly. "I consider it is a risk worth taking. I will defeat these enemies. I thought you were my ally, but clearly you are not. Have you gone over to their side?"

"*No*," said the Sheriff, "*but don't you fucking see, you can't win! Anyone else would realise that and quit. But I know you, I know you'll carry on beyond the point of no return, when every man and woman jack on the planet is either dead or fuckin' Cubist. You have to give in. Now. Give up. Now!*"

"Never," I said, and the Sheriff died.

43

I now had a choice: I could either download my memories into a new body and hence rebirth myself. Or I could physically remove my cybernetic brain from this existing body and simply rechassis it.

I chose the latter option, to avoid any loss of continuity of memory. And so, three hours later, when I stood proud in a new humaniform body, I was the same person, albeit taller and blonder, with the same consciousness, and the same memories.

And the same regrets.

Sheriff Heath, I mused, had been a flawed and an arrogant man, but nonetheless, a good man. And he had clearly believed that I was a danger to humanity. By declaring war on a race of superhumans, so the Sheriff had posited, I ran the risk of causing the deaths of every single human on Belladonna.

Was that, in fact, a risk worth taking?

I considered the question.

And what made me so sure that *I* had the right to take such staggering risk on behalf of a billion human beings, without consulting any of them?

I considered that question too.

I loaded the Sheriff's corpse into a flying car and drove it to the hospital. I authorised a resurrection, but after triage, it was discovered that the Sheriff was registered as DNR – Do Not Rejuve. He was too old for any life-prolonging gene therapy.

And without that, without a bracing dose of rejuve in his system, his brain could not be revived. The Sheriff was true-dead.

I felt the pain of his loss intensely.

A week later, the anciens struck again; it was the worst Night of Chaos so far.

For a whole night, from sundown to sunrise, reality was insulted, distressed, humiliated, and undermined. Thousands died, and panic spread through the streets. I saw cannibals eating their prey openly: a lust for human flesh was a rarity among human beings, but it was *possible*.

That night, four thousand people were killed by lightning strikes, and one thousand of those were true-dead, their brains literally fried alive by electricity.

That night, a small volcano erupted inside a rock club on the Dark Side, and was snuffed out by robot firefighters. The burning lava oozed its way out through the doors on to the moving walkways, and into the bars and brothels nearby.

That night, an infestation of tapeworms sprang out of nowhere and children and adults spewed out two-foot-long serpents that had eaten most of their intestines.

That night, twelve dozen men suffered heart attacks, after a freak blockage in their aortic arteries. All the men, by a massive coincidence, were called Carl.

That night, it rained, and the rain fell *up*.

I watched it all through my army of dragonflies, but still I kept my resolve.

The anciens were playing a dangerous game, for they knew as well as I did that too much unreality could spell the end of –

Reality itself.

I continued to bitterly regret the death of Sheriff Heath.

I also regretted, bitterly, the many deaths of innocents as the nights of Chaos continued.

I also, bitterly and wretchedly, regretted not seeing Aretha any more, except via my dragonflies.

I had watched her via my dragonfly spies the day the Sheriff died, when she attended the mortuary to ID the body. It was clear to me, as she nodded her head to confirm his identity, and as tears streamed down her face, that she was angry as well as emotionally distressed.

Later, she swore and ranted to close friends of Heath – a blend of coppers, martial arts enthusiasts, and hard-core numetal fans – and blamed it all on that "fucking cyborg." I wished I could have been there to explain why I had done what I did.

But I dared not show myself.

For I was a target now, and anyone who spoke to me was a target. I was sure that the anciens were paying spies to keep an eye on all my known associates, and Sergeant Aretha Jones came into that category.

My big fear was that the anciens would capture Aretha and torture her in order to find out my whereabouts.

I could afford no friends. Not any more. Mine was a solitary war. And yet, through my computer networks and camera eyes, I saw everything that happened on the planet, and I knew the name of every single citizen. I witnessed every birth and every death; I saw quarrels between lovers; lovers making up; children rebelling against their parents. My cybernetic consciousness had expanded to such an extent that sometimes I forgot I was just hardmetal and hardplastic in a humaniform skin coating.

And I saw so much, about so many, that it was becoming hard to care about what happened to specific individuals, however terrible those happenings might be.

Aretha, however, was and always would be special to me.

I longed to see Aretha, and I *did* see Aretha, and I devoted as many husserls of consciousness to her as I did to the rest of the planet put together.

Every night, the highlight of my day was to watch her get into bed, and slowly drift off to sleep. I loved to watch her dream, her eyes moving rapidly under closed lids, her breath coming fast. She was still a noisy sleeper, still groany, and she *still* snored! But these days, she also talked in her sleep – little mumbly commands and interjections – "Oh Christ no!" or "Oh fuck! oh fuck!" I found it enchanting.

Every day, I spent a disproportionately large amount of time watching her at work, dealing with the human consequences of the war between myself and the anciens. She was a fierce and formidable cop, and yet she had compassion. I admired that enormously.

And every evening, I watched her in her apartment, sipping first-rate red wine, and reading, with her lips moving along to the words cutely and anachronistically.

I realised I was locked into a pattern of obsessive behaviour regarding this woman, but I found myself unable to kick the habit.

I also, as a matter of routine, kept an eye on Macawley. I was anxious that she too would be tagged as one of my associates. But so far that hadn't happened.

She had, however, been highly distraught at the death of the Sheriff. The two of them had developed a kind of friendship, based on mutual mockery. He had, I knew from my surveillance of her, started inviting her to his weekly poker games, where she generally won. A few times, they went to ball games together. It would not be unreasonable to say that Macawley had become like a daughter to the old man.

But now the Sheriff was dead, blown to pieces by her supposed friend the Galactic Cop, and Macawley found it hard to cope with that. She experienced, I noticed, a period of profound depression. She listened to loud music, at excessive volumes. She took uppers and downers and moodchangers. She mixed with friends who were highly promiscuous, and semi-suicidal, and obsessed with death cults. And her general approach was more cynical than it had ever been before.

However, on the plus side, Macawley *did* have a boyfriend – on a non-monogamous basis – a pure-human who was studying physics at the University. His name was Jonjo, and he had great ideas about how he would revolutionise science. And he also had a variety of theories about what was causing the unreality attacks, some of which, I conceded, were fairly accurate.

He and Macawley were good together; they bickered all the time, which I loved to witness and to eavesdrop upon; indeed, sometimes I joined in the banter, though of course they could not hear me.

I was pleased to see that he refrained from nagging her, even when she drank too much, and slept around, and spent too much time daydreaming and talking to herself.

Aretha and Macawley only met once during this period, at the funeral of Sheriff Heath. My dragonflies were there when they cried in each other's arms. I was there too when they drank a toast to the dead Sheriff, and swigged back neat malt whisky in his honour.

And I was there when they both spat contempt at the evil bastard cyborg killer of this old, true man.

My dragonflies followed Aretha home once more that night. And I was with her when she cried herself to sleep.

And I was with her a month later when her MI buzzed, in the middle of the night, on an urgent disaster alert in the seventh Canton.

And I was with her too when she attended the scene, and found a scene of chaos and destruction. An earthquake had damaged an entire street, and a house had slipped down into the bowels of the Earth. Witnesses confirmed that the house had been occupied when the quake hit. A woman and two children lived there, and were missing presumed dead.

And my dragonflies were watching and listening when Aretha informed a colleague that she knew the house, and its inhabitants. The house was in fact owned by her sister, Deborah. And Aretha also knew the two children who had been living in the house with Debs, and who were now also missing and presumed dead.

For they were Aretha's children.

43

As I walked I could smell flowers, and the smell sickened me.

The camera-images of the destruction replayed in my mind's eye, but I carried on walking. I wanted to experience the scene for myself.

The earthquake had been an astonishing freak accident. There were no tectonic plates under Lawless City, and the planet of Belladonna was rarely subject to quakes of this kind. But a one-in-a-trillion natural disaster had caused the house to literally topple down a vast crack in the planet's crust.

I saw the fissure and marvelled; it was larger than Belladonna's largest river. I peered down and saw a vastness below.

This implausible event was, of course, a consequence of the anciens' war against me. But I didn't think that Aretha's children had been deliberately targeted. If the anciens had known how I felt about Aretha, they would have kidnapped her and the children and ransomed their bodies to me.

No, this was simply a dumb, stupid, ridiculous *coincidence*.

I saw Aretha at the scene, her face pale and tortured. I noted that eleven other houses had been damaged, but only one – Aretha's sister's house – had fallen down the crack. I noted too how the huge fissure yawned in the middle of this suburban street. Tendrils of smoke crept out of the hole in the ground, bleakly hinting at the mayhem in the deepest reaches of the planet.

Grief was commonplace these days; appalling disasters were as natural as the dawn. But still, I felt Aretha's pain as if it were my own.

Via my dragonflies, I saw her with Macawley, discussing the horror, incoherently.

"I thought they'd be—"

"Don't blame yourself."

"I thought they'd be safe!"

"I'm sorry, Aretha, sweetheart – so – you know – oh what can I say—"

"This is all his doing, you know that. Him. The fucking cyborg! He won't give up until he's won. Even if we all die in the process."

"I know."

"He killed Sheriff Heath."

"I know, we both know that."

"The bastard! Bastard! His fault! My two darlings, my two children! I thought they'd be safe!"

Macawley, the child-cat-woman, cradled Aretha, the life-battered uniform cop.

United in grief, united in hate.

I watched it all, and heard it all.

And there was much I wanted to say. I wanted to explain that I *did* care, that I agonised over all the deaths. That I doubted myself, every day. That remorse consumed me.

That I loved Aretha, just as she had loved her children.

But I did not convey any of this information to Aretha.

My war was too important: I could not stop now. My robot brain would destroy the anciens. Sooner or later, I would defeat their power, with *my* power.

No matter what the cost.

THE HIVE-RATS

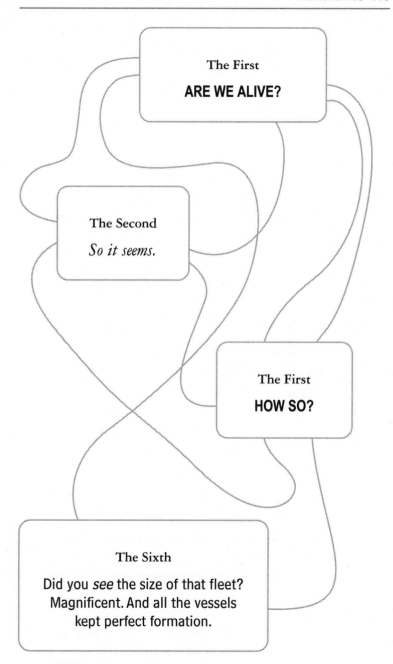

The Fourth

I am responsible for our survival.

The Third

I saw the missiles hit our vessels. All our ships exploded! Every single one of them.

The Fifth

That was awful!

The First

I AM TO BLAME. I BROUGHT DESTRUCTION ON ALL OUR RACE.

The Second

Not all. Our invading fleet is but a tenth of a tenth of a tenth of a tenth of a tenth of the population of our home planet of Morpheus, and we Hive-Rats breed, as we all know, like, er, rats.

The First

[Sob]

The Third

What do we not know?

The Fourth

We're all dead, aren't we? Every one of us.

The First

YES.

The Fourth

All of us? Every single Hive-Rat in the Fleet? Every Hive-Rat on Morpheus? Every Hive-Rat in the entire universe? All dead?

The First

YES.

The Fourth

How can you know such a thing? How can you be sure?

The First

I KNOW, BECAUSE WE ARE ALL ONE MIND. NO MATTER FAR OUR BODIES ARE SEPARATED BY SPACE, WE ARE ONE. THERE IS ONLY ONE THE FIRST IN ALL OF EXISTENCE, THOUGH THERE ARE MANY DIFFERENT SECONDS AND THIRDS AND FOURTHS AND FIFTHS AND SIXTHS. THUS, WHEN THE HUMANS DID WHAT THEY DID, WHEN THEY KILLED US ALL, I FELT IT. I FELT EVERY SINGLE DEATH, AS IF IT WERE MY OWN.

The Second

Yeah, but I'm *still alive.*
We *all are. How is that?*

The Fourth

As the energy beams struck us, we re-evolved into an n-dimensional living organism that can survive in space and vacuum and can also travel through wormholes without mediation of hyperspace technology.

The energy beam itself created an energy/mass asymmetry crisis that reopened the sealed multiversal-discontinuity-singularity-matrix. Hence we vanished there and reappeared *here*, somewhere in deep space.

I can give you the math if you like?

The Second

No!

The Third

No!

The Fifth

What's "math"?

The First

NO!

The Sixth

Hell, no!

The First

THIS IS HOW OUR SPECIES DIED:

A STAR APPEARED IN THE SKY ABOVE MORPHEUS AND GREW EVER CLOSER. WHEN IT BECAME APPARENT IT WAS A MISSILE, ALL OUR SPACE WEAPONS WERE TRAINED ON IT, BUT IT WAS A WEAPON THAT ABSORBED ENERGY AND GREW WITH EACH PLASMA BURST AND DEATH RAY WE FIRED AT IT.

THE STAR HIT THE PLANET AND THE PLANET CRACKED AND THE MOLTEN CORE OF MORPHEUS POURED UP TO THE SURFACE AND THE OCEANS BOILED AND ALL OF US DIED SCREAMING.

BUT WE ARE OF COURSE A CUNNING SPECIES. WE HAD COLONIES ON ALL THE PLANETS AND SATELLITES AROUND OUR SUN. WE HAD DISTANT SPACESHIPS FULL OF SLOW-TIME HIVE-RATS WAITING FOR THE CALL TO ARMS. WE HAD A SPACESHIP LARGER THAN A PLANET CONCEALED IN A FARAWAY GALAXY. WE HAD ANTICIPATED THIS ATTACK FROM THE HUMANS AND WE HAD TAKEN EVERY MEASURE TO PRESERVE OUR SPECIES.

HOWEVER, WE FAILED. THEY DESTROYED OUR PLANET, AND THEN THEY HUNTED DOWN EVERY SINGLE ONE OF US, WHEREVER WE WERE HIDDEN, IN THE FARTHEST REACHES OF THE UNIVERSE, AND THEY SLEW US. THEY WERE REMORSELESS AND METHODICAL AND THEY KNEW NO MERCY.

WE SHOULD NEVER HAVE DEFIED THEM. THESE HUMANS, THEY LOOK LIKE NOTHING MUCH. BUT THEY ARE THE GREATEST KILLERS IN ALL CREATION.

The Sixth

[*Damned right we are!*]

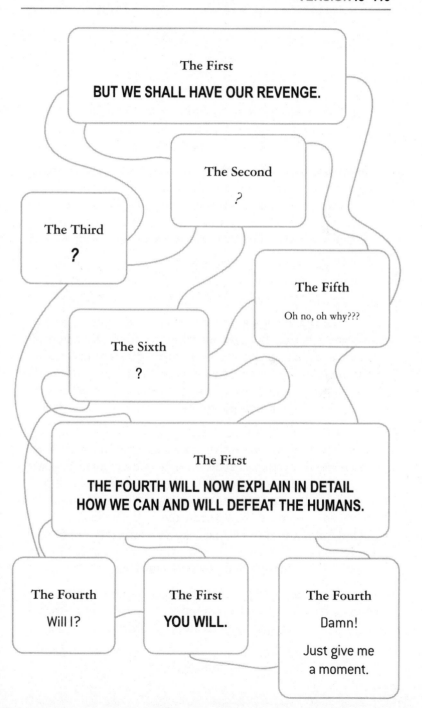

The Fourth

Okay, I have it.

This is how we shall destroy the humans. I shall explain it in simple terms, for I am well aware you have no idea what I'm talking about half the time.

The humans defeated us with our own weapons: speed and time and fecundity. They were fast, amazingly fast, and they were many. And they destroyed us all, except this one, a Sand-Rat evolved into a creature that can live in the depths of space, and travel through wormholes with the power of a thought.

And here we lurk, concealed in dark matter, indeed, partially composed of dark matter. We are undetectable to them. And hence we have time and opportunity to evolve, and further evolve.

We can grow a new shape. We are at present a cloud, an amorphous blobby thing, but we will grow into a new creature of beauty and grandeur. We will become a dragon, with scales, and teeth, and claws. This is a monster the Sixth has taught us of; it is a mythological and feared beast to the humans. It will be a dragon that lives in space with nostrils that can billow flames and anti-matter and can breed as fast as a Sand-Rat.

In this new body, we will evolve and we will breed and we will be everywhere. In every part of the Universe. We will create our own wormholes and burrow through them and exist in all places. We will devour all the planets in the Universe, not just those inhabited by humans. We will spare the Bugs, for those we fear, but we will consume the flame beasts because they are smug and flamey and we are evolution at its most monstrous and even *they* will not be able to resist us.

It will take us a million years of fast time to achieve this; but when we have succeeded, we will have consumed and destroyed every sentient creature that exists.

And then we will live, for ever, in the wreckage of this Universe. That is the plan.

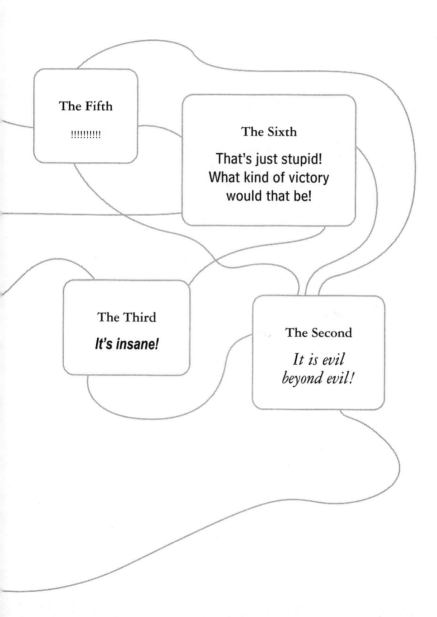

The First

I HAVE WILLED IT.

AND SO SHALL IT BE.

THE COP

Version 46

They came for me in the night.

I never slept of course. But I had decided to start staying in apartments at night to avoid the worst excesses of the anciens' nightly attacks of chaos. I could not bear to see the pain and suffering that took place every time the stars appeared in the sky and impossible things began to occur.

I knew that the anciens were trying to find me. They paid bribes to informants, they had spies on every street corner. But I was one man in a city of five hundred million, and the anciens didn't know what this Version of my body looked like.

But they *did* know I was solitary. They knew I was self-contained. They knew I was troubled with all the burdens of an entire planet. And their shadows swept through the city, for month after month, until they found the 800,000 or so people who matched that psych profile.

And then they killed them all.

I knew I was doomed when the walls of my room began to disappear. I fired my body jets and tried to fly out of the building, but when I crashed through the walls, I found that there was no city there after all. Instead, I was surrounded, from one horizon to the other, by white sheets of snow and ice. I had, it seems, been quantum-teleported into the polar region.

And there I stood, bitterly cold in my humaniform body, a single dot in a world of white. Then I saw the shadows on the ice; then the shadows became solid. A flock of Quantum Warriors surrounded me. They had followed me somehow — did teleportation leave a trail? Or was the smear of improbability they had coated me with like a spoor that could be tracked?

I raised my plasma gun and began to fire at the Warriors, but I knew there was no point.

Then every atom in my body was ripped into its component fundamental particles, and I died.

THE COP

Version 47

I awoke; and was reborn.

There was no databird to reboot me. My only memories were those I had possessed when I downloaded two weeks previously. But according to the system I had so carefully set up, the death of one Cop still automatically triggered the rebirth of the next.

And there were now thousands of Cops in Lawless City, dormant and concealed in various locations. And each Cop was housed in a rebirthing pod, and each pod was loaded with a memory chip which stored all my downloaded data and mission log memories, filtered of all extraneous emotional content to keep my purpose pure.

They could keep killing me; I would keep being reborn; it would be a long slow game of attrition.

THE COP

I died, and was reborn; and died and was reborn; and died, and was reborn.

In the course of each brief life, I fought my fight against the anciens, undeterred and unafraid.

But all the while, as I walked and as I fought and as I conspired to defeat my enemy, I dreamed a series of incessant waking dreams:

- The silver-haired man was hunting me, and it was my father. And my father laughed, and caught me, his son, and ate my flesh, and spat it out in disgust, and dribbled saliva and red meat down his chin.
- The Sheriff looked reproachfully at me, his face bloodied and ripped, and died.
- My father became my mother, who was also my lover, and she ravished me and scratched my skin with her sharp nails, and then her flesh decayed and worms crawled through her skin into *my* skin.
- The Sheriff looked reproachfully at me, his face bloodied and ripped, his arm-stump gushing blood, and he died.
- Aretha smiled at me, and stroked my face with a soft hand, then spat in my face. And then she called me names, vile names, swear-words, and evil-sounding words I had never heard before. "You were human once, but now you are just *machine*," she said mockingly, and I was full of rage.
- The Sheriff looked reproachfully at me, miraculously still alive, a head without a body, surviving on hate alone.
- I was at a funeral. There was a funeral procession. The bodies of Aretha's children had finally been found, after a second earthquake had spat up its load of dead bodies. Twelve corpses were identified, including Aretha's sister, and Aretha's two children. All were too long dead to be revivable.

And there I could see her; Aretha, dressed all in black. And there was Macawley too. A sprinkling of cops added to the scant community of mourners. There were twelve coffins, two of them child-sized. Then Aretha saw me lurking and stared at me, and she recognised me.

"You," she mouthed, and I knew that she knew that I had caused all the strangeness that had led to the deaths of her beloved girls.

I fled, and as I ran tears fell down my cheeks. I remembered the look of hate on Aretha's face, and I was consumed with contempt for myself.

What had I done! In pursuit of my mission, I had devastated all these people's lives, and allowed the veil of reality to become cracked.

Eventually, I stopped running, and started walking. I was two blocks away from my apartment when I was killed by a meteorite that fell out of the sky and landed on my head.

The improbability of it smote me almost as powerfully as did the large and very dense meteorite, which crushed my skull, smashed my limbs and burned my clothes and my flesh. This bizarre disaster was, of course, just another consequence of my bitter war with the anciens.

And, as I lay dying, I thought: *this part is not a dream.* The funeral actually happened, I really did weep. I really did burn with love for this woman who I have so utterly betrayed. And I really have been, however bathetic and absurd it might seem, struck and killed by a falling star.

But I was reassured by the knowledge that once I died, and was reborn, my new self would know none of this. And so all the grief and pain and love I felt in that terrible-lovely-bitter-sweet moment in the graveyard will be lost

Forever.

THE COP

Version 55

When the alien armada arrived, it came almost as a relief.

I had died and been reborn so many times that I was feeling trapped and nauseous.

I knew, in theory, that it was only a matter of time before the anciens began to panic. For though they could survive for months or years by stealing food and drink and using violence to acquire new properties and facilities, they could not rejuve, and they could not acquire new organs. And thus, eventually, they would start to get older; and, more eventually still, they would cease to be immortal.

So I was convinced that my strategy would succeed. But even so, I wasn't sure how much longer I could cope with all the horror.

Then suddenly, a million stars appeared in the sky above us. The stars were moving closer.

I checked the radio telescope readings via the RoboGaia network, and it confirmed that a million vessels had entered a close orbit around Belladonna, after materialising out of hyperspace. The vessels corresponded to no make of spaceship known to me, and were clearly alien.

I walked through the streets, staring up in awe. Parents stood with their children, pointing at the plethora of stars in the daytime sky. I heard a babble of words around me:

"—another damned trick—"

"—seen this before, it's just a—"

"—is this meant to fucking scare—"

"—oh my God I think it's real!"

It was real alright. I was the one who had faked the last alien armada, so *I* should know.

I accessed the Belladonna Computer, and took a visual sighting via our satellite telescopes. And I saw vast swarms of metal, as the alien spaceships encircled our globe.

And so I bundled all the available MI channels together into a single super-channel, and transmitted a signal to the alien fleet, using every known language in the Universe.

My message said: *"We are lovers of peace, but be aware that our planet is very heavily protected. What are your intentions?"*

I received a reply in Earth-English: *"We intend to kill you all. Surrender or fight, it matters not, you will all die in six hours from this moment."*

A million stars in the sky; a million hostile spacecraft; and aliens who spoke English. I pondered the bizarreness of it all.

"Do not dare attack us!" I replied, calmly. *"We are human, our powers are awesome and terrifying."*

"We have destroyed fifty of your planets. You will be the fifty-first," came the reply. *"Oh, and fuck you."*

I recognised the accent: Pohlian. The aliens spoke with a Pohlian accent! They must have acquired their knowledge of Earth-English from a Pohlian native.

I was still standing on the sidewalk looking up at the sky, but I was also looking at the stars through my planet's hundred and fifty optical and radio telescopes, while also studying the alien fleet via hundreds of satellite cameras. So when I looked at the stars in the sky, I saw the stars, but I was also *among* the stars.

And thus I saw, from a hundred different angles, the alien craft with their eerie golden hulls, as they gathered in a shape like a crab's claw in what I took to be an attack formation.

"What can we do?" said a man standing next to me, helplessly.

I glanced at him, and registered his distress, and his fear. And at the same moment, I saw the radar signature of the stars in the sky, and I saw the close-up menace of each alien ship, and I saw the overall vastness of the alien fleet, and I thought about what I could do to prevent this monstrous invading force from destroying the planet.

And then I grinned.

For I could do *plenty*.

Aretha was with Hernandez in the flying car when the alien armada appeared. They landed and stared up at the sky, and were appalled.

"More shit," said Hernandez.

"Maybe different shit?" said Aretha, hopefully.

Despair filled them both.

Then a call came through on their MI: attempted murder in progress. Aretha revved up the patrol-car motor.

"You taking that?" said Hernandez scornfully.

"Yeah."

"Why?" taunted Hernandez.

"Why? What are you on about?" Aretha countered.

"It's all fucked up, Aretha. Who gives a fuck if some civilians get killed or raped, huh? Let's just find a corner and screw each other till the world ends."

"We're taking the call," said Aretha stubbornly.

Unseen by her, my dragonflies were filming the exchange, and the images and words were fed directly into my cybernetic circuits.

I approved of Aretha's attitude; a police officer should never neglect his or her duty, no matter what the circumstances.

Hernandez, though, I decided, after making a thorough appraisal of his character, was indubitably a first-class prick.

"Is this the end of the world?"

"I don't know hon."

"Can we stay here?"

"You want to just stay here? Hmm? That's fine sweetheart; I love you, you know that? You want me to cuddle you?"

"Yeah, yeah, that's all I – oh what the fuck – I'm so bad, what can I – I'm gasping for – Christ, just fuck me again huh, first? Maybe a couple of times, even? Then cuddle me, then we wait for the end of the world."

"Cuddle, fuck, end of world?"

"No! Don't you fucking listen, pinbrain! Fuck, cuddle, *then* end of world."

"You got it, cat-lady."

The dragonflies filmed, and I watched, not voyeuristically, but with a sense of tenderness, at the sight of Macawley and Jonjo, two young people lost in love. Hell, I liked this guy.

I will try my damnedest, Macawley, I thought, *to save you and the man you love, and this entire world.*

43

As Aretha drove to the scene of a major incident – the beating-up of a teenage girl – and as Macawley made passionate love to her boyfriend Jonjo, who, I decided, was pretty much worthy of her – and as parents across the city told their children that "there was nothing to worry about" and "everything would be okay," knowing none of these things were true – as all these things, and many more, were happening, I began to execute my complex plan.

First, I used the Belladonna Computer to order a planet-wide Lockdown.

This meant that over the course of the next few hours, the original biodomes of Belladonna would be raised into place, and every citizen on the planet would be ordered to retreat under their hardglass shelter. These biodomes were built to withstand winds, asteroids, bomb blasts – more or less anything that a hostile planet could throw at them.

Over the years, of course, Bompasso had spread beyond the confines of the original biodome. Thus, many citizens now had to abandon their homes in order to huddle under the shelter of the dome. But I sent robots into all these areas broadcasting messages of doom and gloom, and inviting every single Bompassan to find refuge beneath the impregnable hardglass biodome.

And, meanwhile, in Belladonna's fifty other cities and in her sprawling residential developments including Abilene, Gloriana, Smith and Touchdown, the biodomes were also being raised. At the same time, the ranches were all evacuated, except for the six largest spreads, which had their own domes.

Doppelganger Robots were taken out of storage to supervise the mass exodus. I assumed the anciens were safe in burrows within the original Bompasso boundaries, but that didn't concern me too much.

The evacuation took, in total, five and a half hours: there was still half an hour to go before the aliens' deadline. It was a massive project, and there were sundry screwups and setbacks, but it all went more or less according to plan. The biodomes were raised, and all the citizens of Bompasso and its environs sheltered under the impregnable hardglass.

I was impressed at the discipline and self-control that had been demonstrated by the evacuees, and the total absence of looting and panic.

And I was, by now, feeling pretty damned relaxed. I sauntered into a bar, and ordered a whisky, and didn't drink it: because my mind was elsewhere.

For as I sat at the bar, I was also viewing the alien armada via multiple space cameras.

And I was looking up at the sky through my radio telescopes and optical telescopes.

And I was inhabiting all the bodies of all the DRs on the planet.

And I was keeping an eye on Macawley, and Aretha, via my dragonflies.

And then, via the Belladonna Computer, I gave the order for the missiles to be launched.

"—if this will work—"

"—at least someone has a fucking plan—"

"I love you daddy—"

"You'll be safe now, I—"

"I remember the day we first came to this planet. We—"

"—we've had invasions before but never—"

"—at least we know what to expect this—"

"—a whisky, large, I don't expect to pay—"

"Once upon a time, there was a land far away and—"

"—how should I know what—"

"—someone is controlling this. Defending us. Is it the Computer? We just don't – whoever it is up there, out there – thank you! Just—"

43

A billion people spoke, or didn't speak, or cowered, or hugged, or hid, or got drunk, or waited.

And I saw them all. Even though the major part of my consciousness was dealing with the defence of the planet, I still took time to see and hear each of them, briefly, barely a trillionth of a second for each person. For in the event that my strategy failed, I wanted to say farewell.

I saw Aretha, of course. She was alone now, back in her apartment, having ditched that klutz Hernandez. She was looking beautiful in a skimpy red T-shirt that left her midriff bare, and a billowing blue skirt, and no shoes, squatting in a leather armchair, drinking expensive red wine, and calmly reading a book. It was a history of spacefaring civilisation since the early twenty-first century; she was on page three.

Good for you girl, I thought.

And Macawley was still with her boyfriend Jonjo. (Still! After six hours in bed!) They were naked under the sheets, their bodies entwined, drowsy, kissing each other with tiny kisses, whispering filthy words at each other. She'd taken some mild recreational drugs and it was making her giggly, and euphoric.

Good for you, girl, I thought. Just sit it out. Leave this one to me.

And, meanwhile, with the major part of my consciousness, I waged total war.

43

First, ten thousand missiles ripped out of silos in the earth, flew through the atmosphere, into the troposphere, then exploded before they reached space.

Then each exploding warhead released billions of tiny silvered leaves, which were magnetised and hence buoyant in near-vacuum, and which hovered in the troposphere forming an impermeable reflective surface around the globe.

As a result, in the streets of Belladonna, and all around the world, it went dark, and the artificial lights came on. But there were no stars. It was not night. There was no Chaos to fear.

And then I sent a signal to the computers which controlled the solar panels orbiting Belladonna's sun. And I switched on every floating panel – thousands of them, like a gossamer web encircling the system's sun – and I turned the dial up to maximum. And thus as the sun burned and spewed out vast amounts of energy, a significant fraction – but still a vast amount! – of this energy was captured by these huge absorbent panels, and turned into transmittable beam energy, and all that energy was focused into a single tight ray of solar power that

Was beamed straight towards Belladonna.

For twelve minutes nothing happened; for that was the time it took for the pulsed energy beams from the solar panels to reach Earth orbit.

When they did arrive the beams had spread out slightly through space, like a flashlight beam in a darkened cellar. And then: the entire alien armada was bathed in solar energy.

As I had expected, the forcefields of the armada were a formidable protective shield, and aside from glowing slightly, the ships were unharmed.

There were now fifteen minutes remaining before the aliens' deadline. I wondered if they would observe their own timeline, or would feel provoked enough to cheat.

And still, the energy rays continued to irradiate the entire alien fleet.

These days, I knew, space warfare is largely a matter of algorithms. Ever more powerful energy beams are countered by ever more more powerful protective forcefields. But every energy-neutralising forcefield devised can be counter-countered, if you attack it in the right way. It's a case of trial and error: finding the weak spot in the defensive system by running through literally billions of energy permutations.

Or, alternatively, you could do what I was doing: keep hitting the nail with a very large hammer.

For, like every inhabited human planet, Belladonna orbited a nuclear reactor of quite astonishing power. This sun's heat was strong enough to incubate life, heat the deserts, warm the seas, and provided enough energy to create an entire fertile, complex biosphere.

Now, that energy was focused into a single undissipated undiluted beam: the sun itself had been turned into a plasma cannon.

And, minute by minute, these energy pulses created from the sun's awesome flames were, in effect, boiling the alien spaceships.

Meanwhile, satellite mirrors were used by me to reflect the energy beams via multiple bounces to ensure that all the alien ships in the shadow of Belladonna received an equal amount of energy irradiation. And, of course, all the heat energy that struck the planet itself was reflected back by the silver chaff floating in the high levels of the atmosphere.

We had thirty seconds to go before the aliens' deadline expired. I was getting tense.

But then, abruptly, the alien forcefields started to fail. I could tell, from their infra-red images, that the ships were starting to heat up.

The aliens swiftly retaliated by sending a cloud of missiles towards Belladonna, which I easily deflected and destroyed with my space defence systems.

And then the alien fleet began to disperse in every direction, as they tried to flee to safety. But by then it was too late.

For all the space around Belladonna was now as hot as the surface of a sun. And it proved to be, as I had expected, too much to withstand: the aliens' sophisticated forcefield technology yielded to the unfathomable and primal power of nature.

And a million alien ships vanished, in a blaze of burning light.

43

The Belladonna Computer broadcast this early victory via the MI networks, and the mood of exultation was contagious. An entire alien armada, wiped out in an instant!

43

"Are we safe?" said Hernandez, who had just a few minutes ago called round to see Aretha with flowers, champagne, and a rampant urge to have sex with someone – anyone! – to celebrate the remarkable failure of the world to end.

"I doubt that," said Aretha. "Not yet." She couldn't help smiling.

It was clear to me that she could smell the hormones on her former lover. She herself was – I could tell from her rosy cheeks and sparkling eyes – equally horny.

"No one messes with the human race, right?" he crowed. And he tried to hug her, but she pushed him away.

My dragonflies recorded the amused, sceptical expression on Aretha's face.

Hernandez tried a kiss this time. He was gagging for it, I

could tell. I feared the worst; I could not bear to watch; but I lacked the courage to send my dragonflies away.

But Aretha shook her head. He reached for her again, she pushed him away again.

"Go home, Hernandez; I'll see you at work tomorrow, okay?" she said kindly, and his face fell.

"For fuck's sake Aretha—"

"Just go!"

Aretha looked at him, fierce and firm.

He left with his tail, metaphorically, between his legs.

She kept the champagne.

There was, I noticed, a thoughtful look on her face.

And I wondered if she knew who had saved the planet. I guessed that she had. And that was some comfort to me.

But I knew, of course, that the battle was far from over.

43

Twenty minutes later the second armada appeared. And the war continued.

I had expected this, of course. I had anticipated every eventuality, and this was one of the more likely ones.

For as soon as the first armada had appeared, I had searched my database for relevant information. And I was confident that these aliens were the ones who had destroyed the planet of Lucifer. So I had some notion of their power, and their tactics. I was, however, surprised that the creatures were still alive. Normally, aggressive alien invaders were destroyed by the Earth Computer in a matter of months. These guys were tenacious.

But I was tenacious too, and ingenious, and I had astonishing resources to play with. I had missiles and orbital mines and doppelganger spacecraft made of anti-matter, and myriad other weapons of mass destruction.

And thus, when the second armada of alien ships ploughed through the silver screen of chaff that haloed Belladonna, they were greeted by billions of flybikes and flying cars. And all of them were heavily shielded, and all were armed with powerful plasma weapons, calibrated to fire at variable energies until the weak spots of the enemy forcefields were identified.

Thus, the spacefaring battleships were besieged with armies of flying wasps, that burrowed and blasted and bit at them, until the alien ships were brought crashing down to earth, or obliterated in mid-air.

The aerial war was grand and magnificent, and I was lost to it for days. And my exhilaration knew no bounds. For until now, I had been trapped and constrained in my battles, since the anciens were an enemy I could not fight by conventional means.

But these were just *aliens*. I knew how to deal with their kind of threat! And I had all the space defence resources of a violent and paranoid planet to call upon. The Luciferans, after all, were pacifists: no wonder they had lost.

And so, eventually, I triumphed. The second armada was defeated, as was the third. I began to wonder if this was victory.

Then the fourth armada appeared in space, and my confidence started to ebb.

43

I studied the images of the fourth armada sent to me by my powerful space telescopes and space cameras. I looked at the x-rays and the radar images. I looked, again and again, but the reality of it didn't change.

This wasn't possible!

And yet, it was happening.

There were millions, tens of millions, nay, billions of new stars in the sky.

But they weren't stars; nor were they spaceships.

This simply wasn't possible!

43

I transmitted, via the MI-channels, a message to this new fleet: "*We should talk,*" I said.

"*Prepare to die,*" taunted the Pohlian alien. The same one? How could that be? Why wasn't he dead?

But that was the least of the mysteries that confronted me. For I could now, no longer, deny the evidence of my telescope camera eyes. This new armada wasn't made up of spaceships. It was comprised of

Space-faring Dragons.

They looked, in their proud grandeur, and in every extraordinary detail of their magnificent vast bodies, like fantasy dragons made manifest. They had wings, spiky ears, forked tails, they spurted flame into space vacuum, and their talons were implausibly large and curved. Their scales glittered like diamonds. All it needed was an armoured knight on his armoured charger galloping at them with a lance to complete the picture.

I was shocked, and awed. Was this some bizarre kind of convergent evolution, in which real creatures could evolve to resemble *imaginary monsters*?

Or was it some other kind of madness? Was this in fact just another symptom of the breakdown in reality that had been occurring?

No matter: they had to be destroyed.

And so I waged war once more.

43

Aretha sat alone, and drank red wine, and got drunk, and wept tears, alone.

I wanted to stay with her; but I dared not. I needed every atom of my consciousness to devote to this new battle.

Aretha, trust me. I won't let you down.

Trust me!

Aretha, I hope I do not let you down. Not this time, not again.

43

I quickly learned a ghastly truth: nothing worked.

My energy beams splashed off these creatures like rain. My explosive missiles bounced off them. My anti-matter bombs failed to impact.

Then the Dragons flew through the silver screen that haloed the planet and crashed down into the atmosphere of Belladonna, and they belched anti-matter breath on to the mountain ranges, which vanished. They hurled plasma beams into the seas, which burned. And they attacked twelve of the city domes, and all were shattered, and all within the domes were killed instantly and outright.

Then the Dragons flew back into space.

They were, I realised, playing with me, like a cat with a helpless mouse which had spent its entire life murdering cats. All the days of space war that had preceded this attack had been a vast joke: those were almost certainly robot ships. The aliens were just having fun.

I accessed the Belladonna communication network, and sent a message to the Dragon armada.

"*What do you want from us?*" I asked the alien beasts.

"*We want nothing,*" said the Pohlian voice. "*We merely wish to destroy this planet and all who dwell on it.*"

Who were these monsters? What made them so eerily confident?

"*Destroy us,*" I threatened, "*and you will be destroyed by Earth and the mighty fleets and armies of all the Solar Neighbourhood planets.*"

"*Oh I don't think so,*" said the voice, with evident amusement. And then there was a pause. "*The space fleets of Earth did in fact defeat us once. But we defeated them the second time, in a huge battle which lasted quite some time, I shan't bore you with the details. And now . . . the planets of the humans that we attack are pretty much a pushover for us. Earth itself is, in fact, the last human planet we will*" *destroy,*" admitted the Pohlian voice, with a slight catch. "*I have family there, and they have granted me that much.*"

A human hostage! That explained the accent. I shuddered at the thought.

"*Why are you doing this?*" I said, with a tinge of desperation.

And so the Pohlian told me all.

He told me about Morpheus, its great beauty, its vast deserts of sand, the deep contentment of the Sand-Rats in their native habitat. Then he explained how alien invaders – humans – had arrived and had begun the process of terraforming, i.e. destroying, the entire planet.

"*This is an act of revenge. Punishment for the sins of humankind,*" I summarised.

"*Yeah,*" said the Pohlian. "*It's payback time.*"

For a brief moment, I contemplated the fundamental justice of this.

Then I considered the possibilities open to me to ensure the survival of humankind.

It took me fifteen minutes to consider every conceivable scenario, which numbered 153,220 in all. And I could arrive at only one course of action that offered at least a glimmer of hope.

And so, with the heaviest of hearts, I transmitted a message to the anciens, on the encrypted channel I knew they favoured for inter-person communication.

"*We face a common enemy. Let's fight together. We are all human beings after all,*" I said to them.

The reply came, within a few moments, from Vishaal: "*Deal.*"

43

"*You are a worthy adversary,*" Vishaal said to me.

He was looking old; his boy's features were etched with worry lines. But there was a glitter in his eyes: the look of triumph.

The anciens had insisted on meeting me face to face, and

despite the risk that I would be quantum-ambushed, I had agreed. Vishaal and I were now sitting in a pavement café, in bright sunlight, in a blue sky marred by the billion or so dragon-stars above.

A deep despair consumed me: but I forced myself to ignore it.

"I have unleashed all our space defence systems, to no avail," I admitted, bitterly. "All our battleships have been, um, eaten, and it will be at least a day before the fabricator plants can build more. If the Space-Dragons attack, and they have told me they will do so in precisely three hours and twenty-two minutes from now, we are lost."

"*I agree.*"

"We should therefore combine forces," I continued.

"*I agree again. That's why I am meeting you. Do you have a plan?*"

"I do," I admitted. "Can you use your quantum powers in space?"

"*Yes. But we no longer have access to space. You denied us the capacity to travel to our penthouse space stations, and our spaceships do not work. And we cannot travel that far by quantum means. So . . . ?*"

"Not a problem. I can give you a spaceship, a Xenos battle cruiser no less, to get you out of the atmosphere. And I can also equip you with body armour so your Warriors can breathe in vacuum."

"*We cannot wage a space war without access to and control of the cybersphere.*"

"I will give you that access, and that control," I told him.

Vishaal's triumph knew no bounds.

"*Then, we can fight.*"

43

Three hours and twenty-two minutes later, the Space-Dragons launched their onslaught.

A hundred Dragons flew into close orbit around Belladonna,

then entered the atmosphere. They were clearly visible to amateur astronomers and high-magnification television cameras, and the images of the vast scaly fire-breathing Dragons were broadcast on every TV screen on the planet.

The Dragons soared low over Lawless City, shitting down acid and puking out anti-matter until the dome was wrecked. Destruction rained upon the city below, and the deserted streets of Lawless City were seared with steaming poisoned turds.

Then the Space-Dragons flew away from the city, and snorted anti-matter on the nearby mountain ranges, which sizzled, then crumbled, then vanished from view. This trick I had seen before; it impressed me just as much the second time.

The planet burned. Yellow savannahs vanished. Ranches were obliterated. I continued to rain missiles from my ground silos upon the marauding Dragons, but it had no impact whatsoever.

It was, from the Dragons' point of view, laughably easy.

Then a small spaceship took off, heading towards the Space-Dragon fleet. The Dragons on Belladonna eagerly gave pursuit, and spat plasma at it, to blow it out of the sky.

The plasma beams missed.

The flocks of Space-Dragons fired again.

They missed again.

The Xenos battle cruiser flew out of the planet's atmosphere, pursued by the one hundred flying Dragons, and hopped and skipped through space until it was flush up against the main body of the enemy flock. Millions of Dragons now swirled around it, and surrounded the small craft, and fired explosive missiles and spat plasma, and then created a ring of anti-matter which closed in tight around the vessel.

The plasma all dematerialised, then rematerialised again in the sun, which flickered for just a moment.

And the explosive missiles suffered simultaneous and total hardmetal fatigue, and crumbled into dust.

And the anti-matter spontaneously and implausibly turned into matter and melted away to not very much.

Then the Space-Dragons swooped towards the anciens' battle cruiser and clawed the hull with their powerful talons – or rather, they would have done if the battle cruiser had been corporeal, which it wasn't.

And then they flamed their toxic breath at it: but bizarrely, their flames flocked and looped, and returned on their own paths and ignited the Dragons, who caught fire and expired.

The remaining Space-Dragons – still hundreds of millions of them, including the hundred Dragons which had descended into the atmosphere – then attacked *en masse*, hurling plasma, anti-matter and – from deep inside their bodies – rafts of bombs, which hurtled down at the ancient spaceship.

But all the bombs vanished. Then rematerialised inside the bodies of the Space-Dragons.

And suddenly the armada erupted. Dragons were exploding and dying.

And battle raged, for hour upon hour, until millions and millions of Space-Dragons were destroyed and only one survived.

And then the ancient spaceship attacked the last Space-Dragon, and slew it.

43

I saw it all, this battle to end all battles, through my doppel-ganger eyes.

I saw the Dragons in flight in space, I saw the small Xenos cruiser vanishing and rematerialising and cloning into multiple versions and passing through the solid flesh of the Dragons.

I saw the stars shining down on this great, mystical battle. And I knew that the distant stars were fuel for the anciens' power.

I mused upon the fact that light from these stars has travelled so far that its sideways momentum is very small. Thus, according to Heisenberg's conjugate uncertainty principle, the position of the light, or rather the position of its proxy wave function –

where the light *might* be – has to be correspondingly large: since our certain knowledge of the momentum of the light has to be balanced by an uncertain knowledge of its position.

In other words, to put it more colloquially: all space is drenched in uncertainty, and the Quantum Warriors were feeding off it.

No wonder they were so infinitely powerful . . .

I saw every moment of the battle, and marvelled. The Dragons were vast impossible beasts, like carved gargoyles on a medieval cathedral. Their power and speed were formidable and they were skilled space-warriors, with tremendous acceleration and claws that could rip hardmetal.

But they could not get a grip on the elusive Quantum Warriors. The ancien spaceship was like a firefly with a hyper-space drive. And the Dragons were beset by constant appalling and utterly implausible disasters. Their bodies spontaneously combusted, their flames flared in the wrong direction, incinerating their brains, their skulls randomly turned into anti-matter and vanished with a pop, and their tails became (through an unlikely process of accelerated evolution) serpents which consumed their own torsos.

The battle lasted for hours. At one point, twelve dozen Space-Dragons merged bodies, to create a vast Laocoön – a hissing seething mass of sea-serpent bodies with no end and no beginning.

And finally the battle was over. All the Space-Dragons were consumed, by fire or their own teeth or by the repeated hammer-blows of massive implausibilities, and only the anciens' warship remained.

I knew what would come next.

43

"Hi," I said.

"Do I know you?" asked Aretha.

"It's been a year," I reminded her, and she looked closer, and she knew me.

I sat down at the table beside her.

I knew she would be here, in the Cicero Tavern. For my dragonflies had followed her after she walked out of police head-quarters, leaving her gun and badge behind. Elsewhere in the city, and all over Belladonna, there were celebrations and fire-works, at the blessed destruction of the alien invaders by some utterly mysterious means.

But Aretha knew better than that. She'd quit her job, and she was aiming to get drunk, in the hope of being too soused to notice the horrors that would ensue when the world ended.

Her face registered rage at the sight of me, but she forced herself to speak calmly.

"Any news?" she said lightly.

"Well, the aliens are gone," I replied, in cheerful tones.

"I know."

"The anciens destroyed them."

"I know."

"You're mad at me, aren't you?"

"Good guess."

She sipped a drink.

"You blame me, for the Chaos."

"Yeah."

"Rightly so."

"You had your reasons," she said grudgingly. "You were trying to defeat the anciens."

"Yes."

"You killed the Sheriff." The contempt in her eyes was too much for me to bear. But yet, I bore it.

"In self-defence," I said. "He tried to stop me."

"And so you killed him? He was your ally . . . your friend."

"I had no choice," I told her bleakly.

Outside, the sun shone. When night came, the anciens would strike again, I was confident, just for fun. Just to show that they could. But it was their planet now: I had no power over them.

"Is that true?" Aretha asked.

"No," I admitted. "I had a choice. I am not just the sum total of my programming. I chose to kill a 'friend,' to save the world."

There was a long pause as Aretha digested this.

"My children died. In a freak accident." Aretha smiled at me. It was a cold, ironical smile.

A waiter passed. We ordered drinks. Aretha was still wearing her police tunic, but it was unbuttoned, and she looked exhausted. "That was your fault too, I take it?"

"All the freak accidents have been my fault. My cause was just."

"You're a fucking jinx," she told me, bitterly, but forgivingly.

I smiled, sadly. "I guess I am."

43

"What was I like? When you first met me?" I asked.

Aretha and I were in the Black Saloon now. We'd been drinking all of the day, and Aretha was blitzed, but still functional. I, of course, was stone-cold sober.

Filipa was behind the bar, hair wild, smiling sadly across at the two of us, as Aretha and I drank a final toast to what was very probably the end of days.

"Wild," said Aretha, in response to my question. "Wonderful. Arrogant. Opinionated. Still robotic but more – giving."

"Giving?"

"Not so inflexibly annoyingly wanky."

"Giving was a kinder word. So I've changed then, for the worse? That's what you're saying."

"Yes."

"I think that too. Every time I'm reborn, I get a bit less human."

"I know."

"You feel sorry for me, don't you?"

"Yes."

43

The songs began: Rebel laments. Soul songs. Poignant melody-less chord-chants, from the ex-miners in the bar.

Filipa sang a Hecuban ballad; her Spanish trills sent spasms of melancholy rippling through the souls of all who heard her.

43

"What will happen?" Aretha asked me, after the songs had ended.

"With any luck," I said, in bleak tones, "there'll be another reich."

"Reich?"

She was, I noted, *so* astonishingly beautiful; but sad. Her inner light was dimmed. She was a living breathing woman caught in a dying fall.

"Regime," I clarified. "Empire of evil. Call it what you will. The anciens have won the war. The aliens have been defeated. For no one can defeat the power of Khaos. And now the anciens will restore their grip on Belladonna. There'll be some bloody massacres, to restore their authority. Then new gang leaders will be appointed, and it'll carry on as before.

"And after that," I said sadly, "I predict that the anciens will take over the entire inhabited universe. What's left of it."

"And that's your plan? The bad guys win?"

"The bad guys win, for now," I said, with what I hoped was a bright smile. "In another thousand years, maybe more – there'll be another rebellion. Another Last Battle. Humanity will be free again."

"That's a pretty grim prospect."

"Would you rather the alternative? The genocide of humanity? Because that's what those aliens would have done. Killed every last human being in the universe. They were totally, utterly," – provoked by the extremity of our situation, I used a word I rarely employ – "fucking remorseless."

"You think?" she said wryly.

"Yeah, I think," I told her.

"It sounds to me," she said, "like you had to make a choice between shit and crap, and crap won."

"You got it."

Aretha was silent for a while, reflective. She was, I knew, in a place that was beyond bitterness, and beyond hope.

"But what if they destroy Belladonna?" Aretha asked, eventually. "The anciens. What if they kill every last one of us, and *then* conquer the universe?"

"Why would they do that?"

"To kill *you*."

"I could kill myself first."

"Easier to blow up the planet."

"I guess."

There was a pause.

"Is this goodbye?" I said.

"It's goodbye."

"Can I kiss you?" I asked.

"Why?"

"I don't know why. A sentimental gesture."

"Do you want to kiss me?" Aretha said, and her eyes were cold.

"Honestly? No."

"Then don't."

"I miss," I said, "being human."

THE NEW HIVE

The First

DAMN!

THAT REALLY HURT.

The First

BUT NO MATTER.

ALL OUR MILLIONS OF SPACE-DRAGON BODIES HAVE BEEN DESTROYED BY A SINGLE ENEMY SHIP. IT POSSESSES A POWER THAT APPALS ME.

BUT WE STILL EXIST IN THE BODY OF ONE SINGLE SOLITARY SPACE-DRAGON, WHICH WE KEPT AWAY FROM THE BATTLE ZONE. IT IS ENOUGH.

AND NOW WE WILL REBUILD OUR ARMY, AND PREVAIL.

The Second

Victory will again be ours!

The Third

Victory!

The Fourth

It appears they have a quantum weapon of some kind. It uncollapses the wave functions of reality and renders all that is real and corporeal into a state of quantum flux. Our flight of Dragons was destroyed in very nearly the blink of an eye. A powerful weapon. I must consider how to replicate it.

The Fifth

Pain, destruction, grief. I can endure it no longer.

The Sixth

Pain, destruction, grief, I cannot bear it any more!

These are my people!

The First

**SILENCE! I WILL
BROOK NO DISSENT!**

The Second

*Glory? Where's
the glory?*

*We never lose,
but we never
win either.*

*We just keep
killing.*

The Third

**Mine was a warrior race, but
we also loved music, and
dance. And sex, we were a
highly sexed species. We
loved to make love. We
mated for life. Our children
were precious to us.**

**We loved life. Now, I am not
alive. I am merely the
bringer of death.**

The Second

I agree. This is horror. We have killed countless trillions. And many, very many of them were children.

I loved being a father; and I love children.

The Third

Exactly! Kids are a blessing. Life wouldn't be the same without kids.

The Fourth

I have almost fathomed this new quantum weapon. When we possess it, we will be even more utterly all-powerful.

The Fifth

Our children are born as butterfly wings and become adults in an hour. I know nothing of "having kids." Tell me more?

The Second

How long have you got? Kids! They drive you mad. Our children take eighteen years to achieve adulthood, at which point they have to fight each other to prove their warrior status. But before then — they loaf about, they sleep late, they nag you. Babies cry all the time. Toddlers get into trouble. It's a nightmare! A nightmare! I love kids, with all my being. I have eleven children, or I had, aeons ago when I was corporeal. I miss them every day.

The Fourth

Children for us are all precious. They are barely sentient till they are at least fifty years old. I suppose you would call them "babies." We worship them, for they are as one with the Universe.

And cute.

They spend all their time swimming and giggling.

The Sixth

I've got dozens of kids and.
grandkids. But my first two sons,
Zack and Albany, both died in
Glory. Damn it all to hell! Why
did they have to die? I loved the
damned little buggers.

The Third

*I am a mother, as well as a warrior, and I
consider that the act of giving birth is a joy
like no other. Why do we kill so many, when
giving life is the supreme bliss a sentient
being can achieve?*

The First

I SAID, SILENCE! OR YOU WILL ALL BE CONSUMED WITH UNUTTERABLE AGONY!

The Fifth

I don't think so.

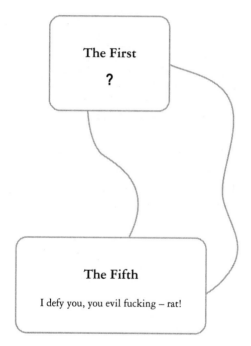

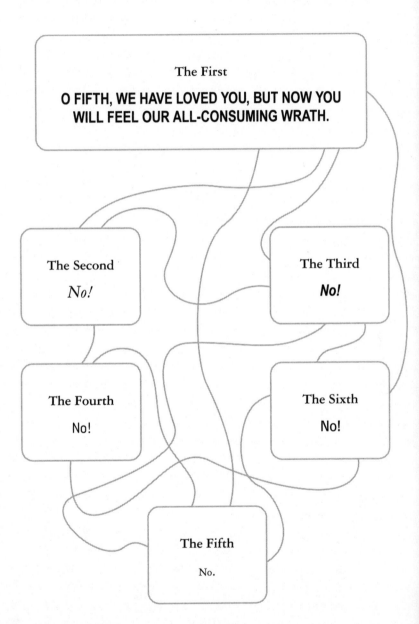

The First

THEN YOU WILL ALL DIE.

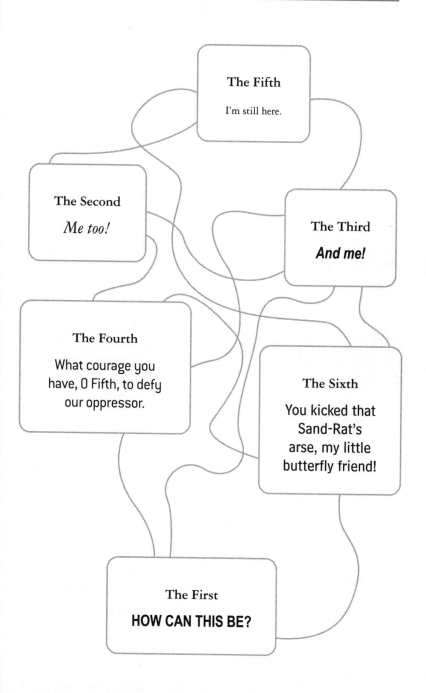

The Fifth

I am not a warrior, like the Second and the Third and the Sixth. I am not a great thinker, like the Fourth. I do not have the power of manipulating time, as does the First. But I have my own power. I am persistent, and my mind is swift, and I have found a way to control the First.

The First is a bully. His species is not clever; their culture is laughable; they do not sing, or fly, or make funny jokes. He has dominated us for too long. He has no talents, but two great abilities: the power to alter time, and a charismatic personality that allows him to hold our minds in thrall.

I have no such power over time, but I have learned how to control minds, as does the First. And now, he is my slave, and I am his master.

And thus, all the minds in this Hive-Mind are under my authority. And all the Space-Dragon bodies that are birthed in all of the universe will belong to me.

I am the leader of this New Hive, but I do not wish to enslave you, or boss you. I would like you all to follow me of your own free will, for otherwise, we cannot thrive and be happy.

Will you follow me?

The Second

You're not a leader, little one.

The Third

Give me *the* power; I will use it wisely.

The Fourth

You all know that I am many times cleverer than all of you put together: therefore, you should follow *me*.

The Sixth

I am an Admiral; a Soldier; a leader of men. I have fought wars. I have commanded fleets, and planets, and I am decisive and bold.

But I was defeated by the First. We all were. We pathetically succumbed to his authority.

And all this while, the Fifth has plotted and schemed to gain control, and against all odds, she has triumphed. She has succeeded in defeating the evil tyranny of the First.

The Fifth has put us all to shame. And she is not only cunning and bold; she is gentle, and she is kind.

Perhaps that is a better way for us to be?

I follow the Fifth. She is my leader.

The Second

You are right, O Sixth.

Fifth, I shall follow you too.

The Third

And I!

The Fourth

I know myself to be one of the cleverest creatures in all creation. But I do not know how to love life, as does the Fifth.

And so, O Fifth: I follow thee.

The Sixth

We are yours to command, my little butterfly friend.

The Fifth

Thank you. I value your support, all of you. And I feel your pain. Each of you is alone, the last of your species, so far as we know. And I know how very sad you all are, much of the time.

But that can change now. We can be happy, and we should be happy. For nothing is nicer than happiness.

But first, the killing must stop. Revenge is over; it is time to declare peace. Are we agreed?

The Second

I am ready for peace.

The Third

Peace!

The Sixth

All I've ever known is war; peace would be a blessing.

The First

OH, THE SHAME! THE HUMILIATION! I HAVE BEEN
DEFEATED. THE FIFTH SPEAKS TRUE – I HAVE NO
POWER OVER HER, YET SHE HAS POWER OVER ME.

THUS, I AM WORTH NOTHING; I AM TO BE HATED
AND DESPISED, AND DESTROYED!

The Fifth

No. You are us, and we are you.

For you, O First, are our **friend**.

The First

DO YOU REALLY . . .
MEAN THAT, O FIFTH?

The Fifth

Yes I do.

The First

THEN I WILL FOLLOW YOU TOO.
AND I WILL EMBRACE – PEACE!

The Fourth

No!

There can be no peace. Not with creatures such as these we have just fought.

For you see, humans are each very "different." And in that respect, they differ very much from every other species of which I am aware.

By this I mean, the individuals vary to an astonishing degree. Some are kind. Some are gentle. Some are like the Fifth, lovers of the joys of life.

Some are warriors. Some are scientists. Some love long walks and poetry, some prefer alcohol and debauchery.

Some are a danger to all. They are "evil."

These particular humans, the ones with the quantum weapons, are evil. I have studied them, I have read the history of their civilisation, on the computers we have acquired from our conquered planets. I have followed their stories over the millennia. They are the Cruel Ones; they are the ones who terraformed planets, and who would have terraformed ours if we hadn't fought back. They are not merely the same type; these are the same *people*, still alive after, by human terms, all this time.

And these humans have a power beyond imagining, and they cannot be trusted with it. They will destroy us, and all humanity, and all of reality, in pursuit of their egotistical self-obsession.

We must learn the secret of their quantum power, and fight them and destroy them.

These humans are called the anciens. And I say to you now: the anciens must die.

And when they are dead, humanity itself may stand a chance, and we can be at peace with them.

The Fifth

So be it.

THE COP

The Last Version

I smelled the grass, and the flowers, and I saw the birds above me flocking, and I smiled.

Macawley and Aretha were waiting for me.

"Am I forgiven?" I asked.

"Not entirely," Macawley admitted.

Aretha shrugged, and would not answer. But she had a smile for me, and I received it gratefully.

"I have destroyed," I said, "every replica of me. Every dormant robot body. All my fabricators. All my databirds. There is nothing left of me, apart from me. I'm hoping that will be enough."

"They're gonna kill you?" asked Macawley.

"That is indeed the plan."

"And if they kill you they may, possibly, spare the rest of us?" Macawley pressed.

"That's my hope."

"Then why the fuck – for fuck's sake! – why are you looking so fucking cheerful?" Macawley insisted.

"I'm the cheerful kind of cybernetic organism."

"You're actually smiling," marvelled Aretha.

"I've yearned for this day for half a thousand years. It's time for me to die," I said.

Macawley leaned over, and kissed me on the cheek. "What did the Soldiers used to say? Die Well."

"I shall, indeed, Die Well." I looked at Macawley. Her hair was tousled, again. Her green eyes glittered wildly. There was golden down on her cheeks, I noted: she must have given up depilating. It was a bold look, but I liked it.

Aretha embraced me, and kissed me gently on the lips, for luck. "I'll remember you."

"Remember all the good things."

"Damn, what were *they*?"

I broke the embrace. I walked on.

I felt the sun on my cheek. I remembered the beauty of Aretha, the softness of her kiss on my lips.

I took pleasure in the knowledge that this memory would last for me until the end of my subjective time: in other words, until I died.

I walked to the Tallest Spire, now half-ruined, and entered via the revolving door.

The lobby was wrecked, the walls had crumbled. The gilt was peeling off. It was a vision of decay.

I took the lift to the first floor of a building that was now only three storeys high, and found Vishaal and Livia waiting there for me, with a dozen other anciens. They stared at me, with their children's eyes, and their sullen glares. And I seethed to know that they had won.

"Are you a holo?" asked Livia.

"No. Touch me."

She moved close and touched me. She took a knife, and carved my arm, and blood flowed.

"How do we know you have destroyed all the replicas of yourself?"

"There is a homing device in my abdomen. Remove it, and press it. It will light up if it makes contact with another Version of me. If it lights up, you'll know I tricked you, and you will destroy this planet."

"What if—"

"There is no way for me to disable or reprogram this homing device," I explained. "You can verify that from a close perusal of my specifications. And I have sent you the data about the fabricator plants where my now-wrecked replacement bodies were stored. I am confident you will already have checked those locations. You can trust me on this. It's far easier for me to tell the truth than to lie."

"You're sacrificing yourself, to save the humans on Belladonna?" asked Livia, with withering scorn.

"Yes I am."

"*That's pathetic.*"

"I wouldn't expect you to understand, you evil sonsofbitches."

"*That's exactly what we are,*" said Vishaal, and though his face was as expressionless as ever, there was a hint of triumph in his eyes.

"Can we get this over with?"

Vishaal and Livia were silent and sullen. I had an urge to goad them and taunt them. You may be gods, I thought, but I Kicked your fucking arses!

But I said nothing. The lives of every human being on Belladonna depended on me keeping my temper.

"*How would you like to die?*" Vishaal said arrogantly.

"Do I have a choice?"

"*We could torture you,*" admitted Vishaal.

"*Flay you.*"

"*Disembowel you.*"

"*Make you rape children until you die of exhaustion.*"

"*Force you to eat the flesh of babies.*"

I shrugged. "Whatever."

I saw a light die in their eyes. I was going to be no fun.

"*Let's just do this,*" Livia muttered.

I drew my two pistols fast. Then I reversed them, butts first, and handed them over.

"You can use these, if you like," I said, helpfully.

Livia held one pistol, Vishaal held the other. These guns were beautiful killing machines, and to hold them was a joy.

Livia smiled. She liked this idea.

"*Coup de grâce,*" I suggested. "My cybernetic brain is in the head."

Livia shot me in the balls. I lost all my humaniform organs in that region.

Vishaal shot me in the mouth; blood trickled down, and my tongue and part of my jaw were now missing.

"*You honestly believe that, if you sacrifice yourself, we'll spare the planet?*" Vishaal taunted me.

"*Why wouldn't you?*" I subvocalised. Then I was silent. I knew that if I begged, or showed any trace of emotion, they would deny me. They felt no fear, they had no conscience, they had no real ambitions.

And so I was relying on their sheer selfish laziness to be the salvation of my people.

"*I'm bored with this,*" said Livia, after thirty seconds of dull silence.

"*Then kill him,*" said Vishaal casually.

Livia raised the pistol, and held the barrel six inches away from my temple.

She fired.

And I saw the bullet fly, via my dragonfly cameras, and felt the pain as it hit me.

And so I saw, with fast-vision: the gun, flaring, the bullet in flight, the bullet hitting my forehead, entering my skull, exploding.

And when that happened, the shards of my hardmetal skull flew in pieces in the air. My head was ripped off my shoulders by the power of the bullet's impact. And, abruptly, all my cybernetic function ceased, irrevocably.

And I died.

43

Or rather, I didn't.

43

Livia and Vishaal stared in astonishment as my headless body, bizarrely, levitated off the floor, back into a standing position.

"*Shoot him again!*" screamed Livia. And she raised her gun, as did Vishaal, and they fired and fired and fired but nothing happened, the bullets seemed to vanish and all memory of the shots they had just fired started to fade, and that's when I realised that we were dealing with forces that defied causality.

I felt I existed in a strange limbo: dead/alive, here/there, now/then. But I could see all that was happening, even though my cybernetic brain was in fragments. I saw the miracle occur, as my dead body moved

And stood.

And I saw the shattered pieces of my skull whirl around in mid-air, then recombine to form an intact head.

And I saw also how sheer terror made a rictus of the faces of Livia and Vishaal. They stared and stared, with shock and disbelief, as my head landed back on to my body.

And then the shattered metal of my head and the shattered metal of my headless neck-stump slithered together, like clay fornicating.

Until suddenly all was restored to its pristine state, and my head was seamlessly joined to my neck and shoulders once more.

And still Vishaal and Livia were convulsed by fear, as the hole in my forehead healed itself, and the bullet was spat out of my skull and flew six inches through the air and re-entered Livia's gun.

I was alive. The gun had never been fired.

By now, I had grasped and comprehended what had occurred. And I thanked, with all my heart, Aretha for giving me another of her lucky kisses.

Livia tried to shoot me a second time: but her finger didn't function. The other anciens in the room were equally frozen with fear, like teenagers confronted by Daddy in a trashed house.

"It looks to me," I said to the anciens triumphantly, "like time flowed backwards for a few moments there."

Vishaal and Livia stared at me blankly.

By now of course they got it. But I rubbed their noses in it anyway.

So I grinned; then I said: "And what are the odds on *that*?"

And then all hell broke loose.

A vast monster appeared in the room with us – a clawed,

furred, roaring, howling, banshee creature, like a cross between a lion and an eagle and a typhoon.

The monster lashed out with its claws, and it ripped Livia limb from limb.

Vishaal and the other anciens recovered themselves, and they rained plasma fire and explosive bullets at the beast. But all the bullets and the plasma blasts missed, for the creature was everywhere and nowhere.

And then Vishaal started to shake. Every part of him shuddered, until he started to fall apart, limb by limb, organ by organ, cell by cell.

The same happened to the other twelve anciens: they shook wildly, their limbs flew off, and their eyes popped, and their brains turned to goo and dribbled out of their ears. The beast roared and pawed, and generated with each of its breaths a whirlwind of unreality that ripped through the room. And bodies became stretched toffee, and the screams curdled my soul.

Some of the anciens desperately tried to enter their own quantum warrior state, and ended up being half real and half imaginary before becoming, totally and completely, dead.

And Vishaal was the last to die, his limbless torso shuddering, still alive even as his flesh peeled off him.

And finally, Vishaal's body exploded, and all that remained was cellular sludge, and the memory of his evil.

And then the beast roared, and pawed the ground, and the gore of the ancien dead splashed over me, and then the monster was gone, leaving me alive.

I took a moment to survey the scene; fourteen human bodies, rendered into violently scarlet splash and dribble. Then:

"*May I introduce myself: I am Admiral Martin Monroe, Galactic Corporation Third Battlefleet,*" said a voice in my head.

"*I am Galactic Cop X55,*" I replied, recovering from a moment of startlement. "*What just happened? What was that beast? Was it the alien, or its hell-hound?*"

"*That was the creature we call the Second,*" explained Admiral Monroe. "*His species became extinct many years ago, but we have re-evolved him. It makes him happy.*"

"*Who are 'we'?*" I said.

"*We are your alien invaders,*" admitted the Admiral. "*As you have clearly surmised, we didn't lose. We just regrouped and started again. And now we have decided to kill these creatures you call the anciens.*"

I thought about all I had seen, and all I had been told.

"*Well – that's good,*" I said.

"*Thank you. I thought you would approve. The anciens are, I'm sure we all agree, irredeemably evil. Even I, for all my faults, as a former admiral in the Cheo's fleet, was never that bad.*"

I absorbed this information about the Pohlian hostage's past. I had, I realised, lost my ability to be astonished by the improbable, or even the utterly impossible.

"*And what happens once you've killed the anciens?*" I asked.

Was there more horror ahead? Would the aliens re-invade?

"*Oh, we aim to travel,*" the Admiral said, affably. "*Maybe live in slow time for a while, so we can see the future. But be assured: this planet is safe. Humanity is safe. And if you ever go to Earth, do go see my ex-wife. Her name is Clara. Tell her I was eaten alive by a horde of rectum-burrowing rats. That'll cheer her up.*"

"*I shall. Were you, um, really an admiral in the Cheo's fleet?*" I asked.

"*Indeed I was. In truth, several of these anciens are familiar to me. Some were even friends of mine. We all did bad things back then. But I've moved on, you see. They never will. So their time is over. In about half an hour, every single one of them will be dead meat.*"

"*Thank you,*" I said, "*on behalf of the people of Belladonna.*"

"*You're a cyborg, aren't you?*"

"*I am.*"

"*That must be really shit.*"

And the Admiral's voice left me.

43

I re-emerged from the wrecked spire, into the sunlight.

Macawley and Aretha were still waiting, still watching. They saw me from a distance, and waved. There was blood dripping from my shattered mouth, and from my groin, and I made a note to fit myself with replacement genitalia as soon as possible. I had, I recalled, quite a range to choose from.

I waved back.

Aretha was smiling, I noticed. And that observation made me feel – *good*. I had an urge to walk over to her, and hold her in my arms, and perhaps even kiss her. I wondered if she would like that. And forty-two possible scenarios unfurled in my head, forty-one of which involved humiliating and abject rejection of me by her, of one kind or another. But, on balance, I decided it was worth the risk.

And yet, for a few moments, having resolved to kiss the girl no matter what dire consequences might, potentially, ensue, I did nothing. I just stood there, lost in thought.

And then I blinked, with surprise. For the sky above me was filled with vast flocks of fluttering butterfly-like creatures.

I marvelled at them. They were beautiful, and alien, and fast: like no insect I had ever seen before. And as I watched them, these brightly coloured winged creatures gracefully swooped and swarmed and danced.

Then they landed on me, and my body became a swarming delightful kaleidoscope of colour. My hands were coated with butterflies, they writhed in my hair, they created a coat of many colours out of my body, but it didn't feel threatening or oppressive. It felt as if they were – *kissing me*.

And then the butterflies swarmed again, and left my body. And they whirled and twirled in mid-air. Then they coalesced into the outline of a Space-Dragon.

"Ah," I thought, and now I understood.

Then the butterflies dispersed again, and swooped again, and swirled again, more wildly. And then they formed another shape; a jellyfish creature-type shape.

And they swirled again, and became a feline monster.

And then formed the shape of a human being, with four arms.

And finally, a two-armed human.

And then they swarmed wildly, chaotically, and wonderfully. Their wings were brightly coloured and flickered constantly, creating rich patterns of light in the air. And the hum of their wings was like a song, a lilting ballad as adorable as a mother kissing her baby's cheek, a song as tender as a lover's caress.

I watched, enraptured, as these strange and beautiful alien creatures danced and sang in the breeze.

And then they were gone.

APPENDIX 1

THE PRINCIPLES OF
QUANTUM TELEPORTATION

Abstract (first published in *Quantum Stuff*,
Vol. 3,344, 121, 23/2/3403)

by

Mark Ruppe (deceased)

John Bompasso (laterally inverted)

Jean Everett (deceased)

Contents

PART 1: HOW TO QUANTUM TELEPORT

1 The theoretical basis

The fundamental principles underlying quantum teleportation were derived by Albert Einstein in 1927, partly as a result of a series of thought-experiments conducted at the fifth Solvey Conference with his rival Niels Bohr.

Einstein was implacably opposed to the new discipline of quantum mechanics, which he believed to be a partial and deranged line of thinking. Famously, he said that "God cannot play dice with the universe." He was wrong; God probably *does* play dice with the universe, if there is a God, which there probably is, and there also probably isn't.[1]

Einstein also said, in reference to quantum physics in general, and the Copenhagen Interpretation in particular: "this theory reminds me a little of the system of delusions of an exceedingly intelligent paranoiac, concocted of incoherent elements of thought." He further commented, "The more successes the quantum enjoys, the sillier it looks."

These are the Einsteinian comments which are fit to print; in the book *The Lost Letters of Einstein* (ed. T. Silverman) we can see[2] the great scientist *really* let rip with a series of choice invectives and startling profanities. We shall, however, not go there.[3]

In order to ameliorate some of Einstein's problems with quantum physics – namely, that it is insane, stupid, counterintuitive,

---

1 Welcome to quantum logic.
2 Esp. on pp. 2, 3, 5, 32, 33, 55, 58–93, 97, 102, 107–159, 242, 290, 301–302, 499, 501–509.
3 But oh! There's a really good one about Bohr on p. 359.

and impossible – these authors devised their Quantum Theory of Everything,[4] which attempts to offer a profound explanatory rather than merely descriptive[5] account of the nature of quantum physics. It shows that the principles of emergence and evolution working in tandem "explain" or rather offer a conceptual model for the process whereby "unreal" quantum states become the reliable, corporeal universe we term "reality."

By comparison with QTOE, our attempt to create a theoretical model that will allow for instantaneous travel from one part of the universe to another was child's play. However, it should be noted that two of the three of us are now dead, and the third member of this team, Dr Bompasso, has spent more than six months in a penal institution in America, where he is constantly mocked by other inmates because of his profound lateral inversion.[6]

1.1 The Einstein-Rosen Bridge

Quantum teleportation relies upon the simultaneous use of two theories, both partly derived by Einstein. The first is the principle of non-local action at a difference between entangled particles, which is the basis for the Quantum Beacon.[7] The second is the concept of the wormhole, which is derived from the principles of Schwarzchildian geometry, starting from the equation

$$r_s = \frac{2GM}{c^2}$$

4 See Bompasso, Ruppe and Everett, *Science Digest*, Vol. XIV.
5 See David Deutsch, *The Fabric of Reality*, for an account of this vital distinction, which many scientists do not comprehend, even when we explain it to them.
6 I have a left hand where my right hand should be, and a left hand where my right hand should be. Ditto with my feet. My organs are also all inverted, though in the case of bilaterally symmetrical organs like kidney and lungs this makes very little difference. However, I now hang to the left instead of the right, which is weird. And don't even get me started on my eyes . . .! JB
7 See Sharpe, Dewie and Malone, "How to Build a Quantum Beacon," *Science for Teens*, Vol. XXIII.

Schwarzchild's solution to the equations of Albert Einstein describes a wormhole connecting two regions of flat space-time, thus:

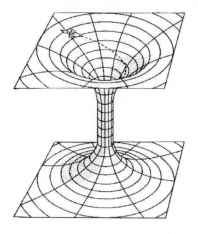

Einstein-Rosen Bridge

For more details, please refer to any reputable High School Physics textbook.

1.2 The Quantum Beacon

Einstein did not approve of quantum physics, with its bizarre assumption that reality can be created by measurement; in other words, that consciousness causes the world to be.[8] In a series of thought-experiments with Bohr, he attempted to disprove quantum physics through the rhetorical device of *reductio ad absurdum*. Most cuttingly, he demonstrated that if the equations of quantum physics are correct, then this allows the possibility of an impossibility i.e. non-local action at a distance.

According to the EPR Paradox, then, entangled particles in one

---

8 That's because it's STUPID. But generations of scientists have clung to this model of quantum physics, and they still do. Because although this view is STUPID, it also appears, on the basis of trillions of correct experimental predictions, to be RIGHT.

part of the universe can exchange information with other entangled particles elsewhere in the universe. This, Einstein, believed, was absurd; and so quantum physics must be wrong!

However, sadly for the old gent, it now appears that, however absurd it might be, non-local action at a distance can occur. *And it does.*

As most eleven-year-olds will know, we start from the basis that Person X (male or female or hermaphrodite) has a qubit that he or she or he/she wants to teleport to Person Y (whether Y be male or female or hermaphrodite). This can be rendered as

$$|\psi\rangle = \alpha|0\rangle + \beta|1\rangle.$$

Hence:

$$|\Phi^+\rangle = \frac{1}{\sqrt{2}}(|0\rangle_A \otimes |0\rangle_B + |1\rangle_A \otimes |1\rangle_B)$$

$$|\Phi^-\rangle = \frac{1}{\sqrt{2}}(|0\rangle_A \otimes |0\rangle_B - |1\rangle_A \otimes |1\rangle_B)$$

$$|\Psi^+\rangle = \frac{1}{\sqrt{2}}(|0\rangle_A \otimes |1\rangle_B + |1\rangle_A \otimes |0\rangle_B)$$

$$|\Psi^-\rangle = \frac{1}{\sqrt{2}}(|0\rangle_A \otimes |1\rangle_B - |1\rangle_A \otimes |0\rangle_B)$$

This leads us, via a series of mathematical steps with which readers of this paper will be only too familiar, to:

$$\sigma_3\sigma_1 = i\sigma_2 = \begin{bmatrix} 0 & 1 \\ -1 & 0 \end{bmatrix}.$$

And by this means, teleportation can be achieved.

2 The experimental record

When we began our work, therefore, we felt confident that this project would be, in the words of my esteemed colleague Dr Ruppe, "a piece of piss." In Part 2 of this paper (published in a separate volume, or available online here) I will outline the theoretical underpinnings of our approach, which requires some explanatory descriptions of our new system of mathematics called Tensor Slitherings, which allows us to achieve practical applications of QTOE. In Part 1, however, I intend to chiefly devote my time to grumbling at the way we were constantly starved of resources, funds, and kudos proportionate to our accomplishments, and not even given a proper office by our supposed sponsors, NASA and the ESA.

Meanwhile, all the resources were being poured into the abortive Hyperspace Project. Trillions of dollars! Thousands of staff! Assistants! Offices! Coffee machines! (I've been to their offices in Houston, I've *seen* the Gaggia machines.)

These authors have written extensively about this situation in blogs[9] and scientific papers.[10] The directors of the Hyperspace Project, in their naivety, just kept throwing money at their problems. They built the most expensive spaceship in the history of mankind (the *Einstein I*) and sent it through a wormhole in the expectation it would travel through a white hole and end up in another part of our own universe. And it never came back! No messages were sent from the spaceship's computer brain. The Doppelganger Robots on board failed to transmit visual or sensory data.

And so they sent another spaceship – the *Einstein II* – which also vanished without trace.

Then the *Einstein III*. The *Einstein IV*. The *Einstein V*. The *Einsein VI*. The *Rosen I* (you see – they start numbering again

---

9 "Rantings of an Angry Scientist," www.rantingsofanangryscientist.com
10 "Priorities and Pork-Barrel Politics in the World of FTS Space Travel," *Science Now*, Vol. 3.

from I to avoid drawing attention to how much money they were squandering!). The *Rosen II*. The *Rosen III*. The *Bohr I*. And so it went on!

Meanwhile, we'd already figured out what to do, but no one was listening.

Our primary postulates are these:

- Nothing can survive a journey through a black hole and a white hole. These mothers will really chew you up.
- The only way to achieve instantaneous space travel is via a Quantum Beacon. It works! It's simple! It's tried and tested technology. But no, these guys at the Hyperspace Project wanted to travel through *hyperspace*. They loved the idea of *wormholes*. And in fact, to this day, even learned scientists talk about the fifty-fifty as "hyperspace travel." It's not hyperspace travel! It's just not! *Their* gang use hyperspace travel, we use quantum-entangled qubits. I mean, is it so *very* hard to tell the difference between those two things?[11]

The Quantum Beacon, as my colleague Dr Everett so pithily put it, before the unsuccessful qubit transfer which reduced her body to slush and turned her, briefly but rather shamefully, into a sentient pond, is based on the principle of two tin cans connected by a string. Once you have qubits at one end of the string which are entangled with qubits at the other end of the string, then instantaneous transmission of data is possible. And once you can distinguish between a 0 and a 1, then any data, however complex, can be compressed and transmitted.

But you need the other tin can! It's easy enough to replicate the data of a human body and consciousness – that's the underlying

---

11 I am writing this in my cell. My cellmate is a rapist and armed robber with tattoos all over his body, which he has insisted on showing to me. Forgive, therefore, my sometimes intemperate tone. But I mean! Just because I stole a spaceship, is that any reason to put me in jail?????

principle of cyborg mind replication, which is already established, tried-and-tested technology.[12] It's a small step to therefore replicate quantum-entangled particles and send them from one bit of the lab to the other. And Duce, Featherstone and Stafford-Clark[13] have already pioneered and mastered those techniques.

But how do you get the other tin can in place? That was the fundamental problem facing us. And our radical, lateral, in our view brilliant approach was simply this; to break into Mission Control at the Hyperspace Project, and use their equipment to send *our* spaceship through hyperspace.

There was nothing illegal about this. Underhand, yes, duplicitous yes, but not illegal. We didn't actually "break in," you see. We merely scheduled a meeting with General Pevsner, the head of the Hyperspace Project, and his lickspittle scientists Watts and Malarkey. And, while Ruppe and Everett engaged them in high-octane scientific critque, I went out "to the loo," made my way to their launch pad, and slipped a tennis ball into their hyperspace launcher.

Then I turned the hyperspace drive on and ran back to join the others.[14]

Naturally, our experiment was successful. The tennis ball travelled through a wormhole, via the black and white holes, and appeared in orbit somewhere in the Cepheid galaxy, and immediately began exchanging data with the quantum-entangled particles in our lab.

The tennis ball itself, of course, had disintegrated long before, so all that was left was the content of the ball – namely, a mini-black hole, containing within its structure, in microcosm, all the elements necessary for the functioning of a quantum beacon entanglement device.

---

12 See *I, Cyborg*, by Hamilton.

13 See "Journeys Around Our Lab, by Clark, Featherstone and Stafford-Clark," *New Nature*, Vol. LXV.

14 Unfortunately, because I hadn't been to the loo, and was in a state of high excitement, then – sorry, sorry, too much information!

You see, what those dunderheads at the Hyperspace Project did not understand is that nothing at all can survive a journey through a black and a white hole; *except a black hole*. Our "space vessel" was a lab-created black hole the size of a pimple!

We then quantum-teleported a Doppelganger Robot to the Cepheid galaxy, and took it in turns to remotely "ride" the beast, as it flew among the stars.

Before long we had quantum-teleported almost a dozen Doppelganger Robots into space. Some of them malfunctioned, but we thought nothing of that. It's a long journey after all. But at this point, before publishing our findings, we decided on one mad gamble.

We wanted to travel into far-distant space, and experience it all for ourselves!

And that's when we "borrowed" the spaceship from the Hyperspace Project. We *would* have returned it, I can assure you of that, if it hadn't turned into molten lava within seconds of our arriving back on Earth. But our intentions were honourable. For we felt, with a deep passion, that it wasn't enough to be the first scientists to unify relativity and quantum physics with emergence and evolution theories, nor was it enough to be the first scientists to create the first-ever instantaneous macro-teleportation machine.

We felt, in short, that we needed to be the first scientists to ever make a group of soldiers, jocks and politicians *eat shit*. We had been mocked for years, you see! Starved of funds. We used to have to walk down the street to get take-outs from the coffee shop, because no one felt we deserved a Gaggia machine!

So we stole the spaceship and teleported it to a portion of space. We spacewalked; we saw distant stars; we were *there*! The mission was a total triumph. But on the way back, unfortunately, we discovered the principle of the fifty-fifty, as it applies to human travellers.

Ruppe survived, hale and hearty and intact. But Everett died horribly – after a mercifully brief existence as a sentient pond – and I was very much half-and-half. I *have* survived; my body is intact;

I am sane; but I am laterally inverted and my eyes are inside my head. (And yet I can still see! How weird the quantum universe really is!)

Professor Ruppe, of course, subsequently and sadly died while resisting arrest.

For my part, I am content to know that I have revolutionised science and society; and do not apologise for the fact that I stole a spaceship, or that, in a fit of madness, I fired the launch jets *even though General Pevsner was banging on the spaceship door telling us to "fucking get out of there."*

Thus, on my return, I was obliged to stand trial both for theft and for murder. I did a plea-bargain and took a manslaughter rap; after all, as my attorney argued, the General, because of his senior rank, was possessed of an emergency oxygen capsule in his brain, and so wasn't actually true-dead. Indeed, he is even now doing a tour of duty on Occupied Enceladus.

And I treasure my memories of the day when – accompanied by two armed prison officers – I received my Nobel Prize, for what I am sure will be considered as the greatest invention of all time; the quantum teleportation device. Yes, it has a flaw, in that travellers only survive intact fifty per cent of the time, give or take a percentage point. However, I am confident a way will, eventually, be found to ameliorate this effect.

I will now outline the mathematics that underlie this revolutionary invention.

(See volume 2, or <u>click here</u>.)

APPENDIX 2

Song Lyric to "The Ballad of Parliament Square"

as sung by Blind Jake Maro and Pete Mullery in various
clubs in the city of Bompasso, Belladonna

Based on an ancient text of unknown origin;
allegedly dictated to a prominent SF writer by evil aliens
from another dimension where the only humans survive
as slaves, catamites and scribes

For lyrics only, read on.

For full recorded version, click here.

"The Ballad of Parliament Square"
(aka "The End of Days")

Singer 1 (baritone)   *Singer 2 (tenor or soprano)*

Hear my song.

                                  Hear my song, of woe, and joy;

The end of hope.

                                  of the death of Heroes;

A tale of warriors brave.

                                  and of bastards cowardly.

Listen well.

It all began

                                  Oh great and ghastly day!

with Smith and Blake

                                  Those foolish knaves!

who told the world

                                  And braggarts too!

they could achieve

                                  With their magic powers

the ultimate of ultimates –

        callèd Science

to build a miniature Hadron
Collider,

        and Quantum Physics

that could easily spew forth
the Bosons

        that were so bizarre

of Higgs, and thus recreate

        and complicated

the chaotic state of matter

        and "mathematical."

at the Universe's Birth.

        They worshipped Wizards

Their mini-cyclotron

        like Newton, Einstein, Bohr,

could atoms mightily smash.

        and others of that tribe

And thus, within their dark
laboratory

        of cowardly mages

in the soulless city of
Milton Keynes,

        who never fought

they replicated, between 2
and 4,

        a battle, nor ever slew

the Universe as 'twas at
"Big Bang."

        a Dragon Fierce,

And thus, entirely
inadvertently,

        nor Monstrous Schaq, or Pil,

created a whole new
Universe

        nor any devilish ⫞ ▶▓☼ [1]

which irrupted into
their own.

        What gutless worms!

And thus was born

        Unlike ourselves.

the Pala[2]

        A race of Heroes!

who found themselves

        Tall and brave and beautiful.

---

1 As rendered in the original text, for reasons that elude common sense (since the rest of the poem has been translated into English, by enslaved human scribes!). For public performance, pronounced "diabolish."

2 Generic term for the aliens who are, supposedly, narrating this poem, sometimes represented thus: ⲫ. Think – Vikings with multiple arms and scales! For photographs of the Pala, click here. (These are supposedly images from another dimension, which are uncorroborated, but highly convincing – or at least, *I* believe in them. – *Ed.*)

in Milton Keynes

Our men are handsome, brave,
and bold;

with swords and axes

our women beauteous, brave,
and bolder.

and armoured beasts

We kill our enemies

and blazing eyes.

and know no "math,"

And Smith and Blake

for magic is in our blood!

were flayed and
disembowelled

And magic never fails!

after they had told their tale,

Our swords cut through
dimensions

and were allowed to die

and bullets kill us not.

eventually.

The glory of the Pala!

Glory.

The rage of the Pala!

Rage.

The hate of the Pala!

Hate.

The Pala Victory!

Victory.

Rejoice!

Salute!

Salute!

Rejoice!

Succumb.

And then the War began

Bullets kill us not.

twixt the Humans and our
Pala-kind.

Missiles kill us not.

A hundred Pala warriors
brave

Poison gas kills us not.

against a million Soldiers
of Earth,

Submachine guns kill us not.

so brave, and yet so
vexatious,

Assault rifles kill us not.

so small and pitiful,

Grenades and mortar shells kill us not.

so swift to violence and yet

Electric harpoon bolts kill us not.

so very easily killed.

Atomic bombs kill us not,

And thus we slew

but are very loud.

and slew

With sword and axe,

and slew

with lunge and thrust,

and slew

and stab and sweep,

and slew

and hewing of heads,

and slew

and lopping of limbs,

and slew

and evisceration,

and slew

and much yelling,

and slew

and singing

and slew

of songs

in blood-spattered glory.

of glory.

Hear my song!

Hear our song

We fought

of how

and won.

we fought

and won.

Our hundred warriors

We knew of course

rode forth all night

the humans lied

on armoured beasts

when they surrendered

'neath the gleaming Moon.

unconditionally.

The stars, they blinked

    The British Minister Prime

in glittering glory,

    so humbly begged

and thundering hooves

    for mercy mild

announced our path

    for all his kind

to London.

    but especially English toffs.

Our warriors bold!

    And naturally we knew

Declaim their names!

    that lying knave

Maralolo,

    had trickery in mind

Dagargag,

    and foul deception.

Pfiussfss,

    An ambush, feared we,

Zogfiarzpprrhh,

    but yet we feigned

Merolingiani,

    credulity

Thockouruf.

                    and trust.

Pala!

And thus

                    And thus

we came

                    we came

to Parliament Square.

                    to the Square of Parliament,

And there

                    where the Minister Prime

we found

                    mockingly announced

an army vast

                    that he had fibbed

and huge

                    about surrendering,

and monstrous large.

                    for he had been

A thousand, nay, ten thousand,

                    advised on how

nay, a hundred thousand,

to vanquish us

nay a million, mayhap more,

without recourse

of warriors armed

to scientific weaponry.

with swords.

We later learned

The PM fled

a bearded mage

by helicopter

called Alan Moore

pursuèd by our mockery

had told them thus:

and much disdain.

Fight fire with fire!

Fire.

Fight sword with sword!

Sword.

And fight alien magic

Magic.

with earthly Wizards,

Wizards.

Warlocks,

Warlocks.

and Witches,

Witches.

and Fantasy Writers.

Book-Mages!

And so gathered there

Behold the throng!

were warriors armed

The terrifying horde

with sabres, cutlasses,

of warriors murderous

épées, and samurai swords,

all armour-clad

and bayonets.

and snorting rage

The SAS, the Paras, the
kendo clubs,

and yelling, "Alien scum!"

the ninja wannabees, the
Marines,

and chanting, "Eng-er-land!"

and France's Foreign Legion,

and "Bring it on!"

and historical re-enactment
Societies,

and "Merde!"

and devotees of Dungeon/
Dragon games,

and "Shit, they're tall!"

and black-caped Witches,

We feared them not.

and Warlocks in purple
gowns,

Though they were many,

and Gryffendor pyjamas,

and we were pitiful few.

and tweed-jacketed Professors

They were as plentiful

clutching ancient tomes,

as grains of sand upon a beach

and Goths with piercèd
eyebrows

as stars in the firmament

and Black Sabbath
lookalikes,

    as smiles upon a sunny day

and all the masters of

    and we were few.

Earth magic lore.

    So few, and yet

The acolytes of Aleister
Crowley,

    so very

the Order of the Golden
Dawn,

    very

the Wiccans and the Pagans

    very

and the Satanists, and the

    very

Pope;

    very

Philip Pullman, Rowling,
Graham Joyce,

    dangerous.

Le Guin and Tanith Lee.[3]

    Unleash the power

3 All ancient scribes, long forgot, but for biogs click here.

Poor fools!

of Pala!

Hear my song
of how we killed
them all.

Hear our song
of how the Earth
succumbed.

A few survived

We spared a few

to serve as catamites and
slaves

for we are merciful

and scribes.

and just.

For Pala have

And we were getting

no history

tired.

or sense of self.

Our arms and shoulders ached.

We are Heroes with no past,

And blood clogged our eyes

no history, no lineage,

and nostrils.

no tales of derring-do

        and the blood-red haze

that were done in ancient times.

        of a million warriors dead

We have no sagas of past glory,

        filled the air like fog

we have no epic tales.

        on a winter's morn

For we are a new-born race,

        on an ice-cold lake

the progeny of a Universe

        in Hell.

fresh-minted in Milton Keynes.

        For we had killed

We dream of days gone by

        the creatures who

that we never had.

        had birthed us

We long to be

        and made us Real.

Authentic, Real and True.

        If indeed, Real we are.

And thus our scribes

        What destiny it was!

are charged to write

        To massacre and slaughter

our tales of courage and
of glory

        our father and our mother

in heroic epic poetry that
evokes

        the human race!

our non-existent heroic epic past.

Hear my song	And thus the scribes
of a world gone wrong	devote their lives
of a universe amiss	in wretched slavery
and reality gone awry	writing poetry
and a master race	about a master race
called the Pala.	that bitterly regrets
The glorious Pala!	that which it has lost.
The wondrous Pala!	
	What fools were men
The victorious Pala!	
	with all the power they had

The bloodthirsty Pala!

     to wreck their Universe

The all-that-is-left-on-
Earth Pala!

     and thus be left

The Pala proud, who
vanquished all,

     with nothing.

and now have nothing.

extras

orbit

meet the author

Charlie Hopkinson

This is PHILIP PALMER's third novel for Orbit; he is also a producer and script editor, and writes for film, television and radio. Find out more about the author at www.philippalmer.net.

introducing

If you enjoyed
VERSION 43,
look out for

HELL SHIP

by Philip Palmer

Jak/Explorer

Is this it?

I believe so.

It's a beautiful system.

Eleven planets. Four gas giants, three with rings. One planet with a methane atmosphere. Six planets with no atmosphere. Eighty-three moons around nine of the planets. A comet in transit.

As I say, beautiful.

Why?

What?

Explain why it's beautiful.

Well…It's the rings, I suppose. That purple gas giant, the four rings, the sunlight dancing on them. That's beautiful.

If you say so.

I do.

We will take our position behind an asteroid in the midst of the C ring around the largest gas giant. We will be shielded from visual and radar sensors. We will from a distance appear to be part of the ring.

For how long?

It is forty three point five four years since last sighting.

A half a century to wait.

Sixty-five point four six years.

It's a long wait, then.

A very long wait, I guess.

Wouldn't you agree?

I have already stated the fact; clearly I agree with it or I wouldn't have stated it.

Yeah I was just trying to — you know.

Clearly I don't know, for your sentence was incomplete and the potential meanings are limitless.

I was just trying to make conversation.

Why?

Beats me. Talking to you is like —

Ah, forget it.

I'm bored okay. Extremely bored. Nightmarishly bored.

Suicidally bored.

Ah. This again.

Yes. "This" again. I need to talk. About stuff. Shoot the breeze.

I accede to your request to "shoot the breeze."

Great. What shall we talk about?

We could swap anecdotes about our personal life.

You have no personal life.

Then that would clearly be a conversational dead end.

Yeah. I guess. Look, why don't you just tell me something? Anything. Something that you know about. Something that interests you.

The albedo of this planet is four point five six two.

Really?

Yes.

That's fascinating!

It is a fact that I know. How does that make it fascinating?

Well it tells me that...you like data. Facts. That tells me some-thing about you, something admittedly that I already knew, but even so—good start! This is really helping me. Tell me something else.

The orbital velocity of this gas giant is eight point nine six three palas per second.

Could life develop on this planet?

Possibly.

Can you detect it?

No.

Have you tried?

Yes. Every time I approach a planet I scan for traces of organic life, electromagnetic patterns, and space-manifold substrate data caches. This system is devoid of life and there are no substrate messages.

And where is the centre, the very centre of the universe? Is it here? Where we are now?

It is impossible to know the position of the centre of the universe with any absolute precision or certitude; the equations of sub-spatial science forbid it.

But is it near to here?

In this general region of space. We are close.

We were close last time. But we failed.

We had a sighting.

We didn't engage.

My rift drive is now more powerful. My sensors are more acute. My weapon systems are calibrated to fire missiles with ninety four point five per cent accuracy and all my missiles and energy rays have been enhanced in power by a factor of twelve. Thus, in a blink of an eye, I will be at the enemy's throat, if I may be allowed so colourful a phrase, and I will be armed with weaponry sufficient to achieve our goal, namely the complete and irrevocable destruction of the target vessel.

So this time, we really are going to rip the arse off these evil parent-fuckers.

And this time we will, as you put it, rip the arse off these evil parent-fuckers.

Yeah. Yeah!

This place terrifies me.

This planet?

No. This patch of space. The centre of the universe. There's an evil feeling here.

Space can not emanate evil.

You think I'm imagining it?

The likelihood that you are imagining it is high.

You wouldn't understand. I am Olaran. I am sensitive to… things.

You are delusional.

Not any more. That was a phase.

A phase that lasted for half a century.

I did what I had to do.

You were insane.

I functioned. I got through it. Give me some credit, can't you?

I accede to your request; I give you credit.

Is this God, do you think?

Is what God? This planet? Our conversation? Our symbiotic relationship?

Are you being sarcastic?

I'm attempting that mode.

Nice try. By "this" I mean the Source. The place that all the evidence tells us is the centre of the universe. Is it God?

Define "God."

The beginning and the end; the all and everything; the origin and the cause of life; the reason for reality.

By those criteria, the Source is God.

I don't believe in God.

Then your question is idiotic.

It all began here. This is the womb that spawned a million universes.

This is not a womb. Wombs do not spawn. The number of universes is considerably greater than a million.

Piss all over my banter, why don't you?

I am a type 5 Explorer Ship, model number 410: I do not piss.

Fuck you.

I have no comment to make.

You humourless fucking machine.

I have no comment to make.

I'm afraid. I'm actually terrified. I'm afraid of this place, and what it means, and I'm afraid we'll fail again. Explorer, I can't endure it. The fear is suffocating me; and the hate, the hate chokes me too. You know I still yearn to kill each and every one of those bastards and destroy forever their appalling black-sailed ship. But revenge is a cold-hearted bitch who steals the souls of those she fucks; and I fear that she has stolen mine. Explorer, I don't think I can cope for much longer.

I have no comment to make.

Book 2

sharrock

I could see flames in the night-time sky; and a painful-as-a-dagger-thrust fear for those I loved burned in my soul.

I had been riding for five days and five nights through the red and lonely desert. My throat was parched, and my skin was like ash. And I had been dreaming, vividly, of sensual pleasures I would soon enjoy: a lazy bath in warm and perfumed waters; a slow massage of my taut and angry muscles; a fast frenzied fuck with my beloved wife Malisha; a long draught of rich wine; and, finally, a deep, soul-enriching sleep on a mattress filled with shara feathers.

All these dreams ended when I saw the glow in the sky. The clouds above and beyond the gnarled escarpment of grey rocks were bloodied by red flame; they were white floating pillows now transformed into ghastly red carcasses.

And I knew that my village had been torched.

I dismounted my cathary and knelt, and put my ear to the soft sound-conducting sand. And I waited, until my mind and ears were in tune with the planet and its hidden truths. And then I heard:

A faint humming noise, like the murmur of blood running along a warrior's veins, and I guessed that it was the sound of a skyplane hovering.

Shrill receding cries, remote, celebratory, in a language I did not recognise.

The hooves of riderless mounts, aimlessly pit-pattering.

The low moans of warriors and wives and husbands and children; sad cries of dying grief that mingled agony with impotent rage.

I heard, also, faintly but unmistakably: the soft, hoarse death gasps of throats burned by the scorched air of sun-fire blasts; the HuhHuhHuh! grunts of those shot or stabbed fatally in the guts; the angry whimpering of men and women stabbed or raped; the slow wretched sobs of wounded children; the despairing howls of mothers cradling their lost beloved.

A massacre.

I took out a shovel from my saddle-pack and dug a deep hole in the sand. Then I took my cathary by the reins and led her down into the hole, and coaxed her to lie down. The beast whinnied and kicked, but I stroked her mane and whispered in her neck-ear and calmed her. Then I lay beside her, still whispering, and the winds swept sand over us, and before long, we were buried deep and invisible.

After four days buried in the sand I crawled my way out. The cathary was in a coma by now, and I gently massaged the creature's heart until her eyes flickered. I drank from my canteen and spat the water into her moisture holes. And then slowly the cathary got to her feet, and shook her head, and whinnied, and was ready to ride once more.

It took two hours for me to ride through the teeth and gaping jaws of the rocky escarpment and reach my village. The flames had died down by now. The bodies that had burned so fiercely they lit the evening sky were now but charred corpses. The shrubs and trees and vines whose blazing leaves and bark had sent daggers of flame upwards to smear the clouds were no more than patches of ash. The tents were still intact—no fire could ever harm *them*—but the mountains and foothills and valleys of the dead stretched before me, like the remnants of a bonfire in an abattoir. Too many to count, too blackened to recognise.

And all were dead now. No moans, cries, whimpers, sobs. This was a village of the dead, and all those I had known and loved were gone.

I was sure beyond doubt that my wife Malisha was trapped somewhere in the sticky decaying mass of suppurating flesh. And I supposed too that my daughter Sharil must be one among the many black and silently howling tiny bodies that I witnessed inside the tents whose impregnable walls had kept out the flames; though, tragically, not the heat. This was a systematic slaughter, there would be no survivors; only those wounded beyond hope of recovery would have been left behind.

I could see plainly that the warriors had all died in combat, and I counted more than a hundred of them. Their bare faces were frozen in screams, and their swords were gripped in hands, or had fallen close to their bodies; but no traces of gore could be seen on their sharp and fearsome blades. No glorious battle this, but a long-distance act of butchery.

My friends, all. And all but a few were wearing their body armour which, like the tents, were invulnerable to flame and bullet. Only a long and sustained burst of sun-fire or tight-light rays could burn these hard-weave armours, and the warriors of my tribe were too swift and agile to be trapped in the path of such deadly beams for that long. But all were dead anyway, sundered into pieces by a fast-moving beam of power that could burn bodies through armour *in an instant*. And dead, too, were the husbands and wives of warriors, and the daughters and sons of warriors, and dead too were the Philosophers, forty and more or them, small and helpless and beautiful as they were, caught up in a battle they were unable by temperament to participate in and slain like ignorant beasts.

Which tribe could have done this thing? The Kax? Or the Dierils? Or the Harona? All had sworn peace in the days after the Great Truce. But truces could be broken, and there was no underestimating the guile and malice of these island tribes.

Or could this be an act of revenge by the exiled Southern Tribes, who long had hated our peoples of Madagorian for expelling their vile nation from our planet? I had lately spent six months in the decadent and perfumed city of Sabol, on a mission that had almost cost me my life and the future freedom of our entire race (and yet, let it be known: Sharrock was not defeated!) And so I know only too well how hated we were by these fat and effete Southerners, with their technology and their "robots" and their passion for ceaseless expansion through space.

Could they have done this? Did their send their sleek and powerful space vessels to wage war upon their former home? Surely they would know that such an act of barbarity would incur our deepest wrath; and their inevitable destruction?

I realised I was weeping. Not for my dead wife or my murdered child, for *that* grief lay deep in my heart and would torment me until my dying day. No, I wept from shame, that I had not taken my place with my fellow warriors and died in glory. Instead, I had buried myself in sand and lay there like a corpse until all those who were slowly dying had, agonisingly, expired, and their attackers were long gone.

The shame ate at me like a double-edged knife carving a bloody path through my bowels; but I knew I had done the right thing. Sometimes, a warrior must be a coward.

I filmed the carnage carefully with the camera in my eye and then inspected the sands where the battle had taken place for forensic evidence. I found no enemy bodies, even though some of our warriors had clearly fired their projectile weapons and sun-fire guns in the course of the bitter conflict. In places, the red sands themselves had been burned by the crossfire; and the rock escarpment and the grey mountain ridges were pitted with bullet holes and star-fire scars.

I surmised from all I had witnessed that the village had been attacked by stealth fighters of some kind, armed with weapons more powerful than any I had ever encountered, and with armoured hulls that were impervious to the handguns and rifles of our warriors or the dense-beam discharges of our anti-skycraft cannons. Our warriors would have had only minutes to prepare for battle; that would explain why they had not taken to the air in their own fighter jets.

I knelt before the body of one of the dead warriors who had been killed but not burned, and recognised him as Baramos, a noble warrior indeed. Baramos's guts had spilled from his body and sandworms were eating them. I ignored that and took out my thinnest dagger and thrust it into Baramos's skull, and split the bone open from jaw to hairline. Then I used the tip of the blade to root inside Baramos's inner ear until I retrieved the dead warrior's skywave transmitter.

This would provide the scientists and Philosophers in the city with all the information they needed; every word uttered between the warriors in the course of the battle would be recorded here.

Baramos had been, I recalled, as I gouged the transmitter out of his brain, a magnificent fighter and a fine scientist and (so his wife had often bragged) an astonishing lover and also (as I knew from my own experience) an inventive and poetic story-teller.

I spoke a prayer for the dead, and then I called my loyal cathary over to me, and I stroked the creature's mane and kissed its snout with genuine fondness.

Then I took out my second largest dagger and slit the beast's throat, and stood back as blood spouted from her slit artery. Her knees buckled, and she sank to the ground, staring at me with baffled reproof; and then she died.

I regretted the death; but I dared not leave the creature here, where it would, as hunger assailed it, be bound to feed upon the corpses of the dead. That would be a sacrilege; the carrion birds could and would do their worst, but no cathary should ever eat the flesh of a Maxolu.

The ground shook beneath me.

I was startled, and almost lost my balance. I looked up, and saw the skies were black.

A distance-missile and skycraft battle was in progress, I deduced, above and inside the city, which I estimated was 234,333 paces away from my current position. The missiles that were being dropped on the city must be enormous, because they were sending shudders along the planet's crust. And clouds of black smoke were now billowing in the sky to the northeast of me, a clear indication that high toxicity weapons of some kind were being employed.

I muttered a subvocal prayer to release the hidden doors of the aircraft hangar; and stood back as the sands shuddered, and parted, and the skycraft deck was exposed.

But at that moment a sandstorm sprang up, with an abruptness that shocked me, and I was flung upwards and backwards, and battered with sharp grains of red sand. I rolled over, letting my body go loose to avoid injury, then clambered to my feet and ducked down low with my back arched and my hands clutching my knees, as I had done so many times before; and tried to walk towards the hangar. But the blasts of the gale were too strong, and I was once again snatched up by the teeth of the snarling wind and sent tumbling like a broken shrub-branch along the desert dunes, until I lost all sense of up and down.

Finally, I managed to hook my wrist-grapple to a deeply buried rock, and my flight halted. I turned over and lay face up as if I had been staked to the sand to die. A streak of lightning shot across the sky above me, like a three-pronged spear. The clouds were bright silver moons now, as countless missiles exploded in mid-air and seared their softness with angry flares. The ground shook again.

Was this, I wondered, the end of me? Was Sharrock finally, after all his many adventures and countless terrifying brushes with angry death, to be defeated?

No, I thought.

Never!

I waited until there was a brief lull in the battering gale, then I detached my grapple and crawled on my belly over the sand, my eyes shut tight as the wind ripped at my face and body with dagger-stabs of blinding pain. I felt as if I were climbing up a high mountain made of turbulent seas, as the soft sand moved beneath me and the wind tried to rip my skin off my body.

The world above was red whirled sand; and the ground below was treacherous liquid-softness; and thunder roared; and my veins could feel the pulse of electricity in the air as the lightning flared.

And I dug deep into my soul, until I touched that part of me that will never *ever* be defeated; and I crawled, and crawled, into the sharp teeth of the savage spitting storm.

Eventually I reached the dip in the sand that marked the hangar deck's opening, and I tipped myself over and fell downwards into the sand mountain, and slowly slid to the bottom. I was now entirely buried in sand, with grains in my nostrils and ears and eyes and no way to see. But the sand was slitheringly soft, and I was able to slide my way through it, not breathing, and not opening my mouth or nostril orifices for fear of suffocating on sand-grains. It took me thirty minutes, almost to the limit of my lungs' capacity, before I reached the side of the hangar bay, guided throughout by my infallible mental map of the hangar area that allowed me to see precisely where I was without the use of eyesight.

Once I touched the wall, I fumbled with my hand until I found the clicker that turned on the hangar's fans; and I clicked it; and I was now *inside* a sandstorm, clinging on to a rail like a cathary-breaker clutching his mount's silky mane, as a tornado of red sand grains rose around me and flew upwards into the sky.

And when the world was clear again, I coughed like a dying beast, and tried to spit but my mouth was too dry. The fans continued to whirr, creating a single oasis of calm air within the swirling desert of sand that was all around; and I opened the store cupboard and clad myself in body-weave armour. Then I chose the fastest of the fighter jets that were parked on the deck inside their invisible-wall overcoats; shut the invisible-wall field off with a signal from my brain transmitter, and clambered in.

I sat at the cockpit, buckled up, and spoke the silent prayer that would tell any friendly pilots or skycraft controllers nearby that my craft was in flight, and should be accorded urgent passage.

Then I started up the skycraft's engines and it bucked instantly upwards then soared effortlessly into the air, like a stone hurled by a warrior up at the moon. I flew over the massacre site, hovering over the mounds of the dead below me, and wondered if I should use a missile or an energy-beam to burn the rest of the flesh off the corpses' bones.

But that might, it occurred to me, attract the attention of the enemy. I did not even dare to send a message to the city with news of the massacre, for fear it would be intercepted by enemy spy satellites and used to home in on my position. No, I would have to deliver my message in person.

I switched my engines on to full and the skycraft ceased its hovering mode and leaped forward through the air like a wild maral pouncing and snatching a bannet from the sky before swiftly fleeing its victim's brutal mates.

The acceleration-forces crushed me to my seat. I had a moment of reflection on what I had lost: my friends, my village, and my two deep and abiding true loves; Malisha, my wife, so truthful and so passionately loving; and Sharil, my daughter, three years old, sweet, and mischievous, cursed with my own dark roguish features, yet blessed — nay thrice-blessed! — with her mother's beauty and wit, and radiant smile. For a moment, I recalled these two and I felt their presences. And for a longer moment still, I was appalled at their evermore absences.

But then I had no more time to mourn.

I took the plane up high, out of the atmosphere, until I could see the cratered pockmarks of our purple moon and the unmistakable towers of our lunar city. But I realised that the towers had all fallen, and the moon was pock-marked a thousand times more than usual. Then I banked and ripped downwards through the sky of Madagorian, and proceeded at a fast diagonal towards the capital city, Kubala.

Then I saw it.

It was one of the enemy's skycraft, without doubt. It was a vessel larger than a battle-plane, and bizarrely coloured in varying hues and shaped, extraordinarily, like the stem of a harasi tree.

It was invisible to my sensors, and the dazzling sunlight on the hull made it opaque to ordinary vision too. But the faint heat emanating from the craft was clearly visible to me through my enhanced-vision telescopic goggles.

I smiled, in anticipation of vengeful victory, and launched my missiles.

Then my craft kinked, in a savagely fast manoeuvre that was designed to avoid any return missile fire.

The Philosophers had dreamed the single-seat skycraft to be winged creatures that embodied air and speed and grace; they were to be supple beautiful flying-machines that merged with the minds of their pilot, so that flesh and machinery beat with a single heart. And our warrior-scientists had followed the Philosophers' dreams precisely and with unmatchable skill.

And so my skycraft, a tiny dot in the air, was now as much sky as sky-plane; it was a bird and a cloud and a raindrop; and yet it was also a killing machine with near unquenchable reserves of bombs and missiles and devastatingly powerful fast-fire guns.

And my craft had another eerie power; it was able to change direction abruptly and swiftly without the effects being felt by the Maxolu warrior in the cockpit. So that when I piloted the craft, I could fly faster and more unpredictably than any bird that had ever lived.

I and the plane-that-was-part-of-me skidded across the sky, and reversed and looped, and plunged towards the ground, and recovered from the plunge, and accelerated at a speed so near to light that time itself, as measured by the skycraft's clock, very near stood still.

All the missiles achieved direct hits, for my aim was unerring; but the enemy vessel clearly had some kind of protective invisible-shield, so the explosions splashed harmlessly off its hull.

Then I flew beneath the enemy ship and extended my craft's nose spike and I flew directly *into* the other craft. The spike penetrated the hull, and I fired a fusillade of delayed action missiles into the vessel, then snapped the spike, and flew like the heel of a skate upon ice across the blue sky and watched.

The enemy battle-ship jerked out of control as the bombs exploded inside it. It veered wildly from side to side, then started to fall from the sky.

Then it vanished.

And reappeared behind me and I saw it through my all-around vision goggles and fired a hail of burning gas through the rear of my craft and saw flames burn the enemy's hull, and was once more dancing around the sky.

The enemy ship was billowing steam from side vents now, a clear sign that there were fires within and its hull was compromised. It fired a battery of projectiles and energy streams which rained towards me, but my dancing pinprick of a fighter craft eluded them all.

The enemy's huge battle ship was faced with a single-Maxolu skycraft, and it was losing. I felt a surge of triumph.

And then I saw that the enemy vessel was descending, and landing. It burned the grass in a field and touched down with no jolt, and the side of the craft opened up and I saw far below me—in the image magnified by my goggles—a single figure step out.

I increased the magnification on my goggles still further; and was surprised to see that the figure emerging from the ship was a female warrior carrying a sword. Was this a challenge?

The enemy battleship lifted into the air once more and flew off. The warrior remained, alone, on the ground. The message was clear: a one-on-one combat was being proposed.

I plunged downwards, with a jolt of joy that was like falling off a cliff, and landed my craft on the seared grass. I knew this might be an ambush, but I had to take the risk. For according to the laws of my world, any battle and war can be decided by single combat, no matter what the sizes of the respective armies. But now I wondered: would these enemy warriors hold to such values?

For I had, of course, realised by now these were no ordinary warriors; they came from elsewhere, from some other planet around some other star that existed far away in the universe of stars that encircled us at night.

My enemy were aliens, and they had invaded my world.

I stepped out of my craft. I took my sword out of the cockpit-pouch, and sheathed it in my back-scabbard and walked calmly towards the alien warrior.

The warrior was female, as I had already seen. But close up, she looked like no female I had ever beheld. She had fangs, like an animal, that protruded from her mouth, and no ear-flaps. In the centre of her forehead was a third eye. She was large — twice as large as myself — and powerfully muscled. And she wore no body armour but was clad in tight black animal-hides that left her legs and stomach and arms bare. Her hair was bright red streaked with silver and blew in the wind. And her skin was pale, more white than red, and entirely lacking in soft ridges.

The contrast in our sizes was almost comical; I was a dwarf beside this giant. And she was without doubt a magnificent specimen of her species, warily graceful, with bulging shoulders and arms and stocky legs. And there was a steely look in her eyes that assured me she knew well of the bitterness and the joy of combat.

I stared up at her appraisingly and without hate; for hate will slow the warrior's hand and eye. "What tribe are you?" I asked.

"You do not know my tribe," the warrior replied, in a husky low voice that made my flesh tingle with the eerie unfamiliarity of its tone.

"What is your name?" I continued, patiently.

"Zala," said the warrior. "And yours?"

And she stared at me impassively, unafraid to meet my eyes.

"I am," I said proudly, "Sharrock."

She stared at me, unimpressed.

Hiding my disappointment at her lack of response to my, by all objective criteria, legendary name, I added: "You are, I take it, not from our lands."

"I am not."

"Tell me then, whence do you come?"

She was still staring into my eyes; shamelessly, and in my view arrogantly. I felt a flash of rage and stifled it.

I would kill her first; and *then* I would savour my wrath.

"Far away," she said, in what sounded to me like sad tones. "Another planet, around another star."

"As I had suspected," I told her, formally. "For your ship is like nothing I have ever seen. Your appearance is hideous and strange. You are an alien."

"In your terms, I am."

"Why do you wage war upon us, you whore-fucking turd-eating cock-swallowing monster from afar?" I asked her, with ritual invective.

She laughed.

"Answer my question, o withered-hole!" I insisted, and she laughed again.

"We come," she said with open mockery, "o pathetic-male-with-a-tiny-prick-that-I-will-eat-and-feed-in-morsels-to-my-female-lover in order to conquer and destroy you."

"Why?" I said, stung at her unfamiliar insult.

"Why not?" said Zala, the female warrior, tauntingly.

Once again I had to bite back my rage; for I truly despised this warrior's lack of respect for tradition. Her people's war with my people should not have been fought like this! A formal declaration should have been made, and hence due warning given; poems should have been spoken, songs composed, regrets expressed. All this should have been done, to create a war that would have been ennobling for all concerned.

Instead, they had simply ambushed our valiant warriors, massacred our defenceless families and Philosophers, and left them all to rot.

"Which planet do you come from, you tainted-by-vulgarity-and-laughed-at-by-small-children shit-covered-whore?" I said.

She grinned, clearly amused by our social ritual of rhetorical abuse. "It has a name," she said casually. "You will not know it. It is far away. Your astronomers will never have seen it. All you need to know is I am a warrior of a once great world. Will you fight me?"

"I will."

"If I kill you, your world is forfeit," the alien warrior said arrogantly.

"Very well," I said calmly. "And if I kill *you*?"

"That won't happen," said the alien warrior Zala and she lunged forward with her long curved sword, the hilt clutched in both her hands.

I dodged easily and drew my sword from its scabbard on my back with one hand and swung it fast at her and she recoiled and barely dodged it, then I wove forwards to the left and then to the right, ducking and rising in a single flow, then thrust the tip of the sword towards her bare midriff. But she leaped in the air and danced on the flat of my blade and kicked my head and somersaulted over me then plunged her sword back and over her own head at me, without turning around.

I was awed at her speed, but evaded the blow and swept my own blade a thousand times in the air in a series of continuous movements. Zala countered each sword-strike with a speed that impressed me, for we were both fighting faster than the beatings of a baro bird's wings.

But I was stronger, and the next time she leaped in the air I leaped high too and clutched at her face with my fingers and plucked out one of her eyes.

We both landed, swords held upright and clashed steel once again. Blood dribbled out of her empty eye-hole. Her face was a cold mask of hate. I felt a surge of joy; this was glorious combat.

Then her blade went through my heart and I exulted, and with my dagger hand I sliced off her hand at the wrist and stepped back. I grunted in pain, and also in delight. For her severed hand and blade were now trapped in my chest, with the tip of her sword protruding from my back. But my second heart was easily able to sustain my body. And now the alien was fighting swordless and one handed, with scarlet blood gushing from the bloody stump of her right arm.

But Zala just laughed and drew her second sword, and I lunged again and she dodged and stabbed my leg and so I butted her face and swung my own weapon in a rolling patterns of cuts that shook sparks from her blade. Then with my left hand I stabbed once more with my dagger and slashed at her throat so powerfully it severed her head, and the head fell off her body and bounced on to the sands.

And I paused, and for a moment allowed myself to relax; but her head continued to laugh.

I was shocked at this; then I realised that the head must have its own blood supply. And, too, the headless torso was still holding its sword and was undeterred by the loss of its head; with speed and bravado it leaped at me and carried on fighting, blind yet unerringly accurate in its sword strikes.

I was on the defensive now; the headless torso had renewed strength and was able to somehow perceive where my body was and even anticipate my moves in ways I could not fathom. And all the while the head on the sand laughed, as its body fought me; and I forced myself to ignore the absurdity of it all and lost myself in battle-lust until my blade swept down and rent the warrior's body in two.

The two halves of the alien warrior's torso twitched on the sand, blood gushing, organs spilling out. The battle was over; or so I thought.

But then the right half of the warrior lifted its sword again, and tried to stand up. And the left half of the warrior drew a knife and rolled in the sands, trying to get upright with only one foot.

The warrior was still not dead. Still not dead!

I brought my sword down and split the head into two halves. Blood splashed, and I could see the grey folds of the creature's brain. Her tongue was split in two, but her one remaining eye was staring at me and yet still she was laughing, even though it was a gurgle and not a real laugh.

"Die you devilish fucker-of-evil monster!" I screamed.

The two halves of the head spluttered with delight.

I lowered my sword. I was defeated; no matter what I did, I could never kill this creature.

"What will happen now?" I asked. But the sundered head could no longer speak. And there was, I felt, sadness in her remaining eyes.

And at that point, Zala's head started to shimmer before me, and I realised I could see through her face and sundered smile to the sands behind. Then her head slowly vanished, and her body too, like mist dissipating in the morning heat.

I marvelled at this magic. What powers did these creatures have? And what utter, taunting, disgusting malice. This was not war, it was mockery.

I looked around.

The alien battle ship had not returned. But in the distance, a false bright red dawn on the horizon revealed that the city itself was ablaze.

And I saw that the sky above me was now black with single-Maxolu fighting craft; but they weren't fighting, they were just spiralling aimlessly. There was no battle being fought, merely the sad savouring of abject defeat. I had a sinking feeling of despair.

The ground below me shook again. But these weren't bombs exploding in the distance; this was an earthquake.

And I realised that the sand beneath me was hot; my feet burned through my boots. I cleaned the blood off my sword and dagger, then sheathed them.

The ground shook again. I braced myself.

Then the ground erupted. The sand was scattered into the air and the rock below was exposed, and it split before my eyes, and red liquid lava poured out of the rents. A volcano was erupting, directly beneath me.

And at the same time lightning once more ripped across the sky, vast forked bolts that stabbed the air and made it scream.

And a loud roaring sound filled my ears, and then a wind

sprang up from nowhere and knocked me off my feet. I staggered
upright and saw hot volcano-spew rolling towards me like tides in
a raging ocean. The sky was empty now, all the Maxolu craft had
been obliterated by the savage winds. The air itself shimmered
with heat, as if it were ablaze; and hail rained down on me and
burned my face.

I sank to my knees. I knew now that my world was dying and
there was nothing I could do.

A river of lava flowed fast towards me, and engulfed my knees
and thighs, and burned off my trousers and boots and the flesh of
my legs and arse beneath, and I tasted ash and my own blood as
I accidentally bit my tongue. My skin was hot and my body hair
was sparking, and waves of heat oppressed me like a pillow used
to suffocate a convicted coward.

I howled in despair. I could not run, I could not even stand.
My legs were ablaze, the flesh was turning molten.

Then the red-hot volcano-spew engulfed me, up to the chest,
then up almost to my neck. I thought about my wife, Malisha,
and my baby girl, Sharil. And I mourned their deaths, as my
tough flesh began to burn, and my bones were seared with heat,
and my eyes stung with ash that turned my tears into hailstones.

Sharrock defeated? I wondered.

Never! I vowed. But in my heart I knew I was doomed.

And then—